D0231338

 **Libraries** | **Hillhead Library**
348 Byres Road
Glasgow G12 8AP
Phone: 0141 276 1617

This book is due for return on or before the last date shown below. It may be renewed by telephone, personal application, fax or post, quoting this date, author, title and the book number.

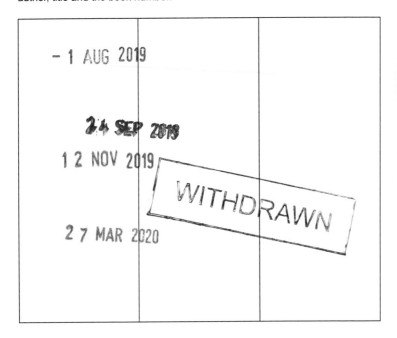

- 1 AUG 2019

24 SEP 2019

1 2 NOV 2019

WITHDRAWN

2 7 MAR 2020

Glasgow Life and its service brands, including Glasgow Libraries, (found at www.glasgowlife.org.uk) are operating names for Culture and Sport Glasgow.

Glasgow
CITY COUNCIL

# TEARS
OF THE
# DRAGON

# TEARS
OF THE
# DRAGON

# JEAN
# MORAN

HEAD
of ZEUS

First published in the UK in 2019 by Head of Zeus Ltd

Copyright © Jean Moran, 2019

The moral right of Jean Moran to be identified as the author
of this work has been asserted in accordance with the
Copyright, Designs and Patents Act of 1988.

All rights reserved. No part of this publication may be
reproduced, stored in a retrieval system, or transmitted in any form
or by any means, electronic, mechanical, photocopying, recording,
or otherwise, without the prior permission of both the copyright
owner and the above publisher of this book.

This is a work of fiction. All characters, organizations,
and events portrayed in this novel are either products of
the author's imagination or are used fictitiously.

9 7 5 3 1 2 4 6 8

A catalogue record for this book is available from
the British Library.

ISBN (HB): 9781788542555
ISBN (XTPB): 9781789543391
ISBN (E): 9781788542548

Typeset by NewGen

Printed and bound in Great Britain by
CPI Group (UK) Ltd, Croydon CR0 4YY

Head of Zeus Ltd
First Floor East
5–8 Hardwick Street
London EC1R 4RG
WWW.HEADOFZEUS.COM

*Black Christmas, no snow.*
*High fences, no freedom.*
*Sunburst, cloud and black rain.*

# 1

*Hong Kong, 1941*

There was only one car on the Star ferry, about to head away from Hong Kong to Kowloon. The vehicle was uninteresting, but the woman sitting behind the steering-wheel was exceptionally good-looking, her hair dark and her features strikingly imperial.

Her companion was fair, and her eyes were shining with excitement. 'Rowena, I might get drunk this evening.'

'Pace yourself, Alice. The night is still young.'

'We're the only car. Did you notice that? Though that chap over there has a bicycle.'

Most of the foot passengers were huddled around the exit, keen to disembark as quickly as possible. The bicycle was slung over the man's shoulder.

Close by a broad-set man, wearing a black tunic over Chinese-style pantaloons, was leaning over the side rail, looking down into the black water, a smouldering cigarette clinging to the corner of his mouth.

Rowena glanced at him briefly. She didn't care who else was on the boat. All she cared about was that she'd put some distance between the hospital where she worked in Hong Kong and a night of enjoyment. They might indeed get drunk – though she reminded herself she had to drive back. Or they might dance until dawn, exchanging lustful glances with the hordes of servicemen also heading for the lights of Kowloon. 'I'm looking forward to this. Thanks for coming.'

'No worries. I'm looking forward to it too. In need of it, in fact. Being a nurse isn't all glamour and uniforms, you know. I dreamed of bedpans last night. Been dreaming of them all week.'

'You're a good nurse, Alice. I – we appreciate you.'

'I'm not sure the male doctors are as appreciative as you are, Dr Rossiter.'

'No need to be formal. We're not on the ward now.'

'It's nice to know that I'm more than a skivvy. Not all doctors are like you, Rowena.'

'That's because they're men.'

'Let me tell you this as a girl from Brisbane – it could be worse. They could be Australian men.'

The throaty blast from the ferry's horn drowned their laughter, signalling that they were about to dock.

Carefully averting his eyes from the women in the car, the man leaning over the rail took one last puff on his cigarette and threw it into the sea.

Alice got out of the car with the starting handle. She gave it a turn but it kicked back.

'Give it another go,' shouted Rowena.

She tried again, but the same thing happened.

'Blimey. It nearly took my arm off that time,' she said, rubbing her shoulder.

The man who had been leaning over the side rail silently nudged her aside, took the handle from her and gave it a single turn. The Austin's tinny engine gurgled into life.

'Thanks... Oh. He's gone.'

At eight in the evening, heaving with humanity, the streets of Kowloon were plunged into startling brightness by a sea of neon lights when there was power – and flickering infrequency when there was not.

'Buy, buy, buy!'

The car windows were swiftly wound up.

'We'll boil like lobsters,' said Alice.

Rowena laughed. 'The lesser of two evils.'

'Whose crazy idea was this?'

'Mine! There's a war on, Alice. It might be our last chance to kick up our heels, sing and dance until dawn.'

'Fat chance. We're back on duty tomorrow.'

'Until midnight then.'

'What's that dark place over there?'

Jostled by street-sellers and soldiers on leave, there was plenty of time for Rowena to glance to where Alice was pointing.

'The real China. Kowloon walled city. KWC for short.'

Alice wrinkled her nose at the ramshackle buildings between the main thoroughfare and the old city. 'They look like they're ready to fall down.'

'Some bits of them do – when it's been raining.'

'I can believe it. We're not going in there, are we?'

Rowena smiled. Alice was all front, brave as could be, but underneath she quivered. 'Do you want to?'

'No, thank you. I thought we were going to a club.'

'It's a bar, not a club. Connor's Bar. It was recommended.'

Alice pointed at the substantial stones of the walled city. 'But it's not in there. Tell me it's not in there.'

'Of course it's not. Nobody bothers the people inside that place. Even the Hong Kong police have no real jurisdiction.'

'But we're safe out here?'

'Of course – as far as we can be.'

Alice shook her head despairingly. 'Rowena Rossiter, I don't know why I let you talk me into this.'

'You know you wanted to.'

Alice demurred. 'I must be as mad as you are, then, and to think you're a doctor.'

'You have to admit it makes a change from yet another foxtrot with a pimply officer at the country club, the officers' club or whatever.'

'You can say that again. I take it good old Reggie's still in pursuit?'

'Uh-huh.'

The crowd divided like a tidal wave, nudged aside by the bonnet of the Austin motor car Rowena had borrowed from Reggie, her would-be and so far unsuccessful seducer. 'Good old Reggie,' she murmured.

Alice laughed. 'Will he expect payment for the loan of his car – if you know what I mean?'

'If he does, I shall remind him that he's a gentleman and the son and heir of another.'

'Oh, yes.' Alice smirked. 'One has one's reputation to think of.'

'Sharing a bed with Reggie Stuart is not the stuff that dreams are made of.'

Reggie had been pursuing Rowena for months. Dinner, theatre and other diversions having failed, he was obviously hoping the car would do the trick. Rowena had other ideas. She didn't fancy Reggie. He was too much like every other officer stationed in Hong Kong, an outpost of empire that didn't even warrant a full complement of military personnel – it was minimal, especially when compared with Singapore.

Silk stockings made a rasping sound as they slid out of the car, the humidity of the day lingering to dampen their armpits and have them dabbing their handkerchiefs against their top lips.

A figure flickered almost out of vision into a dark alley, immediately attracting Rowena's attention. Then her eyes picked out the name of the store on the corner of the alley and the sign above it. 'House of Peace. This is the one.'

Alice followed her into the alley. 'How did you know what the sign said?'

Rowena stopped and pointed, her finger following the form of the Chinese character. 'That top bit is a roof. The bottom bit is a woman. One woman under one roof is peace. Two women under one roof mean war.'

'Put like that, it's pretty obvious.'

Rowena looped her arm through Alice's. 'It'll be fine. Trust me.'

'If you say so. Bit dark, though.'

'This is it.'

Above the blank surface of a dark red door a solitary sign, unadorned by any decorative feature, declared they'd arrived at their destination – Connor's Bar. A figure in black dissected the shaft of light from the briefly opened door, then was gone, swallowed by the inner depths of the alley.

'Are you sure it won't be all uniforms and rounded vowels? I mean, it is an English name.'

'Irish, actually. Trust me.'

The door might have been plain, the sign inconspicuous, but the interior was far from it. The smell of sandalwood, spices and something tellingly sweet seeped out and enticed them in.

Rowena entered as though she owned the place, a dream in green silk, her glossy black hair coiled around her head.

Alice followed nervously. 'You never told me it was like this,' she said, in a hushed voice.

'That's because I didn't know it was.'

'What?'

'Sorry. The truth is I'd heard a rumour about it and just had to take a look, but didn't want to come by myself.'

'Rowena! How could you?'

'You're good company.'

'Reggie might have come.'

'Reggie would cramp my style...' Rowena held the door open as she took it all in, a place that had been recommended as exciting and surprisingly different. Black and red walls. Dragons painted on the ceiling, believed by the Chinese to bring luck.

Booths adapted from the frames of bridal beds lined the walls, only the roofs and sidepieces remaining, their panels ornately carved. The part where newly-weds had once consummated their marriage had been removed, replaced by bench seating around an oblong table with richly carved legs. Lit only by frugal lamps, the features of those inside were indistinct, a mix of shadows and burning brightness, like the candlelit expressions of men in old Dutch paintings set against gloomy backgrounds.

The best-lit booth contained a group of Chinese businessmen playing cards beneath a suspended lamp with a green glass shade shaped like a coolie's hat.

The light laughter of a woman sounded from one booth, the hushed whispers of shared secrets from another. Someone was singing 'The Flower of Killarney'...

*'Mavourneen's the flower of Killarney,*
*The fairest of all to me...'*

As she hummed along with the traditional tune, Rowena's attention wandered to a white fedora sitting on a table next to a glass tumbler in a darkened booth. A slight movement told her that its owner had crossed his legs. Like his hat, his trousers were white. She couldn't see his face but sensed he was looking directly at them.

Ignoring him, she headed for the bar. 'Let's get some drinks.'

The glow of the back bar gave enough light for the barman to work and for them to notice his slightly nervous expression.

The singer at the other end of the bar was now belting out 'Molly Malone', another traditional Irish song.

'And music too,' Rowena murmured to Alice, as she opened her purse. 'Two gin slings, please.'

The Chinese barman didn't budge but stared at them, glass in one hand, a towel in the other, as though they'd grown horns.

Rowena held a banknote between finger and thumb. 'Didn't you hear me, barman? Two gin slings, if you please.'

He shook his head. 'No ladies served here.'

Rowena frowned. 'I beg your pardon?'

*'As she wheeled her wheelbarrow,*
*Through the streets broad and narrow...'*

He shook his head again, more vehemently this time. 'No ladies. No serve ladies.'

'We're not tarts, if that's what you think,' Rowena declared.

Alice turned nervous. 'Let's go.'

The barman's eyes slid sidelong to the end of the bar. He seemed disinclined to interrupt the singer, whose companion was raising a glass to his efforts.

'Boss. These ladies want drinks.'

The singing stopped and the vocalist turned round. His companion followed suit.

The two men, wearing white dinner jackets and ties, exchanged brief looks. One picked up his glass and drank. The singer peeled away and came closer.

'Ladies.' His tone was less than friendly, but Rowena kept her smile in place, noting that his eyes were sea blue, his hair brindled brown and copper gold.

On hearing Alice's sharp intake of breath, she grabbed a handful of silk at Alice's waistline just in case she cut for the door. 'We'd like a drink, please,' she said, in her most beguiling voice.

'I'm sorry. We don't serve unaccompanied ladies.'

'Judging by that accent, I suppose you're Connor.'

'I suppose I am.'

'You sing very well.'

'Your flattery's welcome, but it won't get you any drinks. Women alone are trouble. It's the bar's policy not to invite it.'

His expression was unyielding and his voice without humour.

'We're not whores. We're not looking for men. We came here for a drink and to have some fun while we still can before the fighting starts.'

'We don't allow unaccompanied women to buy drinks. They have to be with a man.'

'Let's go,' said Alice, turning away from the bar, her face flushing.

Rowena pinched a bigger bunch of her dress and her flesh. Alice yelped. 'I'm sorry, Alice, but I won't go. I will not be treated like this.' She turned back and faced him. 'I insist that you serve us. In fact, I will not move until you do.'

A muscle ticked beneath his right eye and his jaw seemed to harden. 'You can stand there all night if you like, but if you're not with a man you will not be served. That's the house rules.'

Rowena looked him up and down. 'Army, navy or air force?'

'Do you care?'

'I care that you should know we're respectable women.'

'I don't know you.'

'Surely at the officers' club...'

His look was steady, his gaze cold. 'Like I said, I don't know you. Now get going.'

'And you don't know the officers' club?' She looked tellingly around her. 'I don't understand. I'm assuming that like everyone else you're in the army but your name is in lights above the door of this bar. How did you manage to swing being in the army and indulging in a little business enterprise? Shouldn't you be getting ready to fight?'

'I didn't say I was. Anyway, there's no rule saying I can't run a sideline, as long as it doesn't interfere with my duties. I have a manager.'

She could tell by the tightening of his expression and the stilted outpouring of information that her insinuation had hit home. She made the decision to go one step further.

'You're a deserter. That's it, isn't it? You both are.' She looked past him to the other man, who had remained at the end of the bar, smiling over the top of his glass. He was definitely a pale shadow of Connor, not so masculine, finer-boned, slimmer-faced, which made her wonder about them. Not just friends, perhaps. Still, none of her business.

'Are you deaf or just stupid?' he asked.

'I beg your pardon?'

'My manager takes care of everything. This is my friend's and my little nest egg, something to come back to once this bloody war is finally over. Not that it's any of your business.'

He grabbed her arm and propelled her towards the door. 'Out.'

'Connor. Excuse me.'

An arm protruded from the mysterious darkness of the bridal bed booth, the hand waving the white fedora.

The voice was unlike any other she'd ever heard, like ice grating over gravel. It made her legs turn to water.

'I know these ladies, Mr O'Connor. I can vouch for them. Kim Pheloung, Dr Rossiter. We met at the country club. We played tennis. Matched pairs. I won. I always win. Please,' he said, waving his hand at the empty benches on each side of his table. 'Join me. Might we have two gin slings, Mr O'Connor?'

Connor looked her up and down. 'Doctor? Did I hear that right?'

'Yes. I'm a doctor and if things really do get going, I'm not going to be out and about enjoying myself for a very long time. That's why I came here this evening. You wouldn't begrudge me that, would you? Seeing as you're likely to be in need of my services if an invasion occurs and you're injured.'

The Irishman looked as though a war was going on inside him. He looked at the man at the end of the bar.

A slight smile came to the other man's face. 'Oh, go on, Connor. If they're known to Kim it has to be okay.'

Rowena sensed Connor was beginning to waver. He didn't believe that the man in the booth knew her, but neither did she. She'd remember a voice like that. She let go of Alice's dress. 'Come on,' she whispered.

The height of the canopy was such that their host in the white suit could only half rise as they sat down, bending from the waist in a slowly executed bow.

When he sat down again he patted the seating to either side of him. 'Please. Sit, ladies. Sit.'

Rowena sank gratefully beside their benefactor, trying to recall exactly when he'd beaten her at tennis – a game she seldom played though she'd been told she had the reach and long legs that marked a good player.

'You spring on the balls of your feet,' somebody had told her. She hadn't been sure what that meant and it hadn't made her any keener to get more involved in the game.

As the drinks were set on the table, their host exchanged a few words in Chinese with the barman, then it was chin-chins and smiles all round as they clinked glasses.

Over the top of hers, Rowena noted his refined features, the high cheekbones, the long fingers and a complexion like burnished bronze. Like a Greek warrior. Long black glossy hair. A proud bearing. Like a prince, the kind she'd once dreamed of when she was younger.

It was hard to tell how tall he was, but she guessed he was less than six feet. He smelt of sandalwood and his teeth flashed white in stark contrast to his glossy skin. Deep-set dark eyes regarded her from either side of a straight nose. His eyebrows were arched, like a woman's, as though they were plucked to shape, but thicker and blacker than any pencil could make them.

In short he was breathtakingly beautiful but with a dangerous veneer. Like a snake, thought Rowena, a beautiful creature that is both alluring and deadly.

'In case you're wondering, no, we did not meet playing tennis. I said that purely for Connor's benefit. My grandmother was in St Luke's private clinic. I saw you there. A female doctor. Most memorable. I would have preferred a female doctor for my grandmother and voiced my preference. Alas, I was told you were unavailable.'

'I specialise in obstetrics. I would guess your grandmother is of a venerable age?'

'A doctor-midwife?'

'You could say that. Alice here is on her way to being a senior nurse.'

'That's my dream,' said Alice, raising her glass and emptying it of the remains of her drink in one quick gulp. 'Cheers. I needed that. I've never been refused a drink before – if you don't count when I was underage or tried to get into a men-only bar back home.'

Kim smiled politely but seemed to close his ears and eyes to her presence, Rowena feeling the full force of his admiring appraisal. Her face warmed. She wasn't given to blushing and refused to do so now. To control her embarrassment, she sought a diversion.

The lively strains of the fiddle resumed, accompanied by the banging of masculine hands on the bar top as though it were a drum while Connor played another tune, this time 'Star of the County Down'.

Kim waved his hand at the barman for more drinks, which came quickly. As the glasses were set down, Kim's slender fingers clamped on Yang's hand. Rowena saw the panic in his eyes, the draining of colour from his face as Kim uttered words she did not understand.

Yang tried to protest, but Kim had the last word – whatever that last word happened to be. She guessed it to have been threatening.

Unnerved, Rowena allowed her gaze to stray to Connor and the other man, her feet tapping in time to the music. She was humming the tune, then joining him in the chorus.

*'From Bantry Bay unto Derry Quay,*
*From Galway to Dublin Town.*
*No maid I've seen like the brown colleen,*
*That I met in the County Down.'*

'You like singing, Doctor?' asked the man they were with. The grim expression was gone, replaced by one of gentlemanly benevolence.

'I do, and I like music that makes me tap my feet.'

He nodded tersely as though he didn't really approve.

One song had finished and another had begun. The strains of a more subdued melody came from the other end of the bar.

'So what do you do, Mr Pheloung?'

'Please. Call me Kim. I am a silk merchant – among many other things.'

'Are you rich?'

Rowena frowned at Alice, who had a tendency to speak without thinking.

'What?' Alice whispered.

'I'm sorry, Mr Pheloung...'

'Kim. There is no need for an apology. I am a wealthy man.'

Alice glowed at the answer. Rowena was more sceptical – after all, they were not far from KWC. Mr Pheloung had admitted he had other interests besides silk and he wouldn't be the first businessman with a foot in both legal and illegal trades. That was how things were in Hong Kong.

'Do you live in Kowloon?'

'When necessary. My real home is close to Shanghai. There are more banks there than there are in Kowloon or Hong Kong.'

'Is it a big house?' asked Alice, her eyes wide with interest.

'Yes.'

Rowena peered at him through a pall of smoke from the cheroot he was smoking and the ones he had handed to them. It was unnerving to see him looking back at her in exactly the same manner, enough for her to parry the look with a question that almost bordered on rudeness.

'Pheloung is not a Chinese name.'

Smooth eyelids fell halfway over his eyes, making her feel like a bird trapped between the paws of a cat. It occurred to her that he had not liked her questioning his name and thus his origins.

'One day you'll push it too far,' her brother Clifford had said to her.

One day she might, but she was not convinced that today was the day.

'I am of mixed parentage, a true citizen of the world.'

Rowena smiled, but did not admit that her grandmother had been from India – not with Alice present. Mixed blood tended to set one apart from those of pure European extraction. Her complexion was fairly brown, a bit like the colleen in the song Connor had just sung, though her hair was jet black, not chestnut.

At the other end of the bar, Connor was singing another Irish song, about whiskey this time.

Kim's dulcet tones broke through the tune, grabbing her attention. 'The Jockey Club employs a most wonderful chef,' he said.

She heard Alice gasp, a sure sign that she was impressed. Only millionaires were members of the Jockey Club and in the last century only Europeans were allowed to join. This man obviously had the thousands of dollars needed to pay the exorbitant joining fee. Not only that, he must also be acceptable to the very cream of Hong Kong society. Kim Pheloung had to be seriously rich.

'I heard that the food is good,' Rowena said, sliding a second cheroot between her lips.

His eyes smiled through the lighter flame as though he believed she'd dined in the company of millionaires and autocrats. Perish the thought! But she had seen it from the outside and heard about the food.

'Then it will be an experience shared between us.'

She drew deeply on the cheroot, letting the smoke go no further than the back of her throat before blowing it out. She kept her eyes on him, smiling secretively, almost bashfully, as she considered his invitation.

'Saturday night at eight. Ask for me by name.'

'I'll try.'

'Try?' His arched eyebrows were coupled with a wry smile.

'Perhaps you should give me your business card – just so they know I'm really meeting you there.'

'And just so you know I'm telling the truth that I am a member.'

'I don't mean to be distrustful...'

'I quite understand. Here. Take this. They will recognise the inscription – should you be asked to prove anything, which you will not.'

'I couldn't possibly.'

'Yes, you can. Catch.'

She caught it with her left hand.

'You are left-handed, Doctor?'

'Some of the time. Ambidextrous, actually.'

'A woman of many talents. I look forward to seeing you on Saturday.'

Reaching for his hat, he got to his feet and slid past her, the backs of his legs brushing against her bent knees.

'Ladies,' he said, lifting his hat and bowing from the waist. 'I apologise for leaving, but I have business to attend to.' He looked directly at Rowena. 'Am I right in thinking you look ravishing in red?'

'I prefer blue. I don't own a red dress.'

Something flickered in his eyes. 'No matter. Perhaps red another time.'

'Well,' said Alice, after he'd gone, 'shooting above his station a bit. I know he's got money, but really... Are you going to keep the date with him?'

Her friend was intimating that he was not European: going out with him could lead to gossip.

'He behaved like a gentleman, which is more than I can say for Mr O'Connor and his friend.'

The smoke of the cheroot curled and twisted before her eyes.

'Don't tell me you fancy him,' Alice said. 'He's not one of us. Different worlds, if you know what I mean.'

Rowena thoughtfully stubbed out the half-smoked cheroot in the ashtray. 'Don't you think it strange that he didn't offer to drive us anywhere – the hotel where we might be staying overnight or back to the ferry, or even the whole way home? He must have known we'd driven here in our own car.'

'Reggie's car,' Alice reminded her.

'Whatever.' Rowena got to her feet. 'Mr Kim Pheloung knew we came by car. How did he know? He didn't see us arrive – at least, I wasn't aware of anyone spying on us.' She tossed the silver cigarette lighter in her hand and smiled at the weight. Solid silver and given to make her feel obliged to accept his invitation.

The music finished.

Rowena stood up and clapped.

Fiddle and bow dangling from his left hand, Connor nodded. 'Thank you.'

'"Star of the County Down" is a great favourite of mine. My grandfather was Irish. He served with the Indian Army.'

'You have a fine voice.'

'I'm glad you think so. I'd like to hear your voice again Mr O'Connor. If you allow me back here.'

Something seemed to shift in his eyes. 'It might be possible.'

She smiled. 'Goodnight, Mr O'Connor.'

'Goodnight.'

The light from the bar diminished as the door closed behind them.

She was about to walk away but stopped as 'Star of the County Down' started again, this time in slow tempo.

'Listen.'

Alice stopped too.

The smell of China was all around them and the alley was a little forbidding, but the music was magical. They didn't move from the spot until the lilting strains of the Irish ballad finally faded away.

'Are you going after her?'

'Why should I?'

'Because the *taipan* likes her.'

Connor balked at the word Harry had used. 'A *taipan* refers to the head of a legitimate business. I would suggest Pheloung's business is far from being that.'

'Somebody should warn her that he's a gangster and to be careful.'

Connor sat himself on his favourite stool at the end of the bar, plucked the strings of his fiddle and gestured to the barman for a drink. 'It's not my problem.' All the while he was hearing her voice in his head and thinking of her forthright manner, the colour of her eyes, her hair, and the fact that she was almost as tall as he was.

'Yes, it is. You liked her. I could see you did.'

'You're reading too much into my appreciation of her having a fair voice.' Connor defiantly knocked back his drink.

'You didn't need to serve them. You could have stuck to your guns but you didn't.'

'Damn!' The stool crashed to the floor and Connor kicked it behind him in frustration.

The men playing cards looked up, but swiftly returned to their game, glancing up again at a cold draught as Connor slammed the door behind him.

He saw her as she was about to open the driver's side door on a cream-coloured Austin. Her friend was already sitting in the passenger seat. 'Doctor!'

Her hair shone like glass and he wondered whether it smelt of flowers like that of the Chinese women he'd known.

The moment she saw him her expression hardened, though the trace of a smile played around her mouth. 'Have you come to apologise or to ask me back to sing with you?'

His face altered to match hers, but his smile was more guarded. 'No. I came to warn you about Kim Pheloung.'

She gave a half-choked laugh. 'It's none of your business and, anyway, he behaved like a gentleman, the only one I've met this evening.'

A retort bristled on his tongue, but he swallowed it. 'I don't care if you don't think me a gentleman. I can understand why. But it takes more than fine clothes and money to make a gentleman and Kim Pheloung isn't one.'

'And you are?'

'Have it your own way.' He turned his back on her and headed for his bar. Harry and he didn't need women around them. They certainly didn't need her.

When he came back in, Harry grinned. 'Did you tell her?'

'Yep.'

'How did she take it?'

'She didn't.'

'You saw the man who came in earlier.'

'A triad gangster.'

'Who works for Pheloung. Yang said he's having her followed.'

Connor paused in putting his violin back into the battered black case. It had once belonged to his mother's father and the old man had passed on his skills to his grandson. 'Why would he be doing that?'

Harry shrugged. 'I could hazard a guess that he's fallen in love.'

'Kim isn't capable of love.'

'Probably not. He sent Yang out to check where his man had got to. He was supposed to come back.'

'Probably lying in an alley with a knife in his gut – victim of a rival gang. Either way it was a bloody cheek to send Yang on an errand. He works for us now, not him.'

'Don't upset him, Connor,' warned Harry, his brows meeting over the bridge of his nose. 'We have to keep on the right side of him if we're to stay here, old boy. Otherwise our little foray into private enterprise is over.'

'If the Japanese come we'll be back to full-time soldiering anyway.'

'But they won't. Trust me, old boy. Their legs are too short and their eyesight is bad.'

'Just as well. Hong Kong is incapable of defending itself. Just a rock in the sea.'

'Did somebody important say that?'

'Hmm. Churchill, I think. It usually is nowadays.' Connor fastened the clasps of his violin case and headed for the door.

'Where are you going at this time of night?'

'To warn the woman. Then it won't be my fault if he gets his claws into her.'

'Why are you taking the violin?'

'I'm thinking that if music can calm a savage beast, or whatever it is, it might have the same effect on a woman like her. She can't be difficult to find. There aren't that many female doctors around. Anyway, I'll follow the car.'

Her room was on the first floor, looking out over a garden that was trying to be English but failing. On opening the balcony doors, the sound of tinkling water from a fountain came into the room through the billowing muslin curtains.

Kicking off her shoes, she rubbed at the nape of her neck and began unbuttoning the bodice of her dress but stopped when she fancied she heard a fiddle and singing coming from the garden. Was 'Star of the County Down' really being played outside or was it just in her head? She looked down into the garden.

The glow from her room fell on his features, his laughing eyes, and the smile on his face when he saw the surprise on hers.

'What are you doing here?' she hissed, the balcony rail damp with dew beneath her hands as she leaned over it. 'Male visitors aren't allowed. It's a nurses' home.'

He took the bow off the strings. 'But you're not a nurse. You told me so yourself. You're a doctor. Is that not correct?'

'I still have to abide by the rules.'

'Ah! I hate rules. It's true, I think, that they're meant to be broken.'

'Go away.'

'I can't. I won't. I have to speak to you. Warn you about our friend in the white suit – though calling him "friend" is stretching it...'

'I know what you're going to say. I won't listen.' She reached behind her for the brass handles of the balcony doors, meaning to shut him out and force him to go. What he said next caused her to pause.

'The man collects women. I thought you should know that.'

'I've known a lot of men who collect women – some without their wives knowing,' she said, smiling ruefully.

'What I mean to say is, he's bad, a real bad lot.'

'And you're Irish.'

'What's that supposed to mean?'

'That the Irish have a reputation for being a little wild. My grandfather was wild too.'

'How about your grandmother?'

Rowena winced. 'That's none of your business.'

'Kim's more than a little wild. He's dangerous. He'll eat you alive.'

'I'm not on the menu at the Jockey Club.'

Connor's steely blue eyes suddenly fixed on her bare shoulder where her unbuttoned bodice had slid down her arm. 'You might be.'

She swiftly pulled the bodice back into place. 'Look,' she said, lowering her voice and turning to see if any lights had suddenly flashed on, 'you have to go.'

'Can I see you tomorrow and explain further?'

'I don't need you to explain.'

'Very well. How about I go away now and tomorrow night I take you to a little Irish pub I know where they allow me to play and sing to my heart's content? You can sing too. How would that be?'

'My grandmother loved Irish songs.'

'Obviously a woman of taste.'

She smiled at his comment. If only he knew. Her grandmother had had the most melting brown eyes, the blackest of hair, and her sari had made a swishing sound when she'd moved. 'She was.'

'Then she would approve of you coming along with me. Wouldn't she?'

'You are incorrigible, Mr O'Connor.'

'Eight o'clock tomorrow evening.'

'It's a date.'

'I don't suppose there's any chance of you asking me up for a nightcap?'

'I don't suppose there is.'

She was still smiling as she watched him vanish into the night. His initial refusal to serve her with a drink no longer mattered. His music and his voice were still in her head.

# 2

Reggie Stuart wanted to take her to dinner on the night she had arranged to meet Kim Pheloung but had been persuaded to settle for lunch on Wednesday in the British-run café across the road from the house she shared with three nurses.

'Did the car behave appropriately?' He was reminding her that he had done her a favour so she owed him one in return.

'I can't see you on Saturday. I'm on duty at St John's maternity clinic. They're having trouble getting staff at the moment. Once that's over, it's a rest and back to the military facility they've set up at St Stephen's. They're short-staffed. The army need my help.'

'Tonight?'

Tonight she was off with Connor O'Connor to the Irish bar, but Reggie had been kind. She didn't want to hurt him. Prodding at her lunch, she felt a pang of guilt for leading him on and decided there and then that she had to put him straight.

She placed the cutlery to one side of her plate and leaned back in her chair. 'Reggie, we're friends and I don't think we can ever be anything else.'

'Well, that's putting it pretty bluntly.'

'I can't help it, Reggie. That's the way I feel.'


Connor arrived in a double rickshaw, his fiddle gripped firmly between his knees. He looked her up and down appreciatively. 'You're certainly wearing the right colour. You look very fine. Very fine indeed.'

'Green. I thought it the only colour to wear to an Irish pub.'

It was just off Nathan Road and, judging by the raucous welcome, Connor was very well known. He bought her a gin sling without asking her what she wanted and settled himself down with a double whiskey. Everyone else seemed to be drinking Guinness.

'I thought all Irishmen drank Guinness.'

'I like a whiskey,' he said, raising his glass after he'd found them a pair of chairs and a table. He leaned close and whispered, 'To tell you the truth I don't like the black stuff.'

Shouts began to ring out for him to get to his feet. 'Give us a tune, will you?'

Connor began with fast-moving jigs, which set feet

tapping. Those who knew the words sang them in loud slurred voices.

A few more drinks and a few more tunes.

'The next song I'm dedicating to my lovely companion. She's a doctor so she is. Can you believe that?'

Rowena found herself blushing as she became the centre of attention and a great roar of approval went up when Connor introduced her. 'My very own Star of the County Down – or in this case Hong Kong.'

Putting his fiddle aside, he began drumming on the table and singing 'Star of the County Down'.

By the end of the evening, she was singing and dancing with the rest and even drinking a glass or two of the famed black stout.

He helped her back into the same double rickshaw they'd arrived in. Hong Kong was still buzzing with life in the dimly lit bars where more was offered than drink. Soldiers, sailors and airmen mingled with the merchant seamen of all nations and the girls who hung around the docks.

She felt his arm resting on the folded hood at the rear of the rickshaw, jolting slightly in time with the footfall of the runner pulling them along.

'Did you enjoy yourself?' he asked.

'Didn't it look as though I did?'

'Aye, but what's outside doesn't always reflect what's inside.'

'Inside and out, I enjoyed myself.'

'I'm free Saturday.'

'I'm not. But, then, you already know that.'

'You're still going to see him?' He sounded incredulous.

'Kim. Yes. Why shouldn't I?'

'I've already told you, he collects women.'

She laughed. 'You mean like another man might collect stamps or antiques?'

'Something like that. Yes.'

She eyed him reproachfully. 'Are you saying I'm as sticky as a postage stamp or an antique?'

'That's a silly thing to say and is not what I'm meaning at all.'

In an angry movement, he removed his arm from along the back of the rickshaw. 'I'm trying to put this as delicately as I can. He's—'

'A criminal.'

He looked surprised. 'Basically, yes.'

'So how come you know him?'

'It's business.'

'So you consort with criminals?'

He shook his head. 'No… No, not in so far as the business is concerned. As I told you, it's something to occupy Harry and me when we're not tramping the parade ground or cleaning our guns.'

'Harry was with you the other night.'

'That's right. He's my senior officer and business partner. It's how we deal with the soldiering side of our life – a chance to let off steam.'

She thought of the way they'd looked together, similar in appearance, wearing the same clothes.

'We're just friends,' he said suddenly, as though reading her mind.

A fine shower of rain was misting the darkness when they finally arrived back at her house. A lamp flickered on in an upstairs room splashing a pool of light onto the narrow strip of garden. Suddenly aware that they were not alone, two figures in the doorway broke apart and hurried away.

'I'm not going to ask if you'll be inviting me in for a nightcap because I know you won't.'

They alighted onto the damp pavement.

'True.'

'And you'll be off to dinner with Kim Pheloung, no matter how much I nag you not to go.'

'That, too, is true.'

'I don't suppose you'll give up your career, marry me and wander round the pubs of Ireland singing while I play my fiddle?'

Laughing, she shook her head. 'You have to be joking.'

'Oh, well. Early days.'

'I've had a wonderful time.'

'We need to have wonderful times while we still can.'

She nodded, her smile persisting. 'I feel like Cinderella. No carriage and fine horses, just a rickety old rickshaw and a bloke between the shafts with very strong legs.'

'You make me laugh.'

'Good. Goodnight.'

His kiss was soft. 'I'll be calling on you again. I think tomorrow might be a good idea seeing as you're off with that other fellow on Saturday.'

'You're very pushy, Connor O'Connor. You don't own me, and neither does the other "fellow".'

His smile was beguiling. 'Not yet.'


As they had agreed, he came calling the next night, his violin tucked beneath his arm and wearing his uniform, strong legs in shorts, shirt undone at the neck.

She was wearing a blue silk dress embroidered with a silk flower on each shoulder. As the evening was warm, although it was December, her hair was fixed with pins into a cottage loaf style so her neck was exposed.

'You look a picture,' he said, taking her hand and kissing her fingers. 'Not much of a limousine, but the best I could do. The man between the shafts is Yang's brother – you may recall my barman?'

'I thought he was your manager.'

'Both.'

His smile lit the night and made her heart pound.

As before, the pub was packed with people, smoke, loud conversation, while the smell of Guinness and whiskey hung in the air.

A shout went up as Connor entered. 'Come on, man. Play us a jig.'

'Be fair, lads. You'll give me time to get a drink for me and my lady here.'

'Enough to wet your whistle.'

'Keep yourself sober for singing – and for wishing your lady a goodnight later on.'

'Or giving her a good night later on...'

'I'm sorry if they offended you. They're out for a good time.'

'I'm having a night in an Irish bar. It's only to be expected. If I can't take it, I shouldn't come through the door.'

After he'd brought her a drink and found her a spot to sit, Connor was lost to her, lost in traditional Irish music, songs that made some cry and jigs that made them dance.

Sweat soaking his shirt, he kept going, stopping only to get her another drink or down one of the beers or whiskeys bought for him by his audience.

When his fingers were sore and his voice cracking, he came back to sit with her.

'That was wonderful.'

'I was thinking the same about you. You're wonderful to sit here and understand what I was doing.'

'Did I understand what you were doing?'

'I think so. Go on. Tell me.'

She looked around the young men, who were all drinking and smoking too much and laughing too loudly. 'You made them forget. Nobody knows for sure what's going to happen next, but I think most people realise that Hong Kong is vulnerable.'

'A moment to enjoy themselves and forget they're soldiers. I do my best.'

'You have a heart of gold.'

'Now don't get too sentimental, Doctor.'

'Stop calling me Doctor. My name's Rowena.'

'Does that mean we're more than friends now?'

'If that's what you want.'

He leaned closer and stroked her nose with his fingertip. 'I want you as a lover. And before you refuse me, I know it's a tried and tested line, that it could be our last chance to feel alive and that I might be dead by this time next week, being a soldier and all that. So what do you say?'

Her jaw dropped. 'What? You're nothing if not blunt, Connor O'Connor. I'm shocked.'

There was humour in his eyes when he smiled. 'I was just testing the water.'

'No, you were not. You meant it.' She looked at him accusingly, but couldn't stop the smile, then the laughter.

He joined in, braced his arms around her and pulled her out into a dancing space, him bawling a song in her ear as they swung around. 'Early days, you'll say, but you are my star, Rowena. Have you any objection to that?'

'No.'

The rickshaw rumbled on through the darkness, the lantern hanging around the runner's neck throwing a fragile light into the blacked-out streets.

Rowena shivered. 'It's so dark.'

Connor's arm lay warm and solid behind her. As the rickshaw tossed over a bump in the road, his hand gripped her shoulder and brought her closer. 'Like the world,' he said.

For the first time since meeting him she heard fear in his voice. 'Tonight was wonderful.'

He put his arms around her. The gentleness of his kiss and the softness of his lips surprised her, and all the time she heard his words in her head, what he'd asked her, and despite herself, she did not find his suggestion objectionable.

She asked herself if wanting what might very well be one last moment of passion was so wrong.

The sounds of the night, the crispness of the air and the darkness made her feel as though they were somehow separate from the world, master and mistress of their own desires.

'Do I get that nightcap?' he asked suddenly.

She hesitated. 'I'm on duty in the morning. If it wasn't for that...'

She looked up into his eyes and he stroked her hair.

'I'm a good lover.'

'And I'm a good doctor. I owe it to my patients to be alert tomorrow.'

'I'm on duty for the next few days. I won't be around. It'll be next Monday before I'm back here, asking again for a nightcap. Do you mind?'

She shook her head. 'No. But it might only be a nightcap.'

'I don't think so.' He stroked her hair. 'Whatever happens, you're every song I ever sing, every tune I ever play. It's for you, Dr Rowena Rossiter. Just for you.'

# 3

Connor O'Connor. She was doodling his name on a writing pad, over and over again. The man remained fixed in her mind, like a bookmark that kept a favourite page or chapter. And that's what he is, she thought. A favourite page I want to revisit.

Kim Pheloung was also in her mind. Just thinking of him made her tingle all over. She imagined the softness of his skin stretched without a crease over the hard muscles beneath. Connor had insisted that he was a good lover, but she couldn't imagine being in bed with him. Kim, though, created images of their bodies entwined in silk sheets, the smouldering of perfumed candles, the lilting music of a harp or a flute.

She picked the lighter out of the pocket of her white lab coat and looked at it, turning it in her hand. The dinner date at the Jockey Club would bring welcome relief to her busy schedule, though so, too, would another night with Connor O'Connor.

Two attractive men in her life, but of the two Kim, the silk merchant, was the most intriguing.

Alice was still pressing her to rethink her dinner date at the Jockey Club.

'I've nothing else on,' she said to her friend, 'so I may as well go.'

'The singing Irishman won't be available?'

'Not until Monday.'

'Are sure about this?'

'About Connor? Of course I am.'

'No. The other. The foreigner.'

'You don't like foreigners, do you?'

'I didn't say that, I'm just not sure about him. How do you think he makes his money?'

'He's a silk merchant. That's what he told us.'

'I suppose that's all right.'

'Do you ever know that much about your date before you go out to dinner with him?'

'That's different. He's not one of us.'

'You mean of European descent.'

'That's exactly what I mean. You don't have anything in common and that includes background.'

'So I should only date men I can relate to.'

'It makes sense to stick to your own kind.'

A look of whimsy came into Rowena's eyes as she smiled. 'Didn't you ever want to fly away on a magic carpet with Sinbad when you were a little girl?'

'No. I did not.'

'I did. I used to read *One Thousand and One Tales*

*of the Arabian Nights.* I always wanted to fly away on a magic carpet with Sinbad – or Aladdin. It didn't matter which.'

'*Weeell*, I did read them, and I did quite like them, but...'

'They were foreign.'

'They were just stories.'

'Of course they were.' Rowena sighed beginning to lose patience with the conversation.

'And what about Connor? Will he continue to serenade you with his Irish flattery and that honey brown voice?'

'Honey brown, is it?'

'I heard him playing his fiddle outside your window, and I saw him drop you off the first time, then the second. Grand limousine. No expense spared.'

Reggie phoned again to ask her out on Saturday night and again she gave him the excuse that she was on duty when in fact she was keeping her date with Kim Pheloung at the Jockey Club. Unfortunately what had begun as a lie became truth.

'Serves you right for lying,' she muttered to herself, on being told that she was needed on duty on Saturday evening.

'Mrs Chandler has come in early. She's getting pains on and off. Although birth isn't imminent it's not far off, and Dr Mercer has broken his ankle.'

'Playing golf?'

'He got in the way of his opponent's hefty swing.'

'Well, that's all right, then,' said Alice, when Rowena told her.

'Shame. I was looking forward to it.'

'You'll have to tell him.'

'Of course. I'll give the club a ring and ask them to pass on my apologies. After that I'd better keep my date with Mrs Chandler and see when she plans to have her fourth child.'


It was gone six o'clock in the morning when twenty-seven-year-old Mrs Joan Chandler gave birth.

Aided by a midwife, Rowena was present, but once it was all over she handed the cleaning up to the nurses. An hour or two later, she visited the ward to see how Mrs Chandler was getting on. 'A beautiful baby girl,' she said. All babies were supposed to be beautiful, so the words fell like raindrops off a roof. This particular infant had a slightly Roman nose and a wrinkled red face. 'Have you thought of a name for her?'

'Yes,' said Mrs Chandler, with a rueful grimace. 'I thought I'd like to call her Enough. That should give my husband a strong hint.'

Rowena was still chuckling when she gained the double doors that led to the outside world, a new dawn and her chance to get home and sleep for the next six hours or more.

There were arches along the front terrace of the

hospital, which gave shade to the wards and offices beyond the metal-framed windows. At this hour solid darkness was giving way to the slate grey before dawn.

Rowena rubbed her tired eyes with forefinger and thumb. In her mind she could already see the water splashing into the bath along with a good handful of pink and yellow bath salts. Until her eyes were assaulted by a pale green Lagonda with chrome exhaust pipes hugging its gleaming paintwork.

Kim Pheloung, the dinner date she hadn't been able to keep, was leaning back against the car in a casual fashion, one leg folded across the other at the ankle. The brim of the white fedora shadowed his face and one hand was posed ready to whip it off in a pronounced wave of acknowledgement.

Sensing her there, he did just that, bowing slightly from the waist.

The sight of him, his sheer exoticism, took her aback. His black hair was shoulder length and tied in a thick bunch at the nape of his neck, a plait turned in upon itself. His smile was slow and languid, silvery wrinkles radiating like sunbursts at the corners of his eyes.

She felt an overwhelming need to apologise. 'I'm sorry I couldn't make our date. You did get my message?'

'Yes, I did. I came to take you for dim sum.'

She was about to say that she wasn't hungry, then decided that perhaps she was. Without a word, he opened the car door and, although reluctant to forgo her bath and catch up on her sleep, she did so.

In her head Alice was warning her about Kim Pheloung, and Connor had told her he was dangerous. She told herself she deserved to be indulged. She had enjoyed being with Connor, but he wasn't there. Kim Pheloung was. A bad boy he might be, but she had to award him top marks for consideration. 'I'm starving. You must have read my mind. I still have your lighter.' She fiddled in her pocket.

'I said you can keep it. As a gift.'

The open-top car was the perfect antidote to a night spent on a hospital ward bringing a baby into the world. A cool breeze tugged at her bound hair, a style she always adopted when on duty. Wisps blew across her face until she could no longer peer through it to see the road ahead.

'Let your hair down. Let it blow free.'

She hadn't realised he'd been watching her. Feeling strangely daring, she undid the clips and the snood until her hair fell onto her shoulders.

'I like that better,' he said, glancing at her sideways, then returning his attention to the road, relatively empty, given the hour, though the street traders were setting up shop and sunshades were bobbing around a multitude of shop fronts.

She'd anticipated him taking her deeper into Chinatown to a place unknown to her and most Europeans and thus something of an adventure. 'Where is the dim sum house?'

'I will surprise you.'

'No kidding,' she murmured, as the car pulled up outside a building she'd only seen from a distance. 'This is Victoria House.'

He nodded. 'Built on the land that once surrounded an ancient temple. Only the garden and a dovecote remain.'

'I'm impressed.' She gazed at the handsome portico of an exclusive apartment block. Like the Jockey Club, nobody lived there unless they had enough money to keep their own racehorses, a limousine and a handsome motorboat in the harbour.

'Forgive me, but I don't believe this place has a restaurant, and even if it did, it wouldn't be serving dim sum at this time in the morning.'

With a flourish of bravado, he swung open the car door. 'No. I will be serving you breakfast. Everything is prepared.'

There were three steps leading up to double doors. A large man of inscrutable expression and shoulders as wide as a barn door bowed stiffly. He was matched by another man on the other side who, like him, wore traditional garb, had a wispy beard and a long pigtail.

Swirls of ironwork in the guise of leaves, vines and snarling dragons formed protective panels over the doors, which the two men swung open simultaneously.

To hesitate was normal and she couldn't help but question her common sense when she entered the building. Alice had been right – she hardly knew this man – and if Connor was right, too, she could be walking into danger.

'Come,' Kim said to her, extending his arm around her back and gently but firmly easing her forward.

'I've never seen a block of apartments with guards at the entrance.'

'Security is very important to me. I run various businesses from here and also entertain when necessary.'

'Am I necessary?'

'Come.'

The doors had closed behind them with a sharp click. Ahead, another man dressed in similar fashion to the guards dragged open the iron grille of the lift. His hair was grey, but his expression was as inscrutable as theirs had been. He moved quietly and smoothly. Even the metal grille closed with a satisfying thud rather than a clang.

They began to ascend, Rowena clasping her hands in front of her, her fatigue overridden by her sense of adventure and the beguiling man who wanted to serve her breakfast.

A glance at Kim reaffirmed her view of him as beautiful, with fine features and refined taste. He intrigued her.

'I suppose you live in the penthouse.'

'It is like living in the tallest tower of a great castle. It has the best view in all Hong Kong. I see the ships coming and going in Victoria Harbour, and on a good day I can see all the way to Macau. I'm sure you'll be thrilled by it.'

'I'm not sure I can give it my all. I've been on duty all night.'

She'd already apologised in the car and told him about Dr Mercer.

'The man should take more care of himself,' he had responded. 'It was unfair of him. I was looking forward to seeing you, as I am sure you also were looking forward to us having dinner together.'

'Duty called. I cannot apologise enough.'

'It seems duty rules your life.'

'It does.'

'A great shame.' He looked tellingly at her. 'I wonder what kind of man it would take to make you forget duty and put him at the centre of your world.'

She couldn't help laughing. 'A very exceptional one.'

The lift whined to a halt, the grille dragged open by a small Chinese woman with downcast eyes, grey hair and tiny feet.

Rowena winced. They were lotus feet, broken and bound when she was a child and now only a little more than three inches in length.

The now outlawed practice of binding feet made her want to harangue and educate the ancient emperor who had demanded it be done. On the whim of one man countless women had been deformed. Worse, it hadn't died out with his death but continued through the centuries, from the most powerful to the peasant following the despicable custom.

Kim cupped her elbow in his hand and guided her into an opulent penthouse where a wall of windows looked out over the most imposing vista in Hong Kong. Below them a flock of white doves flew in and out of a pagoda dovecote. Around it were carp ponds, fountains and the bright yellow of many flowers.

'My garden,' he said. 'In the midst of all these buildings. Do you see the flowers? Chrysanthemums.'

The woman, who had followed them, remained silent and still until Kim turned to give her his hat and his jacket. When she bowed, he did not return the courtesy.

'Come. See the view.' He swept his arm towards it, like a ringmaster inviting the audience to look and be amazed.

'You weren't exaggerating,' murmured Rowena.

Spread out in a far-reaching vista, the Perfumed Harbour resembled a multi-coloured mural of colour, brightness and light. Liners and warships, sampans and junks all cheek by jowl against the backdrop of jumbled buildings. Far beyond the city the lilac hills of mainland China were collared with halos of floating mist.

'A lovely view. And your garden is beautiful.'

'Is that all you can say? A lovely view? Your eyes must be extremely tired.'

She looked at him and smiled. 'Not as much as my feet.'

He clapped his hands and the woman with the lotus feet appeared as if out of thin air. He pointed at Rowena's feet and said something.

'I asked her to get you slippers,' he explained, as the woman shuffled away. 'I also asked her to massage your feet before you put them on.'

'I don't want to put you to any trouble.'

'No trouble. I am not offering to do it myself.'

Rowena frowned. 'I meant the old lady. I understood that much.'

His eyebrows rose and his face glowed with pleasure. 'You understood? I am pleased to hear that. The foreigners here expect us to speak their language. For you I will speak in English.'

He did not ask her why she frowned but she felt compelled to tell him anyway. Of course he wouldn't regard the woman's feet as anything but normal.

'That woman. I cringe at the thought of her pain.'

'Please sit down,' he said, indicating the sweeping dimensions of a scarlet sofa positioned to take in the most panoramic of panoramic views.

Embroidered silk cushions were ranged along its full length and gave off the smell of herbs and dried flowers when Rowena leaned back.

He had ignored her comment about the bound feet, but she couldn't get the woman out of her mind, imagining the pain she had endured.

'Whatever would possess somebody to do that to their daughter?'

His jaw tightened. 'She would not have found a husband if her feet had been big.'

'But they're broken.'

'She suffered pain for her husband and he valued her for it. He also sensed her vulnerability – her dependence on him.'

As Rowena attempted to control her disgust the

woman came shuffling back with her sleeves rolled up and a pair of black velvet slippers dangling from her hand.

Kim explained to her that Rowena did not require a massage, just the slippers. The woman nodded and knelt down.

Her hands were gentle as she took Rowena's foot into her lap, took off her shoe and replaced it with one of the slippers. She repeated the same process with the other foot and gave no sign of surprise when the slippers only just fitted.

Rowena studied the top of her head. She reminded herself that the outrage had been carried out when the woman had been a child, little more than a toddler, when the bones had been malleable, but all the same it would have been a painful process.

The slippers were comfortable, as were the cushions at her back.

'I cooked breakfast before I went to collect you. Are you refreshed enough to eat?'

She stared at him. 'Before you collected me? How could you have been so sure I would come?'

'I knew you would wish to apologise and take breakfast in lieu of dinner. It's in the kitchen. I will ring for it when you are ready. In the meantime...'

Coffee was set on an ebony side table inlaid with mother-of-pearl flowers in pastel shades of light green, pink, yellow and white, glowing like the inside of conch shells. The rich smell made her stomach rumble. 'Delicious,' she said, after taking a sip.

'And now breakfast.' He clapped his hands.

'No... I have to go. I have to get some sleep.'

'Breakfast first.'

'I'm sorry, I don't really fancy dim sum at this hour. It's a little too early.'

'Exactly what I thought. I have cooked eggs, bacon, toast and marmalade. I also have good-quality butter. It's imported from New Zealand. Come. Eat.'

He lifted a cover in the centre of the table.

'That is so unfair,' she said, though she was delighted.

He pulled out a chair for her. 'Eat.'

She was halfway through the meal when something occurred to her. 'I would have thought a man like you would have his servants wait on him.'

'No servants. I wanted an intimate moment with you, as we would have had at the Jockey Club.'

She had never been the kind of girl to be embarrassed by a male comment, but on this occasion she felt her face was on fire.

'It is true.'

'But you don't know me.'

A controlled smile curved the corners of his mouth. 'But that is the whole point. I wish to get to know you. I decided this when I saw you at Connor's and he refused to serve you – though, as I told you, I had seen you before at the hospital.'

Rowena frowned over the last piece of toast she had every intention of eating before she reached for another cup of coffee. 'What do you think of Connor?'

'He is honourable enough.'

She sat back against the comfortable cushions and eyed him quizzically. 'Are you honourable?'

'What do you think?'

His deep-set eyes looked at her in such a way that she wanted to close her own in case he was capable of influencing her thoughts. 'I'm thinking I should be going to bed.'

'I, too, am thinking this.'

Rowena pushed the coffee cup away and got to her feet. 'I meant I should be away to my own bed. I'm on duty again tomorrow.'

'But at least you will have Sunday to recover.'

The moment he got to his feet, she realised she'd misconstrued. 'That's very considerate of you.'

'You sound surprised.'

'I just... well... You've gone out of your way to get me here.'

'But not to seduce you.'

She hardly noticed him gliding closer until she smelt the hint of spice and sandalwood, with the unmistakable pungency of eau de Cologne.

She kept her head bowed as she took off the slippers and slid her feet back into the black loafers that she reserved for the wards.

The old woman followed them to the lift, dragging the outer grille across after them. As it descended, the woman's feet, almost triangular in shape, were there before her eyes, prettily encased in a pair of embroidered slippers the size a four-year-old child might wear.

Before the lift thudded gently to the ground floor, she thanked him for breakfast.

'I gave you breakfast so you must give me something in return.'

'I can see you again, if that's what you want.'

'Ah, yes. Dinner. I will think upon this.'

The bulky men in black silk tunics pulled back the grille of the lift, running to tug open the heavy double doors, bowing as Kim escorted Rowena to the car outside.

She tied a scarf around her head and put on a pair of sunglasses that half hid her face. 'I'm beginning to flag a bit. It was a long night.'

'Not so much as you would have flagged if you had not sampled my very good coffee, though I would have liked you to eat more breakfast. However, you can go home to your bed and sleep. You have been fed. There is nothing else you need to do. Rest. I will be in touch when convenient.'

'I can't promise not to be on duty.'

'I cannot promise to be tolerant of your erratic lifestyle.'

'Erratic? I don't think it's erratic.'

'You will rest.'

It sounded like an order, but as her eyes were beginning to flutter shut, she didn't bother to argue.

It was nine o'clock in the morning when the car pulled up in front of the nurses' home, which was some way from the hospital.

'I have to go now.'

His mood seemed to have changed, his eyes flickering over the crowds already thronging the streets, early on a Sunday morning.

'Thank you for picking me up.'

He nodded, his dark pink lips set in an unbroken line, like iron. His eyes made her feel as though she was an exotic plant being carefully nurtured until it was time to be picked.

She watched him drive away, feeling a strange mixture of fear and excitement. He made her head swim and her blood race. She wished he had offered her half of his bed. She would probably have taken it.

Unlike Kim's home, there were no guards to open the doors of the nurses' home where, as the only female doctor, she was forced to live.

On a whim, a forlorn hope that he might have returned, she looked down the road and was surprised to see that more people than usual on a Sunday morning were crowding through the streets. Perhaps some kind of celebration was going on, though she couldn't hear fireworks. Hong Kong loved them, the displays and explosions sometimes going on all night, cascades of fiery brightness lighting the sky.

'You need to go to bed,' she murmured, her eyelids drooping.

A group of nurses, including Alice, were clustered at the bottom of the stairs, talking nineteen to the dozen, as her mother used to say, and looking decidedly anxious. It wasn't normal to see too many people around at this hour, perhaps one or two nurses off to the hospital or some staggering back, keen to get to their beds.

'Rowena! There you are. Have you heard what's happened?'

Rowena's thoughts were elsewhere. It had suddenly struck her that Kim had not asked where she lived but had brought her straight here. How could he have known that?

'What is it, Alice? Have you won a sweepstake? Broken a nail? Or have you finally met your Prince Charming?'

Alice's face darkened. 'It's worse than that. A lot worse. The Japanese have bombed Pearl Harbor. The Americans have entered the war.'

'And about time too,' said Rowena, and yawned again.

Alice's expression was unchanged. 'Rumour has it the Japanese are heading this way. It's our turn next. What are we going to do, Rowena? What the bloody hell are we going to do?'

# 4

Across the water in Kowloon, Connor's Bar shook to its foundations. Glasses and bottles tottered and tumbled from shelves. Pieces of the old ceiling smashed onto the canopies, snapping them in half, carved uprights standing at warped angles, the seating ruptured, the tables splintered.

Amid the crashing plaster, splintering wood and broken window panes, Connor and Harry hunkered down as another explosion rocked the roof from its supports and sent the front wall tumbling to the ground.

Yang, his face creased with misery, came out from his place of safety beneath the stairs. He was covered with dust. 'What now, boss?'

Harry threw him the oversized key to the front door. 'That's why we're here so bloody early this morning. Keep our key with yours. We might need it sometime or other. In the meantime it's all yours. We're called to arms. Bloody nuisance, but there you are.'

Yang stared at the vast iron key.

'We'll be back for our share of the profit after the battle's won,' added Connor, as he grabbed his violin case and scarpered.

'If we get back,' muttered Harry, as he rushed out after him.

Heads bowed, the pair scrambled out of the gap where the door had been, clambering over the mangled wreckage of what had been the front of the building.

Orders were being shouted by men in khaki, police and screaming merchants, attempting to save what they could from the devastation.

A crowd of Chinese were thronging towards the walled city in the hope that its ancient walls would remain when everything else was in ruins.

'My word. The walled city's still standing,' remarked Harry.

'It'll take more than a Japanese bomb to destroy that place.'

Their kitbags landed with a thud on the rough boards of the army vehicle that had come to collect them and they climbed in after them, Connor still carrying his violin.

''Bout bloody time,' shouted the driver. 'Don't you know there's a war on? I work for the army, not you two buggers.'

The driver was known to them and would do more or less anything they asked as long as they paid him. Cash, booze or cigarettes, he'd accept them all.

Connor and Harry grinned, said nothing but shared a packet of army-issue Woodbines between them.

'Good while it lasted,' said Harry, blowing a pillar of smoke into the air.

It had been Harry's idea to buy the bar. Connor had reminded him that they were in the army. 'As senior officer I have to pull rank, old chap. We're opening a bar. It's an order.'

'Then I've no choice – except I want my name above the door. Connor's Bar's got a better ring than Harry's Bar.'

'But not an out-and-out Irish bar.'

'No. A bit of a mixture. Irish and Chinese. The Chinese like a drink, a bit of music and a game of cards as much as the next man.'

Glad to have Connor as a partner, Harry hadn't argued, though they realised they could have only a part-time interest, which was why they had employed Yang, the previous owner, to manage the place. 'You can call us sleeping partners,' they'd explained to Yang.

'Yes,' he'd said, nodding vigorously. 'When you fight or sleep, I run bar.'

'We'll mostly be sleeping until the war comes to us,' murmured Connor.

The occasional visit was about all they could manage but it was enough – for now. They'd employed a simple logic mooted by Harry and agreed by Connor.

'It does not appear that our services are required yet by His dear old Majesty King George, so we might as well occupy ourselves making a few pounds for ourselves and having some fun. I've always wanted to own a pub, you know, one of those whitewashed places in the country with a thatched roof and low ceilings, the ale drawn straight from the tap.'

Connor had looked at him in amazement. 'You frequent nightclubs. I've been there with you, so I have.'

'Ah, yes, but a man can dream, old boy. A little place in the country...'

The only thing the bar in Kowloon had in common with an English pub was that it had a bar. Under Yang's ownership it had sold plugs of opium and long black pipes. The beds had been just that: beds. It was Connor who had suggested they convert them to seating alcoves.

Yang had been desperate to sell and not just because he wasn't making any money. His opium den had been doing well enough, but there was a price to pay, not just to a criminal gang running a protection racket out of the walled city, but to a big crime lord who controlled the opium supply in Hong Kong and increased the price whenever he felt like it.

Connor looked thoughtfully down the length of his cigarette. 'I suppose old Yang will revert to his former trade without us around – poor bastard.'

Harry nodded. 'Unless—'

He didn't finish his sentence. The lorry jolted as part of another building crumpled in a yellow-ochre dust cloud.

'Out! Out!'

It was Harry barking the order. Connor tumbled out with him, keeping low as they scurried for cover.

They found themselves enjoying the relative protection of a defensive position, connected by a narrow path to a sequence of redoubts squeezed among those buildings that were still standing. Dust stung their eyes, clogged their ears and hung like a pall over what remained of the one-storey army offices and the main gate into the cantonment.

Connor headed for where he should have been, skirting a contingent of Canadians who were busily assembling a field gun. Unfortunately their equipment had only just arrived and although the Japanese had been across the water in Canton for some time, the tempo of preparation was only now accelerating.

Despite the enemy bombers, the rattling of machine-guns, the fear swirling around him, Connor thought of the bar and smiled. How crazy they'd been, a pair of serving soldiers setting up a Chinese-style bar and making a success of it, a brief and pleasant interlude.

As a sergeant major, it was his job to assess the situation on the ground, barking orders, making sure men and machines were where they should be. Harry had reported to Headquarters, where maps would be spread, pins representing their fragile army moved around in the hope that they would prevail.

The truth was that they were undermanned and lacking in heavy armour.

His concern increasing, he looked up at the sky, hoping against hope to see their aircraft attempting to tackle the invaders. There was nothing. He concluded that none had even got off the ground.

Teams of Canadians and Indians took turns on the newly assembled field gun, sending shell after shell skywards.

Connor mopped the sweat from his brow. How swiftly things had changed.

The moment he saw Harry and other officers running out of Headquarters and waving their arms, he knew the game was up. 'They've landed on the island. Head for the boats. We're to defend Hong Kong.'

After ordering his men to positions where they could best be used, Connor had a word with the man who had become his closest friend. Concern was heavier than dirt on Harry's face.

'They're streaming south, coming our way. We're outnumbered.'

Connor sneaked a smile. 'No chance of a drink at Connor's Bar, then.'

Harry shook his head. 'No. Anyway, it's not as cosy as it was.'

Connor wondered at how they could still make jokes in such an alien world. To keep a hold on sanity, he thought. That's what we have to do in any way we can. 'Do we know where they're heading?'

'Fort Stanley way.'

'The hospital.'

'Is she there?'

Connor shrugged. 'I don't know.' He didn't say it, but he hoped she was. She'd intrigued him, and although they hadn't ended up in bed, he was sure it would happen sometime. In the meantime he had a war to fight.

'Are you two brothers?' asked a Canadian officer.

Connor laughed. 'Him an English gentleman and me an Irishman? Now that's something of an insult.'

'You look alike and you're always together.'

'That's friendship for you.'

He saw a questioning look flash into the man's eyes. He knew what it meant, but there was no time to deflect any accusation that might come. Nothing did. A bullet from the guns of a low-flying Zero took off the back of the Canadian's head.

Connor blinked, and then he was off, shouting and shoving. 'To Hong Kong. Get the bloody boats and get to Hong Kong.'

# 5

St Stephen's had been a school before the war had begun in Europe, but as the possibility of more fighting swept eastwards, it had been requisitioned and turned into a military hospital.

A number of people working in private clinics and varied disciplines of medicine had volunteered to serve there if the need arose. Until Saturday evening there had been only a skeleton staff in situ, army doctors readying themselves for an influx of injured men. Following the bombing of Pearl Harbor and the dire news that the enemy army was coming their way, the need had intensified. The number of army medical staff had been swollen by civilians, doctors and nurses all keen to do what they could.

The buildings were set in a green landscape bordered with deciduous trees. Even now, with enemy planes screeching overhead and people running in all directions, the buildings and grounds still looked as though they had been transplanted from Surrey.

A contingent of Punjabi soldiers closed the gate the moment they were through and began setting up a machine-gun post. The gates, they informed their driver, would not be opened again except for emergencies.

'I think we'll be getting quite a few of those, Sergeant,' Rowena remarked.

It turned out she was right. The emergencies came, ambulances and other vehicles carrying injured soldiers of all nations.

Rowena asked for a duty roster. Sister Alice Huntley lingered in case there was also one for the nurses. A senior surgeon with gold braid on his epaulettes said, 'There is one but we can't see it lasting for long. There are too many casualties. We'll all have to muck in until things are sorted.'

She didn't ask in what way things might get sorted, but exchanged a look with Alice, set her jaw and said, 'We'd better get on with it.'

Leave was more or less suspended. Nights out in Hong Kong were no longer an option. The neon lights had been turned off. A strict blackout was in force, the only light being from the few searchlights that were still in operation, their thick beams sweeping the sky.

Gradually the trickle of casualties became a flood. Kowloon was first to fall, though most of the casualties had been ferried to facilities closer to the harbour, church halls, canteens and the private clinics that had once catered for the wealthy of the island.

The sound of shells got nearer. The Zeros were strafing the hordes of refugees running for shelter.

Camps sprang up around the periphery of the hospital, though for the most part the dazed and frightened Chinese were kept out of the main grounds, which were gradually filling with brown tents housing hundreds of soldiers. Artillery was stationed closer to the boundaries, the throaty sound of firing continuing all day and most of the night, spent shells scattered everywhere.

Rest breaks for the medical staff were few and far between, mostly grabbed on the run.

After a particularly tiring week of no respite, but continuous work to staunch blood and save lives, the strain was beginning to tell.

Over a late-night whisky and soda, Rowena found herself sitting in the staff bay with Alice and a Chinese nurse. 'You should soak some cotton wool in cold tea and put it over those bags beneath your eyes,' she said to the Chinese nurse.

The woman blinked, smiled and promptly fell asleep.

Rowena turned to Alice. 'Was it that boring a suggestion?'

'No. We've all got the same bags. It's like a uniform.'

'Hope I get rid of them before I'm thirty.'

Alice sighed. 'I'd just like to reach thirty.'

They fell silent as they considered the probability of doing so.

Rowena frowned. 'I refuse to die before I've had another moment of fun. Dinner with a handsome man. Dancing at the Peninsular Hotel. Drinking with officers in crisp uniforms not stinking of death.' She smiled. 'Most of all, I'd also like to go to an Irish pub and sing "Star of the County Down" with Connor O'Connor one more time.'

'That's a long list.'

'And so little time.'

She didn't mention Kim. Alice didn't approve and they had enough to think about at present.

'That night we had in Kowloon sticks in my mind. I really enjoyed it. Was that the last time we dressed up to the nines?'

'I think so.' Alice sighed and scratched at her hair, which she hadn't washed for a week. 'I've got a new silk dress. A little man down some backstreet alley made it for me. I've only worn it once.'

Rowena thought of her favourite shoes, high-heeled with a peep toe, such a change from her loafers, which offered undoubted comfort but were far from glamorous. Was it really too much to ask to have some fun amid all this hard work and the horrors of war? 'Damn it. Let's get a pass, just for a few hours.'

Alice, who had been trained to look up to doctors, never failed to be surprised by Rowena's daring. 'Do you think we can swing it?'

'I'm going to try. Anyway, there seems to be a lull in

enemy action. I haven't heard a plane today. There's a place in the village nearby, a small bar run by the son of a Dutchman. It's not much, but okay for an hour or two.'

'If they let us.'

'Let's see if they will.'


Dr Black eyed Rowena cynically when she asked if there was any chance of leave. 'That's a very difficult question deserving of a carefully thought-out answer.' His baggy face looked baggier than usual. For a moment he seemed about to refuse her request. The telephone interrupted. He picked it up and frowned at whatever the person at the other end was saying to him.

'No. I would prefer that you didn't do that and I will hold you responsible for the consequences.'

Whoever it was appeared to insist on whatever they were asking. Dr Black looked defeated. 'If that's an order, I suppose I have to put up with it. But I don't like it. We're a hospital not a fortress or a defensive position. And I don't care what you say. We're bound to draw enemy fire.' The phone clicked as he returned it to its cradle. His frown deepened and his eyes were lacklustre.

Thinking he might have forgotten she was there, Rowena transferred her weight from one foot to the other, clearing her throat to remind him of her presence.

He looked up as though he'd just awoken, shook his head and smiled sadly.

'You're welcome to try to get out of this place. I wish I could. Quite frankly I feel as though I'll never get out of here. Enjoy yourself.'

She saw the concern in his eyes. He seemed to be seeking a source of strength to see him through what he felt was coming. 'It'll be just the two of us. Sister Huntley and myself.' He had not asked for any details. She'd felt obliged to give some in the vain hope that visualising young people having fun might cheer him up.

'Two, four or sixty. It matters not.'

Later she told Alice how hopeless he had seemed. 'The poor man's drained. At times he wasn't looking at me at all but far off, in another world.'

'Are we still going out?'

'You bet we are, but first we're putting up the Christmas decorations.'

Alice had strung bits of cotton wool on cotton thread and was hanging them in front of the windows. Rowena had decorated a potted palm with bits of silver paper and stars.

'What you doing, girls?'

The patients were intrigued. Descriptions of the decorations were relayed to those who could not see, lying in bed with bandages around their eyes.

'Spangles, stars and snow.'

'Can't wait to see it.'

'Looks lovely,' said those who could see but couldn't move.

'So glad you appreciate our efforts. Fingers crossed regarding mistletoe.'

'Mistletoe be blowed. I don't need any of that stuff to give a nurse a kiss. You too, Doc, if you play your cards right.'

Despite the fear that flashed from patient to patient, nurse to doctor each time a bomb exploded or a plane flew overhead, there was laughter.

Rowena helped Alice down from the wooden steps she'd been balanced on and saw the pensive look on her face. She knew immediately that Alice was having second thoughts.

'Do you really think we should be going there? To those bars? I mean, is it likely they might think we're on the game, like the bloke in the bar in Kowloon did?'

'He didn't think that. I've been out with him since, remember? He was fun. Really fun.'

She purposely sounded exuberant though she was reining in her own misgivings. Maintaining a normal life was central to their wellbeing and that was what she told Alice. 'You have to remain in control of your life and carry on as normal. Alice, the first casualties are in. We both know there's more to come. This could very well be our last chance to grab a moment to ourselves.'

'I know you're right, but... you're more daring than I am. Sometimes I think I should never have left Brisbane.'

'Don't worry. It'll turn out to be an experience you'll remember for the rest of your life.'

'However long it is,' Alice retorted grimly.

Rowena paused in brushing her hair and forced a smile. 'You're right to be scared. We all are. I certainly am. We're making a memory. Enjoy it. It'll be something to tell your grandchildren about in the far distant future.'

'I hope I get to have grandchildren.'

'I've every intention of doing so. I intend having a lot more sex before I die. No Imperial Japanese Army is going to make it otherwise.'

Alice looked both amused and appalled. 'Would you really? Not just anybody, surely.'

Rowena eyed her reflection. 'No. Not anybody.'

'I quite fancy one of those Canadians, especially the one who told me he used to be a lumberjack.' She giggled. 'Looked it too, judging by the size of his biceps. Imagine having them around you. Gives me the shivers.'

Rowena smiled. 'I've got my own imaginings, thank you.'

'But not the man on the flying carpet. The Oriental.' Alice was wearing a disapproving look.

'I wish you'd stop calling him that.'

'What should I call him?'

'The man who bought us drinks, which enabled us to stay.'

'Okay. Him. So what's the attraction?'

'He intrigued me.'

'Does that mean you'd have dinner with him? When all this is over, of course.'

'Why not?' She frowned. 'He knew where I lived. Drove me straight to the door – and he wouldn't be pinned down when I asked him where he was from. Did you notice that?'

'Perhaps he was ashamed of his background. I mean, he could be anything.'

'Profession, yes. But why be evasive about his origins?'

Alice shrugged. 'Beats me.' She looked at Rowena enquiringly. 'What you said about having more sex before you die. What would you do if he was the last man left alive? Would you really... you know... sleep with him?'

'Sleeping? I truly think that the most preposterous word to describe a night of passion.'

'Never mind the word, would you let him?'

'I don't know him. Perhaps.'

'Oh, Rowena. You can't mean you'd do that just so you get grandchildren.'

Rowena burst out laughing. 'For goodness' sake, Alice. I'm a doctor. You're a nurse. We know how to deal with... consequences. Besides, I don't think it's going to come to that. Anyway, there's a whole battalion of Canadians out there to choose from.'

At the very last minute before they left the building and took the road down to the main gate, Dr Black beckoned to them from the other side of the ward.

The pair of them stood in front of him, feeling like naughty schoolgirls.

'Two hours. No more.' A reflective expression appeared in his eyes when he saw Rowena's face fall and he sighed. 'You're young. Be back before the witching hour.'

He turned away, looking purposeful, but she could tell by the slope of his normally square shoulders that he was very tired.

★

It was seven in the evening and a filigree sunset shimmered through the treetops and fell like orange muslin over the extensive lawns in front of St Stephen's.

Rowena and Alice set out down the spur of the main drive, which swerved in the direction of what had previously been the preparatory school, its classrooms commandeered as overspill wards. The main road swept down to Fort Stanley, a British settlement built on the ruins of an older one.

The planes that had been absent that morning came round in the early evening. Although a large red cross had been painted on the roof of the hospital, the enemy aircraft still dived at the building, dropping bombs and strafing anything that moved.

Alice's steps slowed as they got closer to the main gate.

Rowena tried to sound reassuring: 'Keep going. Just an hour, but a little respite.'

It was unrealistic to think the lull would last. As the Japanese Army advanced, the hospital would fill with groaning men and the swift, sharp movements of medical staff as they fought to stem the tide of blood and death with scalpels, saws, scissors and bandages.

The soldiers on duty threw them admiring glances as they walked by.

'Handsome buggers,' murmured Alice, a wicked grin lifting one side of her mouth. 'Just look at those shoulders.'

'Just look at those thighs.'

Alice covered her mouth to mute her laughter.

Rowena smiled at all those who smiled at her. Such young men. Such brave young men. Such muscular bodies. 'One more time before I die,' she muttered.

Despite the sudden return of the sound of shelling, they kept going. It was Rowena's plan to walk down the drive and along the road to the cluster of houses and two or three bars just a few hundred yards from the main gate. Originally there had been only the one bar, run by the Chinese Dutchman, but more had sprung up almost overnight once it was obvious that the school had become a hospital to be staffed and defended by British military personnel.

The enterprising bar owners had been proved right and were very happy to be patronised by soldiers in need of a drink and everything else a Hong Kong bar could offer. That included prostitutes, female and male.

The main gate beckoned, wide enough to drive a tank through. It should have been so straightforward and there should have been nothing to stop them – but there was.

'Get out of the way.'

The soldiers frantically pushed them back, forcing them against the bushes that fringed the guard post.

The smell of petrol and the grinding of engines preceded a convoy of army vehicles. Men crowded the trucks both inside and out. Rowena was reminded of a swarm of bees. Those for whom there was no room on the trucks walked, marched, limped and used their rifles as walking sticks, all gazing ahead to the white-painted building, seeing the red cross on the roof as a sign of refuge.

Rowena knew immediately that they wouldn't be going anywhere. Already she was thinking of how many bandages would be needed, how many syringes for painkilling drugs and the new penicillin.

The soldiers were from a cross-section of the British Empire, Canadians, Indians, British and Australians, with machine-guns strapped to their shoulders. Some of the Canadians looked like fresh-faced boys who'd not long arrived, their ruddy complexions the result of lives spent in wide open spaces, where prairie land went on for ever and forests were thick with trees that grew so tall they blanked out the sky.

The Punjabis were tall and of aristocratic bearing, their beards and turbans more telling than their uniforms, advertising who they were and where they were from.

'Number one machine-gun to the left of the gate. Number two to the right. Fall back three and four over there and over there...'

The orders of an officer were repeated by the barked

orders of another man, whom she instantly recognised.

It was Connor.

Alice noticed too. 'Isn't that...?'

'Connor of Connor's Bar fame. The man who wouldn't serve us a drink but who can make the most wooden feet dance a jig.' She eyed him with dismay, not because she wasn't pleased to see him but because she knew that his presence meant things were bad and could only get worse.

The column of men fanned off, obeying orders, the hefty throng that had marched through the gate thinning into a tail, running off in all directions in response to more shouted orders.

'What do we do?' Alice asked nervously.

Rowena frowned. 'I don't know. Oh, sod it. Come on. Last-chance saloon!'

Alice made to follow Rowena around the red and white pole that served as a security gate to the hospital. A guard came out of his box, crossed his weapon over his chest and barred her way. 'I'm sorry, miss...'

'Doctor.'

'I'm sorry, Doctor. Nobody is allowed to leave.'

'I have permission from Dr Black for us to spend what little leave we have in the local bars – fly ridden and seedy as they might be. That's as far as we're going.'

'Things have changed.'

The officer who had intervened, spoke with the refined voice of Surrey drawing rooms and the cadets of Sandhurst. She recognised him as Harry, Connor's senior officer but also his friend. 'How much have they changed?'

'Too much.'

'We do have permission.'

'Fine. Go ahead if you want to get your head blown off.'

'We have passes,' said Rowena, offering him the pieces of paper Dr Black had signed.

He glanced at the signature then tore the passes to pieces and threw them up into the air. The wind sent them scuttling over the gravel path and grass verge.

'Connor!'

He saw her and strode over. 'What's going on?'

'The girls thought they were going for a night out. I'm afraid I had to disappoint them, old chap. I'll let you explain our position. Hey! You over there...' Harry strode off.

Connor braced his hands on his hips. 'The Japanese are coming this way. I think you'll find the bar owners have got the message and shut up shop.'

Rowena sighed and exchanged a brief look with Alice, whose usually pink cheeks were now ashen. 'I think we're going to be needed.'

'I think you will,' said Connor. 'Now you'd better get inside. It's not going to be very pleasant out here. Oh, but if you could just take care of this for me...'

He reached into the pile of kitbags that soldiers were identifying and taking to their billets in the brown tents on the front lawn. He handed her his violin case. 'Take care of it for me until sometime in the future when we can dance a jig and sing our hearts out.'

She felt privileged. He was putting his most precious possession out of harm's way.

'One more thing – just in case I don't get to do it ever again.'

The kiss was short and sweet. It took her by surprise and she couldn't help fingering her cheek. When again would she be kissed?

She ran back to the hospital, the violin clutched to her chest, a semi-hysterical Alice behind her.

The sky filled with enemy aircraft. The make-up she'd put on with such happy anticipation streamed down her face.

# 6

Men flowed in endless eddies back and forth to machine-gun posts, their tents and rest areas, the tracks of their feet flattening grass and creating muddy trails across what had been pristine green lawns. The air smelt of oil, sweat and fear. Clutches of men hovered over their weapons, one set replacing another at regular intervals, eyes peeled, trigger fingers ready for action.

At mealtimes the smell of bully beef and boiled potatoes vied with the more appetising smells coming from the Indians' food: they were more at ease with the local cuisine, making good use of saffron and paprika, rice and chicken.

Too weary even to unwind the mosquito net and lie down to sleep, Rowena stood at the window of her room. The first casualties were enough to keep everyone on their toes, but her gut feeling of more to come brought dryness to her throat and heaviness to her heart. If she thought she was tired now, it was likely nothing to the exhaustion to come – though she prayed it would never happen.

She saw Connor moving through the mass of men, imagined him doing his best to reassure with glib or saucy comments.

So many men. So young. Against a staccato accompaniment of sporadic machine-gun fire, some ate, some slept, some shaved, some cleaned their rifles, and the Sikhs unwound their hair, bringing it round from their shoulders, washing and brushing it, then coiling it into a topknot and rebinding their turbans. Their naked brown torsos made her think of her grandmother. Her skin must have been as glossy as theirs. No wonder her grandfather had disobeyed his British family and married her. How could he have resisted?

Alice came in just as she was giving in to the idea of trying to rest before duty called yet again. At least she might sleep a couple of hours, perhaps even four...

As the only female doctor, and there being no single rooms available, she had chosen to be billeted with Alice, sharing a room that overlooked the front lawns. When they had time they would sit on the deep window ledge and, despite the threat of stray bullets or shrapnel, watch the unfolding scene, wondering how many of those young men would be injured or killed, how many they would save to fight another day.

'I'm bushed,' said Alice, taking off her starched headdress and scratching her head. 'Is there any tea?'

'There is, but it's cold. But there is lemon and sugar.'

'That'll do me.' Alice kicked off her shoes and lifted the pot.

Rowena yawned as she began to undress. 'It's been a long day.'

'We're managing quite well, though, don't you think?'

'I'll be fine if I can get hold of a new pair of feet. How about you?'

'Ditto. My feet are killing me.' Alice's eyes went to the window. All was darkness except for the few embers from some impromptu cooking fires and the flashes from explosions in the distance, which were gradually getting closer. 'The Irish oaf asked about you today. He hoped you were looking after his fiddle.'

'He's not an oaf and I am looking after his fiddle.'

Unwilling to hear Alice's rather jaundiced view on anyone who wasn't from the same stable as herself, Rowena changed the subject. 'This is my last pair of stockings. And they've got a ladder. Hope I can get some more.'

'He said you had a grand voice and hoped you'd bump into each other, though he did say he was a trifle busy. I said, "Guess what? Dr Rowena Rossiter is also a bit busy these days. So is everyone."'

'I wouldn't mind some new underwear too,' Rowena mused. Stockings and silk camiknickers lay on the small chest of drawers at her bedside, but they were three years old.

'He was aching to see you,' Alice went on, 'but when's

that going to happen in this place? I told him I wouldn't blame you if you vowed never to see him again or look after his fiddle, seeing as he wouldn't serve us that night. And do you know what he did then? He apologised. Fancy that!' When Rowena failed to rise to the bait, Alice tried again: 'Still, at least he's white. No matter how rich a man is, it's best that you have some things in common. If you know what I mean.'

She was referring to Kim Pheloung. Rowena did not want to hear that. 'Goodnight.'

She was bundled up beneath the mosquito net, her back towards Alice. That very evening she had run into Connor on the front colonnade. They'd stood facing each other.

'Do you think anyone would see if I kissed you?' he wondered.

'Would you care if they did? Would I?'

'Damn it.'

Connor had kissed her anyway. His lips tasted salty and he smelt of sweat and cordite, but she didn't care. He felt warm and alive and made her feel the same way.

'Sorry you couldn't get away for your night out,' he finally said.

Her shoulders heaved with a sigh. 'I don't think any of us will be getting out for some time, do you?'

He shrugged. 'Probably not. Do you think I might kiss you again?'

She laughed, more lightly than she had for days. Big

as he was, he seemed so boyish. 'I think we should.'

'I think so too. It could be an age before we get another chance.'

She told herself that she was only doing it to give him support, a sweet memory to cherish. On reflection she knew it was more than that. She needed support and a sweet memory as much as he did.

'I have to go.' She disengaged first, then attempted to side-step him, but he countered it with a side-step of his own.

'I meant it about your singing. You've got a grand voice. My mother had a grand voice too.'

'So have you.'

'You're keeping the fiddle safe?'

'Of course I am. I put it in a cupboard down in the boiler house. Nobody goes there.'

She'd felt guilty that her thoughts were wandering in another direction but told herself that thinking about Kim Pheloung was a form of escapism. It would help her get through all this and whatever was to come.

Now Alice was still wandering around in her underwear, one foot resting on a chair as she began unfastening her suspenders and carefully curling her stockings down her legs. 'Have you seen those Indians? Stripping off to the waist and washing out front. And their hair! Longer than mine. Longer than yours,' Alice said suddenly.

'Can't say I've noticed,' muttered Rowena, pulling the sheet up to her chin. 'Goodnight.'

Something in the room buzzed for a while until it was

skewered on the blade of the ceiling fan. Beyond the window crickets sang into the night and the clattering of men, their armaments and their cooking pots, softened as they fell into fitful sleep.

At first she thought it was Alice's snoring or gunfire that had awoken her. Her eyes blinking open, she stared into the darkness her arms folded beneath her head.

His voice, unaccompanied by any instrument, drifted up to her window.

She smiled. The same song again, but not just a song: it was a message. He was telling her how he felt, that she was the colleen from County Down though her hair was nearly black and her eyes grey.

Smothered by darkness, Connor O'Connor lay on his side beneath a tree whose slender branches fell like a scented curtain before his eyes. He knew instinctively that she had heard him and, after checking on Harry and a few other things, he'd found this place, a perfect spot from which to observe without being seen by anyone in the grounds or in the main building.

A convenient stone pillowed his head. An opium pipe, long and black, containing the residue of the last smoke, lay cradled in the crook of his arm. Harry had taken it into his head to try opium but he had been unable to smoke it once and leave it. He was hooked. 'I aim to try everything in life, dear boy. After all, we don't get long on this earth, do we, so what have we got to lose? Give it a try.'

'Why should I?'

'Because you and I are soul mates. You'll always do what I want.'

'I don't do what you want. I help save you from yourself.'

'And those who would do me harm, old boy. And those who would do me harm.'

'Not tonight.' Tonight Connor had taken the plug and the pipe from him. 'Until matters improve, Harry. In the meantime you'll be needing your wits about you. You're the man in charge. There's men depending on you.'

Harry hadn't argued and Connor had made a sharp exit before he could change his mind.

Their friendship had begun on a foul night outside a pub in Catterick. Connor had come out of the pub. Harry had come from who knew where, cigarette holder poised in slender fingers, cap set jauntily to one side and smiling like a dockyard tart.

'Oy. Look at 'im.'

Connor could still hear the raucous twang of a Liverpool accent behind him. Harry had been under threat. Officer he might be and rightly respected but, like others before them, the men had sensed something else.

Connor could still hear the way Harry had greeted them. 'Nice night to be camping out,' he'd declared, in a sing-song voice.

'Camping out' was not the best expression to use in

front of common soldiers, whose favourite topics were football and women.

Dusk had been falling so, despite the blackout, it was easy to see one man smash the neck off a beer bottle and move in on the officer. The other two followed, one flinging a cigarette end to one side, another hurling off his jacket. Heads lowered, the three had circled Harry, like wolves scenting blood.

He remembered the look in their eyes: partly hatred, but also fear, as though he, being different, was a threat to their masculinity.

Connor had been on his way back to barracks, but one look at the glitter in the major's eyes, and he knew he had to stay.

The three men appeared not to notice that Harry found their behaviour amusing.

'Fag,' snarled one of the men.

'A queer officer. That's all we bloody need,' said another. 'Bound to get us killed. Bloody pansy.'

The man with the bottle moved first, the broken glass arcing over Harry's shoulder, missing him by inches as he stepped aside. Another man moved forward, straight into his fist. The third took only one step and found himself yanked back by his collar, swung round to be flung against the pub wall.

Connor gripped the wrist of the bottle-wielding man before he could take another swipe. One punch and his victim went sprawling.

After that he and Harry had eyed each other speculatively.

'I trust you don't mind me saying this, old boy, but you and I look devilishly similar.'

'To some extent.'

'And you're not a queer. I would know.'

Connor smiled at the memory. He didn't know why they had clicked, but they had, though he did wonder how Harry had made major. Class and position would have had a lot to do with it. Normally he didn't tolerate upper-class people like Harry, but there was something about him that he liked. No matter their differences, right from the start he'd felt obliged to look out for Harry, to be his friend and try to dissuade him from the worst of his excesses.

Her footsteps were so soft that he didn't wake up. She looked down at him sleeping peacefully, wanting to lie down beside him. If she was to die shortly, she wanted to lie just once more with a man she felt she could trust and love.

On seeing the opium pipe cradled in his arm the smile fell from her face and her retreating footsteps were swifter than those that had brought her there.

Back in her lonely single bed, she bunched the bedding round her chin telling herself that a man with such an addiction was nothing but trouble, yet she couldn't get him out of her mind. You could help him, she said to herself. Addicts could be weaned off it.

All was flux and bewilderment and habit was a way some people found to cope. In such turbulent times she could not condemn him out of hand. Worse things would happen before this terrible time was over.

★

'Connor! Where the devil are you?'

Harry sounded angry.

Connor hid the opium pipe in the long grass behind him. He would retrieve it later.

He dived behind the tree and came out the other side. Harry saw him and presumed he'd been to relieve himself.

'Sorry to interrupt you in full flow, but—'

The sudden barrage from enemy guns lit up the night. 'Shit!'

Harry ducked one way and Connor the other. Then they were up, running for shelter behind a bastion of sandbags, though only long enough to analyse what was going on and what to do next. Men who had been sleeping came out of their tents, and those on duty began to shoot. The rat-a-tat of a machine-gun out-chirped then silenced the crickets as the branches of trees were blown off or burst into flame.

Ambulance bells jangled, ruining the night and setting nerves on edge. A whole fleet of the cumbersome green vehicles trundled through the main gate, the red and white pole wavering overhead.

Relief etched on their faces, men clinging to the sides jumped off once they were within the hospital grounds. Some fell to their knees, others stood to attention the moment they could, waiting to report and to respond to orders.

Medical staff poured out of the main door of the hospital, the doctors' white coats flapping, nurses attempting to pin their headdresses to uncombed hair. One or two were wearing no stockings, frowned on usually but in this situation nobody cared. Speed was of the essence.

Connor spotted Rowena and raised his hand in something resembling a salute.

To his surprise, she gave him a blank stare, then looked away, almost as though she wasn't too sure who he was. He was puzzled but there was no time to ponder.

Stretcher after stretcher was unloaded and it wasn't too long before the last passed through the main entrance of the old school building.

The barrage stopped to be replaced by enemy planes, diving low, then dropping their bombs, strafing anything that moved with their wing cannon. Bullets pinged all around sending tufts of grass high into the air, and explosions lit the night.

A tired-looking messenger on a beaten-up motorcycle passed Harry his orders, which he tore open and read.

Connor looked straight at the man. 'How bad is it?'

The messenger was wearing a bandage over one eye. 'They've landed at Tai Koo.'

'They reached it days ago. Where are they now?'

'Don't know the name of the place, but they're not far behind us.' His voice shook and Connor was sure he could smell urine.

'Pissed yourself?'

'Shit myself, more like.'

'Get yourself a cup of tea.'

There was no way he was going to tell him to take a bath because they needed to preserve water for drinking just in case it was cut off. None of them would be bathing for the foreseeable future.

Harry shared the content of the written orders. 'We're to hold our position, defend the hospital until it's safe to drive the remaining civilians and medical staff away.'

'To where?'

'Victoria Harbour.'

'Does it still exist?'

Harry shook his head. 'Buggered if I know.' He threw back his head and took a great gulp of air. 'Orders are orders. Christ, I'm dying for a smoke.'

Connor knew he didn't mean a cigarette and, not wanting to be questioned, he ducked away.

The once pristine interior of the hospital stank of blood, vomit and unwashed bodies. Nurses, doctors and other medical staff did their utmost to keep standards up, determinedly calm despite the extreme circumstances.

Like everyone else, Rowena did what she had to do while trying not to puke or break down and yell at every man in the room that they shouldn't be doing this, that war was not an end unto itself but wholesale destruction.

While she was pushing a man's intestines back into his abdomen, she forced herself to think of lovely things from her youth, the smell of her parents' garden, the cheeky grin on the face of her brother, the silly boys who'd set their caps at her, not realising she would never make the kind of wife who kept house, had children and vied with her neighbours as to who had the cleanest windows and the whitest nets.

Blood spurted from beneath her fingers, splattering her white coat and spotting her chin.

Behind her momentarily closed eyelids, she imagined rosebuds. When she opened them again the blood was no less real, smelling metallic, and redder than the rosebuds she'd imagined.

'Rowena.' A gentle hand landed on her shoulder. Dr Black looked kindly but concerned. 'There's nothing more you can do for this poor chap.'

She looked down to see the dressings she'd applied were thick with blood, her hands too.

'You've been on duty for six hours.'

'So have you.'

'Take a break. That's an order.'

★

Outside, the early-morning light softened the brown tents against which tired men sat with their heads on their knees in air thick with smoke. A few of the medical staff lay full stretch on the grass, their arms crossed over their faces. The sound of explosions and firing was edging closer, yet they had to rest, had to operate a small bubble of normality.

Every nerve in Rowena's body screamed for rest, yet her mind refused to shut down. She was reliving the last few hours, triumphant about those who had survived, traumatised by those she'd been unable to save.

'Cigarette?'

Her fingers trembled, the cigarette sliding down between her finger joints. She knew it was him, and even though she'd seen the opium pipe she really didn't care. With hindsight she wished she'd lain down beside him, perhaps even had a puff of the pipe. What did she have to lose? The war was crowding in on them, only explosions and gunfire for now, but soon the slaughter would be here, breathing into their faces.

Connor gripped her wrist so that her hand was steady. He began patting the pockets of his sweat-stained shirt. 'No matches. Damn.'

'Never mind.'

With her free hand, which was shaking as much as the other, she sought out the lighter given her by Kim Pheloung and flicked it with her thumb again and again. Connor took it from her, studied the inscription on the bottom, then fired it into life, lighting her cigarette then his.

She inhaled deeply, closed her eyes and let her mind soar with the smoke as she exhaled. Then she laughed.

Connor frowned. 'What's so funny?'

'I don't smoke. Or I didn't before coming to Hong Kong.'

'You smoked that first time I saw you.'

She nodded. 'Yes, but only because you'd annoyed me and Kim... Mr Pheloung... offered me a cigarette.' She looked at her shoes, noted the spots of blood and instantly took another puff. 'It all seems like a lifetime ago.'

'Seventeen days.'

'Are you sure?'

'Seventeen days between Pearl Harbor and today. You know what day it is?'

She looked at him blankly before it came to her. 'Christmas Day.'

The staff had planned to sing carols for the benefit of the patients, but they hadn't had time.

'Did you hear me singing beneath your window the other night?'

Smiling hesitantly, she nodded and debated whether to tell him that she'd seen him cradling an opium pipe. She decided not to mention it. Not everyone continued the habits they'd picked up in war and perhaps he wouldn't either. Instead she said, 'You made me feel like Juliet.'

He threw back his head. 'Hah! Romeo and Juliet. Now there's a thing.'

She saw his smile slip away as he turned his head, his craggy face and deep-set eyes seeming to see beyond the boundary of trees. A dust cloud shrouded them. It was suddenly accompanied by the sound of gunfire, a tidal wave of men flowing beneath the branches.

'Go inside. Now!' He pressed the lighter into her hand, turned away and broke into a run. 'Get inside,' he shouted, more urgently, over his shoulder.

She hesitated long enough to see him racing towards the main gate, bellowing orders all the way.

Gunfire sounded from all around, not a barrage, but rifles and machine-guns, bullets pinging close by, and met with the opposing gunfire of the troops guarding the hospital entrance.

The attack they'd feared was inevitable had come. Rowena ran back to where she would be needed the most.


At first Connor felt gut-wrenching nausea, but once the adrenalin had kicked in, his mind and body were in unison. He'd heard it said that being in a battle was like sex: fear of failure and excitement set the blood racing and the heart beating faster.

'Get down behind those bloody sandbags. Mark your target. They're coming. You there, don't gawp, get your head down or it'll be blown off!' Harry Gracey came running from the other direction, his long legs eating up the ground. His face was haggard, his eyes sunken. 'This is it then, Sergeant Major Connor O'Connor.'

Fear lending speed to her feet, Rowena dashed into the main ward and shouted, 'They're coming. The Japanese are coming.'

Nobody moved until Alice flapped her hands in mute helplessness. 'What do we do?'

The gentle hand of Dr Black landed on Rowena's shoulder. 'There's nothing we can do but carry on.'

None of those listening could help but be calmed by what he said and the way he said it. Everyone went back to what they'd been doing, regardless of the fact that all hell was breaking loose outside.

'No Christmas turkey today, then?' asked the man who had been blinded by an exploding shell.

Another responded. 'No, mate, unless you count us. We're the bloody Christmas turkeys and about to be stuffed!'

Those patients still savvy enough to know what was happening could tell from the return fire that they were outnumbered.

Just before midday and against a back noise of bombardment, Dr Black approached Major Gracey and asked if it was possible for them to evacuate the hospital and perhaps surrender as far away from it as possible. 'I did protest about the army setting up within the grounds of the hospital. I believed then as I believe now that it could only serve to draw enemy fire. It seems that I was right.'

Harry Gracey refused. 'I'd love to, old chap, but I have my orders.'

From the ward window at the front of the hospital, Rowena heard what had been said and saw the unyielding rigidity of their jaws, the stiffness of their bodies. It was like watching two male buffalo about to lock horns and do each other serious injury.

A bomb blast blew the windows inwards, frames broken like matchsticks, glass flying through the air and onto the beds, injuring those patients who could not move.

Rowena was knocked to the floor. She saw her knees were bleeding, cut by shards of glass.

She heard the panic around her, more explosions, gunfire and the screams of injured men. Another blast, and clods of lawn flew through the broken window. Her immediate thought was that this could be the last day of her life. Suddenly something hit the back of her neck. Her gasp almost turned to laughter when she saw a Christmas bauble roll across the floor, unscathed.

One man after another was brought in bleeding and worn out. The sound of explosions and gunfire was less prolonged, especially the return fire of their men manning the machine-guns. Nobody wanted to say it out loud, but the defence of the hospital was drawing swiftly and inexorably to a close.

'They'll have to surrender,' said a patient. 'It can't go on.'

'It won't. You can tell we're finished. Bloody well finished.'

'What's likely to happen?' Though she was shaking, Alice's voice held firm.

Rowena's eyes hovered over the injured men lying helpless in their beds, the nurses carrying on with their duties, the orderlies, non-combatants, some conscientious objectors and Chinese locals who hated the Japanese for the wholesale massacre in Nanking.

They deserved to survive, but Alice had asked a serious question.

'The Japanese have a code of honour called *bushido*. I read it somewhere,' she added, in response to Alice's enquiring look. 'We need to appeal to their sense of honour. Nobody can be as bad as we've heard they are. There has to be some human decency in them somewhere. We throw ourselves on their mercy. This is a hospital after all. My plan is that everyone wears a Red Cross armband. Can you check that we still have some in store?'

Alice told an orderly to go and look. 'Keep everyone busy. That's the plan. Yes?'

'Yes,' said Rowena, and began her round, checking wounds, marking the notes for the senior doctors, an ulcer here, a suppuration, an oozing that could be infection, a wound that was slowly beginning to knit into a scar.

She did her best to present a courageous exterior to hide the terror she was feeling. Although she wanted to believe the enemy would respect the medical staff and the injured men, there was no guarantee.

The orderly returned with the armbands and Alice put him in charge of distributing them. Manufactured from stiff cotton, they were for the Chinese and other volunteers, to give them some kind of immunity when transporting patients close to enemy lines. Until now there had been no need for them because the Allied army had not been operating close to enemy lines. Their effectiveness would be proved now the enemy was on their doorstep. Rowena only hoped they would work.

*

Rapid gunfire preceded the enemy's arrival, bustling little men, dressed in pale khaki, thrusting bayonets at anyone still daring to put up a fight. Splattered with the blood of their men, Connor and Harry fell back to the tents where men were piling sandbags in a useless redoubt.

Harry aimed his revolver over the top, got the Japanese officer in his sight and pulled the trigger. Nothing happened.

Connor steadied his rifle.

'Stop.' Harry laid a hand over his. 'It's over.'

From where they were, it was as if the world stood still. The only scene filling their sight was that of the machine-gunners being bayoneted, some by as many as three Japanese soldiers, plunging naked steel into their guts then sawing through their necks.

'I have to stop this.'

Harry's voice was hushed but held immense strength.

Connor knew it wasn't his business to question the actions of a senior officer, but at least he could add some support – however futile it might be.

For Connor the only light moment in all of this was seeing a pure white handkerchief tied onto the bayonet of his gun and held aloft. Harry strode out from behind the redoubt and Connor followed at his right hand.

'If I die, remember your promise you'll get my remains back to England. My mother would appreciate it. I would appreciate it.'

'I might have to kill a few Nips before that happens so I may not be around myself.'

Harry's lips twisted into something that only partially resembled a grin. It might have been a grimace. 'You're a brick, Connor.'

'Say that again?'

'No more jokes. You heard what I said.'

With Harry leading them, waving a white flag, the men fell in, faces bloodied and blackened by a mixture of sweat and dirt.

The butt of a Japanese rifle slammed against the side of Harry's head, sending him down on buckled knees. A second butt slammed against the other side. Connor was given the same treatment. They lay on the ground, waiting for disembowelment or beheading, surrounded by a forest of bayonets poised and ready to strike.

'This is it,' Connor said. 'And there's bugger-all I can do about it.'

He did not close his eyes, but smiled up at the assembled imperial soldiers with their black eyes and their moon-shaped faces, his last view of life as he waited for death to strike.

Another soldier barged in, and raised the butt of his rifle.

'So much for getting you home,' Connor murmured, and everything went black.


A phalanx of conquering Japanese soldiers stood squarely on the lawn in front of the hospital, officers at the front, swords hanging at their sides.

Bravely, Dr Black and his second in command stood at the top of the steps leading to the entrance, wearing their white coats over their uniforms. More male medical staff stood behind them, then the nurses. Rowena had voiced her intention to stay on the ward, hoping her presence would help calm the patients.

Alice and two other nurses stayed with her, the three softly singing 'Away in a Manger' as they worked, their voices made oddly sweeter by fear.

The sounds from outside, guns firing, shouting and screaming disturbed a normality that was too fragile to hold onto. Everyone did their best to get on with what they had to do, sometimes freezing in the process of turning down a sheet or changing a dressing.

The nurse standing nearest the door had a good view of what was happening outside. She stood as though frozen, her face as white as the clean sheet she carried over her arm.

Rowena felt her fear and the rising tension around them. 'Nurse. What is it? What's happening?'

The nurse turned back to her colleagues with frightened eyes. 'They've taken the doctors away.'

'Did you see where they went?'

The nurse shook her head.

Suddenly there were screams as the double doors to the ward crashed open. Faces stiff with fear, those nurses who had been in the opposite ward barrelled into them, closely followed by half a dozen Japanese soldiers.

Rowena counted how many heads. Six nurses left of those who had been outside. With a sinking heart she remembered there having been more than that.

Orders were snapped out aided by the butts of rifles dividing Chinese from Europeans.

The Red Cross armbands so lately distributed were torn from their arms with almost enough force to pull joints out of sockets.

Two soldiers pushed the Chinese women towards the exit.

'We're being set free,' one whispered.

Rowena staggered as she was shoved with the rest of the women, all herded to one end of the room.

Patients unable to get out of bed and defend themselves lay there helplessly, their faces contorted with fear. The man who couldn't see was the only one lying completely still – except for his lips as he silently said the Lord's Prayer.

Even in the depths of winter, Hong Kong was never cold. Rowena could smell her sweat, though felt no heat. Fear covered her body like an icy cloak – or a shroud.

More soldiers swung through the doors, their faces twisted with unfathomable expressions, their arms lunging forward as they moved through the ward to the first bed, the first patient, one after another, bayoneting chests, stomachs, even eye sockets.

'No!'

It was an exclamation, but Rowena said it only softly, her hand to her mouth, eyes wide with horror.

Men were hanging over the sides of their beds, blood staining the once-white sheets. Only the blinded man seemed at peace, his head on the pillow, his arms close to his sides and a hint of a smile on his face.

Rowena felt Alice's arm slide through hers. 'Don't let them separate us. Please. I'm so scared.' Her eyes were squeezed half shut and her chin was trembling.

'I won't. I promise.'

Bayonets already slick with blood gained more as the bodies of those already fatally injured and the dead were stabbed again and again.

This was bloodlust. She'd heard of it but now bore witness to what it really meant: warriors drunk with power and revelling in the act of killing, the sight of blood.

Was Connor dead?

Fear and terror, small screams, gasps of horror.

They could keep close but there was nothing either of them could do to stop this. Alice was close to breaking point. Lies were as good a reassurance as anything. She winced with each thrust of a bayonet, each battering of a man in his bed, but Rowena kept her eyes open so that she wouldn't forget, the images imprinted on her mind as they would be on a camera, a record for the time of retribution or judgement.

The soldiers stopped the slaughter when an officer, with a stocky body and wearing glasses, entered the ward. Not having seen him, those at the far end of the ward finished off the man in the last bed before coming to attention.

The women kept close together as the officer strode stiff-legged, glancing at each bed in turn grunting and jerking his chin each time his accompanying adjutant said something.

An interpreter, thought Rowena. That man has to be an interpreter.

Stout legs parted, hands behind his back, the officer stood in front of them, like a fighting cock come to collect the prize hens.

Rowena was as scared as any of the others – most were

trembling, some close to tears. She and one or two others held their heads high. Most of the European women were taller than the stockier Japanese, which meant the officer was forced to look up at them.

The officer's face stiffened, his chin jutting out further than his nose. 'You will bow to your Japanese conquerors.'

The women looked at each other.

When they didn't respond, the adjutant stepped forward and slapped the nearest woman on the cheek, her head jerking to one side with the force of the blow.

'Bow to Japanese officer.'

The other women gasped in horror. Only Rowena stayed silent, her mind reeling. Her compatriots were afraid. She also sensed their loathing, which might lead to disobedience, which in turn could lead to death. 'Bow, ladies,' she said, taking the lead and bending from the waist. Through clenched teeth, she added, 'Bow to the victors.'

Their reluctance was tangible, but slowly they followed her lead.

'For now,' she whispered to herself.

The officer eyed the nurses. Despite everything, they were still neat and tidy in their uniforms. His gaze settled on Rowena. His fingers felt the collar of her white coat. 'Why you not wear nurse uniform?'

'Because I'm a doctor.'

'Doctor? Woman doctor?'

'Yes.'

She kept her eyes lowered. She knew she had to appear

submissive, at least when he was facing her. That was how it was in his society. Women were objects and had no power. All the same, an insane sense of pride had stopped her denying her profession.

He eyed her with interest. 'I speak English very well, yes?'

Breathing a sigh of relief that he hadn't taken offence, she nodded. 'Yes.'

'How well?' He tapped her face, the precursor to a slap.

'Very well. Yes.'

Their watches were taken, even the ones the nurses wore pinned to their breasts. After that came wedding rings, necklaces and earrings.

She tried to hold on to it, but a gold crucifix was torn from a Dutch nun who had fled to St Stephen's for shelter. Blows rained down on her but she kept it in her fist until one side of her face was battered and bruised, her eye beginning to close.

'This is intolerable.' Rowena kept her voice down, but could not ignore what was happening. She stepped forward, her limbs trembling as she bowed so low her head was level with the officer's waistline. 'Please. The woman is hurt. Will you allow me to tend her?'

'No.'

Rough hands, accompanied by shouted orders she did not understand, and she was pushed back into line. Lucky, she thought, but felt for the poor nun who was dragged off by two soldiers on the orders of the officer.

More barked orders, more pushing, shoving and prodding with rifle butts.

The women gasped but maintained a kind of calm as they were divided into threes.

'Out! Out!'

'Please keep close,' murmured Alice, as they were herded into the corridor that led to the old classrooms at the back of the building.

Rowena clasped her hand and that of Tansy, another Australian, the third member of their trio.

One last push and they were in a small room, perhaps a staff or study room for a teacher or student.

The door closed behind them and they heard a key grating in the lock.

Alice almost swooned with relief. 'Oh, my God,' she said, hands folded beneath her racing heart. 'Oh, my God.'

With a shaking hand Tansy took a cigarette from a crumpled packet. Her hand shook further when she tried to light it with a match.

'Here. Let me.'

Oddly the soldiers had failed to search the pockets of the white coat that, as a doctor, was her only uniform. Rowena took out the lighter and lit Tansy's cigarette.

'What do you think happened to the nun?' said Tansy, the smoke exhaled with a deep sigh.

Rowena shook her head. 'I don't know.'

In the depths of her pocket she felt the silver of the lighter grow warm with the rubbing of her fingers. She was in no doubt of its value should she need to barter it for food, water or even her freedom. For now she regarded it as a talisman, something that had survived the first phase of their incarceration.

The fate of the senior doctors was preying on her mind. There was no way of knowing where they were, though she still hoped that as doctors they would be respected.

Tansy nodded at the pocket containing the silver lighter. 'How come they didn't get that?'

'They seemed only to take what they could see. It was in my pocket and they would have had it if the officer hadn't arrived.' She took it out and studied the Chinese characters etched on the bottom. Another world, another night. A gift from the man she knew as Kim Pheloung.

A scream followed by the sound of sporadic gunfire brought her back to the present. The killing continued, but sounded now as though it had speeded up and was coming from the direction of where the dark brown tents had been erected on the lawn.

Triumphant shouts followed.

'*Banzai! Banzai!*'

'Bastards!' muttered Tansy, head hanging over her cigarette.

Alice slid to the floor, her back against the wall and her face buried in her hands.

There were shouts from the living soldiers. 'Bloody Nips, killing wounded men.'

More expletives shouted in an Aussie or British

regional accent. She strained to listen for an expletive delivered in an Irish accent, but none came.

Instantly more gunfire. More screams.

Alice clamped her hands over her ears.

Tansy puked into a wastepaper basket.

Rowena shuddered, still waiting to hear Connor bawling at the enemy, though it would be more sensible if he kept his mouth shut. The only other reason for his silence was that he was lying out there with the others, unable to sing or shout ever again.

'Can't anyone do anything to stop them?' Alice implored, out now from behind her hands.

'Not yet. Not today, not tomorrow or even next year. But they will. Eventually.'

She wanted to believe that the main killing spree was over and the survivors, men, women and children, would be taken as prisoners of war.

Tansy pushed sweaty tendrils of reddish brown hair off her face. 'Sorry about that.'

'No need to be. I'm just about holding mine back.'

Neither of the nurses had asked her what she thought might happen next and she was grateful for that.

Time went on. Nobody came.

The windows were closed and the room was getting hotter.

Alice slowly dropped her hands from her ears. 'Do you think we could open a window?'

'I don't think it would be wise. At least the blinds are down. With the sun streaming in we'd roast like turkeys.'

'I was looking forward to Christmas dinner – even though it was chicken and not turkey. I made some paper hats, not enough to go round, but still...' Tansy's voice trailed away.

Rowena thought about taking off her white coat, but decided against it. Perhaps holding on to some symbol of status might be advantageous.

There was nothing to do but wait.

She studied Tansy's taut expression and the way her clasped hands tightened, released, and tightened again. She was holding on, but it wouldn't last. She clasped her own hands together. They felt icy cold, as though there was no blood left in them.

She decided against giving a pep talk because she was as scared as they were at what might happen next. But it made sense to take their minds off their fear... 'I'm thirsty. We've been in here for, what, two hours?'

'I'd tell you the time if I still had a watch,' Tansy said grimly.

'They took mine too,' Alice said.

'No matter,' said Rowena, getting to her feet. 'We need water. Food too.'

'What about the lavatory?'

'Use the fire bucket or the wastepaper bin.'

Rowena hammered on the door. 'Hey! Can anyone hear us? Somebody!'

She hammered again, aware that Tansy and Alice were staring at her back with frightened eyes.

'Should you be doing that?'

'You've just said it yourself. We're thirsty.'

'But...'

She guessed they felt safer with a door between them and the enemy. She did too, but they had to have water.

'They're coming.'

The tramping of boots heralded the unlocking, then swinging open of the door. Two soldiers entered the room. She stepped back, wondering if it was appropriate to bow. One of them pushed hard at her shoulder and shouted something she didn't understand.

'We need water,' she said, making a cup shape in front of her mouth. 'Water.'

They didn't speak English but understood her action, if their mimicking of it was anything to go by and the shared laughter that followed.

One went away, closing the door behind him. The other remained, studying each woman in turn, standing in front of one, moving to another with steady measured footsteps, smiling all the time as he moved his bayonet in circles around their hearts and stomachs.

When they shrank away from him, he laughed and repeated his actions, with little stabbing movements, making them jump back each time he did it. Only once did he lower his bayonet to reach out and touch Tansy's luxuriant hair, the colour and texture seeming to fascinate him.

Alice gasped when he placed his hand on her breast and looked about to push him away.

'Don't.'

Rowena's hushed warning stilled Alice's hand but diverted his attention to her.

She flinched when he laid the cold steel blade against her cheek. A little more pressure, the skin would break and blood would flow – as it would with a scalpel. Fashioned from the same substance, hard steel, yet the scalpel was used to heal and prolong life, the bayonet to intimidate, maim and kill.

He grinned and muttered something, increasing the pressure of the steel against her cheek. A small nick, a sharp pain and, as she'd feared, blood trickled warmly down her face.

Holding back a scream wasn't easy, but logic told her to keep her head and hold it high.

Over his shoulder she saw Alice thrust a fist into her mouth, eyes wide with terror. Tansy was retching though there couldn't have been anything left in her stomach.

His grin vanished and something else came to his eyes. The bayonet retreated. He waved it at her in a downward direction and barked an order. She knew he wanted her down on her knees.

Alice whimpered, both hands now covering her face.

Tansy was taking deep breaths, her chest heaving.

Rowena had no choice. She sank to her knees, looked up at him and gulped as he reached for the front opening of his trousers.

Just as what she most feared seemed imminent, the door opened. The original guard and the adjutant appeared, carrying enamel pitchers. The adjutant set down a pitcher and ordered the guard to set down the two he was carrying.

The guard who'd drawn blood from Rowena's face sprang to attention.

The adjutant looked at her and frowned. 'What is happening?'

She wiped the blood from her cheek with the back of her hand and, without waiting for permission, got to her feet.

The adjutant's head jerked round from her to the guard. He asked a question. The guard gabbled an answer that might or might not have been the truth.

Whatever he'd said was badly received. The adjutant slapped his face on one side, then the other. His glance at her bloodied face was uncompromising in that he did not care for the guard's explanation but neither did he wish to draw things out. 'You have water,' said the adjutant. 'Imperial Japanese Army is merciful towards women and will be more merciful when your generals have surrendered.'

Rowena gulped. The garrison had not yet surrendered. She dragged her thoughts back to the immediate, the here and now of their continuing existence. 'And food. When can we have food?'

An odd silence fell on them all, three members of the Japanese military and three female medical staff.

The adjutant's eyes fell on each of them in turn.

Rowena's jaw hardened. She wanted to ask him to explain how torturing and bayoneting patients in their beds was merciful but knew better. Instead she asked the whereabouts of her fellow doctors.

The adjutant's look hardened, his eyes like two black beetles beneath his brow. 'Officers. Not doctors.'

He turned on his heel, leaving her stunned and speechless.

When she turned, Tansy and Alice were drinking from the pitchers.

'Didn't you hear what he said?'

They stared at her. Then Tansy said, 'It's terrible. But there's nothing you or any of us can do. Drink, Dr Rossiter. Even if they're dead, we have to survive.'

'Yes. To tell the tale. If we survive.'

'Do you think they're dead? The doctors?' asked Alice.

She gently bathed Rowena's bleeding cheek with water and her own handkerchief. Her voice sounded as though it were coming from the bottom of an oil drum, hollow and empty as though all the life had been sucked out of it.

Rowena brushed her hand away. 'How the hell would I know?' She drank from one of the pitchers.

Alice winced.

'I'm sorry,' said Rowena, her palm flat on her brow. 'The tension's got to me. I really thought...' She gulped back the ugliness of what might have happened if the adjutant hadn't arrived to stop it. 'I'm truly sorry.'

Alice looked away. Tansy muffled her sobs with a thick strand of hair she pulled across her face.

The room had no furniture, just a desk, the bin and the fire bucket. The three women perched on the desk, their backs resting against the wall.

'We should try to get some sleep,' said Rowena. 'We may need it. I don't know about you, but I'm losing track of time.'

'It's Christmas,' said Alice. 'I've always been happiest at Christmas.'

'Ah, yes. Presents, plum pudding and roast potatoes,' murmured Rowena.

Tansy's voice wavered as she said, 'A stocking. I love Christmas stockings.'

'Not the ones in packets given to you by an admiring officer?' Rowena sounded more amused than she actually was.

'And chocolate. What wouldn't I give for a bar of Fry's Five Boys?'

They tried singing carols, Rowena going out of her way to sing the jollier ones like 'God Rest Ye Merry, Gentlemen' eventually getting round to 'Silent Night', their voices trembling when they reached 'Sleep in heavenly peace'. So many were sleeping for ever. She only prayed that Connor wasn't among them.

'Wish we were at peace,' said Alice.

Rowena mentioned their night out in Kowloon. 'We were certainly on an adventure.'

Alice's laugh was brittle, but it helped when Tansy asked her to tell her about it.

Rowena left her to get on with it. Her mind was outside, with Connor and the dead men scattered across the lawn.

Time dragged on, second by second, minute by minute, hour by hour. They dozed, cried and prayed, sometimes making the odd cryptic comment. Their spirits lifted on hearing gunfire or aeroplanes flying overhead, then dived at the sound of enemy cheering. The planes were Japanese.

As dusk descended Rowena, crunched up semi-foetal style against the whitewashed wall, turned her head and looked up at the window. She debated drawing up the blind to see what was going on. Did she dare?

'The sun's gone down.'

She stared at the blind expectantly as though some time soon it would wind up by itself. Taking a bold leap of faith, she went to the window and tentatively rolled it up.

'What do you see?' Alice sounded hopeful.

'Nothing,' said Rowena. She let the blind drop. 'The outside shutters are closed.'

A lot of buildings in Hong Kong had shutters, no windows with glass panes. The hospital had both. It appeared the shutters had been closed and fastened from the outside.

The room had turned dark. Rowena went to the light switch. Nothing happened. 'The mains must have gone down and the oh-so-clever Japanese haven't found the generator.'

They all knew the generator was in the basement. Keeping Connor's violin dry, thought Rowena, and almost smiled.

'Do you think he's dead?' asked Alice, as though she'd read her mind.

'I hope not. I'll miss him playing the fiddle and singing. It did make me tap my feet.'

'And our foreign friend?'

She frowned. 'I would prefer to be with him now than here.'

Alice shivered. 'So would I, and that's saying something coming from me.'

'We'll never see the likes of him again, not unless they allow visitors at prisoner-of-war camps.'

Neither voiced the fear that they might never get to a prisoner-of-war camp.

'I wish they would bring us food,' said Alice, bending over her arms, which were wrapped around her stomach.

'I don't,' said Tansy, averting her eyes from what she'd spewed up earlier.

'I'll get us some.' Rowena did as she'd done before, rapping on the door, more furiously this time.

Muffled conversation came from outside, laughter, shouts of derision, then the tramping of army boots. The door swung open to reveal four privates standing there, glassy-eyed, a bottle of stolen whisky passing from one soldier to another.

The three women looked at them with frightened eyes. Even Rowena had lost some of her nerve, but resolved not to show any sign of fear, to appear confident, to take the opportunity to ask for food and more water.

The men stared, leering at each woman in turn, licking their lips, sipping the whisky.

'We haven't had anything to eat all day,' she stated, and made movements with her hands, fingers together as though she were taking food from a rice bowl to her mouth.

An exchange of words and smiles between the men, then a coarse hand grabbed her shoulder and pulled her out of the door. Another hand pressed into her back. In her peripheral vision she saw the alarm on her colleagues' faces. 'Looks like I have to collect it,' she called, over her shoulder.

All bravado vanished as the door behind her was closed, the key turned in the lock. She was alone with four drunken men. Although her instinct told her otherwise, she held on to the belief that they were taking her to fetch food – or perhaps to ask the commanding officer or his adjutant for permission to do so.

Prodding her with their fists or their rifle butts, they pushed her all the way past the wards she'd known so well, the beds now empty of the injured men that had lain in them and soaked with blood, the smell like scorched metal on the air.

When her steps slowed the butt of a rifle jabbed into the hollow of her back.

'Out. Out. Out.'

Outside? She froze. This had to be the moment they were going to shoot her.

This is it, the end of your life, she thought, and stumbled as her legs threatened to buckle beneath her.

On they went, out of the door to a quiet courtyard at the back of the hospital. It was a shady place that used to be pleasant, but even here there was the smell of blood and the bodies of the Chinese women who had thought they would be freed. Her blood ran like iced water in her veins at the thought of her body being piled on top of theirs. So much potential. So much youth. All over.

They pushed her out of the courtyard and onto the path that wound through aromatic bushes to the chapel, a holy place set apart from the main building.

Her heart raced, drumming so loudly she could hear her pulse in her ears, like tinnitus but louder and far more frightening, fatal and final.

These men from a different country, different culture, different religion, had no need of a Christian chapel, but that was indeed the direction in which they were heading... unless it had become a mortuary.

Double doors of gleaming mahogany were pushed open. The chapel smelt of incense, candles and the wax polish recently used on the wooden pews. It was very cold and desolate but perhaps the only place not smelling of blood.

No lights were switched on, no candles lit. The light from a dying day shone through windows situated on each side of the altar. The altar cloth was missing, along with the silver candles and other church vessels that had once graced the house of prayer.

Like the hospital wards, the chapel had been decorated for the Christmas service, cotton wool snow falling in straight skeins in front of the windows, spiky bamboo shoots bound with tinsel and ribbons, glass balls and angels made from clothes pegs, gowns from scraps of bandage, dried grass woven into wings.

Rowena stood with her back to the altar facing them, her fear rising as the muttering soldiers heaved a pew against the closed doors. She knew then what they were going to do. No doubt they would eventually kill her. In her mind she was taking off on a flying carpet, an escape from reality, into a dream world.

They chattered excitedly as they laid their weapons aside, flung off their caps and formed a circle around her, grinning as they undid their trousers.

In a strange move she herself didn't quite understand, she began to take off her white coat, the item she'd foolishly believed would act as a shield. For some reason she didn't want it sullied with their touch or with her blood if they killed her.

'Do you mind?' she asked, as if having their permission really mattered, but spoken for her benefit rather than theirs.

She didn't know what they said to each other, probably that she was keen on what they were about to do, since she'd taken off her coat.

When they saw that was all she was taking off, they came at her in a rush, tearing off the rest of her clothes, knocking her to the floor, holding her there, arms above her head, legs spread.

Above her, a trio of angels made from clothes pegs and ragged bits of material swung from tinsel.

She didn't struggle, but lay there with her eyes fixed on the Christmas decorations, willing her mind to be somewhere else and totally separate from her body.

# 7

Connor rubbed at his ear and the blood crusted around it.

'Can't hear a bloody thing.'

'Really?'

Connor had done nothing much to infuriate the guard who had clouted the side of his head with the butt of his rifle, except to help a man from the ground who was trying to keep up even though his arm was broken. 'Worth it,' he muttered to himself.

He could stand the pain of his busted eardrum. Living with the sight of the man he'd helped was more difficult. He'd been knocked down, then bayoneted, his guts overflowing from his stomach.

Now the dead man was one of many being carried to the bonfire of bodies already blazing, helped by a little petrol from a British jerry can.

Flies were swarming around the piles of dead, which included those who had been manning the machine-guns and others who had put up a fight before Harry had waved the white flag. No more than a quarter of the original military force was left.

They worked steadfastly and silently, slinging one body onto the funeral pyre before going back for another, their faces grim set and eyes filled with tears.

The worst thing about it was that they recognised those they now carried. Connor could still hear the mighty laughter of one of his Indian sergeants, the mouth-organ music of a Canadian chap.

The next body was that of Dr Black – not a fighting man but an army doctor. His second in command had also been slaughtered. Harry took his arms and Connor his legs.

'One, two, three.'

Another body on the fire.

Hearing Harry sobbing, Connor touched his shoulder. 'Bastards.' He swiped at his eyes.

Three nurses, the ones who had been marched away from the rest on the first day lay dead and half naked. Neither man needed to be told that they had all been raped before they were slaughtered, the head of one almost severed from her body.

Connor's hesitation in picking her up earned him another jab in the back with a rifle butt, but he didn't care. 'I'm getting there. Have a little respect.'

He cricked forward under the force of the blow, but still took his time lifting the woman from the ground.

This time he held the arms but called Harry to place his hands beneath her head. Someone else carried her legs, so at least she'd go whole into the afterlife.

At long last there were no more bodies but the flattened grass and rust-coloured patches of blood where they had been. The fire sizzled with running fat and the smell of burning flesh sickened some enough to empty their stomachs, others their bowels.

'Something for the diary,' whispered Harry.

'They'll kill you if they know you're keeping a record.'

'They'll probably kill me anyway. One way or another. Christ, will you look at these blisters? Whatever would my dear mama say? Or my father, come to that. "You're an officer, son, and should be treated as such." Tell that to the sour-faced sod over there!'

Tired, thirsty and hungry, following their grim work, Connor, Harry and their men slumped to the ground only to be goaded upright by their captors.

'Up, up, up.'

At sight of the officer in charge, Harry stepped forward and saluted.

'Colonel. Permission to speak.'

The colonel looked him up and down from his lesser height with what could only be interpreted as the utmost contempt. 'Why you salute me? You are coward. Japanese do not surrender. A soldier is no longer a soldier when surrender. You bow. Like slave, servant or woman, you bow.'

Connor slowly moved closer to his friend's side. Harry

could be so bloody unbending when he wanted to be.

'Bow,' he whispered. 'Stop being a fucking lord of the manor and bow.'

For a moment he thought Harry would remain defiant. A little pause, but then, to Connor's relief, he reconsidered and bowed as low as he could from a height far greater than that of his captor.

'We have only been given a little water and no food. My men... we are hungry and tired.'

The blow came from out of the blue and had not been ordered. Harry crumpled to the ground, eyes rolling back in his head before they closed.

At first glance Connor presumed him dead. Sick to his stomach, soaked in sweat and drowning in anger, he fell to his knees.

Harry's eyelids flickered.

Connor glared fiercely up at the colonel. 'Knock me down too, but if you want more work out of us, we have to be fed – or we might just as well jump into that bonfire of yours right now.' He waited for what might be the final blow.

Although he knew how dangerous it was, his look was fierce and uncompromising.

Never far from the colonel's side, the adjutant translated. The colonel's jaw flexed as he weighed his options.

Connor silently congratulated himself that he'd guessed right.

Finally the colonel's nostrils flared and his eyes were

on fire. He grunted before barking orders, clipped his adjutant around the head, who, once the colonel was pacing back to his command post in the heart of the hospital, clipped a subordinate, which Connor found somewhat amusing – except he knew that in the Imperial Army, based on the old Samurai system, abuse filtered down from the top to the bottom and he was the next in line.

The slap when it came sent him reeling, but he refused to fall, staggering, then returning to a standing position, shoulders back, stomach in and head held defiantly high.

'Just get us the bloody food,' he muttered, blood trickling from his lip and into his mouth.

Harry had been out cold and had not witnessed the goings-on. It was a couple of hours before he struggled to sit up.

'Jesus,' he said, rubbing the side of his head. 'I'm going to christen that a Japanese kiss. Are you deaf?' he asked quizzically.

Connor touched his ear. 'No. Are you?'

Harry grinned. 'I might be, though I did hear food mentioned. I take it that was your doing.'

'All Irishmen have the gift of the blarney.'

'And on an empty stomach too.'

Connor grinned and rubbed at his bloodied lip. 'I bloody well hope so. Got a slap for my trouble, though.'

It turned out that Harry was right: an hour later two

guards appeared, carrying a heavy cauldron that smelt of something nourishing.

Harry took a scoop of it into his mess tin and Connor did the same. Not having the luxury of spoons, they tipped their heads back and let the mixture flow into their mouths. After that they analysed what they had just eaten.

'There's rice.'

'Bit of veg.'

'Chicken?'

'What's the brown stuff?'

Connor picked out a piece that hadn't totally disintegrated. It tasted sweet.

Harry also found a piece. 'It's cake. They've chucked everything in there. Even cake. Doesn't taste too bad, though.'

Connor grinned. 'I'm guessing it's not cake but Christmas pudding. Well, there's a thing.' He swallowed the last of it, drank some water and picked out a tree behind which he'd relieve himself. It turned out to be the one where he'd hidden Harry's pipe and stash of opium. There wasn't much left of the tree, the upper part having been blown off by artillery fire. There was no sign of the pipe and its contents.

When he got back Harry was sullen. 'I'm guessing we're looking forward to a grim future.'

'I'm guessing that food is going to be the centre of our world. Or rather the lack of it.'

*

By lunchtime of the following day their evening meal was nothing but a cherished memory.

They'd been marched all the way to Hong Kong harbour on no food and little water. Hungry and exhausted but still defiant, they had joined the main contingent of the defending garrison where the Rising Sun now fluttered above the governor's palace in place of the Union flag. The imperial Japanese command had taken it over, along with a few other auspicious buildings, including the Madison Hotel, where enemy aliens – those who were still alive – were being ordered to assemble.

'As an Irishman, I shouldn't mind,' Connor said to Harry, his eyes taking in the red and white flag flapping in the wind. 'But I do.'

Harry sighed. 'I wonder where they'll take us. China? Or Japan? No, not Japan. Too far away.'

'I suppose that depends on how much territory they've occupied.'

'Well, let's hope they don't get as far as Singapore. That would be a disaster.'

'There's a fair few prisons in Kowloon.'

'Yes, old boy. There certainly are. Pity the poor refugees who were there. The Japs will have caught up with them.'

Connor guessed that Harry's thoughts about the fate of the refugees who had fled the Chinese civil war were in tune with his own. But they'd both seen enough death and were disinclined to talk about the probability of more.

'Looks as though we're about to get something to eat and drink.'

Connor nodded to where a contingent of Chinese was working their way around the huddles of men, ladling water from a pail. Another had what looked like balls of rice piled in panniers swinging from each shoulder. The Japanese soldiers bullied them, driving them into a huddle as a collie might a herd of sheep.

'Seems we're not forgotten,' said Harry, slapping his thighs gleefully.

'This could be the high point of our day,' Connor added.

When a pannier of rice balls swung into reach, they both dipped in.

'Hi, boss,' the man whispered.

When they looked up, they saw enough of the face beneath the coolie hat to recognise Yang, their one-time barman and previous owner of their short-lived but relatively successful business enterprise.

Their own hands and others around them dug into the feast piled into Yang's panniers.

'They must not see us talking. Pretend you are paying me,' Yang whispered. He held out his hand, jerking it under Connor's nose at the same time cursing him in Chinese.

'That's all you're getting, you Rangoon rogue,' shouted Connor.

'I not Burmese. I born in Sham Shi Po. Sham Shi Po, hear me, you British soldier? You know where that is? You should go there soon, and then you will know.'

Harry paid Yang with the last piece of change he had in his pocket, the only coins not taken. He grabbed the Chinaman's wrist. 'You got a spare pipe? Some opium?'

Connor grabbed his arm. 'No, Harry. Listen to me. You've got to keep your wits about you. We've got to survive. Think of your mother.'

Harry stared at the rice he still held uneaten in his hand.

Yang passed Connor another rice ball.

'I hear what you say, Yang,' Connor said quietly, and for a moment their eyes met in mutual understanding.

Hearing a shout from a guard, Yang turned away. He muttered in Chinese as he stepped over other men, giving them rice balls and demanding money, which he sometimes got.

Connor locked eyes with his superior officer. 'Did you hear what he said?'

Harry nodded. 'Yang was born in Kowloon yet has just insisted that his birthplace was Sham Shi Po.'

'So it's Sham Shi Po. The old refugee camp. We were right.'

Harry nodded. 'Seems like it.'

Sham Shi Po in Kowloon had received thousands of refugees following the Japanese invasion of China and its ongoing civil war that had been raging for years. The numbers had surged following the slaughter in Nanking. Now, if they'd interpreted Yang's outburst correctly, they were to be taken by boat across the bay and interned in Sham Shi Po.

A number of motor torpedo boats along with an assortment of junks had been requisitioned to ferry them to Kowloon. Their numbers swollen by non-combatants, civil servants, businessmen, their wives and children, the process was taking hours to complete.

And still they came.

Over the heads of those sitting on the ground or on what was left of their bundled belongings, Connor spotted a small group of dusty women.

Harry noticed them too. 'I do believe the latest arrivals are the residual female medical staff of St Stephen's. Still alive, though not entirely unscathed, methinks. Is your doctor among them?'

Connor nodded slowly and got to his feet. 'Yes. She is.'

A guard ran towards him, ordering him to sit down again.

Connor raised both arms in surrender. 'Permission to use the latrines,' he shouted, then patted his crotch with one hand.

The guard nodded. 'Go.'

Connor made his way to where a number of buckets were positioned behind a canvas screen. He had to pass the women to get to them, close enough to see if she was there, perhaps even exchange a word or two.

He nodded at them, his eyes swooping over their heads to where she stood looking oddly alone, although others crowded around her.

'Good to see you.'

'Do you happen to know where they're sending us?'

He recognised the nurse named Alice, but wasn't sure of the names of the others though he knew them by sight. They all looked glad to see him, except Dr Rossiter. His chest tightened at the sight of her close up. There were deep hollows under her eyes, her cheeks were bruised and blood had dried at the corner of her mouth. She looked withdrawn, hugging herself protectively, and showed no sign of the confidence he'd seen in her from the very first. His stomach churned at the probable reason, which caused him to curse his own sex and wish he had not been born a man.

He doubted it would work but managed anyway to adopt a cheery smile. 'I'm not sure where you're going, but me and my friends are off to Sham Shi Po for an extended holiday.'

'Don't ask me what happened,' said Alice, her voice barely audible, her eyes fixed on Rowena. 'They took her first.'

He knew what she meant and in knowing a terrible rage rooted him to the spot. 'I want to kill them.'

'One day you might get the chance. I hope you do.'

He eased his way through the other women until he was standing as close to her as he could get.

'Rowena?'

She gave no sign of having heard him.

'Dr Rossiter?'

The white coat she wore on the wards was filthy and smeared with blood. She was gripping its lapels with both hands, hugging it around her as though it was a protective suit of armour.

She backed away when he attempted to touch her.

'Rowena. It's me, Connor O'Connor, the man who should be performing on Broadway, not stuck here with a load of short men in khaki. They're not my type at all.'

Her eyelids flickered. When she looked at him it was as if she couldn't quite work him out.

As far as he was concerned, there was only one thing to do.

Softly and at a slow tempo, he began to sing the song they'd sung together when they'd first met. '*She looked so sweet, from her bare brown feet to the tip of her raven hair...*'

He sang as much of it as he could before his presence and voice attracted the attention of a Japanese guard and a rifle slammed across his back.

'Move. Move.'

As he was pushed away, he saw a flicker of recognition in her eyes. Suddenly her lips moved, formed his name but no sound came out. She made a second attempt and this time she was audible. 'Connor?'

'It's me and, never fear, for you'll never see the back of me.'

Brighter now, her eyes followed him and she raised her hand as he was bundled away.

He received another glancing blow before he was obliged to dip behind the canvas screen where, despite the freshness of a Hong Kong winter, the buckets stank.

'Too many people, too few buckets,' he muttered.

On coming out again his attention was drawn to where the Japanese commander saluted a man alighting from a pale green Lagonda.

'By Paddy McGinty's whiskers...' he murmured, his brow furrowed in surprise and fear.

A man wearing the customary black of a triad henchman, got out from behind the steering wheel, went to the back passenger door and bowed as he held it open.

Wearing his customary white fedora, his crisply tailored suit, Kim Pheloung alighted, raised his hat and seemed to be exchanging pleasantries with the Japanese commander. It was also noticeable that not once had he bowed, almost as if, thought Connor, the two of them were of the same status, equals in whatever dealings they had with each other.

What dealings? wondered Connor, and scowled.

Not only did Kim Pheloung control the Hong Kong opium trade, but the criminal element of Kowloon paid him homage in the form of protection money, a portion of profit from their activities. He had ruined Yang's business, and he and Harry had had to pay him a premium for allowing them to operate. He had also encouraged Harry's addiction.

Loyal only to his own greed, Kim didn't care who was in power and was known to bribe any Hong Kong police who would take his money. Now it seemed he was currying favour with the new power in the land.

A conversation ensued, followed by a waving of

hands, intense discussion, accommodating smiles and the passing of a parcel from beneath the bowed head of Kim's chauffeur to the imperial officer.

For a moment they disappeared inside the hotel where pre-war dances and concerts had taken place, the haunt of officers and wealthy civilians. They came out a short while later, shaking hands, saluting in their own individual ways, the officer in the military manner and Kim raising his hat.

Connor's eyes narrowed. 'I'm wondering what you're up to, Kim, rogue that you are.' He said it softly but was under no illusion that business was being done. Money would be changing hands.

'Go! Go!'

Unseen by him at first, a guard was giving him an order and swinging a rifle, leaving him in no doubt that he was to sit down.

He did as ordered, making his way back to where Harry was hunched over his knees, his body sometimes twitching, his head jerking as though he were dreaming, still chasing the dragons induced by opium.

His attention went back to Pheloung. 'Now that's a man with many sins to answer for.'

To his dismay he saw Rowena being separated from the other women and shepherded to the car. 'Oh, Christ!'

Nobody heard his exclamation. Nobody could know how angry he was for what Rowena had gone through and how afraid he was for what she would face next.

He wanted to race through the crowd and drag her out

of the car but would likely get a bullet in his back before he got within ten feet of it.

He fancied she looked for him before getting in, nervously smoothing her hair, which was tied in a bunch at the nape of her neck. When the car drove away it was hanging loose and Kim was running his hand through it as though removing the very last pin.

He stared at the spot where the car had been, willing himself to remember her steady grey eyes, her smiling lips and the sound of her voice singing or her feet tapping in time with a tune.

Her departure left him feeling useless because Kim had done what he could not do: he'd saved her from an internment camp – for his own reasons no doubt. He'd seen how Kim had looked at her that night in his bar, wondered how he'd known so much about her, who she was, where she worked and the mode of transport she'd used to get to Kowloon. One of Kim's henchmen, a thickset man dressed in black, had entered the bar before Rowena, bending low and whispering into Kim's ear: the man who was driving the car today.

Where was he taking her?

It was rumoured that Kim had a house in the walled city. Nobody knew how he'd come to live in such a place. Although forgotten, the only people who should be there were government administrators, but they hadn't been seen for some time, not since Japan had invaded Manchuria. The prison at Sham Shi Po was some distance from there and, in his heart of hearts, Connor had to accept that he would never see her again.

One thing he knew above all else was that what Kim Pheloung wanted he made sure he got, and once somebody was in his grasp the only way to escape his clutches was in a coffin.

# 8

Her hair was loose. She knew that much. Her thoughts, normally so wide-ranging and energetic, had contracted and become guarded. She was still clasping the collar of the white coat she always wore on duty, holding it and both her hands tightly together.

'There's no need for you to do that. You're safe now.'

Long cold fingers attempted to prise her fists open so she would let the collar go, but she hung on fearing that if she did so she would be exposed body and soul to an uncaring world.

Time was of no importance. Hours, days or years could have passed. The pain was still there. The horror. The clawing hands and thrusting bodies again and again and again.

He made a second attempt to prise her hands apart, but she still wouldn't let him, her grip unyielding as iron. She never looked at him, not so much as a glance. Neither was she really aware of the touch of his hands, teasing her hair out into long dark locks, caressing her cheek and telling her to count on him from now on. Just him.

She kept her stony gaze on the road ahead, if there was a road.

She saw nothing but them.

Heard nothing but them. Felt only the clawing of their hands, the thrusting of their bodies. Smelt the stink of male sweat.

Awareness of where she was and who she was with didn't begin happening until she felt a rush of salt air on her face that sent her hair streaming out behind her.

She saw the water they were crossing, short chops of turquoise and indigo, black, yellow and green, and the prow of a boat rising and falling with the motion of the water.

The stiff breeze cooled her brain. The nightmare visions were still there but lessened. She touched the crusting of blood at the corner of her mouth and tasted salt but wasn't sure whether it was seawater or dried blood.

'Don't worry. We will get you cleaned up.'

So. He was watching her. She touched her cheek and winced. 'Why?' Her voice was little above a whisper and caught swiftly on the breeze, but he heard and, apparently, felt the need to explain.

'Since the time of Genghis Khan, conquerors have taken women as prizes. I will not ask for the details unless you wish to tell me.'

She didn't answer. As yet she wasn't sure who this man was, though he seemed vaguely familiar. Instead she opened her mouth, swallowing the fresh air as though it were oranges.

Her throat felt sore when she tried to speak. She took one of her hands away from her collar and pressed it to her neck. 'I don't want to talk about it.' Her voice was barely above a whisper.

'Then you need not.'

She eyed him nervously, still not sure who he was and why she was with him.

His eyes were like dark holes beneath the brim of his hat, unfathomable, like deep, dark wells.

The car slowed and she cowered when they reached a checkpoint on the other side of the harbour in Kowloon. Just the sight of the uniforms made her feel sick because she could do more than see them: she could smell them. Taste them. She slunk further down into the seat so her knees were almost touching the floor.

The car did not come to an abrupt stop but was waved through, as though this man was important. Was he? She wasn't sure. He was wealthy, she knew that much.

He spoke. 'We met at the hospital, then played tennis at the country club. We also met at the Jockey Club. Do you not remember?'

She frowned. Bits of what he said seemed to ring true. If she could just retain those bits and add others when and if they came back to her... 'Your name's Kim.'

'That's right.'

'Where are we going?'

'To my house. It is in Kowloon Walled City. The

ancient walls have defended the city for centuries. You will be safe there.'

The breeze flung her hair across her face when she turned back to the checkpoint. To her great relief nobody appeared to be pursuing them. 'They did not stop you.'

'Why should they?'

She cast around for some reason, noticing the driver's hands on the steering wheel. They were big hands, the fingers thick and square-ended. Seeing the wheel move beneath those hands was strangely hypnotic.

Hands told a lot, she thought. She looked at Kim's hands as though she had never seen them before, yet she had. He'd told her she had. Half-memories bubbled into her mind.

They were strong hands with slender, tapering fingers. His nails were polished and overly long – like a woman's but more so – yet still he appeared exotically masculine, like a prince from *The Arabian Nights*. Ah! That was it. A favourite story helped her to fill in the details.

'I remember you now, but only bits about you.'

He glanced briefly. 'I hope they are the best bits.'

She frowned as though that would help her catch the vestige of memory that could so easily fly away. 'You gave me breakfast. I remember that.'

'Breakfast was in lieu of dinner at the Jockey Club. You stood me up.'

His mouth opened, his eyes crinkled. He was laughing, but silently, a strange phenomenon. It made her think that the memory did not amuse him.

'I can't remember.'

'What do you remember?'

She looked down at her hands, frowned and thought very hard. 'The war started. I remember that. I remember people running and the air-raid sirens ... and St Stephen's...'

Stating the last words caused bile to rise from her stomach. The nightmare. Christmas Day. That was what St Stephen's meant to her.

'It's best you forget all that. It is nothing to do with you now. You are safe and no longer a participant in the warring of great powers.'

She thought his comment slightly odd, but had no appetite for confrontation. Both the present and the future were foreign countries in which she could not yet be interested. The recent past was still with her, a festering wound that would not easily heal and a barrier to whatever had gone before.

He didn't press her to tell him what had happened, if she'd been treated badly or well, and for that she was grateful. She did not want to speak about it.

The harbour and the checkpoints were left behind. The heaving mass that was Kowloon began to look familiar even though she couldn't recall visiting this place more than once.

Women hanging from overhead balconies were throwing rice-paper notes containing their price lists to the short men who suddenly looked taller since their takeover of Hong Kong and its adjacent territories.

The red robe of a prostitute leaning over a parapet parted at the front, thanks to a draught from a side alley. She wore nothing underneath but her thighs were tattooed with writhing dragons, their fangs meeting either side of a mass of wiry pubic hair.

Rowena was more intrigued by this than shocked.

Ahead loomed the walled city of Kowloon. Around it a cloud of dust shrouded the vague outlines of trucks, dust-covered labourers and the soldiers guarding them.

Suddenly huge stones crashed from the wall to the ground, causing the prisoners and the men guarding them to scatter in all directions. Gradually, the men were reassembled and the dust began to clear.

The man sitting beside her stood up and spread his arms, his face full of pride. 'See this?' he said. 'I supply these men. They are taking stone to extend the runway at Kai Tak airport.' He sat down once he'd imparted the information but the self-satisfied expression remained.

A man who seemed to be overseeing the gang bowed as the car went past. Kim did not acknowledge him but stared straight ahead as though such obsequious courtesy was his due.

They drove past the fog of choking dust and straight into the old city, coming to a halt outside the entrance to a traditional Chinese house with red pillars, blue-tiled steps and green dragons painted on either side of the door.

The driver got out first and bowed as he opened it. The man she now remembered as Kim got out first and extended his hand to help her.

Hesitantly she disengaged the fingers of one hand from the front of her white coat and accepted his assistance. She was instantly struck by the other-worldliness of the place, the home of this most exotically fascinating man. Lucky charms and magic words written on tin hung between each pillar, tinkling like bells in the gentle breeze, and half a dozen cats lounged on the warmer spots, spitting and snarling as she walked within a foot or so of their unsheathed talons.

'This is my house. Come.'

Only to a rudimentary extent did she take in the finer details of the cats, the lanterns, the painted walls and the wooden buttressing holding up the lower balcony.

The interior smelt of incense, sandalwood and lotus blossom. In striking contrast with the brightness outside, it was a place of cool shadows, soft silks and dark wood.

He led her out through another door into a courtyard crowded with chrysanthemums, their heavy blooms like miniature suns, round and perfectly golden. She recalled seeing the same flowers before at another place, a garden beneath a high window from which one could see the whole of Hong Kong.

'The flowers...'

'The queen of flowers, first grown in Japan but I have long loved them. They are the emblem of my house, my family.'

He pulled on the chain of a brass bell hidden among the leaves of a miniature red-leaved Japanese maple. 'We are prepared for you,' he said, and smiled. 'Just as we were before.'

The same diminutive woman who had waited on them back at his property in Hong Kong came tottering out behind a servant girl carrying a tray.

She said something to Kim, which sounded quite pleasant.

'My grandmother welcomes me back. She welcomes you also.'

Rowena found herself doubting the woman's welcome. She had beamed at her grandson but had avoided looking into Rowena's face.

The hands of the servant girl wobbled as she placed her burden on the low table. Some tea spilled onto the tray.

The old woman growled words at her, like a dog about to bite, then punched the girl in the ribs.

Rowena looked up at Kim. 'What did your grandmother say?'

Kim smiled. 'That the girl is Han and has big feet. It is only to be expected that she is clumsy.'

With trembling hands she poured the tea into her parched throat. Over the rim of the cup she followed the rolling gait of the small woman with the tiny feet.

Kim noticed. 'You are staring. It is impolite.'

'I can't help it. It seems so... barbaric.'

Kim stopped drinking from the fragile gold-edged tea dish. 'It was tradition.'

'Were your mother's feet bound too?'

His change in expression made her think she'd said the wrong thing. 'No.'

Whatever the circumstances of his mother's unbound feet, she wasn't going to hear about it.

The tea warmed her blood and perhaps jolted her memory. 'Why am I here? Where are my friends? I remember now. I was with my colleagues from the hospital. We were rounded up and were being taken somewhere.'

'You do not want to go where they have gone. It is best you stay here. Here there is food and drink, water for you to bathe in, silks for you to dress in and to lie on. And there is me, here to look after you. You will trust me. You will be happy.'

She rubbed at her forehead disturbed by the resurgence of memory that she'd willed herself to preserve in vivid detail. The memories had jagged edges, like broken glass, and they would be painful to fit back together. 'Will I ever be able to leave here?'

'Not while the war is going on. You are an enemy of Hirohito and the Empire of the Rising Sun. The emperor's army will shed much blood in his name – including yours.'

'Well, that's clear enough.'

Yes, it was clear, but it was also troubling. She looked down at the tea, the rice balls, which had been sweetened with honey, rolled in flour and deep-fried.

'Take one. These are very special. My grandmother's recipe. I know you have not had much to eat of late. I intend making sure you do eat. Please. Take one.'

At first her stomach curdled at the thought of eating, but after one bite she discovered just how hungry she was. The rice balls were delicious and she told him so. 'I'm very grateful you whisked me away from wherever I was destined to go, but I'm worried about the others I was with.'

'I am sorry. I have some influence, but not enough to press for the release of all enemy aliens. My priority was to have you released and, with a little persuasion and some very good whisky, I achieved that.'

'I didn't mean to sound ungrateful.'

'Do not worry about it. You needed my help. Anyway, there is still the prospect of us dining together. I am determined that we will do that.'

'At the Jockey Club?'

'It can be arranged.'

His smile was full of the confidence of one who knows when to be bold, when to be tender and when to swap sides in times of trouble.

She shook her head. 'I can't...' She paused as she fought to find the reason why she didn't want to be seen out dining anywhere.

'I understand,' he said, before she had the chance to continue. 'Very bad things happen in war, but it is behind you now. I will keep you safe within the walls of my house. I want to take care of you. It has been bad. Very bad. China sheds many tears for its children, but the dragon will rise again. As you may have noticed we believe in lucky charms, and the greatest one of all is the dragon. China considers itself the dragon and, although it weeps now, has vowed that it will rise again. Whether it does or does not, I will be there to assist the victor.'

She rose to her feet. 'I should really be with them.'

Suddenly everything around her seemed to be swimming in a violet haze. Her legs buckled, but his arm was around her so she didn't fall. He pressed a cold hand against her forehead. 'You are very hot.'

'I'm so tired.'

The sound of her voice seemed so far away.

He let her sink onto the velvet-covered divan, heard him give orders, then footsteps coming and going.

There was comfort in being cared for.

He had the Han girl bathe her, attend to her injuries and put her to bed. She let it all happen, uncaring who might be in the room when the girl stripped off her dirty clothes, but vaguely aware that she had not heard him leave.

The air was cool upon her naked flesh. The girl rubbed her down with herbs and oils, brushed her hair so it fanned over the pillows and applied more ointments to her face, the bruises and cuts on her body, her breasts and between her legs.

Daylight had diminished by the time she was falling asleep in a bed with a canopy, wooden walls on three sides and a curtain across the front. The buttercup-yellow pillows were soft and the overhead canopy, side walls and curtains kept the light away from her tired eyes.

Tonight, this first night in the house of Kim Pheloung, the demon faces did not come and neither did she hear herself screaming, beating the empty air with her fists. Fighting back only happened in her dreams. At the time she had feared what might happen if she did fight back, had stared at the Christmas decorations and pretended that she was flying away on that magic carpet. Tonight she was closer to that escape than she had ever been and the smiling prince on the flying carpet with her was Kim Pheloung. Tonight she slept deeply.

Kim stretched full length on a sofa against silk cushions smoking a cheroot. On the opposite sofa lay his grandmother, eyes half closed as she puffed on her opium pipe.

'She sleeps.'

'She would, though I did not put too much in her tea. You did not drink?'

'I pretended to.'

His grandmother half raised her wrinkled eyelids and studied him shrewdly. She wasn't always sure she liked her grandson, but she loved him because he was of her blood and looked after her. 'Why her?'

Kim smiled. 'I like exotic blooms. You know I do.'

His grandmother scowled. 'She's foreign, like a weed in the flowerbed.'

'She's a doctor.'

His grandmother was surprised at this, just as he'd known she would be. 'And that's your reason?'

'Doctors are not gods. Women are not goddesses. Both need to know that.'

'I don't like her being here. It will come to no good. If the British find out...'

'That I rescued one of their own? They are no longer the lords of Hong Kong. They are defeated.'

Her eyes narrowed further as though the smoke was stinging her eyes. 'And the Japanese?'

'I paid an agreed price.'

'With one man only, not the entire Japanese Army. I hope she proves worth it.'

Alarmed by his wilful obsession, she closed her eyes and pretended that she was at one with the opium in her pipe. He was her only grandson and it was her duty to protect him – even from himself.

# 9

Killings and beatings had continued until the white flag fluttered in meek surrender, but if Hong Kong thought that was the end of it, it was sadly mistaken.

There were still beatings, still killings but, as Connor had speculated, their labour was valued. In time the Allies would counter-attack and the Japanese High Command knew they had to be ready. In the meantime he would await his chance to escape, whenever that chance might come.

Sham Shi Po had been a refugee camp before the war following the Japanese invasion of China. It now served as a prison for those who had guarded the Chinese refugees. The accommodation was crowded but from the first there was camaraderie of like among like, all men in the same situation, some of whom were civilians, mainly administrators, engineers and public servants. The rest were military.

'You will work.'

That was the order and for the most part it was accepted as better than being bored.

Harry got a slap for daring to ask if they would be paid for their labour.

'Seems not,' Connor grunted.

The sight of the walled city still fascinated and, prior to harvesting the old stone, Connor was surprised at how serene it was at that hour of the morning, although the rest of Kowloon was only barely waking up.

Its history fascinated, though it had a jaded look now its walls were being dismantled. He understood that only a few administrators had resided in the *yamen*, before the war, and had scarpered back to the mainland. After struggling to the top of the wall, sledgehammer slung over his shoulder, he looked into the compound and saw the house with red pillars and a pagoda-style roof. He also saw how well guarded it was and knew that the rumours he'd heard in Kowloon were true. *'That's Pheloung's place.* Just look at those guards. Armed to the teeth they are.'

Connor spent longer than he should have taking in the details. The guards were familiar, big-shouldered men wearing traditional costume offset by American-style gun belts. He didn't need to see the pale green Lagonda to know who lived there.

Harry saw where he was looking.

'Don't even think of breaking and entering, old chap, and before you suggest I might like to accompany you and steal a little opium, forget it. I know when a fad has run its course, especially if I'm likely to get shot trying to steal some.'

The guards were using long canes to keep everyone working. Connor received a lash across his legs, and Harry jumped down from the wall onto the first block of the day before he got one too. Once quarried, the huge stones were manhandled onto the back of trucks, which were taken to the airport where another labour force was engaged in smashing them with hammers to be used as hardcore for lengthening the runway.

Connor had not jettisoned the idea of escaping, but now he was close to where he believed Rowena was being kept prisoner. He voiced his concerns to Harry. 'The dear doctor doesn't know it yet, but she's as much a prisoner as we are.'

'Better fed.'

The labour force was staggered, the same men never assigned the same job two days in a row. Sometimes they were dismantling the ancient walls, at others working at the airport.

Those chosen to work at the airport were obliged to get up at four in the morning to follow trucks already laden with the stone they were to smash. The sledgehammers were distributed on site, counted out and carefully counted in again at the end of the day.

'That's the secret. Hide a hammer,' remarked Connor. 'It should smash a few heads.'

'And where do you suggest we hide it, old boy? Up our jacksy? Sorry, even I have to draw the line at that.'

It was humour – black or otherwise – that kept them going, that and the little extra food they could buy from street traders who came right up to the fence to barter. There was plenty of variety. Rice, vegetables and fish, squawking chickens, their legs tied together, hanging upside down from a pole slung over the trader's shoulder, cigarettes, gin and whisky, no doubt looted from the officers' club before the Japs had had a chance to take it themselves.

Money was the preferred currency but unless it had been well hidden, nobody had any, unless they'd had the foresight to sew it into the lining or seams of their clothes. Some still had wedding rings, wristwatches and the odd coin caught in a deep pocket. Bartering and clubbing together with a few coins or valuables became the norm. United they might survive.

The work was relentless and so were the empty nights. Connor's Irish ballads and traditional folk songs entertained the inmates during the long evenings and helped them forget that they weren't getting enough to eat, that bathing was restricted and that it could get bloody cold if all you had was a single blanket to keep you warm.

When he sang Connor imagined Rowena singing with him and wondered at how quickly the woman had got under his skin. Now his greatest wish was to survive and find her again. There was a long road between now and that happening, but his mother had told him that if you wished hard enough you'd get what you wanted.

He closed his eyes. 'Mother, I wish I was bloody out of here.' When he opened them again nothing had changed. 'Ever the optimist,' he muttered to himself, and smiled.

'Come on, Paddy. Give us a song. I'll accompany you on the mouth organ.' The speaker blew a few notes.

'And I've got a drum,' said someone else, banging with a pair of sticks on an upturned bucket.

After he'd finished doing his bit to entertain his fellow prisoners he would lie in his bunk, still hearing her voice and seeing her hair blowing in the wind as Kim Pheloung had driven her away. Would he see her again? Perhaps he would glimpse her outside Kim's house. Perhaps she would take a walk in his direction.

It was a faint hope, but all he had.


The faint hope turned into reality on the slog back from the airport at the end of a long day. His hands were raw from the stone dust, his feet sore from being on them all day and walking back and forth from the airport to the camp.

The sweat pouring into his eyes cleared the grit from them. That was when he saw her.

The Lagonda was easily recognised: the chrome was shiny, the paintwork pale green and highly polished. Kim's car.

His steps slowed, and although his eyes burned from

the remnants of stone dust still in them, he kept staring, his spirits soaring because she was still alive. There was still a chance.

Looking well groomed and cared for, she was sitting next to an old woman with a sour expression.

His steps had slowed, but he badly needed to stop, to stare, perhaps even to wave.

With that in mind he paused and began to rub at the small of his back, acting as though it was paining him. He knew he was chancing a slug from one of the guards, but if she saw him it would be worth it.

At least she was still alive but vulnerable to whatever Kim Pheloung had in mind for her. He'd heard of him taking women before, but never a European. He was a man with a finger in many pies, gambling, opium and prostitution forming the main part of his business empire. Rowena, he decided, represented more to Kim than anything she could earn as a whore. There had to be some reason for the man to find out all he could about her.

Yang had told him a story about another beautiful woman, the wife of a Chinese official. 'He forced her to abort her child, but it was born alive so he forced her to kill it with her bare hands. He had stolen her from her husband with sweet words, then broken her soul until she was his creature, as you would a dog.'

Somehow he had to attract her attention but he couldn't do that unless the car stopped.

'Wait your chance, Connor. Wait your chance.'

The chance came when a pile of loosened stones tumbled down close to the front wheels of the car causing the driver to slam on the brakes. A huge dust cloud arose in front of it. He saw both women waving their hands in front of their faces.

The guards waved their sticks, beating the backs of those men who were nearest, exhorting them to move the stones so the car could drive on.

Although he was nowhere near, Connor ran to assist, bending away from where the stone had fallen, heading for the rear passenger door. Almost whooping in triumph, he got close to the back of the car.

At first she was not aware of his presence, her gaze held by the sight of the overworked men with their ragged clothes, healing scars and blistered feet. Then, suddenly, she saw him, saw through the stone dust covering his face and dusting his hair.

'Doctor.'

The most wonderful smile lit her face. 'Connor! It's so good to see you.'

'My star. You've just lit up my heaven. Not that it's much of a heaven. A pretty dirty one, as you can see.'

'What's happening here?'

He jerked his chin in the direction of the dust cloud that only now was beginning to settle. 'Stones from the old city wall to Kai Tak. A new runway.'

'You look thin.'

Grinning perversely, he grasped the loose folds of his shirt. 'It's a new diet they've got us on. Rice, rice and more rice. What I wouldn't give for a spud and a rasher of bacon.'

'Is that all you're getting? Just rice?'

'There's sometimes bits of fish or meat in it, stuff we don't recognise as edible. We buy a bit from the locals outside the fence, but money and valuables are scarce. The Japs saw to that. They've robbed us blind.'

Her eyelids flickered. 'I've no money to give you. I wish I had.'

'I didn't ask. I'll get by somehow.' He followed her glance to the old woman beside her who was engaged in haranguing the driver to get going. He was telling her he had to wait for the stones to be moved and permission from the Japanese Army to continue their journey.

'His grandmother,' she whispered.

'Is Kim treating you all right?'

She didn't answer but furtively searched in a silk purse hanging from a gold rope over her shoulder. Unnoticed by Kim's grandmother she slipped something smooth and shiny into his hand, closing his fingers over it so it wouldn't be seen.

There was no time for her to say anything. The old lady's scolding stopped as the guards waved and shouted at the driver to get going. The car jolted forward.

Connor slid the lighter into his pocket but didn't rush to get back to work. Feeling sick for her safety he followed the progress of Kim Pheloung's car until it disappeared into the hidden world of the walled city and wished he could run after it. The British had rarely entered the

Chinese enclave and neither did the Japanese. All they wanted was its stone for their own purposes, which obviously suited Kim Pheloung. He was probably selling it to them or providing the truck and the sledgehammers.

That evening Connor ate his rations in silence.

Harry was in close conversation with a young Eurasian man who had somehow managed to slide under the wire to trade. He'd brought food, but Connor knew the main reason Harry had invited him to stay. Tonight he would forgo their conversations, but he didn't mind that. He could still see her in his mind and there for the moment she would have to stay.

'You'll enjoy the meat. It's pork.'

The information was provided by the corporal sitting opposite him. He was devouring his meal with gusto.

'Are you sure?'

The corporal nodded. 'It wandered into the camp and got requisitioned. Not the only one, eh?' He smirked at Harry and his new friend.

After he'd finished his food, Connor helped himself to a mug of hooch that an American inmate had brewed from a minimal amount of sugar and a lot of rotten fruit. Mug in hand he went outside and clambered onto one of the stone buttresses of the old buildings, aloof and aloft from the shabby men around him.

Sitting up there he looked out over the city to where the setting sun was turning the sky salmon pink. The lighter was still in his pocket. For now just touching the hard lump of silver reminded him of her and gave him hope.

In time he might have to barter it for food or medicine, but the situation would have to be very dire before that happened. In the meantime it was part of his present and his past, just as she was. The war would end one day and hopefully they would both live to see it, to have children, to grow old and ponder this part of their lives and the youthful people they'd once been.

# 10

Strands of tinsel were whirling around as though caught in a hurricane sucking in the clothes-peg angels, some of which were blowing little gold trumpets or playing miniature harps. The noise they were making was far from sweet. Not until the yellow light of a noisy city began to creep over the walls and into her room did she fall into a peaceful sleep, the nightmares gone with the darkness.

Despite the application of white cream by the Han girl Luli, Kim commented on the dark rings beneath her eyes. 'You look tired.'

'I don't sleep well. So much has happened.' She gave a little gasp and drew back when his fingertips touched her cheek.

'I will not hurt you, my dear Rowena. Now. Calm yourself.' Unsmiling, he reached out and did it again. This time she steeled herself not to draw back. His fingers stroked her cheek. They were soft and cold and made her want to shiver but she thought she owed him something. He had taken her from a vile place and it was only right that she showed him she was grateful.

'Why am I here?'

'You are here. Accept it.'

'Won't you be punished for sheltering an enemy alien?'

'The colonel passed you into my custody. He is an honourable man.'

'That sounds as though I am still a prisoner.'

'Yes. This is true. But look.' He indicated her surroundings with a sweep of his hand. 'You reside in a gilded cage, not in a dog kennel like the other women. Many of them will die. Japan cannot feed itself, let alone the thousands of prisoners its soldiers have taken.'

'You sound convinced of that.'

'Just as I am convinced I will be on the right side when the surrender finally comes – whoever the victor might be.'

She gathered her legs beneath her and buried her face in one of the silken cushions. One half of her wanted to rebel and demand he take her back to her friends. The other was confused and very afraid.

She started on feeling his hand patting the back of her head.

'All this will pass. You are still the same woman you were, but more so. In future it is all you have to be. A woman. Nothing else.'

She frowned. The woman she had been was slowly being rebuilt as her memories re-formed. 'I'm a doctor. I brought babies into the world. Treated the sick.'

He frowned, his eyes black with disappointment. 'You no longer need to be that. You are now just a woman. Clear your mind of everything else.'

Her head hurt. She touched it and closed her eyes.

'Now,' he said, getting to his feet. 'You are obviously not sleeping well. This we can deal with. My grandmother has many potions to help you sleep better. Do you have nightmares?'

She looked at him over the top of the cushion and nodded. Just thinking about the nightmare made it active again, weaving its way into her mind as though it were yesterday.

'The Japanese soldiers. Lower orders told to die for their emperor. Not that they wish to, of course. Unfortunately these uncultured men revert to type. Peasants and fishermen will remain just that. In time you will forget.'

She heard the contempt in his voice and did not look into his face but flicked thoughtfully at a small blemish in her robe. 'I'm a doctor. I understand trauma. Even with time it will never pass entirely away. I can never forget it, only live with it.'

'You will forget you are a doctor. You will be a woman and will heal. I insist on this.'

He settled himself on his favourite divan, pulled up his feet and stretched full length, his look steadfast and discerning. The blue silk robe he wore fell open exposing his chest, the skin glossy, like honey-coloured jade. 'In time you will tell me everything. I am a man of the world. I will not flinch.'

'But I will. I feel such shame. I don't understand how you can bear to look at me as you do.'

'How is that?'

She swallowed and turned her head, gazing out through the window and across to the bustling south side of the courtyard and the kitchens, storerooms and servants' quarters.

His hands stroked, his look was of desire, yet she couldn't bring herself to say the words. How could he desire her looking as she presently did? How could he desire her knowing what the soldiers had done, how many times they had abused her body? She felt tainted, demeaned.

She kept her gaze fixed on the scene across the courtyard. 'They look busy.'

He nodded. 'The south side suits those who must work. Servants always work on the south side. The family live on the north. All Chinese houses are built so, the south more open to the outside world.'

'I suppose you live on the north side because it's cooler in summer,' she said, thinking it the obvious reason.

'No. It is traditional. It is *feng shui*.'

She felt him looking at her as though he could see beneath the silk robe, her naked skin, see how everything inside was working, some of it battered and bruised.

She blushed under the intensity of his gaze. Although

tears burned at the corners of her eyes, she held them back, refusing to break down. Inside she felt broken.

'I will give you comfort when you need it.'

His voice soothed her troubled mind until he said, 'The men who abused you have been dealt with. I can show you their bodies if you like.'

Her eyes widened. 'They were executed?'

'Yes. By me.'

Some days she spent walking alone in the courtyard, Luli keeping a respectful distance. On other days she found herself confined to her room, the door unmoving when she tried to open it.

'Why am I allowed out some days and not others?' she demanded of Luli.

Luli shook her head. 'The master...'

She asked Kim the same question.

'You spoke to one of the men taking down the stone from the walls.'

So, the old woman had noticed. 'Is that a crime for which I am to be punished?'

'Your looks set you apart from your former countrymen. This will save your life. Do not jeopardise it unnecessarily.'

The chance did not come for her to repeat the action. Now when she went out for a ride they drove into the hinterland of the New Territories, though even up there it was possible to look down on the walled city, rising like a green carbuncle amid buildings thrown, like children's building blocks, around it.

Twisting from the waist, she kept her eyes fixed on the dust cloud and the men working until they were smothered by distance, though his voice still sang in her head.

She wondered whether the boiler might dry out the wood and make the fiddle unplayable. Connor would be heartbroken and so would she if that happened.

For all its comforts, life in Kim's sumptuous house was lonely, the coldness of luxury rarely warmed by human interaction except with him. He dined with her, talked with her and slowly gained her trust.

The only other person she could talk to was Luli, but their conversation was stilted and narrow, Rowena reluctant to divulge her history or discuss Kim in too great detail.

He had rescued her, but she was still unsure of his reasons and did not dare push him any further. If he could kill Japanese soldiers with apparent impunity, he could easily kill her, yet all he showed her was kindness.

Explaining that his business dominated his life, Kim was away most of the day returning sometimes after she had had supper and gone to bed. At first he stroked her hair tentatively and his cool fingers caressed her cheeks but gravitated to her forehead, her eyelids, down her nose to her lips, so gently, so softly.

That she no longer winced at his touch unnerved her.

When she closed her eyes she asked herself what was happening to her, but could come up with no answer she wished to face. Instead she imagined she was someone, something else.

I am like a cat, she thought. Touch me more. Hear me purr.

It was two weeks following her arrival when she'd been left alone all day, except for a brief meeting with Luli, that the nightmare came back with a vengeance.

In the midst of her tossing and turning, the silk coverlet tangled around her. Turning in the opposite direction, it fell from the bed, leaving her shivering and sobbing as she relived that dreadful day with fevered horror.

Suddenly the sweaty faces disappeared, the hands melted as a great rush of water flooded over her and swept them away, cooling her inflamed body, yet she did not drown, her breathing slowed. Deep sleep was only a breath away.

Half waking she realised it was not water but the coolness of the silk coverlet, retrieved from the floor and being laid gently over her.

She began drifting back into the deeper sleep she craved when suddenly she became aware that she was not alone: another body was weighing down the other half of the silk-covered bed.

Slowly she opened her eyes, trying to decide if she was in a dream or if this was really happening. The darkness of night was spangled with dots of light coming from lanterns glowing on the veranda outside her window.

As her eyes began to flicker shut, she felt an arm placed across her, a hand gently stroking her shoulder. 'Sssh. Sleep. Sleep.'

At first she tensed, but the softness of his voice was hypnotic, as were the cool fingers stroking her shoulder. Not once did he attempt to slide beneath the silk coverlet, but remained on top, caressing her hair and whispering kind words against her ear, sometimes in English, sometimes in Chinese or Malay.

Eyelids heavy, soothed by his voice, she fell asleep.

By dawn he was gone. She should have been relieved, but his presence had kept the demons away, just like the daylight that was streaming through the window.

The darkness having gone, she fell asleep again, warmly confident that there would be no nightmares now. She was safe.

Luli, the Han servant reviled by Kim's grandmother on account of her big feet, came with the morning, carrying a bowl of water scented with rose petals. With her usual air of subservience, she placed it on a lacquered washstand, standing with head bowed, eyelids flickering from under a ribbon of black fringe.

'You can go now.' Rowena made a shooing motion with her hand, but the girl didn't budge. 'I can wash myself.'

'Zu Mu told me stay and wash you. Make sure.'

Luli had told her that Zu Mu meant 'grandmother'.

'I can do it myself.'

'I do it. She will beat me if I do not and send me back to the mission.'

'Is that where you learned to speak English?'

She nodded and dared raise her eyes to Rowena's face. 'Yes. I learned at mission school.'

'How did you come to be here?'

'The *luoban* needed servant.'

Rowena frowned because Luli had used the word for 'boss' rather than *taipan*, the name usually reserved for the head of a thriving and legitimate business house. It confirmed her worst fears. She'd presumed Kim to be a silk merchant right up until he'd admitted to killing the men who had raped her. Only a man of immense power could get away with doing something like that or buy her from a Japanese commander.

Connor's warning came back to her. He'd intimated that Kim was the boss of a criminal gang, a triad, and, as such, could wield great power. She took the opportunity to talk to Luli, to ask her more about Kim, his grandmother and the other people who lived in this place.

'I cannot tell you any more.' Luli glanced nervously over her shoulder, as if anyone could hear anything that was said through the heavy ebony door that, like everything else in this place, was carved with the lucky symbol, the dragon.

'Can you tell me where the *luoban* has gone?'

She shook her head avidly, her eyes wide with fear. 'No. I must not.'

Rowena frowned. 'Have you been told not to speak to me?'

'I can speak to you, but not too much. It is not my place.'

'Where was the mission you came from?'

'Shanghai.'

'Do you like it here?'

It was the wrong question to ask. Luli was just a servant. She wasn't expected to like it here.

'What if I asked the *luoban* if you could visit me every afternoon?'

Luli looked terrified.

'I won't if you don't want me to.' She thought about how she could persuade Kim to allow Luli to spend more time with her. 'I could ask him if you could teach me some words of Cantonese. I'm sure he'd be pleased if I could say a few words in his language instead of always having to revert to English.'

Luli's tight expression of outright fear lessened.

'Right,' said Rowena. 'That's settled, then.'

A loud banging on the door, accompanied by a demanding shout, had Luli scooping up the bowl and the Turkish towel she'd brought with her.

The door flew open and closed with a bang once Luli had shot through it. The door had no lock but there was a sound of sliding wood. Rowena tried opening it. It didn't budge. A wooden bar on the outside prevented it.

Rowena slumped onto a silk-covered divan. She was

alone once more, with nobody to talk to. She resorted to watching what was happening out in the courtyard or in the kitchens at the southern end of the house.

It was midday when Kim's grandmother shuffled in, her hips swaying like a hula dancer's, thanks to her lotus-flower feet. Swift movement was denied her, but a kind of balancing act contrived to alleviate the pain that walking caused. Luli was behind her, something silky and heavily embroidered over her arm.

Kim's grandmother barked at her, then turned her uncompromising expression to Rowena.

Nervously Luli interpreted what had been said.

'Zu Mu says you are to bathe and prepare to dine with her grandson tonight. You are to wear this.'

Grandmother snapped an order and pointed at the dragon-ended couch in the corner of the room. In response Luli dutifully trotted over and carefully spread out the dress.

Rowena had to admit it was breathtaking. 'It's very beautiful. Shame about the colour.'

Luli translated into Cantonese for the grandmother, who demanded what she had meant by her comment.

'Red isn't my favourite colour. I prefer blue or pale green. Even dark green.'

Again Luli translated.

'Zu Mu says it does not matter what colour you like. Red is her grandson's lucky colour.'

Rowena fingered the heavy embroidery, so elaborate

compared to her own clothes and her beloved white coat, the symbol of her profession. Thinking of her coat prompted her to ask for her clothes.

'I'd like my own clothes. Especially my white coat.'

Luli looked startled.

Grandmother frowned. A long-nailed finger prodded Luli for an explanation, which Luli duly delivered.

The old lady's frown deepened and her guttural tone said everything without the need for Rowena to understand the words.

'No good,' said Luli, shaking her head, her eyes darting nervously between Rowena and the old lady.

'No good? What do you mean, no good?'

Luli looked ready to crumple into a heap. 'Burned.'

'Everything?'

She nodded, studying her feet rather than meet Rowena's expression.

Letting the heavy silk fall from her hands, Rowena eyed the dress. 'Well, that should certainly turn a few heads when I go driving in the car.'

'Oh, no, Doctor. Not go out in cheongsam. Go out in tunic and trousers. *Luoban* ordered this for his eyes only.'

'I'm flattered,' she murmured, though it was only a half-truth. It occurred to her that Kim considered he was doing her a kindness in destroying the clothes she'd worn on Christmas Day back at St Stephen's.

Without another word, Kim's grandmother pushed Luli out of the door, then barred it behind her.

So, tonight he wanted her to dress for dinner. Surely

that wouldn't be so bad. He was a considerate host, the food would be good and the surroundings were aesthetically pleasing. They would dine in great comfort. The furnishings were sourced from a number of countries, his taste a mix of East and West: Turkish rugs, European paintings, silver candlesticks and French-style mirrors with gilded frames.

This must all have cost a pretty penny and Rowena wondered how he'd acquired such beautiful objects, bearing in mind he was a man who took what he wanted, stole rather than bought.

Loneliness was her companion for the rest of the day until Luli reappeared to help her bathe and to massage her flesh with sweet-scented unguents. She sighed as the girl rubbed a scented cream into her skin, massaging her sore elbows, spreading it over her hands and between her fingers. 'The *luoban* will fall in love with you tonight.'

She shook her head. 'I don't want that.'

Luli tilted her head. 'Not want?'

'No.'

Luli shook her head. 'You different.'

'Different from what? From whom?'

'The others.'

Her eyes flashed open. 'Others? Do you mean other women?'

'Yes.'

'I've seen no other women.'

'Not here. Somewhere else.'

'Where?'

Luli didn't answer at first.

Rowena made a guess. 'Shanghai? Are there other women at the house in Shanghai? You can tell me. He told me he has a house there.'

'Yes. That is where they are.'

She sank forward onto her folded arms as Luli continued to rub the creams into her bare back. So, she really was alone here. Perhaps she should feel flattered at Kim's attention, but that wasn't what she was feeling: he made her feel safe, protected by his power.

Evening. Everything was ready. She was wearing the dress, which slid like water over her curves, lifting her breasts, emphasising her small waist, the flare of her hips, the roundness of her bottom.

As instructed, she sat waiting for him at a Western-style table, laden with dishes for them to pick at, to nibble and savour. In her mind she rehearsed asking him when she could leave her room and walk in the courtyard once more, but feared doing so. She was beginning to learn that everything had to be done his way and she counselled herself to be cautious.

A single servant, dressed in black silk, eyes downcast and a white towel over his arm, was on hand to serve but was ordered to leave once Kim had entered, his black silk robe billowing behind him like a parachute, his legs clad in dark blue trousers.

His hair was loose, black silky strands falling around his shoulders and onto his glistening bare chest. The sight of him, like the princes she'd read about, took her breath away. Paper lanterns lit the courtyard outside and linnets sang in a wire cage hanging from the rafters. The scent of night filtered into the room, with the heavy smell of the battalions of yellow chrysanthemums, like harvest moons in the borrowed light.

The lanterns' glow caught the blackness of his eyes, threw shadows onto his features and emphasised the muscles of his chest.

Her practical side dismissed the notion that she'd been spirited away on a magic carpet but her imagination, her need to escape the experiences of St Stephen's, was too powerful to resist. Despite what had happened and despite herself, Kim Pheloung was one of the most intriguing men she'd ever met. She no longer doubted that what Connor O'Connor had told her was true. Kim was less than snowy white. This was the man who had killed the soldiers who had raped her and somehow had got away with it. For that reason alone she could never condemn him. On the contrary, she was grateful he'd taken revenge on her behalf. She felt renewed, her body refreshed, the wounds helped to heal.

'You look thoughtful.'

She smiled. 'I cannot quite believe all this.' She waved a hand at her surroundings. 'In the midst of this war you have this – this haven.'

'My haven. My heaven. Stand up.'

'What?'

'I want you to stand up. I want to see how you look in the dress I have given you.'

She'd never been the kind of woman to flaunt her figure and doing so now she couldn't help but blush. 'Um. Yes. All right.'

She arose slowly from the chair, aware of the flatness of her stomach, the roundness of her breasts pressing against the silky fabric. She blushed even more as his eyes swept over her in the most intimate way.

He nodded. 'It was the right choice.'

She wasn't sure it was: the cut and colour reminded her of the woman she'd seen standing on the balcony, dragon tattoos running up her naked thighs.

To counter her embarrassment she sat down again, tempering it further by asking him why he'd had her clothes burned.

Narrowing his eyes he smiled reassuringly. 'I thought it best. They were in a very bad state. Not worth my laundrywoman's time.'

'I would have preferred to keep my white coat. I studied and worked hard to become a doctor. That coat was my badge of office.'

He raised the rice bowl to his mouth with one hand, his chopsticks in the other, his eyes never leaving her face. 'You do not need it now.'

'It might be needed – I might be needed, if I could get to Singapore.'

He put the bowl and chopsticks down, wiped his mouth with a cotton napkin.

'Singapore has fallen.' He sounded almost triumphant.

Rowena was taken aback. 'Singapore? I can't believe it. Not Singapore. It's well defended.'

The way his expression changed told her he was indeed telling the truth.

'It was well defended. Fortress Singapore is now occupied by the Japanese.'

Shocked beyond belief, she dropped her gaze, her blood curdling at the probability that Singapore had endured massacres just as Hong Kong had.

'Can you get me anywhere else? Australia... or an American base?'

Smiling sadly he shook his head. 'Impossible. The world is at war. The colonel gave you into my custody. I am responsible for your internment.'

'Internment. That means I'm your prisoner. How long will I remain your prisoner?'

'As long as the war lasts – unless other circumstances intervene and curtail your time with me.'

She felt her face drain of colour. 'What are you saying? That you will keep me here even after the war is finished? Or by "other circumstances", do you mean you will have me killed as you did the rapists of St Stephen's?'

'I am not a barbarian.'

'But you're a criminal. That's true, isn't it?' she said, unable to stop herself lashing out with the truth, uncaring if he should repudiate her accusation.

'Opium. I control all of the opium passing through Hong Kong, Kowloon and the New Territories.'

He didn't care that she knew and seemed proud to admit what he was, what he did.

'Why are you telling me this?'

His expression darkened. 'So you know what is at stake in your life. So you know that you should not cross me and that you should be a grateful guest in my house. If not for me you would be starving and infested with lice like your friends.'

His tone was bitter, his eyes hard. He rose from sitting to standing in one abrupt fluid movement, gliding to the door, his silk robe floating out behind him.

Fearing she'd gone too far, she attempted to make amends. 'I'm sorry. I didn't mean to sound ungrateful.'

He stopped at the door, a dark glower on his face. 'I have put myself and my household at risk in having you here. All I ask in return is your respect and your trust. Do I have that?'

One half of her was inclined to be the old Rowena, independent and unbowed, but she'd been so close to the death of others, the smell of blood still in her nostrils. She was not ready to die. She would like to grow old, as she and Alice had discussed. Determination overruled proud defiance. If she was to survive in this house with this man, a different Rowena was required, one who appeared subservient on the outside, her real self hidden within, just waiting for the opportunity to escape.

She got to her feet and joined him at the door, gazing

up at him imploringly, realising deep inside that with one movement from him she would be lost.

As if to confirm her inner feelings, the cool night breeze ruffled their hair, lifting his tresses so that they fluttered with butterfly lightness across her face to entangle with her own.

Standing close to him, she could feel the heat of his bare chest. It was difficult not to drop her eyes and take in its bronzed smoothness. He was muscular but lithe and he smelt of the sea.

Tentatively, she lifted a hand, wanting so much to touch him. At the last minute she withdrew, clenching her fingers into her palm, feeling the dryness in her mouth and the pounding of her heart echoing in her ears.

'I did not mean to offend you.' She found herself bowing her head, the way she'd seen Luli bow hers before Zu Mu, his grandmother. This man held her life in his hands. Defiance needed to be hidden, but having it smoulder away inside would keep her focused and bolster her courage.

When his fingers lifted her chin she saw that, although he was smiling, his jaw was set firm and the hard look in his eyes that she'd seen earlier was still there.

'Tomorrow we will dine again. Nine o'clock. Have everything ready. At nine. No earlier. No later.'

She wanted to ask him if he would come to her bed that night. Her lips parted, the words on her tongue ready to slide out. At the last minute she held them back. Whatever he was doing to her was working. In time she would be unable to help herself, but for now she refrained. In the meantime desire smouldered deep inside, but she held it back, unwilling to admit, even to herself, that she wanted him.

# 11

The next day Luli came in as usual, carrying the bowl of rosewater, the soft white towel and the creams that had helped her body to heal. She brought another red dress, too, this one a dark, blood red, almost purple in a certain light.

'Always red,' she murmured.

'Zu Mu said you may go outside today. You are permitted.'

Rowena felt an instant wave of relief wash over her. At last. Outside meant the courtyard and the sheltered aisles bordering it. It was such a small place, that courtyard, she thought, surveying it through the window, seeing the painted shutters, the fountain, the forest of flowers and green bushes.

Luli had only just left through the ebony door when Rowena opened it and looked out.

Luli glanced round at her and smiled. 'You free now.'

'Being allowed to leave my room hardly constitutes liberation,' Rowena snapped.

The girl looked confused, but Rowena was so eager to get outside that she didn't stop to explain.

In soft slippers, she crossed the wood-tiled floor and went into the courtyard where she stopped, breathed in the air but wrinkled her nose at the smell of overblown chrysanthemums.

Fresh air wasn't all she wanted. She wanted a change of scene. She wanted company.

Rowena followed Luli's path, which led straight into the kitchen on the south side of the house. She stopped and breathed in the starchy air, which reminded her of the smell of wallpaper paste back in England.

The cook and his assistant stopped what they were doing and stared at the handsome woman who had dared enter their precious domain.

'I'd like to help.'

The cook, a little man with a long pigtail and a white apron that folded around him twice, said something to Luli.

'He asks if you do not like his food.'

'Of course I do. I love it, and I would like to learn his skills, or at least some of them.'

He looked pleased when Luli interpreted, beaming with pleasure and gesturing with his hands that he would like her to join in.

He chatted away, pointing at herbs, various spices and the heads of fish floating in greenish brine. Luli couldn't interpret fast enough, but Rowena gestured that she understood, her eyes alighting on familiar ingredients.

There was a light rice dish flavoured with spring onions and egg for lunch, which would be served cold. The evening preparations were more elaborate as they were to be served to her and the master of the house. They were laughing at Rowena's efforts to make noodles when Kim's grandmother entered, the door slamming open, her walking stick tapping angrily on the tiled floor when she saw that Rowena was present.

Anger rumbled from the depth of her being as her voice rose along with her walking stick, falling on Luli's cheek, aimed at and only just missing the cook, who was swifter on his feet than she was. She turned to Rowena, waving the stick and shouting furiously.

Luli was trembling and rubbing at the spots where the stick had landed.

'Tell Zu Mu I understand. She does not want me in the kitchen.'

Luli nodded.

The old lady raised her stick and pointed it at the door. 'All right. I'm going.'

She wished Kim was there so that she could tell him she would like to do something in this house, not just wait for him.

A little later, Rowena was sitting beside the fountain, pulling at strands of gold thread that formed the tails of exotic birds on the tunic she was wearing, when Luli came running out.

On seeing the servant, she sat bolt upright. 'Is Zu Mu still vexed with me?'

Luli, a red mark on her cheek where the stick had hit, said nothing, her eyes moist with tears. She set down the dish and scampered away.

Rowena sat without eating, watching heads bobbing and moving around in the kitchen. A tableau of human life was acting out in front of her, something to watch and wonder about. Fish had been delivered, a pedlar of fruit was enjoying the company of the cook, and men with brushes were sweeping down cobwebs from the overhanging roofs and leaves from the tiled areas beneath the overhanging eaves. Not once did they look up to meet the eyes of the foreign woman, a *gweilo,* an interloper from the Far West, as were all her people.

There was a door from the kitchen to the outside, used by tradesmen and servants. The door Kim had brought her through was ostensibly for the use of guests and family. It led into a cool hallway, where an interior door opened onto the courtyard.

Her attention stayed fixed on the kitchen door, which might be accessible at all times... perhaps even at night.

An uncanny feeling accompanied thoughts of escape, an inner voice suggesting she was safe here, that the aura of the man had been apparent from the beginning and had drawn her to him. It felt almost shameful that she didn't want to escape the undeniable comfort of her situation. He was attempting to keep her safe and she had to be grateful for that. But there was more. She was under his spell and wasn't sure she wanted to be free until the spell was well and truly broken.

★

Although not blinded to the privations of a prisoner-of-war camp, thinking of Alice, Tansy and the rest made her eyes misty and brought a lump to her throat. Hopefully all those she'd worked with had survived. She smiled when she thought of Alice, her opinions and her reaction when she'd taken her out that night in Kowloon. She might not have been adventurous at the time, but if she was still alive, being adventurous was a definite advantage.

A chrysanthemum bloom, too heavy for its stem, startled her when it settled on her shoulder. She looked at it and sniffed its unique perfume, thinking it looked like the sleepy head of a round-faced child. The only time she'd seen such blooms in England had been at funerals.

She eyed it balefully. 'I'd like you better if you could speak.'

Just a flower. She sighed as a few of its petals fluttered to the ground. It was here and so was she.

The sun went down and shadows fell with the night across the courtyard. Before darkness finally claimed it, lanterns of multi-coloured shades danced and tinkled in the night air.

He would be here tonight. When she closed her eyes she could smell his exotic aroma, see again the polished perfection of his bare chest.

'Be still,' she muttered, placing her hand over her heart. Her natural sensuality was battling with her professional self.

Desiring him did not prevent her wanting to know what was happening in the outside world, not just the war but smaller details of Kowloon and whether there was transport to Hong Kong, or in the opposite direction into the interior of China – just in case she changed her mind and escaped before they got closer.

He came to her almost every night, the warmth of his body against her back. In the beginning she'd tensed but now she looked forward to his presence, suffused with a sense of calm as he laid his arm across her, his fingers combing her hair.

Tonight he would come again.

By nine o'clock all was ready. The smell of food wafting across the courtyard from the kitchen was delicious. Cold delicacies had been set out ready for them to nibble before the main course was brought to the table. Fresh fruit was piled in a blue and white bowl in the middle. The whole was a mix of East and West and included a bottle of French wine, the label referring to a vineyard in Burgundy.

The dining chairs, too, were French, moulded in a style more often seen in a château, the seats and backrests upholstered in embroidered silk. Feeling light-headed, she sat down and waited, with nothing but the creaking emptiness of the room.

The French clock, an ornate thing of gilt and cherubs,

ticked resolutely, the minute hand moving on past the allotted time.

A faint sound, like a soft brush sweeping the floor, came to her from outside. Was he back? She hadn't heard the car or his swift footsteps, his and his bodyguards.

When the door opened it was not Kim standing there but his grandmother.

She pretended not to be surprised to see her and asked, 'Is Kim home yet?' Even though the woman spoke no English.

The old woman glowered, pushed the door shut and clambered onto a couch, where she drew up her legs and laid her walking stick beside her.

Rowena's eyes fell instantly to the tiny feet, broken in childhood, forced into unnatural shapes, now encased in tiny slippers decorated with pearls and silk thread.

Pursing her lips, Kim's grandmother glowered once more, then closed her eyes, her hands folded in front of her.

What was she doing there? Merely waiting for her grandson to come home? Unless she was there as a chaperone – but protecting Rowena from whom or what?

She stared at the wrinkled face, the fine brows, and the puckered lips. The old woman's robe was made of heavily embroidered purple silk, the wide sleeves trimmed with black satin.

There was no chance of a conversation, but it felt worse than that. Her presence made it seem that Rowena's was of no consequence, that she was no more important than the pots on the table or the chair she was sitting on.

The darkness closed in, deeper as the hour got later.

She sat listening for the sound of a car but heard only the singing of crickets, a nightingale and the resonant snores of Kim's grandmother.

Sighing with exasperation evoked no response from the old woman.

The French clock hanging on the wall of the Chinese house struck the half-hour and then ten o'clock. Still no Kim.

Feeling hungry, she took one of the sweetmeats from the table, the pastry light and delicately flavoured, melting like a whisper on her tongue.

Sensing movement, the old lady's eyelids fluttered open, then shut again.

Rowena sat watching her, her resentment growing, even though the sound of the ticking clock was now more noticeable than the snoring.

She took another sweetmeat. The last one had been cherry. This was apple.

At last she heard the sound of a car and the screeching of iron gates being dragged open in the compound beyond the inner wall.

Straightening she brushed the crumbs from her mouth and her clothes, listening as the sound of his footsteps on the tiles came closer.

The old lady heard too, grabbed her walking stick and swung her elfin feet to the floor.

He stood framed in the doorway, the darkness of night

and the glow of lanterns behind him. His smile was faint and disappeared when he noticed his grandmother.

Oblivious to his displeasure, Zu Mu took her stick in hand and got to her feet, bowing and prattling as though he were a god not a mere mortal.

Kim looked less than pleased at what she was saying and, although Rowena did not understand his words, his tone was harsh.

Hurt at being spoken to in such a manner, the sparkle left the eyes of the doting grandmother and her fractured expression almost made Rowena feel sorry for her.

She left, but not before throwing a look of pure malice in Rowena's direction, as though it was all her fault and there would be a reckoning.

'You upset her,' Rowena dared to say.

'I did not request her to be here.'

'I thought you ordered her here to be my chaperone.'

'Do I need to appoint a chaperone?'

Rowena couldn't help smiling. 'Not unless you suspect me of taking the cook or the fishmonger as my lover.'

'They would not dare.'

The sound of his scathing laughter made her bold. 'Have you had a good day? Is all well with the world of Kim Pheloung?'

'All is well.'

He began to take off his top tunic, was bare to the waist before he reached for his robe and put it on.

She held her breath. No matter his crimes, he was still a beautiful man. But despite being attracted to him, she had to keep her options open in case the need to escape became inevitable.

'Did you have to travel far today?'

'Here and there.'

He was reticent. She could have asked more direct questions, but she held back. There was a look in his eyes that she had not seen before, guarded but speculative, and somehow she guessed he was about to say something – something she might not like.

He frowned at the clock, then at the table. 'How long has this been here?'

'An hour.'

'Send it back.'

'There's nothing wrong with it. I've already eaten one or two of those sweetmeats – well three, actually...'

'You have eaten? Without me being here?'

His anger was almost palpable.

'You hadn't come and I was hungry...'

His jaw tightened. His eyes blazed. 'I said we were to eat together.'

'But you didn't come.'

'Get rid of it.'

'But I'm still hungry. Even if you are not willing to eat it—'

'No. I will not eat it and you will not eat this stale food.'

With a sweep of his arm, dishes, plates and chopsticks were brushed off the table and onto the floor.

Rowena gasped and stared, first at the broken crockery mingled with food that poor people would envy, then at the anger on his face and the realisation that she had awoken a sleeping dragon.

'You will be seated here at the same time tomorrow evening. You will wait for me to join you. You will not eat until I do.'

She wanted to retaliate, but held her tongue. Kim's arms were hanging at his sides, his fists clenched.

The message was clear. She understood immediately. One word, just one word of defiance, and one of those fists might break her jaw or black her eye.

It was late. The events of the evening were still with her. For the first time she felt afraid of him and as escape seemed a far-fetched fantasy – at least for now – she had to make amends for inadvertently upsetting him.

Could she escape? Her options were few. Stalk across the courtyard when Kim's black-clothed guards were otherwise engaged; climb up onto the fishmonger's cart and bribe him to take her into Kowloon where she could hide while thinking of the next stage of her escape. But how could she do that? She had no money and had given the silver lighter, her only valuable, to Connor.

Other possibilities. She had to think of another way.

Adopt some kind of disguise, perhaps as a boy, or jump out of the car when she was taken driving with Zu

Mu, though that would result in the driver running after her and he was big enough to swing her off her feet and carry her back.

Kim filled her dreams in which he was an emperor and she was his concubine, expected to please him in any way she could.

The French clock chimed midnight. The old house creaked. The singing crickets accompanied the music in her mind, the old fiddle, rattling out a tune, the dancing blue eyes, the tapping of feet, a rich voice outshining them all.

When dreams of Kim vanished and nightmares threatened, it was Connor O'Connor and his music that eased her weary soul.

She started.

What was that?

Gunfire?

It was no dream. More cracks followed. She sat bolt upright.

Logic told her to stay away from the open window, but curiosity guided her actions.

Glowing like red moons, the lanterns hanging from the overhead rafters played on figures without features running through the darkness, male voices shouting and somebody screaming in pain.

She glanced over her shoulder. The bed was empty so it might be Kim.

From outside, she heard his voice, the rapid footfall of

running men, barked orders, and the thudding of bone upon bone.

She grabbed her green silk dressing-gown and hastily slid her feet into slippers embroidered with gold thread.

Mindful of stray bullets, she kept close to the wall, heading for the reception room separating the courtyard from the outside world in the ancient heart of Kowloon's walled city.

The gunfire had ceased. The only sound she now heard was that of a man in pain and guttural tones of alarm.

When she entered the reception hall from the courtyard she saw four men gathered around another lying on the floor, their giant shadows lying like a black cloud behind them, thanks to a wooden lantern at the end of a pole hanging over the supine figure.

The features of all were in shadow.

'Kim?'

He looked up, displeasure spreading across his shadowed face.

'Get back inside. This has nothing to do with you.'

'Is that man injured?'

'Yes.'

'Then it is to do with me. I'm a doctor, remember?'

Ignoring his angry expression and the clenched fingers that failed to grab her arm, she fell beside the man lying on the floor, feeling for a pulse, her fingers dipping into the sopping wet patch in his stomach area.

'I take it the Japanese did this, or somebody who dislikes him – or you?'

Kim's face was like thunder. 'It does not concern you.'

'No. I'm the one who can pick up the pieces and sew them back together. Fetch me boiling water. Bandages. And a sharp knife.'

This time he did manage to grab her. With one jerk of his hand she was back on her feet.

'It is no concern of yours. We have our own doctor. A Chinese doctor. You are just a woman while you are here. Just a woman. Is that not clear?'

She dared to stand up to him. 'So where is this doctor? Where is anyone who knows about medicine? This man could die waiting, and you would have lost a valuable servant. Is that not so?'

Even in the darkness she could see his face contort with anger.

'It is none of your business.'

She winced when he grabbed her arm and resisted when he attempted to march her back into the inner courtyard and towards her room.

'I don't understand.'

'We are not savages. We will deal with it ourselves.'

'But—'

In the deep shadows she saw a small figure hobbling towards them.

Immediately understanding, she looked at the old lady, then up at him.

'Your grandmother is old and so are her methods. Isn't it best that I stay with your man until the proper doctor comes?'

She felt his grip ease and, from his expression, knew he was seeing the common sense in what she was saying.

'Only until then.'

In the meantime Zu Mu had taken temporary charge, bundling up herbs and, with a loud voice, slaps and a waving of her stick, instructing Luli to hand her the hot water and bandages.

Rowena eased her way back to where she had been kneeling at the man's side, probing the wound for the bullet and pressing down on severed blood vessels.

'The bullet has to come out. I would prefer a scalpel but a sharp knife will do.'

Her request elicited a torrent of angry comment from Kim's grandmother, who waved her bunch of herbs at Kim in the same manner as she did her walking stick at Luli.

Ignoring the furore between grandmother and grandson, Rowena repeated her instruction for Luli to fetch a knife. 'A needle and cotton too.'

She also ordered more lanterns. 'Though a flashlight would be better.'

Everything she asked for was provided.

Furious and spitting bad words between her teeth, Zu Mu stalked off, the tip of her walking stick tapping angrily as though the stone slabs also deserved a thrashing.

Not until she was back behind the big screen that divided her quarters from everyone else did the sound of the tapping cane cease. By then everyone was leaning over the British doctor, watching with undisguised interest as she sewed the man's flesh together.

Finally she held up a bullet between her bloodied fingers. 'He is a lucky man. It wasn't too deep.'

'There was no need for you to do that. You will never do it again.' Kim yanked her back to her feet.

'But I—'

'My men know how to sew a wound together. He is not the first injured comrade in need of embroidery. You have done enough.'

His finely chiselled face was disapproving when she'd expected to see only gratitude. 'I wanted to help. It's my profession.'

'I do not care about that. You have no need to prove yourself while you are under my roof.'

She frowned. 'It's not about proving myself, it's what I am.'

'Go back to bed. Now.' He paused and looked at her more deeply than he ever had. 'I will come to you. Be ready.'

Thanks to the open window, her bed felt cold and she shivered as she slid between the silken sheets. He'd said he would come to her and she wanted him to. His habit of lying beside her had aroused surprising feelings. Perhaps, she thought, that was exactly what he'd intended, teasing her with his presence, accustoming her to him lying beside her but showing no desire himself, waiting for her to make the first move.

As a man he was beguiling, but medicine was

important to her. Emotion and pragmatism were fighting a battle, making her feel as though she was on the edge of a precipice, deciding whether to jump or retreat to safer ground. The trouble was she wasn't sure which was which.

Her mind was restless, her body even more so. Throwing aside the covers, she paced to the window and looked into the darkness. The gathered men had gone and she couldn't tell whether a doctor had arrived. She wondered at the whereabouts of the injured man, presuming he was housed with the other men in the south of the house along with the stores and the kitchen.

The lanterns had burned low. Cloaked in shadows and disturbed by a breeze, the round heads of the chrysanthemums seemed to be nodding at her. She imagined them having faces, grinning mouths and staring eyes, just like the Japanese soldiers at the hospital, and began to hate them.


Unseen by Rowena, eyes were watching her from the other side of the courtyard. Zu Mu could not sleep either. She'd been married off at fifteen to a silk merchant and borne one girl child, who had disappointed her in marrying a man of her choice, not one found by a matchmaker. The old woman put it down to the fact that the girl had run wild because her feet had never been bound. When she'd died and the boy child had been passed to Zu Mu to raise she'd given him her all and in turn he had respected her.

Unfortunately she had indulged him too much, denied him nothing and told him he could be anything he wanted to be and do anything he wanted to do.

Her big mistake had been never to chastise him when he did wrong, when he stole, bullied or shunned his former friends for those who lived in the city and showed him a more colourful life, where everything was free and nothing was denied.

He'd collected women as other men might collect butterflies and when he'd tired of them he'd let them go.

This woman was different. The others had been beautiful, but she was European and also intelligent. Why was he obsessed with her when he could have Chinese concubines who would do his bidding and not have an intelligent thought in their heads?

Now she felt he was making a bad mistake. Not only was she angry, she was deeply hurt. This woman, this doctor, was taking her place in his affections and had created a rift between them. She was the one who should have treated the injured bodyguard. She knew who had shot the man and the retribution that was to come, while this woman, this Westerner, would be appalled at her grandson's ways, his cruelty and his cleverness.

Worst of all, he had not listened to her good advice about the woman. For once he had totally ignored her. Her own grandson!

From the very start she'd warned him not to bring the woman under the family roof, counselling that she would be his ruination. He had not listened, so it was up to her to act in his best interests and deal with the matter herself.

Her mind was further made up when she saw the tall young man, of whom she was so proud, moving through the darkness. He was going to her. He would spend the night with her as he had before, teasing her with his presence, waiting for the right moment to take her. It would happen soon. There was no time left. She had to act quickly.

# 12

Disturbed by the sound of men coughing, spluttering and moving into wakefulness, Connor opened his eyes.

The interior of the hut that had once held Chinese refugees was pitch black because it had no windows. A guard stood silhouetted against the encroaching dawn in the doorway at the end of the hut, berating them to get to their feet, to attend *tenko* – roll call – then to march to the old city and, with crowbar and sledgehammer, remove more of the old stone.

He closed his eyes again, wishing he could get back into his dream and watch the bacon sizzling in the pan. It had been so vivid that the smell had made him salivate. He'd been ready to add an egg when the shout had come to get out of bed. It was four a.m.

Months had passed since the surrender and the last time he'd eaten a decent meal. Breakfast today would be the same as it was every day: a bowl of rice, perhaps with a few vegetables. Not enough to live on and certainly not enough to work on.

Work was getting harder and so were their taskmasters. The demand for the runway to be completed rated higher than taking care of the labour force that was building it. He knew, as did everyone else, that they didn't need to conserve slave labour: thousands had been taken prisoner, with more muscles to waste, more bones to break, more stomachs to leave hungry. Supply outstripped demand.

Little time was given to eat after roll-call and the trek to the airfield.

A comment passed like a spring breeze from one man to another. 'Only one truck.' It was followed by groans.

Goaded by rifle butts, the men pressed forward. Those at the front would ride; those behind would walk to the walled city.

Connor looked across at Harry who seemed tired but happy. His Eurasian friend was not around, no doubt having tunnelled or climbed back over the wire to wherever he'd come from. 'Could be we're riding today,' he called.

Harry grinned from ear to ear. 'A second-class ride, old chap, is always better than a first-class walk.'

Their assumption proved correct and they counted themselves lucky to be close to the front of the queue.

Compared to some they weren't in bad condition. Connor was reminded of this when the man next to him stumbled and muttered, 'Christ. I don't think I can walk there today. They'll have to shoot me where I stand.'

Connor glanced at the man who had spoken. It was hard to say for sure, but he looked to be a civilian, his once-plump flesh now hanging from his bones. Connor saw that his feet were swollen, a sure sign of vitamin B deficiency, due to the lack of eggs and other protein. He guessed the poor bloke had probably slept with his feet in water to alleviate the pain. 'You go in front,' he said, stepping back and pushing the man forward.

His eyes met Harry's. His friend had seen what he'd done and stepped further back in the queue. He, too, would be walking. Bulging with men, the truck moved off in a cloud of black smoke, a crocodile of men following, Connor and Harry included. The daily grind had begun.

Every week, sometimes every day, somebody died. Funeral units had done their best to cope with the ominous numbers, but some bodies remained at the side of the road, torn by vultures. The sight was sickening and Connor was beginning to feel that the human race was sickening too. He reminded himself that that didn't apply to everyone. War brought out the best in people as well as the worst.

And nature was still nature. Animals didn't make wars and their lives went on regardless. They gave him hope.

Food was constantly on everyone's mind. What wouldn't he give for a rasher of the bacon he'd smelt in his dream?

He became aware that Harry was smiling at him as they plodded on towards another back-breaking day.

Connor frowned. Sometimes that smile made him feel uncomfortable.

Harry jerked his chin at Connor's feet.

He looked down. The yellow dog pattering along at his side on thin legs gazed back at him. She had a kind look and ribs as fine as guitar strings. A row of distended teats swayed as she walked, which explained the prominent ribs. The puppies had sucked everything out of her and had then probably died, either from natural causes or eaten as a delicacy.

Despite all she might have gone through, the dog looked as though she was smiling, tongue lolling from an open pink mouth. 'And what might you have to smile at?' He glanced at Harry. 'She's a girl and I think she's in love with me.'

'Lucky you. It's about time you settled down.'

'Hah!'

The day consisted of dust, sweat and finally total fatigue. Men walked slowly back to the camp, longing for their frugal supper, a cup of water and the poor pallets they slept on.

The rows of huts that constituted the camp were hardly the most auspicious buildings in the world, but the sight of them after a long day's work was a relief.

A team of Chinese civilian prisoners, a few Europeans and some Indians were building a second fence outside the original one. The Chinese refugees who had lived there pre-war had not wished to escape so a secondary fence had not been thought necessary. The present occupants were a different matter. So far there had been no escapes, but security measures were constantly reviewed.

The fences were scrutinised by the prisoners.

Connor was cautious but Harry was hopeful and kept pressing him. 'Think there's a chance?'

'Cat in hell's once they've built new fences and got some kind of sentry system in place. The trouble is they didn't expect so many prisoners, what with here, Singapore and other places. They're still getting organised.' He knew he was right. The roll-call was a bit haphazard and the Japanese Army hierarchy were not yet sure who of their number was properly in charge.

As the gates closed behind them, rain began to fall and the whole camp was galvanised. Buckets, oil drums and dustbins were utilised to capture rain from an elaborate guttering system running down and along the roofs, every drop precious in a country where, thanks to the harrying of Allied aircraft, the municipal system was less efficient than usual.

As he ran to help, Connor noticed the dog was still with him, her ears dripping with moisture, eyes bright and tail wagging. She'll go away, he thought, as he got on with what had to be done. You can't adopt her. You haven't even enough food to feed yourself.

Tarpaulin sheets that had once covered army lorries were stretched across the gaps between barracks to collect more rain. Every drop might count within the coming days. The system could fail altogether and prisoners might be severely rationed.

When the rations were handed out, supplemented by those lucky enough to have bought from the black-market traders lurking around the perimeter fence, Connor felt the tiredness in his soul and took his share. Bowl in hand, the rice supplemented by a few cubes of corned beef, he climbed onto his favourite concrete block, whose purpose had been to protect Hong Kong, to be used to build a defensive wall. Now the blocks provided a good vantage point from which to observe the city and the scarlet sky left by a setting sun.

The dog lay panting in the shade below him, looking up at him expectantly. Her tail wagged as though he'd said something kind when he'd said nothing at all. Neither did he throw her any food. There was too little. He had to keep up his strength. Give nothing. Survive. That was what he had to do.

He'd eaten most of the frugal evening meal leaving just two pieces of corned beef in the bottom. He glanced down at the dog. 'No good looking at me like that. I'm a big man, working all day on a bowl of rice and a few cubes of bully beef. You'll get nothing from me.'

He turned his gaze back to the setting sun and wished he could walk along one of its rays, jump off the end and find himself far away, a lot further west... a lot further north too. Unfortunately the friendliest islands were to the east. If his reckoning was correct the Hawaiian Islands were in that direction and his safest bet. Despite the bombing at Pearl Harbor the Americans were still in the game, if the rumours filtering from Chinese traders were to be believed.

A slight movement out of the corner of his eye caused him to look down. The dog was sitting with her head up and ears erect, eyeing the shadows between the stones. She was some sort of terrier, but definitely of mixed ancestry.

'What you up to, girl?'

She didn't look away at the sound of his voice but remained stock still.

Connor deduced that she was watching something, as keen-eyed and still as only a perfect hunting dog could be – though almost cat-like in her manner, crawling forward on her belly.

He looked to the darkening shadows and saw a seabird waddling unconcerned, pecking at the cockroaches that had dared to come out from beneath the stones.

The bird did not see the dog until it was too late. Although it was almost as big as she was, she dealt with it efficiently. One toss of her head and its neck was broken.

Connor watched, fascinated, as she tore at its wings and feathers, her sharp teeth gradually exposing the warm flesh beneath. Rice bowl clutched in one hand, he vaulted down from the wall.

'You're one hell of a hunter,' he muttered, and realised what an asset she could be.

Not knowing how she might retaliate, he tentatively stroked her head. Thankfully she went on eating. Connor checked the pathetically inadequate pieces of corned beef remaining in his bowl then peered at the bird's meaty breast. He took a piece of corned beef between finger and thumb, wagging it in front of her nose.

She licked her chops and looked up at him, the bird firmly wedged between her paws.

He eyed the remains of the bird. Only half the breast was gone. The rest was intact. No wonder her coat was still glossy. The puppies had taken all the best from her, but she'd survived on her hunting skills. She was thin, but her condition wasn't bad, all things considered.

The dog got to her feet to sniff at the morsel of tinned meat, then took it delicately between her teeth. The remains of the bird were within his grasp. Broken up and stewed it would make a tasty addition to the rice. 'Here,' he said holding out the last piece of bully beef. 'How about it? Fair exchange is no robbery, so my old mother used to say. How's that with you?'

Again the dog sniffed delicately before taking the beef between her teeth.

Connor's movements were stealthy. Only a little blood oozed from the dead bird, the dog having licked up most of it. He held up the carcass as though it were a trophy.

The dog wagged her tail.

Later Harry laughed when he saw the dog. 'She really is in love with you.'

'And I with her. She's a hunter.' He swung the bird in front of Harry's face. 'She caught this.'

'And ate some by the look of it. What is it?'

'Some kind of heron or crane. Nice bit of meat on it.'

'I'm glad she left some.'

'Can't wait. Meat in the stew tomorrow, and if I'm right about this dog, there'll be more where that came from. She'll hunt for us, won't you, girl?'

She seemed amiable enough and after a little scratching behind the ears she lay down.

'Have you thought of a name?' Harry wondered.

Connor held up his fingers in the V for Victory salute. 'Vicky,' he said. 'Short for Victory – or Victoria.'

# 13

The following morning Luli brought Rowena a message: the car would be outside shortly and she was to go for a drive with Zu Mu.

That seemed strange: they had already been out twice that week. Until now there had never been a third outing.

Rowena kept her face expressionless as though she didn't really care where she was going, when in fact she was very interested. 'Where are we going?'

'I do not know. The grandmother did not tell me.'

Rowena had once had mixed feelings about going out on one of Kim's grandmother's mystery tours – just driving around and looking at the scenery or peering at the huddled shops of the old towns in the New Territories, never in Kowloon.

As usual, Zu Mu gave the driver his orders, striking his shoulder to emphasise where she wanted to go and how quickly she wanted to get there. On the whole they travelled slowly and avoided bumps in the road. She tended to draw her legs up under her, so she was perched precariously on the seat. One jolt and she might easily fall off.

At the old lady's instigation, the driver turned away from their usual route through familiar villages and waterlogged rice paddies along a road Rowena did not recognise, meandering through trees and rows of jagged rocks. They had never taken this route before, yet it seemed vaguely familiar. Was this the way Kim had brought her that first day?

Her suspicion was confirmed when the flat land broadened and the road looked like a ribbon reaching for blue mountains in the distance to their right, and to their left the city that could only be Kowloon, a glimpse of sea visible through a gap in the jagged rocks.

Although parts of Kowloon were in ruins, shopkeepers, tailors, food vendors and others had set up their stalls among the ruins, their need to make a living outweighing their fear of the occupying army.

Some of the shop frontages had been rebuilt in a rickety, haphazard style that only just kept out the elements. Those not so lucky or unskilled in construction laid their wares on chunks of fallen debris beneath a canopy of ragged canvas or tarpaulin. Rowena stretched her neck in an effort to locate the bar she and Alice had entered before their world had been turned upside down. Such a happy memory, though she'd had reservations at the time.

The car edged its way through collapsed buildings, piles of stones and ragged people doing their best to survive. A pang of sadness struck her when she saw a lopsided sign sticking up from a pile of fallen stone. Connor's Bar was no more, yet she thought she saw a pair of eyes looking out at her, not Connor's, but those of the barman who had served them that night.

When she closed her eyes he stood before her, like an actor on a stage, barking orders. She heard again the crack of gunfire and saw the corpses scattered over the once neatly kept lawns at the front of the military hospital. If things had been different, where would they be now?

The bar and the barman were left behind, but a vision of Connor popped into her head and his voice sang in her heart. As they drove along she hummed the tunes he had sung and played on his fiddle. Doing so made her forget where she was and the danger she was in.

The old woman grumbled and muttered in response to her humming, which only made her hum louder, then break into song:

'*From Bantry Bay unto Derry Quay,*
*From Galway to Dublin Town,*
*No maid I've seen like the fair colleen,*
*That I met in the County Down...*'

She was still singing and the old lady scowling when the car swung into the harbour, heading to where the Star ferry still tied up to ply between Kowloon and Victoria Harbour.

Rowena stopped singing. 'We're going to Hong Kong?' She said it softly unable to believe that it was so.

Perhaps they were going to Kim's office, Victoria House, where she'd gone with him for breakfast the day Pearl Harbor was bombed and he'd picked her up from the hospital.

On recognising the car and checking with superior officers, those guarding the incline onto the ferry did not ask for papers. A guard glanced a second time but, on seeing her black hair and aquiline features, perhaps decided she was a citizen of a neutral power that had not yet declared war on the Empire of the Sun.

They were allowed to stay in the car all the way across the water – like two queens, thought Rowena, turning her face into the breeze and drinking in its freshness. The night before, when Kim had come to her bed, she'd expected him to make love to her. His hand had dropped beneath the silk coverlet but only to caress her back and her hip, shushing her to sleep when she began to respond. Her body had been on fire, so much so that she'd almost begged him to take her but some vestige of pride stopped her. She was the one to be persuaded, not him.

Perhaps I should escape, she thought. Perhaps I could jump over the side and swim ashore.

It was a stupid idea. The guards might not hesitate to shoot her, especially if they were in Kim's pay.

There was no point in asking Zu Mu where they were going so she mulled over the probabilities aloud. 'His office perhaps? The Jockey Club? Or perhaps he's having lunch with the Japanese High Command and wishes our company.'

The old lady eyed her grimly.

It was pure devilment to start singing all over again, from the first verse of 'Star of the County Down', to the last, then 'The Flower of Killarney':

'*Mavourneen is the flower of Killarney,*
*And none is so fair as she...*
*The land of the mists and mountains...*'

Zu Mu smashed her stick against the back of the driver's seat, barely missing Rowena's knees.

Rowena glared at her. 'You hate me. I know that. You hate me and I hate you. I've seen your face when your grandson enters the room. I've seen the way you fawn over him as though he were a god, yet he's a man who kills people, trades in opium and goodness knows what else. Opium ruins people's lives. Do you know that?'

The old lady responded, spouting venomous words that she didn't understand but knew were disparaging, condemning who and what she was. A European. A woman not fit to grace her grandson's house. A woman with big feet!

With regret she realised that Fate had taken a hand in her life. Kowloon and now Hong Kong. Here, whether she wanted to or not, was the chance to escape. What would he do if she ran away? Come after her? Seek gratification elsewhere?

When she closed her eyes she could still see and smell his gleaming body, the muscles honed to perfection, the skin like polished wood. Deep in her soul she knew it wouldn't be long before the inevitable happened. Did she really wish to escape before it did?

The sea was calm and the ferry made good progress. The crossing was soon over.

As they rolled down the incline, Rowena experienced a sudden bout of anxiety. If she wasn't mistaken, a faint smile had come to Zu Mu's thin lips and there was a definite change in her eyes. Sheer dislike had given way to what she could only interpret as extreme happiness.

She glanced at the woman's inscrutable face, wrinkled like a long-fallen crab apple. 'If we're not going to Kim's office, where are we going? Are we going shopping? More silks? More seed pearls to sew on your slippers? Though they look like purses to me. Just big enough for pennies, not feet.'

Zu Mu remained silent.

They finally came to a halt in a busy street, the traditional buildings leaning against each other and across to the opposite side. Shops and stalls, street pedlars and labourers jostled for space in the narrow alleys. The smells of food, spices, heat and animals clogged the air.

The driver was ordered to park at the widest end of the alley where a column of rickshaw men slept, leaning on their vehicles, one leg lifted, the foot resting on a naked knee.

Zu Mu barked more orders, raising her stick more

than once when the driver questioned what she'd said to him.

Concerned at their arguing, Rowena tried to follow what they were saying, but they spoke too fast for her to follow. But she was right about one thing. There was conflict between them. They were disagreeing about whatever was about to happen, the driver looking worried, the grandmother forceful, determined to have her way.

At last some kind of agreement was reached. The driver alighted to help Zu Mu down from the car, lifting her as he might a doll or a child. The moment her tiny feet touched the ground, she was dependent on her walking stick to remain upright. At her shouted instructions, a rickshaw driver peeled off from the rank, lowered the shafts of his vehicle and helped her climb onto the ripped leather seating from where she shouted at Rowena to join her.

Rowena wondered how far she could run before the driver caught her and carried her back to the car.

He looked worried, hopping from foot to foot, continuing to bow and ask questions to which Zu Mu gave only clipped answers and a wave of her cane.

For a moment her eyes met those of the puzzled driver. There was more to this than met the eye and she worked out what it was. Neither she nor Kim's grandmother was of a class that took rides in shabby rickshaws – if they used one at all. Rickshaws were the preferred mode of transport for *matelots* on leave wanting to explore the seedier side of the city. Only a few of the very poor used one to get around, and even fewer of the very rich.

Zu Mu was not of the class or nationality to take a rickshaw. Rowena imagined she would have considered it the way the poorer class or a *gweilo* got around.

Once she was seated the driver responded to the old woman's barked instructions. Her voice softened only when she was speaking to her grandson.

The bandy-legged driver, his feet encased in leather sandals that had seen better days, turned the rickshaw so it was facing the way Zu Mu pointed and plodded off.

The alley narrowed. At the very end Chinese characters fluttered on silk banners. In alternate strands, paper lanterns threaded on rope bounced and spun above the braziers of those selling sweetmeats and toasted crickets. The further they went, the more pungent the aroma, the smell contained by the constricting walls of the alley.

'Are we going shopping?'

Her question was aired lightly. She liked the feel of this place, the upper windows of the houses only feet away from those on the opposite side. If she really wanted to, this was her chance to run, so why didn't she?

Smiling, she looked at Zu Mu so the old woman would know she was aware she would not be answered.

To her surprise Zu Mu faced her, her eyes as deadly cold as those of a cobra. There was pure malice in that look, plus a hint of triumph, as though whatever was about to happen had sent her spirit soaring.

Trepidation barely held in check, Rowena prepared herself for the unexpected.

They left the steaming hubbub of the narrow alleys and broke out into the open, passing less official buildings, more humble dwellings, then a road she recognised. Her blood ran cold.

'Where are we going?' She thought she knew, but still had to ask, not that she was likely to receive an answer, just a wider smile. That in itself was worrying. Kim's grandmother never smiled at her, only scowled.

They rattled along, the old lady remaining silent with that satisfied look on her face.

Rowena considered jumping out of the rickshaw and running into the paddy fields, until she spied the contingent of Japanese soldiers marching behind them and a staff car packed with officers some way in front. 'I know this road,' she whispered.

She looked around her to confirm that she was right. This road, she remembered, went to Fort Stanley and passed St Stephen's, the school that had been turned into a hospital that had become a charnel house, the place where many people had died.

Nausea gripped her belly and rose into her throat. She looked accusingly at the old lady. 'You're having me killed, aren't you?'

There was a smug look on her face. Kim's grandmother was taking great pleasure in her discomfort. Only it was more than discomfort. With all that had happened at St Stephen's she was falling to pieces.

She poked the rickshaw driver in the back and asked him where they were going.

He shook his head.

Not that he doesn't know, thought Rowena. He is not allowed to tell.

They came to a fork in the road.

The old woman laughed.

Rowena's heart was in her mouth, her arms spread to either side of her, her fists tight on the folded-down hood of the rickshaw. The right fork was the road she had sometimes walked in those few short days before the hospital had become a slaughterhouse.

The buildings in which she'd experienced the worst ordeal of her life came into view. They looked unchanged, except that the flag depicting the rising sun had replaced the Union flag. 'I can't bear this.' Her throat felt as though it was closing. If she didn't do something soon, she might die through lack of oxygen.

She'd jump and run, damn the consequences. It was her only hope.

Claw-like fingers grabbed her hand, holding it so tightly her fingers began to tingle.

She struggled but Zu Mu clung on.

Closer and closer. The entrance to St Stephen's was just yards away. One quarter of the buildings showed beyond the red flame trees. A little further, and more came into view.

To her relief, the rickshaw driver did not slow or turn

in, but ran on, past the entrance, past the familiar wall, the trees, the fields to one side.

In the near distance there was another building, an official-looking place that Rowena recognised as Fort Stanley. Another entrance, another guard post, more enemy soldiers with guns.

And then it came to her what this was about. Ahead was a prison camp. Zu Mu wanted everything as it was before, her grandson to herself and Rowena locked away from him.

Seeing the rickshaw approach, a Japanese guard held up his hand, ordering it to stop.

Rebellion stirred in her veins. 'Let me go, you old witch. Let me go!'

She struggled against the old woman, kicking at her legs, trying without success to step on the most vulnerable part of Zu Mu's body, her feet.

The little feet kicked at her shins, too high for Rowena to stamp on them.

'You wicked old—'

Zu Mu clung on, shouting at the guard, as though Chinese would somehow translate into Japanese. When he shouted back, the old woman tried a different tack.

'This woman British. Should be here in camp. I bring her here.'

Rowena was astonished. Never once had Zu Mu said anything in English. Now the shrewd old bird had shown her cards, desperate to get rid of her.

Rowena lashed out as the guard dragged her down from the rickshaw. He retaliated with a slap to her face, shaking her so hard that she fell to the ground. He waved away the rickshaw driver, who didn't wait to be told twice, grit spurting out from the wheels as he did a tight turn and ran off as fast as his legs would take him.

In the back, her tiny feet a good four inches off the floor, the old lady threw back her head and laughed.

Sick with fear, Rowena eyed the white building with its metal-framed windows. This time no amount of bribes would obtain her release because Kim would not know she was here. His grandmother had left the car and driver and taken the rickshaw for good reason. She would not tell Kim the truth but would say that Rowena had run away.

One guard gripping her right arm, another her left, she was half dragged, half carried through a gate between high fences enclosing Fort Stanley, which had once administered the British Crown Colony. Now there were guard towers at intermittent intervals, machine-guns levelled at the inmates. As she drew closer, featureless figures beyond the wire became women and children, staring at her with wide-eyed interest, the wind blowing their dry hair across faces as pale as candle wax.

The buildings, people, shouted orders, paperwork and questions all passed in a blur but her fear had subsided. Fort Stanley was not St Stephen's although, some distance behind her, she could see the top of the hospital thrusting above the treetops.

Within an hour fear was replaced by joy as friendly faces smiled and voices called to her. One face, one voice stood out. 'Rowena!'

'Alice!'

They hugged, then held each other at arm's length.

Alice was wearing a pair of white shorts and a dark green top. Rowena remembered that the top used to be quite snug on her. Now it was hanging loose.

Alice noticed her surprise. 'Don't tell me I've lost weight. I already know that. How about you?'

Rowena shrugged. 'Oh, I'm not too bad.' She threw back her head and closed her eyes. 'I'm so relieved. I thought they were taking me to St Stephen's.'

'Welcome to Chez Stanley, your new home – such as it is. You look good – in fact, I'd say you've put weight on. Anyway, our chief medical officer will give you the once-over. It's purely so he's forewarned of any diseases coming into the camp.'

Rowena followed her to the ground-floor medical facility where an examination area was screened off in the far corner.

'I'll take you for tea afterwards.'

Alice nodded at the doctor. 'Do you need me to assist?'

'May as well.'

The doctor asked her the usual questions, had she been sick, had she noticed any change in her breathing, any sores, anything out of the ordinary.

She responded that she was feeling fine and hadn't suffered anything except fatigue.

The doctor peered at her over his glasses. 'And your menstruation is regular?'

'I think...' She stopped. Her life during the last few months had been extraordinary to say the least, so unusual that she'd hardly noticed the more routine things in her life. 'Just the odd spot. That's all.'

'Not unusual in the present circumstances. But I'll examine you.'

'I can hardly examine myself!'

When he had finished, she knew from his face that those few spots were far from a normal monthly flow. 'I would estimate that you're about four months pregnant.'

Rowena bit down on the things she could say, but the sickening truth spilled into a sigh of despair.

Alice lowered her voice. 'I'm so sorry.'

'Fancy,' said Rowena, numbly, as they left the screened-off area, wound their way between the beds and went out into the sunshine. 'I'm a doctor but I never gave it any thought. My mind's been full of so many other things.'

'Whose is it? Not the Irishman's, I take it.'

'No. The enemy soldiers didn't care about my monthly bleed. The baby will have a foreign look about it – if it ever gets born.'

Alice waved her hand behind her. 'Well, you couldn't have come to a better place. There's more doctors and nurses per square foot than there are stars in the sky.'

'My God.'

'It wasn't him, the fellow who took you from the camp?'

'No.'

'Did you...?'

'No. I didn't.'

'Damn rotten luck, though. How the hell are you going to cope with a kid that looks, well, not like us?'

'Don't say that, Alice. It'll be just a child.'

'And a lovely one. But you know what I mean. Not everyone is going to love it.'

'Only those who don't know it.'

'But the Japs are going to be hated after the war – in fact, anyone who looks a bit Oriental will have a tough time. You could always put it in an orphanage.'

'Alice, will you please let it drop? I'll think further on it when the time comes.'

'Of course you will. In the meantime I think I'm going to faint with joy, you turning up here out of the blue.'

'Where's Tansy?'

'She's got malaria. We treat it with whatever we can, but it keeps recurring.'

Someone susceptible would never entirely shake it off, Rowena knew. They would have to learn to live with it.

'Jaundice is our other main problem, along with malnutrition. There's never enough to eat – though you've already noticed that.' Alice plucked playfully at her baggy blouse and the legs of her shorts, which no longer dug into her thighs as they once had.

'And all this in just a few months?'

'Precisely. What the hell's it gonna be like after a few years? If it comes to it,' she added, trying to make it sound like a joke, though they both knew it was a worst-case scenario.

A group of children ran noisily in front of them, riding hobby-horses made from bits of wood, old socks and string. A boy ran at the guards brandishing a wooden sword. They pointed their bayonets at him just as playfully and laughed.

Rowena watched them running away, heard laughter exchanged between the guards.

Humour and joy still existed, even here. For a while it had seemed that nobody would ever laugh again.

Alice laid a hand on Rowena's shoulder. 'Come on. I'll find us that tea I promised you and introduce you to a few people.'

Initially set up as a range of offices, the building was now subdivided into dormitories for the women and children living there. Alice explained that half of the bottom floor catered for families and the other half was used as a hospital.

'Some of the men got allocated here, but only those with families. I can't know for sure, but I think they're the lucky ones. At least they have their families.'

The room on the first floor was long and subdivided into sleeping quarters by large pieces of tarpaulin, coverings for army trucks in a former life. Some women were sleeping, sewing, reading or knitting. One woman looked up from breastfeeding her baby and smiled.

'Alice. And a new arrival?' The booming voice came from a square-shouldered woman sitting behind a trestle table with two others at the far end of the room. Smiling in welcome, she got to her feet and came round from behind the table. She was wearing a gold lamé cocktail dress with a pair of scruffy black plimsolls. 'Excuse the mix of styles. Grabbed what I could when I realised the end was nigh – the end of Hong Kong, that is.'

Alice introduced her as Marjorie Greenbank. 'Marjorie's husband used to work here.'

'How do you do?' She gave Rowena's hand a firm shake. 'You look as though you've been well cared for. That should give you a head start. In time you'll be as scrawny as the rest of us. But we still have tea. Nothing is too bad as long as we have our tea, don't you think so, my dear?'

'Dr Rossiter is pregnant.'

'Oh dear. Never mind. Even more of an excuse for some tea.'

'I'd love a cup.'

'You shall have it. My husband liked his tea, my dear. He also told me the location of the tea and the store cupboard and gave me his key before he was taken.'

'He's not here with you?'

'No. They shot him because he didn't get to Murray Square on time. He missed the less than pleasurable experience of being housed in one of the brothels down near the harbour. Quite a few of us were held there while they tried to work out what to do. Hundreds of us stuffed into the most dreadful accommodation possible. The women there didn't like it either. Interfered with their business, you see. Does Darjeeling suit you? Or I do have a little Earl Grey left. The Assam is favoured by our Indian comrades so I tend to keep it exclusively for them.'

Rowena was amazed that she could talk so casually about varieties of tea in the midst of a prisoner-of-war camp.

'I refuse to lower standards,' Marjorie added, on seeing Rowena's surprise, 'but I'm afraid I can spare you only half a lump of sugar and just a spot of milk. We're running low.'

'I'm fine with black and no sugar.'

Alice went off to fetch a tin of condensed milk.

Marjorie talked above the clattering of crockery and the whistling of the boiling kettle. Topics of conversation came and went, but she chatted mostly about the various embassies in which her husband had served, India where she had met him, and how many applications there had been to join the amateur dramatic society she'd lately set up. 'You look Anglo-Indian. Am I right?'

Rowena was taken aback, inclined to deny her pedigree, but Marjorie didn't give her the chance. 'Don't worry. I won't tell a soul.'

Not once did she ask Rowena where she'd got the silk pyjamas she was wearing, or where she'd been before arriving at the camp, and for that she was thankful.

Tea clutched in their hands, Alice took her outside to a shady spot at the back of the building where rows of ragged washing cracked like gunshots in the wind. A cast-iron bench was set against the back wall. A few of its wooden slats were missing, but there were enough left to support their combined weight.

All around her women were carrying on with their lives, doing the mundane things that would occupy them no matter where they were in the world. It felt strange but also reassuring.

'It's good to be here,' she whispered, smiling as two children threw a rag ball to each other while their mother tied their pitiful clothes to a washing line strung between two saplings.

Alice patted her hand. 'You're with friends, your own countrywomen for the most part.'

It wasn't until she'd sipped her tea that Rowena realised how dry her mouth had been. She had panicked at the prospect of returning to St Stephen's to endure the same ordeal as before.

'I haven't seen you since everyone had to report to Murray Square. You were there one minute and gone the next. Are you going to tell me more of what happened?'

'You saw him collect me.'

Alice nodded. 'Recognised him right away.'

'Kim Pheloung, the foreigner, as you insisted on calling him.'

Alice fidgeted, sipped tea and looked unconcerned, but Rowena wasn't fooled. She answered the question before it came. 'I've already told you, he never touched me.'

Alice looked puzzled. 'So why...'

'...did he pay a bribe to free me?' She shook her head. 'Alice, I still ask myself the same question and don't know the answer. I asked him but his answer didn't make any sense. He told me that the colonel handed me into his custody. I can't believe he got away with it except that the Japanese need people like Kim to keep everyone in line. I suspect he's more powerful on his own patch than they are.'

'Looking at what you're wearing and the bloom on your face, I take it you were treated well, which begs the question, why come here? Was it your decision?'

'No.' She told Alice something of her short stay in the old house within the walled city, of the cool, dark interior, the guards, the servants and especially his grandmother. 'It was she who dumped me here. I wondered why we took a rickshaw. I presume it was because she didn't want the driver of the car to bear witness to her bringing me here. She was jealous that I was usurping her position with her grandson.'

'I wonder if he'll come here and take you back.'

Rowena shrugged. 'Not if he doesn't know I'm here. She's a sly one, his grandmother. She'll probably tell him I ran away.'

'If he did come, would you go with him?'

'No. I've got my condition to think of.'

Thankfully Alice didn't ask whether she would go

with him if she wasn't pregnant, because she wouldn't have been able to answer.

'Oh, well,' said Alice, draining the delicate cup Marjorie had lent her, 'you're safe and will be well looked after – especially when the time comes.' She jerked her chin at Rowena's stomach, which at present was only showing the very slightest swelling.

Rowena looked down into the remains of her cup, noting the decoration of painted roses and gilt around its rim. It was so English, bound to arouse homesickness in a place like this. In her it evoked a different response. 'I don't want it.'

The sun went behind a cloud. A stronger wind had the washing cracking a little louder.

Alice sat silently as she took in what Rowena was saying.

Rowena turned her head to look at her. 'It happened to you, too, didn't it? Don't you remember?'

She shook her head. 'Not really. I was in shock. I didn't want to be there, I didn't want to be me, and I kind of retreated into a bubble. I can't recall the details.'

'Were you pregnant?'

'Yes. A few old recipes from Marjorie Greenbank and my little problem was no more. But it was early days. I was lucky.'

'And Tansy?'

'She miscarried, saved by malaria – though a heavy price to pay.' She looked away.

Rowena sensed there was something more. 'How bad was it?'

Alice hung her head and mumbled into the empty cup. 'It was a breech baby. She went on for days. Luckily – and I say luckily only because the procedure saved her life – there was a surgeon here who'd specialised in obstetrics, but some time ago. Still, he was all we had. So he operated.' She swallowed what might have been a sob. 'He couldn't do a caesarean. He hadn't a full set of tools. The baby came out in pieces. I doubt she'll ever get pregnant again, thanks to that.'

Rowena thought of Tansy's vivacious personality, the colour of her hair and the glint in her emerald eyes. 'I'm about four months gone but I want to lose the baby and only a doctor can help.'

Alice sucked in her breath. 'You're going to ask somebody?'

'I am.'

'But that's taking a life. It's a difficult thing to ask.'

'Somebody will do it.'

'You're a doctor. What would you do if somebody asked you to abort a four-month foetus?'

Rowena bit her lip as she took in the scenes going on around her. Straight ahead one of the children playing with the rag ball ran off, the other chasing him, bawling at the top of his voice.

Rowena watched them. Could she really destroy the life that was inside her? She shook her head. 'I would hate to be asked, but if there were extenuating circumstances...'

'It's your decision.'

'And that of the doctor.'

'Under the circumstances...'

'Indeed. Under the circumstances.'

There was no white coat, no smell of antiseptic or the swish of nurses' skirts as they went about their daily duty, but there were stethoscopes and medical instruments.

She began visiting Tansy daily. The once vibrant personality was no more and her conversation was always the same, as though the previous day hadn't happened and their reunion was fresh not repeated.

'Dr Rossiter,' she said, her voice rasping, as though every word, every breath was painful. 'How wonderful to see you again.'

'And you, Tansy. How are you feeling?'

'A little better.'

Rowena bathed her brow, gave her what comfort she could and also a little of the quinine that the incorrigible Mrs Greenbank had hidden from the Japanese.

Tansy's belief that she was getting better was not supported by her appearance. Her red hair was paler and thinner than it had been and her fresh complexion had a waxy look. Her eyes were sunken, her lips cracked. Her furred tongue licked her lips and Rowena braced herself for the next oft repeated statement.

'I lost it. I lost the baby.'

'Tansy, you mustn't think of it. You have to concentrate on getting better. That's all that matters.'

There was a faraway look in Tansy's eyes. 'I think it was a little girl. I don't know for sure, but I like to imagine it was.'

'You shouldn't think about what happened and what might have happened. Just get well.'

'I don't think about what happened, only about the baby I might have had. I wanted that baby. She would have made everything worthwhile.'

Rowena adjusted her stethoscope and swallowed her anger. She couldn't understand how Tansy would want to keep a baby born as the result of a brutal rape. For her part she would prefer not to be pregnant and the baby not to be born. Tansy had seemingly forgotten the circumstances and embraced the thought of having the child.

'Tansy. Do you remember me visiting you yesterday?'

Tansy's glassy expression wavered and, for a moment, there seemed hope of improvement. Then she said, 'That doesn't matter. I know how busy you are. But you came today. You came today and that's all that matters.' Her confusion worsened with each passing day. After every visit, Rowena went outside to take deep breaths of air, brush at her tears and swallow the pain. It had been wonderful to see Alice and Tansy again, but there was no doubt that rape, the miscarriage and malaria were all worsening her condition. 'I so wanted my baby,' Tansy murmured, just before she took her last breath.

She was buried in the adjacent cemetery, a peaceful place near the chapel, originally laid out in the mid-nineteenth century as the last resting place for the military and their families. Rowena knew that she could cope with the funeral and the cemetery. The chapel, however, was more difficult. She'd had to steel herself to go inside, and stiffened on entering, walking down the aisle to the bare altar, seeing the army padre in his threadbare garb, his bald head shiny in the light from the window. The pews had been chopped up to make coffins. The floor was bare and cold. It was the fifth burial that week, but the first that Rowena had attended.

Beside the grave, she kept her eyes on the roughly made coffin in the grave, only raising them when those gathered began to sing 'The Lord's My Shepherd'.

Rowena did not sing.

Marjorie Greenbank noticed. 'Lost your voice or are you like me? My husband used to tell me that I sang like a throttled hen.'

'My throat's dry.'

'So is mine, my dear. I could murder a drop of gin. How about you?'

Marjorie's forthright manner was enough to lighten the moment.

'I was just thinking.'

'Yes. At this moment I feel quite a rapport with that line about walking through death's dark vale.'

'I would prefer not to.'

'So would I, dear, so would I. But death comes to all of us. It's just a question of when.'

'I'm not ready to die.'

'None of us are. Cedric wasn't. He loved life. Now it's the end of his line. We could never have children, you see. That's what makes his death so final. Mine, too, I suppose – when it happens, neither of us leaving anything behind except material possessions. And they mean nothing.'

'I'm sorry, I didn't intend...'

'I know you didn't, dear, but I meant it about the gin.'

# 14

She didn't know when her attitude changed about the child. Perhaps it was after that conversation with Marjorie or Tansy's death, or perhaps as a result of what happened a few days later. She was lancing the boils of a girl of thirteen or so. The child was listless and starving, like everyone else but also immature for her age.

Her mother was very concerned. 'I thought she would have had a period by now. I did by the time I was thirteen. And I would like to become a grandmother. In time, of course, when she's grown-up and this is all over.'

'Not having enough food can impair a child's development and postpone adolescence. Some calcium might help. Green vegetables and fruit contain some. Condensed milk even.'

There was no point in mentioning butter or cheese and certainly not cow's milk. Thanks to Mrs Greenbank and her late husband, there was condensed milk, but the supplies hidden in the secret place beneath the floorboards were swiftly running out.

Sudden movement in front of the commandant's office turned heads and contributed to hushed conversations.

'Roll-call.'

'*Tenko! Tenko!*'

Women and children began lining up.

Rowena had been on her way through the main door and from there to the ward. She wanted to get on with what she had to do – roll-call interfered with medical schedules. She asked Marjorie Greenbank if she knew what was going on.

'Give me a minute. I will shortly, no doubt.' As one of the few British people in the camp who could speak Japanese, once everyone was standing in line she stepped forward, bowed and asked what was happening.

Standing behind her, Rowena saw the sudden stiffening of her spine.

When Marjorie finally turned, her face was pale. 'We are required to dig a mass grave in the cemetery. We will receive further instructions after that. Can I have volunteers, please?'

Silence dropped like an iron curtain on those present. When only a few married men stepped forward to volunteer, the commandant barked at his men to pull others out of the lines, including some of the women. Leaving everyone in stunned silence, they were marched off, shoulders slumped and sweating fear.

Although the day was pleasant enough, it was as though a black cloud had touched the earth. Whispers coursed from one person to another. Those too sick to leave their beds continually asked questions that nobody wanted to answer. Rowena kept herself focused on the jobs she had to do, though every so often she looked out of the window to see if the grave-diggers had come back.

Everyone in the camp was on alert for their return. There were fears that they might not come back at all, that they had dug their own grave.

It wasn't just Rowena who feared that, if this was so, it might be a new policy and not stop at one communal grave but continue until the camp had been emptied of people.

'Tea.' Alice pressed a cup into Rowena's shaking hand.

'Thanks.'

'There's a chair behind you.'

Gratefully Rowena sat down, rested her aching feet on an upturned enamel bucket and took a sip. 'Thank God for tea.'

'Do you think they'll come back?' Alice resembled a frightened rabbit as she peered over the rim of her cup.

Rowena declined to answer because she had no answer to give, or not one that would bring any solace.

'Should we revolt?' Alice asked.

'Armed with what? A few scalpels and bedpans?'

'It's no laughing matter.'

'I'm not laughing.'

Between sips of tea Rowena rubbed her belly. Perhaps the child would not be born after all. Perhaps she would die before that happened. If only she could believe it was Connor's baby she might die happy, but that was impossible.

Alice was just as frightened. 'I'm so scared that we're all going to die.'

'I don't think so. If they were going to kill everyone, why wait until now?'

She could see from Alice's face that her comment had done some good.

The same kind of thinking was going on around the camp but nobody let it get in the way of their meals, the children's schooling, the laundry, the cleaning, the growing of vegetables and the endless attention to those who were sick.

The feeling of apprehension intensified as evening approached. Some of the inmates were hanging out of the upper windows, hands shielding their eyes as their fellows returned, their steps slow but relief etched on their faces. They were still alive. The grave had not been for them… So who had it been for?

They came in dragging their feet, dog-tired bodies covered with dust and stinking of sweat. A line formed outside the bathing hut where the water supply was as intermittent as the electricity, but less dangerous.

Concerned about providing enough coal to the British-built power station, the Japanese had cut back, plunging whole areas into darkness, and at Fort Stanley they kept only their own headquarters permanently powered.

Skilled engineers among the prisoners had reconnected the supply, though it wasn't entirely safe and everyone was warned not to touch the overhead wiring with wet hands.

One or two of those who had not been involved with the grave-digging attached themselves to the queue for the showers. Heads shook in disbelief, matching the expressions on haggard faces and in sullen eyes.

Alice was one of those who heard the news first. '*They had to dig a big pit. A grave,*' said Alice, in a hushed voice. 'And they have to work tomorrow too.'

Marjorie interrupted. 'The men tried to take on most of the heavy work so the women didn't have to do it. Now they're exhausted. I think you'll find there'll be new diggers tomorrow, and as they've exhausted the men, it will consist mostly of women. They need workers. They need more people.'

Unable to sleep, that night Rowena sat up holding the hand of a dying nun. She had once been in a convent looking after orphaned Chinese children. Somebody said she'd known Gladys Aylward, the missionary who had taken her own Chinese orphans away from fighting warlords to safety, but nobody knew for sure.

In the morning Rowena nodded into wakefulness in time to see everyone milling around outside, long before *tenko* was actually due. Before going down to join them, she closed the eyes of the dead nun. She reckoned everybody needed someone to witness their passing, confirmation that they had once lived.

She wandered out to join the others, her hands dug deep into the pockets of a very tattered white coat to be worn only when she was on duty. The doctors shared equipment between them and also the coat. All of it had seen better days. The more up-to-date medical equipment had been requisitioned for use by the Imperial Japanese Army.

Alice was already there, scuffing at the dust with one foot then the other, a sure sign that she was nervous.

Marjorie was standing up front, waiting to hear whatever the commandant required. When she finally turned to relay what the commandant required, her strong, purposeful manner was absent. Before she could get a word out, soldiers loaded with empty sacks came in and piled them in a heap behind her.

Rowena almost stopped breathing as she contemplated what they were to be used for. They were big enough to take a folded body. She banished the thought. There had to be a more civilised purpose. Cruel as they were, surely they were not contemplating massacring a whole camp?

Marjorie licked her lips. 'Some of you were at St Stephen's on Christmas Day so there's no need for me to go over what happened. You know those killed were burned. Their bones and ashes are all that's left. Permission has been given for their reburial in the cemetery, hence the digging of a communal grave and the supply of these sacks, which are to be filled with their ashes, then interred.'

The sound of sobbing broke out. Rowena closed her eyes and placed a hand over her chest. It did nothing to stop the palpitations brought on by shock, surprise and an overwhelming sense of loss. Ashes to ashes, a few words from the funeral service that seemed to bear no relation to the people those ashes had once been. Kind and dutiful army doctors, British, Canadian and Indian soldiers, nurses raped and brutalised, then killed.

A doctor was not expected to join the column of volunteers that was forming to carry out the sickening task, but she felt driven to do so.

Today somebody else had donned the white coat and stethoscope, but she could not sit idle while this was going on. Like many of those around her, she stepped forward, picked up a sack and a shovel and joined the growing line of sad people faced with a terrible task that, nonetheless, they were willing to carry out.

Marjorie confirmed the details. They were to shovel the remains into sacks, take them to the cemetery for burial and hope, blindly, that somehow they could live with the memory.


In silence they arrived and in silence they contemplated what lay in front of them.

Weathered and tossed by wind and rain, the remains of the bonfire formed a bleak island in a sea of green grass.

'Go! Work! Dig!'

Some sobbed. One or two brought up what little was in their stomach.

'Dig! Now!'

Somebody mumbled a short prayer: 'May they rest in peace, safe in the arms of the Lord.'

They worked in pairs, one digging, the other holding open the mouth of the sack.

The ash was loose and easy to break into. In some places a scorched bone pierced the surface, a grim reminder that this grey morass had once been people. Overnight rain meant the top few inches of ash had formed a damp crust so at first there was no dust. As they dug deeper, the remains were drier, a mixture of powdered bone and wood ash rising in a pewter cloud to coat their faces and sting their eyes.

Sporadic coughing began as they breathed it into their lungs. Rags torn from their clothes were wound around noses and mouths. Salty tears ran from their eyes leaving white trails on pale grey faces. Some dug slowly, some more quickly but always carefully.

In an effort to keep her feelings at bay, Rowena opted to dig furiously, another woman holding open the mouth of the sack so she could drop in the ash.

The shovel suddenly hit something more solid. She reached into the ash and picked out a small round object. A ring. It looked like an engagement ring, which saddened her. Somebody, possibly a nurse, had been engaged to be married. What dreams she must have had: a white wedding, a handsome husband probably in uniform, dreams of a home where they would raise a family. The dream had ended at Christmas in 1941, a black Christmas that would long be remembered by those who'd survived.

A few minutes later she came across a nurse's belt buckle. She picked that out too and laid it to one side with the ring. Eyes wet with tears and sobs strangling her throat, she went back to digging. The sooner the residual remains of the fire were all gone, the better.

The personal items were plucked and put to one side in the hope that at some point in the future somebody would locate the relatives of the dead person and the items could be claimed.

Her throat dry, she pulled the rag mask off her face, took a gulp of air, then water from the ladle hanging at the side of the bucket they'd brought with them. Half a cup only every hour. It wasn't enough but it was all they were allowed.

When the sacks filled, everyone stood silently, staring at the scorched ground.

Looking at that patch, Rowena had expected to feel emptiness, but instead she was about to burst with emotion that was too much to bear. The silence was deafening and the emotion had to come out. She opened her mouth, expecting words of damnation, but instead she sang, her voice rising like a lark in the meadow:

*'O God, our help in ages past,*
*Our hope for years to come...'*

Nobody moved. Even the guards stood transfixed.

Just a few lines and her voice broke with sobs, the hymn taken up by a male voice, then everyone else.

The guards got nervous, pushing and shoving, shouting orders and slamming their stakes or their rifles across shoulders and backs.

Rowena, her voice faint now, sang the last lines:

*'Be Thou our guard while troubles last,*
*And our eternal home.'*

For some reason they left her alone until she'd finished, then she joined the rest in loading the cart before walking back to the cemetery, burdened with the remains of lives that should have been longer.

At first they thought it a mirage, the piper who had somehow preserved both his kilt and his instrument. He saw them at the same time as they saw him, primed his bagpipes and struck up a plaintive lament. The familiarity of his dress and the music did something to everyone there. Rowena felt the burden of pent-up emotion fly with the notes of 'The Flowers of the Forest'.

The piper led them with slow, sliding steps to the last resting place of those who had been human and were now only sacks of dust. The guards, without officers to note their respectful air, stood back, some with bowed heads, others with strained expressions as though they wished they were far away, not party to this.

At the graveside an army pastor stood ready, bare-headed, peering at them awkwardly, thanks to a crack across one lens of his spectacles. His vestments were in as bad a state as those of the medical fraternity, but he held his head upright, leather-bound copy of the Holy Bible clutched reverently in one hand.

The chaplain waited until everything was ready and everyone was gathered, his stance stolid, his face expressionless. He explained he would conduct a non-denominational service.

'I would not want to offend anyone so thought I would mention it. Please feel free to leave if you wish.'

'As if,' murmured Rowena, and jerked her chin at the grave. '*That* is offence enough.'

'*I am the Resurrection and the life...*'

Every so often he raised his eyes to Heaven as a fine ash rose from yet another sack handed down to somebody in the pit.

The task could have been done more quickly by throwing in the sacks, but instinctively two men had climbed down into the pit to see their brothers in arms and sisters of mercy laid to rest in a reverent manner.

When every sack was accounted for, a shower of petals and leaves was thrown in.

'*Earth to earth, ashes to ashes...*'

The last line.

As she joined in with the final amen, Rowena felt the

hatred flooding back. Her life would never be the same again, and how would she cope with her child looking so much like them?

For days, even weeks afterwards, sadness and resentment simmered among the imprisoned residents of Fort Stanley in the form of a stilted silence broken only by the laughter of children at play.

Rowena immersed herself in her work, the only way she could blank the events from her mind. She went about her tasks with her usual efficiency – as far as medical supplies would allow.

Anger rather than resentment burned in her heart. She could not look at a Japanese soldier, even the more amenable ones, without wanting to stick a scalpel in his groin or his eyes, replicating some of the atrocities he and his comrades had carried out. She would probably never have the chance to do that. Their guards sauntered around outside the medical facility, which was for the use of prisoners only. They had their own clinic, though occasionally one would come smiling and bowing with something minor. Those who did this were willing to barter valuables for food. Their punishment if caught was severe, but still they came as if they, too, were trying to lead something resembling a normal life.

Along with their smiles they brought family photographs, proudly pointing out and naming their wife and children.

One day she got close enough to take revenge in an uncommon manner.

'Yashito has a problem with his private parts. I've told him we'd take a look.'

Rowena flinched. That was the last thing she wanted to do to an enemy soldier.

Catching sight of her expression, Dr Anderson, who had once practised in Harley Street, reminded her of her duty. 'He's been able to steal morphine from the army dispensary – for a price, of course.'

'So it's to our advantage, though I don't see why he can't see one of the army doctors.'

'He has a rather bad infection of pubic lice. Crabs, as our own men call it. Face, my dear. He might lose face. Losing face is important to the Japanese and I for one understand that.'

'I see.'

She was still disgusted but also took a certain sadistic delight in his plight, just as soldiers like him had taken in her. The problem could be put down to not washing, a difficult thing in times of war, but there was another cause and that was the one she favoured. It was well known that the Japanese frequented 'comfort houses' set up to administer to their troops. In order to contain the transmission of sexual diseases, the women there were very young, mostly abducted from their homes in Korea and elsewhere. However, containing disease was never easy, and Chinese whorehouses, run by well-established criminal organisations, often undercut the official brothels. To save money from their army pay for sending home, a number of soldiers preferred them.

Aubrey Anderson began inspecting the man's genitals. Rowena turned away, chilled to the bone, though beads of sweat dotted her forehead. She had a strong stomach, but she couldn't bear to look at the man's genitals. The memory was too raw and the aftermath was swelling in her stomach.

Her colleague noticed. 'You all right, Doctor?'

'Fine.'

The man was carefully examined.

'Just crabs,' the doctor said jovially, as he dabbed the man's private parts with DDT. 'If he wants any more of this he'll have to get it from his own doctor. The Japanese Army must keep tons of the stuff. Can you go with him outside and get Mrs Greenbank to interpret my prognosis to this chap?'

The ambling soldier looked nervous at the prospect of hearing what he was suffering from.

Marjorie had been giving a talk about Royal Doulton porcelain to a group of women. Most had come along with their knitting or mending, patching together items of clothing that, under other circumstances, would have become dusters.

'And with that, ladies, my talk on Royal Doulton is over. Next time I'll be talking about Charles the Second and his love of the arts.' On seeing Rowena she grinned. 'Love of the arts indeed. Actresses mostly – and a certain voluptuous young woman who sold oranges!'

The comment deserved a smile, which, in present company, Rowena found hard. Revenge was said to be best taken cold. She wasn't cold. She was on fire. The sight of those sacks, the shovelfuls of ashes and bones...

Marjorie was her usual breezy self and had a tendency to put bad things behind her. 'So what do I tell him?'

'Tell him he's got the pox and is likely to die within the next month.'

'Oh, I say. Poor chap.'

Rowena walked away. She didn't want to see the man's distress: she wanted to relish it. Her smile broadened. In time he'd go to the army doctor and find out the truth. In the meantime he would suffer.

On hearing her return, Dr Anderson looked up. 'My dear. I wanted a word with you.'

'And I with you.'

His eyebrows rose. 'Oh, really?'

'You first.'

'That's very kind of you,' he said, his jovial manner seemingly undeterred by the presence of cockroaches in the skirting and flies settling on his bald head. 'I couldn't help noticing, my dear, that your coat is getting a bit too tight for you. By chance I happen to have a spare one that might suit.' He turned to an upturned tea chest he used as a table.

'That's what I was going to talk to you about. I don't want this to go any further.'

The coat he held was a little less than white, but looked clean enough.

Judging by the look on his face her meaning wasn't clear.

'I'm sorry, my dear. What exactly do you mean?'

She dug her hands into the pockets of the straining white coat she was presently wearing, then raised her eyes to meet his. 'I don't want it.'

A look of uncertainty came to the doctor's craggy features yet she knew he understood. His mouth hung slightly open. He was obviously waiting for her to explain and not wanting to hear the question he feared most.

'I have no wish to bear a child fathered by one of these monsters. I was raped on Christmas Day, though you probably already know that.'

He looked taken aback at her vehemence, the way her lips curled over each word as though they were poison. 'You're not quite too far gone. Four months?'

She nodded. 'Quite a Christmas present, one I didn't want.'

He sat with his head bowed, the loose skin of his neck like a frill upon his worn collar. He was studying his hands, first the palms then the backs, which were speckled with age spots. 'Like you, I pledged to save lives.' His voice was thin and sad.

She knew what he was saying and she, too, had truly believed in that oath: 'First do no harm.' St Luke or Hippocrates? It didn't really matter. She was a victim of a time, a place and an occurrence of the modern day. The centuries had rolled on. 'Do you think that in the circumstances you could do something?'

His eyes dropped from her face to her swollen belly. 'Have you any idea what you're asking of me? I'd have to ignore my professional ethics.'

Rowena pinched her lips between her fingers and squeezed her eyes almost shut. She was indeed asking a lot but knew deep inside what she might do if the child was born. 'It won't make any real difference – getting rid of the child before or after it's born. I recall there being an orphanage in Macau run by a Swedish mission.'

His fingers interlocked in front of him. The tired-looking white coat fell back onto the upturned tea chest. 'I sometimes feel ashamed of my own sex but tell myself they wouldn't act like that if we weren't at war. However, there are times when I'm not so sure. I can understand your hate.'

'The child will look like them.'

'Perhaps.'

'I don't think I could bear it. I don't think I could love it.'

He nodded stoically, then intoned the words she was desperate to hear. 'Tonight. Come at a quarter to midnight.' He turned his back and left her standing there, feeling unexpectedly sad, though tears of relief streamed down her cheeks.

She'd wiped her face by the time Marjorie Greenbank appeared in the doorway, an unreadable look on her face. 'Is something wrong?'

'That man you said would die of syphilis or whatever. He's dead.'

'He didn't have syphilis, just pubic lice, and they wouldn't have killed him. A dusting of DDT would have done the job.'

Marjorie's face clouded with concern. 'Oh dear, but I'm sure I interpreted your prognosis correctly.'

'You did.' Rowena faced the sudden guilt and made a useless excuse. 'I was feeling a little mischievous. He couldn't have died from crabs.'

'He didn't. He committed *hara-kiri*. Suicide.'

'Oh, God.'

'Oh God indeed.'

'I'm sorry.'

'We'll all be sorry about a lot of things once this war is over.'

# 15

Orange, crimson, yellow and pink: sunset.

'Best time of the day, Vicky. Do you hear me? Best time of the day.'

The colours randomly splashed across the sky filled Connor with wonder and always would.

Sitting like a meditating Buddha, cross-legged on his favourite concrete block, he gazed unflinching at the sunset. At times he felt he was flying towards it, its warmth caressing his aching muscles. The sun shone all over the world, anywhere and everywhere, and if he narrowed his eyes he could believe the same of himself: no prison camp or barbed wire, but a verdant land, the sound of birdsong and Atlantic waves crashing onto shoreline rocks.

The house of Kim Pheloung was rose-coloured in the dying rays. The block he sat on was slightly bigger than the rest, the one with the best view of that house. His eyes searched in vain for some sign of the doctor with the fine singing voice, but he hadn't seen her since the day she'd given him the lighter.

He still had it in his pocket, wrapped in the only handkerchief he had left. The lighter would stay with him, never bartered for food or anything else, not until he had a glimpse of her.

He held onto this promise to himself and every night, as soon as he'd eaten, this was where he came. Kim was keeping her in seclusion, a common practice in some Asian societies. If he stretched his neck he could see the tail end of the car in the outer compound. If it had been out, it would have been in the daytime. At night it stayed parked.

Victoria had learned the knack of springing halfway up the concrete block, but the height was too much for her to get up unaided. Claws scraping on the concrete, she yelped for him to reach down and scoop her up. Lying beside him, front legs outstretched, she, too, narrowed her eyes against the sun, two of a kind enjoying the warmth and, for the moment at least, alone.

The camp was overcrowded, but despite being overworked, starved and bored, they all rubbed along somehow. Their days consisted of work and their nights were haunted by dreams of food, freedom and visions of home.

It was one of those nights when there was no glorious sunset, the rain falling and filling the numerous receptacles spaced liberally around the camp that Harry again made him promise to take his remains home. 'The last time I mentioned it, I was rather flippant, but we were under fire at the time. So forgive me for blithering on. You know the mothers of ancient Sparta used to tell their sons to come back from war walking upright or on their shield. Get me home in a bucket if you have to, but get me home. Promise?'

Connor threw back his head and laughed. 'Bloody hell. In a box, a bottle or a jam jar.'

'Anything. In a paper bag if you have to.'

A thoughtful look that was out of character with his normal ebullience turned Harry's handsome features more serious than Connor had ever seen. He knew his friend had sunk a few mugs of hooch, but his expression was sober and his voice was serious. 'I mean it. My darling mother will forever wonder about me if I don't get back – one way or another. So I want you to promise. I swear this is the last time I shall ever ask you.'

'You're obsessed.'

'Yes, I am.'

Their eyes met, and not for the first time Connor felt as though he was looking at a reflection of himself. Even their views on life were similar, both keen to drain it to the dregs. The bar had been part of that, a prankish diversion from the everyday slog of being in the army. It could have won them a dressing down, confinement to barracks, or even a period in a military prison, but that to them was all part of the fun. That was the way they both were, daring to push the boundaries. Luckily they'd not been found out.

'I miss the bar,' said Connor. 'It was a fine adventure. Dangerous, but a fine adventure. And we kept ahead of them all – the army and the underworld.'

Harry thought about it and frowned. 'We defied convention.'

'Damn convention.'

'We could have been killed.'

'Or court-martialled.'

They sank into silence as they contemplated their brush with more dangerous people than the army high command.

It was Harry who broke the silence. 'Where do you think he is, Kim Pheloung?'

Connor's face darkened. 'I don't know.'

'You're thinking of the doctor.'

'Uh-huh.'

'Look on the bright side. She'll have enough to eat.'

Connor had to agree that he was right, but that didn't stop him wondering.

'The bright side will be when a Samurai sword cuts off Kim's head. He'd be one man who deserves it.'

'Too right, old boy. I suspect it wouldn't have been long before he muscled in for a cut of our profits.'

'He's probably got it to himself now. Poor old Yang. I wonder how he's faring, whether he's set himself up in the rice-ball trade. I must admit they tasted good.'

Recalling the day Yang had passed them a message with the rice balls, Harry laughed. 'We set up that bar in defiance of convention. Do you think we were a bit naïve?'

'We didn't allow for a criminal like Kim Pheloung to come along, so I suppose we were. Mind you, I never was one for convention.'

Harry laughed again and shook his head. 'Connor O'Connor, you're a wild man and a bloody good soldier. Did I ever tell you that?'

'Did I ever tell you that you drink too much?'

'Constantly.'

In defiance, Harry helped himself to another mug of hooch.

Connor shook his head. 'I'll see you in the morning. Vicky needs her late-night walk.'

The dog followed him obediently, only inches from his heels. They headed for the narrow strip of grass winding between the dusty compound and the perimeter fence. One step towards the fence, and the guards looking down from their elevated vantage points would fire a warning shot.

By the time they arrived back at the airless hut that was home for the duration, it was lights out. Connor climbed into the bunk beneath Harry's. Vicky jumped in beside him, burying her head in his thigh.

Harry was humming 'Mademoiselle from Armentières', sometimes slipping in a few of the more saucy words. 'I don't suppose it's worse here than being in a military prison,' Harry suddenly exclaimed.

'With these killers?'

'It's war.'

'War without honour.'

'Sssh. They wouldn't like you saying that.'

It occurred to Connor that his senior officer was more capable of living with the slaughter than he was. Connor wondered whether a brooding fatalism lurked just beneath the other man's bluff exterior – he often mentioned getting his remains home. Until now, Connor had always considered himself the hard man, the one who could take care of himself and remain seemingly unaffected by the brutality going on around him. But it wasn't true. He was screaming inside. In the depth of the night he let his emotions run free, tears streaming down his face, licked away by the little dog lying at his side.

'A day out. What joy!'

'You go Tsim Sha Tsui. Lots of work to do,' said the portly little captain, who oversaw their work party. 'Bomb damage. You mend. Take everything with you. Stay overnight.'

Like the other men in the party, Harry had a jaunty air, pleased to be out on the water, travelling on the old Star ferry from Kowloon to Victoria Harbour.

Connor was less exuberant. 'Why take all our things?' He shook his head. 'It doesn't make sense.'

Harry laughed it off, but Connor remained grim-faced. No matter how hard he tried, he could not jettison his gut feeling that there was more to this than being sent to do some labouring in the civilian camp at Fort Stanley.

It was after six in the morning and they'd left their own camp early. The commandant had insisted they leave in time to catch the early ferry, to take what food they could carry and eat it on the boat. Two sticky rice balls per man and a few tomatoes cultivated by a corporal with shaky hands and a stammer brought on by strain: it was hardly a hearty breakfast but the best they'd get all day. The sea air made them even hungrier.

Refusing to leave the dog behind, Connor carried Vicky down the gang plank onto the shore. She'd become a mascot to the mix of regiments and nationalities, not least because she was such a good hunter – some of the meatier and more digestible bits of her plunder went into the pot.

'Hunts like a tiger,' said one of the Indians. 'Not bad for a dog.'

The birds and small animals she caught went some way to augmenting the bland rice, which was sometimes augmented with vegetables or fish, but usually not.

Guards to either side of them, the group of men made an effort to march like an army even though the soles of their boots were worn thin and the uppers were cracked with dust through lack of polish. One or two still owned a tin of polish and made the effort to keep smart. Most were too tired after a long day of labouring, their hands bleeding, their ribs bruised from beatings by the more brutal guards.

'Only months since the surrender, yet to me it feels like years,' Connor commented.

'It's not like an Irishman to be downhearted. Come on, man. Brace your back and march ever onwards! Your country needs you!'

'Hah!' Connor didn't feel like following his friend's advice, but he kept his mouth shut, and frowned when he recognised the building ahead of them.

The perimeter walls and fences around the administrative block had been shattered in the fighting and had probably stayed that way. When they'd first taken charge the Japanese had had no plan in place for prisoners or, indeed, for occupying Hong Kong and the New Territories, Kowloon included. Just recently they'd begun getting up to speed.

Connor tried to convince himself that he and the other men were there because their captors were organising things and they were not about to be put in front of a firing squad. There were the usual shouted orders and an excited exchange between the guards, who seemed to be moving more briskly today, as though, like him, they felt something in the air.

'Not a bad place,' said Connor, eyeing the women hanging up washing, the kids running around, shouting at the tops of their voices even at this early hour. They were skinny, granted, but still full of energy.

An imposing woman, with the shoulders of a sergeant major and regal as a queen, glided towards them. The fact that her clothes were sweat-stained stole nothing from her look of absolute authority.

'Good morning. I know the Nips are about to shout at me for talking to you, but we thought a little food wouldn't go amiss, and seeing as some of our men will be joining you and they haven't breakfasted yet, we thought it only polite to include you in their simple repast.'

'Don't mind if we do, ma'am,' said Harry, a senior officer with as rumbling a stomach as everyone else. 'Major Harry Gracey. How do you do?'

'Marjorie Greenbank. Lady Greenbank. I keep the title bit to myself. People clam up if they think you're upper crust.'

'Really? Perhaps you know my mother. Lady Gracey. Everyone calls her Grace.'

Marjorie frowned as she thought about it. Harry helped her along.

'Her maiden name was Louise Frampton Lyons. She was born in Epsom.'

She threw back her head. 'Ah, yes. Of course I do. We were at school together. Good horsewoman. Good shot too. Could show this lot a thing or two,' she said, indicating the guards with a sideways jerk of her head. 'Well, no good all this nattering. We'll check our store cupboard and see if we can't get a bit of extra food for you.'

'You're an angel.'

'Hardly that. Just a woman doing her bit.'

The guards curtailed this friendly exchange, stepping between Harry and Lady Greenbank, though noticeably showing her grudging respect in response to her imperious glare.

'We'll bring something over,' she called, as they were marched off.

It was a fresh day but getting warmer, as was usual halfway through the year. By mid-morning Connor felt as though his empty stomach was cleaving to his spine. He was sweating and his muscles were aching, not so much because of the type of work expected of him, but purely through lack of food and drink.

A Chinese labourer came round with buckets of water suspended from each end of a pole carried over his shoulder, a ladle passed from one man to another.

'Food,' said Connor to the guard. 'We need food.'

The guard laughed and stalked off.

Connor didn't press his luck. Make the same demand too many times and it gained you a broken rib. Hopefully Marjorie Greenbank would be able to get something to them.

'Will you look at that?'

They were building a perimeter wall that had been damaged by the enemy. They required it to be taken to the same height it had been before but with buttressing and platforms for machine-guns. There were about ten of them in the work gang. The women were not looking at their best, but the fact that they were there made the strongest of the men pine for home.

They were teaching children or washing clothes, and the men stared until they spotted Marjorie Greenbank and four others wending their way towards them. Lady Greenbank was at the forefront, head held high, shoulders back.

'She should have been our CO,' muttered a lowly private.

There was much laughter – but Connor was looking beyond Lady Greenbank to a face he had instantly recognised.

He blinked, unsure at first that it was her: her figure was not as it used to be. She was wearing a shapeless red and white checked dress that reminded him of a tablecloth. It had no waistline but dropped directly from the shoulders, flapping around her shins, her arms like sticks in comparison to her girth.

At the same time as he saw her, she saw him.

'Mr O'Connor.' She blushed as she handed him the food.

The over-large dress confused him. She was shapeless in it.

'Are you okay?'

She nodded. 'Where have they put you?'

'The Kowloon Ritz. Otherwise known as Sham Shi Po. How did you get here? I thought you were with Kim Pheloung.'

'I was, until his grandmother decided she wanted her beloved grandson to herself. She brought me here and turned me in.'

'I'm sorry.'

'I'm not.'

He wondered what had gone on behind the walls of Kim's house, but could not bring himself to ask.

'He never touched me. Just in case you're wondering.'

'I'm glad to hear it.'

'Now eat up. It's not much, but it's all we can spare. Now I'm not sure what these are called, but it's bits of meat, rice and chillies wrapped in a vine leaf. Well, we think they're vine leaves. And these little cakes are made from papaya and some currants we had hanging around. The pastry is made from ground rice and suet pudding.'

Hands dived across him, taking the food and cramming it into mouths.

When there was only enough left for him, she turned sideways so nobody else could grab it. As she did so her dress was blown to one side and Connor saw the curve of her belly.

She saw him looking. 'A memento of Black Christmas,' she said bitterly.

He threw a tiny piece of food down to his dog, needing a small diversion to give him time to think what to say. 'What are you going to do with it when it's born?'

Rowena swallowed and looked away. 'I wasn't planning for it to be born. I'll work something out when the time comes.'

'Hopefully you'll both survive. If you want a husband's name on the birth certificate, I'd be willing. I think you know that.'

'You don't quite understand.'

'It doesn't need to be mine. I like kids. Any colour, male or female. You'll bear that in mind, won't you? That I'm willing.'

Her eyes locked with his and he could see she was on the brink of tears.

'That's very kind of you, but I wouldn't want to burden you with my problems. Anyway, given my present circumstances, there's no guarantee it will survive.'

'Please,' he said forlornly. 'There's enough death in this world. A child is blameless.' A sudden whine reminded Connor that he wasn't entirely alone. 'Sorry. I haven't introduced you. This is Victoria. Vicky for short.'

Rowena smiled down at the little dog, who returned it with her own version, mouth open and eyes apparently laughing.

An awkward silence descended until Connor said, 'If you ever need anything, get word to me. One of the Chinese traders who do business here is bound to come to us. I can't promise miracles, but I'll do what I can. I've still got the present you gave me, well hidden. I can give it to you now if we can go somewhere we won't be seen.'

Before she had the chance to suggest a suitable place, the rest period was over and she was shoved aside, then pushed back with the other women.

The men were being herded like cattle, prodded and beaten if they moved too slowly.

'Finish now! Finish!'

Accordingly they attempted to pick up the tools they'd been using but, with more slaps and prods, were ordered to put them down again.

Connor's feeling of unease returned. He craned his neck so he could see her better, thought again about the lighter and what she could do with it. Better with her than with him. Regardless of the punishment he was likely to receive, he would endeavour to give it back to her. In her condition it might buy her and the baby enough to keep them going until this was all over – whenever that might be.

He glanced around, noting where the guards were standing and where the women were grouped in a small huddle. If he was going to make his move, it had to be soon.

Just when he judged the time was right, he and the other men were goaded with rifle butts into a straight line. More guards appeared and a human fence formed around them.

The stink of men's sweat filled his nostrils.

There were shouts from the main gate, which was swung wide to let in an open-top army staff car followed by a small truck.

'I've got a nasty feeling about this,' whispered Harry.

Connor didn't reply. His chance to hand back the lighter seemed to have gone.

Those in the car got out. Their uniforms were not those of the regular army but as well cut as their superior facial features. They were clearly of the elite and specially chosen.

With a sinking feeling Connor assessed them to be Kompei Tei – Japan's equivalent of the German Gestapo, as quick to hand out punishment and death to their own people as they were to their enemies.

The tools they'd laid down were picked up by Chinese labourers and placed in the handcart in which they'd arrived at Fort Stanley.

Connor's eyes met those of Harry, who mouthed one word that said it all.

'Up to our necks,' Connor mouthed back.

They were ordered to stand to attention while the new arrivals looked them over contemptuously, as though they were not equals, not even human at all.

At a nod from the officer who appeared to be in command, they were loaded onto the truck. Connor grabbed his dog, pushing her inside his shirt so she'd be less noticeable.

One of the last, he looked across to where Rowena and the others stood. The big woman with the square shoulders spoke to one of the resident guards. Whatever he said to her was relayed to Rowena.

His instinct that something bad was about to happen was etched on Rowena's face. Whatever it was made her take a few steps forward as if to warn him of what was to happen next.

She didn't get close enough, her attempt prevented by

the driver of the staff car, whirling round and lashing out with a karate kick to her belly.

Connor called her name and aimed a host of expletives at the guards, promising that one day they would answer to him, that they were all bastards, all murderers, that the time of retribution would surely come.

His outburst earned him blows from the guards stationed against the tailboard of the truck, but he took it all, arms across his chest and bending from the stomach so that no blows landed on his dog.

There were other men in the truck and no room to sit down. There was no other option than to grip the overhead frame that supported the tarpaulin used to shade them from the sun or give cover from rain.

'Not the most comfortable form of travel,' Harry said.

Connor mopped at his bloody nose and winced when he tried to straighten his back.

'Don't worry. We're not going far in this old crate. I understand a bit of the language from my Oxford days. We're taking ship, old man. We're going to Japan to work for a firm called Mitsubishi.'

# 16

The women who had helped her get up exchanged worried looks.

'She's only seven months,' remarked Sister O'Malley, unable to keep the worry from her face, but doing her best to jolly things along. 'Lean on me, Rowena. We'll get you inside. Everything will be all right.'

Nausea rose into her throat as they laid her on the narrow bed – she could feel every slat beneath the thin mattress.

Sister O'Malley brought her a bowl while Alice continued to mop her brow with a wet cloth. 'Whatever did you want to say to our friend from the bar in Kowloon?'

'Marjorie told me they were being shipped to Japan. I wanted to let him know.'

Suddenly her back arched as she fought to ride the pain in her stomach and groin.

A heavy weight bore down between her legs. The child was coming and there was every chance that the kick she'd received had done irreparable damage. Just hours ago she would have preferred it to die, but now she wanted it to live. 'Will my baby be all right?' She heard herself voicing the question many concerned mothers had asked her.

O'Malley's face was impassive, but when Rowena tried to rise from the pillow, her strong hands pushed her down. 'Rest. Baby won't be arriving just yet. Try to get some sleep.'

Sleep came sporadically, along with the pains of childbirth and rape, the two inextricably combined.

Throughout the night, she was aware of soft footsteps and comments when Alice or another nurse checked on her.

There were whispers in the depth of night.

'Are you sure?' she thought she heard somebody say.

'Positive.'

Positive about what? Was the child dead in her womb, thanks to that kick? Or was she dying, haemorrhaging blood? She certainly felt sticky in that area.

Just before daybreak she heard more urgent whispers. Through her blurred vision she became aware of a third person joining the two women at the end of the bed. Forcing herself to open her eyes a little wider, she recognised Dr Anderson. The two nurses parted so he could examine her. He eased himself onto the side of the bed, taking her hand. He leaned closer and whispered so the others would not hear, 'You never came that night when you asked me to do the unthinkable. I know this is a difficult time to ask such a question, but why was that?'

Rowena made an attempt to lick away the dryness of her lips, but it remained. 'I did come, but you'd fallen asleep. I felt I had no right asking you to take a life when you were doing your utmost to keep others alive.'

'And you were having second thoughts.'

She swallowed, and rode the next spasm of pain.

'I suppose I was.' She arched her back as her body was racked with pain. 'Do you think I could stand up so gravity can give me a hand?'

Dr Anderson agreed but seemed a little distracted. She put it down to him having been awoken in the middle of the night following a day on the ward. 'If you think you're up to it.'

O'Malley and Alice helped her to her feet with Dr Anderson standing by.

As she stood upright, fluid trickled down her legs and swiftly became a torrent pooling on the cracked brown linoleum floor.

'You've got a good grip,' murmured Alice. Rowena was holding her hand rather tightly.

'Sorry.'

'Grip all you like, girl. I can stand it.'

The weight inside her began to move, a rolling sensation as the foetus slid down the birth canal. Rowena gritted her teeth and took deep breaths.

'Here it comes.'

'I know.' She gritted her teeth some more, analysing her own body as it went through this, feeling the head emerge, O'Malley turning it so the shoulders would come out laterally to the perineum.

O'Malley was good at her job.

'Just a little more...' She caught the bloodied newborn in part of an old sheet she'd ripped in half for the purpose.

Alice's face appeared above her. 'It's over, Rowena. It's all over.'

Rowena knew what she meant. The process of giving birth was over and so was the child. It had not taken a breath.

Her expression grim, O'Malley wrapped the cloth around the small body.

In her mind Rowena saw the blueness of the baby's complexion, the process of checking for a heartbeat, the look that passed between her and Dr Anderson. His long sensitive fingers followed the same pattern over the stillborn child, checking for any sign of life.

Coming to the same conclusion as O'Malley, he shook his head and turned back to Rowena. 'I'm sorry, my dear. There's nothing we can do. The baby didn't make it.'

Rowena had never expected to burst into tears, but that was exactly what she did as they continued to tend her, delivering the afterbirth and finally laying her on the bed.

Tears were streaming down Alice's face. 'I'm so sorry,' she said. 'So very, very sorry. It looked such a pretty little thing.'

Sister O'Malley passed Alice the bundle for disposal in the oil drum where they kept a fire burning for old bandages and amputated limbs in an effort to keep infection at bay.

Rowena enjoyed a sudden coolness when O'Malley wiped her face with a wet flannel.

''Tis not for you to be sorry. 'Tis that monster who kicked you. Jesus, Mary and Joseph, I curse him to high Heaven.'

Rowena closed her eyes. She was terribly tired, but there were still pains so it would be some time before she could sleep. A single tear squeezed out of her right eye as she remembered Tansy's words, how much she'd wanted the child she'd lost despite the circumstances of its conception. She'd never expected to have such feelings and desperately wanted to tell somebody how she felt. O'Malley was as good a person as any. 'I didn't want it, or at least I didn't think I did, but now it's dead I do. I feel it was my fault for not wanting it. What's the point of entering a world if there's nobody waiting there to love you?'

'That's a silly statement,' scoffed O'Malley.

'What was it, Sister? A boy or a girl?'

'I don't know. I didn't look.'

'You're lying.'

'I'll tell you in a few days when you're fully recovered. You'll take it better then. Now, let's get you cleaned up. Are the pains gone?'

Rowena frowned. 'They should be, but they're not.'

Looking a little puzzled Sister O'Malley folded the sheet down and, using both hands, pressed Rowena's stomach. 'Hmm. Some residual contractions, I think.'

Rowena lifted her head enough to see that her stomach was heaving as though there was something else to expel.

O'Malley and the rest of the team were good and not likely to make mistakes, but this was not a clean regular hospital. The conditions were primitive, the staff underfed and worn out, the outcome of trying to treat diseases that would be so easily treated in different circumstances.

'Are you sure the afterbirth's come away?' Rowena asked.

'Thank you, Dr Rossiter, but we know our job as well as you do. We've already done that and it was entire,' said O'Malley. 'I'll swear on a stack of Bibles that I've left no nasty bits behind.'

'Unless...' said Rowena, her eyes meeting those of the sister.

'Unless...' returned O'Malley, knowing what she was getting at.

Alice was told to put down the mop and bucket she was carrying and fetch Dr Anderson.

'Tell him there are complications.'

Alice looked about to say that he'd only just gone to bed, but on seeing the expressions on O'Malley and Rowena's faces, dropped the lot and went running.

'Aaah!' Rowena arched her back as the pain intensified. Raising herself up on her elbows she gazed at her heaving belly. The pressure between her legs had returned. She was giving birth all over again.

Almost as much sweat was pouring out of O'Malley as there was from her. They didn't need to make comment. They both knew what was coming next.

Dr Anderson appeared at O'Malley's shoulders. 'There's another?'

O'Malley nodded. 'Or my name's not Alexandra Kathleen Bridget O'Malley.'

'With a name as long as that, I have to believe you!' he said, pushing the ends of the stethoscope into his ears.

'May I suggest that she does not deliver standing up this time?' said O'Malley. 'She's tired out.'

'You may, Sister, and I concur.'

Rowena knew that wasn't the only reason. They weren't going to risk this baby falling out too fast and injuring itself on the hard floor. She didn't want it either. Suddenly the dour atmosphere lifted. This baby would be born alive.

Just as before, the fluid came in a rush, but not so much this time, accompanied by the second baby being born, pushing through all the obstacles nature and the world could throw at it.

This baby cried, and to all of them in that dire place it was the most beautiful sound in the world.

O'Malley was ecstatic. 'A girl. A beautiful little girl.'

There were smiles all round. Rowena laid her head on the pillow and prepared herself for what was to come next. She was indeed totally exhausted, and also aware that, once more, she did not want to be a mother.

O'Malley smiled at her. Alice smiled at her, and so did Dr Anderson. It took a great effort to smile back at them, as though she had finally accepted her fate.

In a bid to hide her true feelings, she played along, naming the child, which was always done as soon as possible – just in case.

'What's it to be? Something traditional or something exotic?'

'What time is it?'

'It's dawn. God's made us another new day,' O'Malley declared.

'Then that's what I'll call her. Dawn.'

'Very apt,' said Dr Anderson.

A new beginning was exactly what it should be but when she looked at the black hair matted to the scalp, and saw the shape of the eyelids, the terrible memory came flooding back. Nobody put forward an opinion on which parent she most resembled. Even newborn, the child clearly favoured her father – whoever he had been. Closing her eyes, she turned away, bitter tears squeezing out from beneath her eyelids.

'It's usual to cry. You're exhausted,' said O'Malley.

You cannot possibly know what I'm feeling, thought Rowena.

She looked down at the tiny face, the black hair, the scrunched-up features, and the bitter feelings returned. Despite Dawn's origins, surely any mother would love a child like this, fuss over her and kiss the top of her silky head – but she couldn't. The barrier inside her was like a wall composed of ice a mile high and a mile wide.

As the child was put to her breast, she became aware of O'Malley smiling as she chivvied her to put her hand on the back of the child's head. 'This should come naturally to you. You're a doctor.'

'That doesn't mean I'm a natural mother,' she snapped.

O'Malley looked as if she'd been slapped. Experienced in the sometimes odd reactions of new mothers, though, she recovered quickly, believing that everything would be all right in the end. 'You've been through a tiring time. You'll be as good a mother as anybody. Did I ever tell you my mother had thirteen? Once my fifth brother was born, she decided it was enough and did all she could to get rid of the other pregnancies, cried buckets when they stayed firmly in place, but once they were born, once she'd got over the ordeal, well, she loved each and every one of us.'

After the baby had suckled, she turned her head away, repelled by her own confused feelings of love and hate, refusing to look at the small bundle tucked into the crease of her arm, feeling the warmth nestled against her, even the faint beating of the newborn heart.

'She's a beautiful child,' said O'Malley.

'Yes. She is.'

Even to her own ears, Rowena's voice sounded cold. There was no denying the child's beauty, but her features brought back the memories of that terrible Christmas

Day. She flicked her gaze to O'Malley and saw the sadness in her eyes.

'Doctor, I know what you went through.'

'Do you?' Rowena couldn't help sounding disparaging. How could anyone know?

'I went through the same, of course.'

Rowena gulped. 'I didn't know.'

'Luckily I'm mutton, not lamb, too old to conceive. I count myself lucky to be alive, and that way I can go on. I was spared for a reason, perhaps for you or for all the babies I may deliver in future.'

There was common sense in O'Malley's statement and she said it with conviction. She was a strong woman and was taking a positive stance. Rowena couldn't do that.

'I'll never forget that night for as long as I live. I wish it had never happened.'

'Well, there's no going back. The child is here now. There's nothing you can do but get on with it.'

# 17

'Ever heard of the mad monk Rasputin?'

Connor and Harry were stretched out on their bunks in the cellar of the chemical factory, an airless place where the sound of machinery hummed incessantly from the floor above. The men crowded into the hold of the *Tojo Maru* had been divided into work gangs, some getting the work promised at Mitsubishi, but Connor and Harry were at a chemical plant where the stink of ammonia burned the lungs and irritated the eyes.

Connor's were red-rimmed as he mumbled that, yes, he had indeed heard of the Russian monk who had exerted influence on the Russian royal family. 'And don't tell me that I'm in line to be the lover of an empress.'

Harry laughed, though it wasn't the rich laugh he used to have: it sounded brittle, as though his throat was lined with broken glass. 'Not at all, old boy. What I meant was your beard and hair are as long as his were. You look like

275

a Russian monk, as do I. As do us all, come to think of it.'
Razors were in short supply, and scissors sharp enough
to cut their hair into some sort of presentable order were
virtually non-existent.

Their new home was in a series of cellars beneath the
factory floor where the bunks were stacked in threes
and there were too few latrines for the hundreds of men
living there.

Single-bulb electric lights hung from shrivelled wire at
intermittent intervals the length of their cellar and into
the next.

Vicky was curled up at Connor's feet, which were
swollen from a mild attack of beriberi, the warmth of
her body making up for the fact that he couldn't get his
boots on.

They were working inside the factory but it was
winter and the weather had turned cold. Thanks to
frequent American bombing, and the blockade of vital
raw materials, heating and lighting were rationed and
channelled towards industry rather than for private
consumption, even when the consumers worked in the
factories.

A small bloke from northern England, his sharp face
made sharper by extreme starvation, crept up to them as
though he had something very important to impart – or
something of value to barter. 'Care for a bit of this?'

Connor recognised the can he held up as containing the
lard they used to grease machinery parts. 'What would I
do with it, my friend?'

'Eat it, of course.'

'You're going to eat that?'

'Yeah. Want some?'

Connor shook his head. 'It smells terrible.'

'How about your dog?'

Vicky raised her head, sniffed, then lay down again.

'She's not hungry.'

'One ciggy and you can have a big dollop.'

'I'd prefer the ciggy to the dollop – if I had one.'

'Keep your dollop,' muttered Harry, the dry wood of his bunk creaking as he turned over, pulling his meagre blanket up to his neck.

'Then I'll eat it all myself!'

Whoever was in charge of the factory generator chose that exact moment to pull the switch and cut the power. There were grumbles as the lights went out, then loud cheers when it was followed by the wailing of an air-raid siren.

'Hunker down, lads,' shouted Connor. 'And try to get some sleep.'

Nobody got out of bed because there was no need to. They were locked in and deep down, safe enough unless the factory scored a direct hit.

The building shook in response to nearby explosions and the air turned gritty as dust fell from the ceiling.

Connor heard Vicky whimper. Luckily he was on the top bunk of three, and because he was tucked just beneath the ceiling, he could reach down to his feet where she was curled up to stroke her bristly coat. His dog worried him.

Back in Hong Kong when he'd first found her, Vicky's coat had been soft and reasonably glossy. Now it was patchy and rough, possibly due to parasites.

The walls shook in response to the thunder of the planes flying overhead and explosions close by. The raid went on for some hours, bombs falling on Osaka before the bulk of their payload was delivered to Tokyo.

Once daylight had arrived, Connor swung himself down from his bunk and waited with outstretched arms for Vicky to launch herself into them. 'Are you coming, girl?'

All around him men were stirring, coughing, groaning and spitting up the phlegm that accumulated on their chests, thanks to the dusty atmosphere.

Vicky opened her eyes, looked at him then snuggled back down. Connor had known the parasites were bound to affect her health, but until now she'd had enough energy to prick her ears and wag her tail.

Somebody was calling to a comrade. 'Hey. Arthur. Arthur!'

There were other murmurings of concern.

'Hey. Can somebody take a look at this bloke?' The request was made in a strong Australian accent.

Out of curiosity, Connor followed an ex-dentist called Steve, one of the few of their bunch with medical knowledge. He recognised the man who had offered him a portion of lard. His eyes were wide open with the knowledge of eternity that only the dead possess. Spit drooled from one side of his mouth and his body was already stiff with rigor mortis. In his hand he was still grasping the tin of grease he'd offered Connor. It was almost empty.

Connor took a sniff. 'I smell almonds.'

The comment travelled from one man to another. Those who knew what he was driving at enlightened those who did not.

As a kid they'd had marzipan at Christmas and he'd loved the smell, breathing it in as others might the scent of a rose. It was only later he'd learned that cyanide had the same smell.

'My money weren't on 'im to go next,' somebody said. 'Too fly, I thought. But there, you never know. Anybody win the bet?'

To an outsider, betting on who would die next might seem macabre and unfeeling, but those men lived with death. There was no time and no energy for grieving over the inevitable.

He felt Harry following him as they joined the queue for rations before they made their way up the metal stairs to the factory floor.

'Poor chap. Can't blame him, though. What I wouldn't give for a pork pie or a cake oozing with almonds and sugared icing.'

Connor smiled through the mass of beard that now hid the lower half of his face. 'Food. Our favourite subject. Used to be women.'

'Never.'

He fancied a sudden awkwardness between them. The

truth was that even before the war Harry had rarely talked about women. He knew Harry preferred men and Harry knew that he preferred women. It was enough that they were friends and understood each other and as such it went unsaid.

There were three burials that day. Arthur's was one, plus two *rabusha* – Tamils enticed by hollow promises to work for the Japanese in their newly acquired territories. Burial parties were picked to carry out the job, a much valued chance to get out into the fresh air. As there was only one European, the Tamils would bury the latest casualties.

The civilian labourers were kept separate from the Europeans, their quarters lacking even usable latrines. Also, they were given even smaller rations.

The men tasked with the job filed past. Connor regarded the Tamils' sunken eyes, the cheekbones prominent in gaunt faces. They were like walking skeletons. They'd been promised good wages but they were slowly starving to death.

There would be no mourners at the funeral. Everyone else would work, stopping at midday to eat a bowl of rice mixed with a green vegetable that looked suspiciously like a weed, and perhaps a little fish.

Rarely allowed outside, Vicky had contented herself with hunting and catching rats rather than pigeons. Stewed long enough, they tasted similar to chicken and nobody referred to their origins. Everyone was aware that they needed protein to fend off the more devastating diseases.

During the last few days she'd laid no kill at Connor's feet. At first he'd found it strange. Now he was worried.

'You might have to let her go,' Harry said to him.

'I can hardly put her down. I don't have a gun.'

'Rope? A garrotte?' Seeing the distaste on his friend's face, Harry put up his hands. 'Pax. Didn't mean it old man. Say, a bloke in the next cellar's been making hooch from vegetable peelings. Not much, but worth a taster.'

Connor said he wasn't that thirsty.

'You don't have to be thirsty, old chap, just in need of oblivion.'

For the rest of that day Connor kept his nose to the grindstone, barely looking up when a guard laid a cane across his back half a dozen times, purely because he hadn't bowed deeply enough.

'You're too tall,' remarked Harry.

'And I don't bow low enough. Neither do you, for that matter.'

It was nine o'clock in the evening when he finally dragged himself back down the cold metal stairs that rattled from the tramp of men's feet. The cellar smelt of mould and the lighting was only barely enough to read by. Fresh air was a luxury.

Books were almost as valued a commodity as a cigarette, more so perhaps because they kept boredom at bay. Losing oneself in fiction also helped one forget hunger, aching muscles and the pain of swollen feet, broken spirits and eternal fatigue.

Today's dead in the ground, the minds of some turned to the future. 'Who do you think will be next? Anyone willing to wager?'

The betting on death had already begun.

Connor had expected Vicky to be under the bottom bunk waiting for him, but she wasn't. He checked his bunk, calling her name, in case she wanted to jump into his arms and do her business in a dark corner, which he would clean up and take to the latrine, but she wasn't there.

'Vicky?'

No sign.

'Anyone seen Vicky?'

'Only machines, Paddy. And powder flying up into my face. What is that stuff anyway?'

'Fertiliser of some sort. One bomb on this place and we're all blown to kingdom come.'

'Care to wager when that might be?'

'Care to wager where the dog's gone? I reckon she's found a hole in the wall and crawled out of here. Wonder where it is. Be nice if it was big enough for a fellow my size to crawl through.'

Connor ignored their remarks and set off for the other cellars.

Harry offered to help.

'No need.'

'I'll come anyway.'

With Harry in tow, he asked the same question in the next cellar and the next.

Men were eating, the lucky ones smoking. A few already lay snoring on their bunks.

'Been working same place as you, mate. Up top all day.'

'I ain't.'

The man coughing up his lungs in one of the very last beds spat a trail of green slime into a pot he'd placed on the floor. 'Me lungs are shot. Even the Nips know that. Left me alone today. I tried sleeping, but heard a bit of a kerfuffle. Think somebody fetched her and she went through that door.'

He pointed to the flimsy barrier between the military section and that housing the civilian Tamil workers.

Connor felt a sinking feeling. 'Are you sure?'

'Sure as I can be. I bin here all day coughing my lungs up, mate. Just waiting for the call. Shame, mind, I was looking forward to going back to Adelaide. Keep dreaming of a cold beer... one last cold beer...'

Connor looked to where he'd pointed.

Harry grabbed his arm. 'Connor, if she's gone...'

Two men were responsible for guarding the door between the military prisoners of war and the civilians. Clasping their weapons across their chests they attempted to hold back the Europeans who, although thin, were far taller than they were.

Connor barrelled through, still strong enough to sweep them aside as though they were wooden skittles.

The Tamils and other native workers imported from abroad stared at him with frightened eyes.

He searched their gaunt faces and saw fear in their eyes. 'Vicky? Have you seen her? My dog. Have you seen her?'

At first there was a stony silence, then a low hubbub of conversation, shaking heads and a nervous sinking back against the wall in an effort to escape the man who shouted at them.

Suddenly all hell was let loose as guards came running, reinforcements summoned by the two guards he'd knocked over. Even then he and Harry lingered, noticing that the civilian labourers were even thinner than they were.

'Poor sods,' muttered Harry.

Some of the dark brown men could barely stand and quite a few were just skin and bones, lying on thin pallets, other men attempting to feed them from steaming bowls.

'Time of reckoning,' shouted Harry.

The guards were upon them.

Connor was grabbed by the first wave of soldiers, hitting him with their rifles while dragging him back to his own domain.

Harry was shouting and swearing as only a man of his background could do, the words straight from the gutter, his pronunciation giving them a veneer of civilisation. In broken Japanese he tried to explain what they were doing there, which earned him the same treatment as Connor had received.

The guards swarmed over them, dragging them away until they crashed back into their own area. Other guards, inflamed that they'd dared to attack their compatriots, beat them with rifle butts until their ears, their noses and mouths were bleeding and their spines felt as though they'd been cracked into pieces.

Both men knew that insubordination didn't necessarily mean death, but it did mean a period of solitary confinement in a cell the size of a coffin with no food, no water and no daylight.

Connor tasted blood on his tongue. His brain felt like unset blancmange in a broken mould but he held on to consciousness, determined he'd be the same man when he was released as when he was thrown into the black hole of a cell. He'd seen others broken, some of his own countrymen who hadn't died living with madness, their eyes vacant, their speech slurred and slow.

Starvation didn't help. Without certain vitamins and minerals, the brain became distorted.

'Vicky. I'll come for you, girl,' he shouted. 'Don't you worry about that.'

She's just a dog, said a voice inside his head. 'Yeah. My dog.'

He closed his eyes. Islands of pain throbbed all over his body and his swollen feet felt icy cold. If Vicky was there she would snuggle up against them and they would borrow her warmth. She might even be enticed to a titbit, something as tasty as the Tamils were cooking.

Whatever they were cooking had smelt good. Definitely meat, such a rarity in recent days.

Although only half-conscious, the dying man had been adamant he'd seen Vicky entering the civilian domain, but not alone.

The truth hit him like a sledgehammer. Vicky had disappeared and they were cooking meat. He retched but brought up only bile and, in the unrelenting darkness, he cried.

Light, sharp and painful, pierced his eyes. That was how it was after a time in total darkness.

How long had it been? Three days? Four?

Human contact at last, but at the end of rifles and staves, forcing him to double over.

Satisfied the treatment had made him more malleable, the guards dragged him by his hair and his arms out of the cell.

Sweat and blood trickled into his eyes. Blinking it away, he raised his head to see Harry in pretty much the same state. It wasn't until the guards slung them against a wall that their eyes finally met.

Despite the blood, the sweat and the state of his body, Harry was his usual exuberant self. He grinned. 'This could be it, old chap. Nice knowing you. Remember that promise you made to me about getting my miserable remains back to the old mater. Okay?'

When Connor laughed a spasm of pain racked his jaw and he realised it was broken.

Three days without food and water and his body wouldn't easily straighten but his feet were no longer swollen. His knees felt like water and his legs as though every bone in his body had been removed. He had been looking forward to climbing up onto his top bunk. The mattress was thin, the pillow stuffed with straw, but a great improvement on a stone floor.

'Somehow I don't think we're going home any time soon.'

'Sod it.'

They were dragged out into daylight, the first time they'd been outside for weeks, thanks to the bombing. They were pushed to the ground, their backs against a wall beneath the factory windows. A layer of frost covered the earth and their breath came out as steam.

The guards stayed close, bayonets aimed at their heads.

Connor narrowed his eyes against the light and looked around.

'Fresh air,' said Harry. 'And glad I am to be breathing it.'

'And glad to see they're being hit hard.'

The two of them took in the many bombed buildings, the scorched streets, the signs that an inferno had ripped through the fragile construction of Japanese houses.

While the guards' backs were turned a shower of ragged strips of blanket fell from a narrow window not far above their heads.

With every ounce of what little strength remained,

Connor wound them around his feet. Harry watched him with one eye, the other closed, thanks to the beating he'd received.

'I don't want a bullet in the head. I prefer to stand in front of the firing squad,' Connor explained.

A few pieces of raw fish followed the blanket, which they devoured quickly, wiping their mouths on the ripped material, which Connor then bound to his feet. 'At least our stomachs won't be rumbling.'

'That would be terrible. Put them off their aim, old chap. And I for one would like a clean death.'

'If we're to have one at all.'

The guards became mobile when a truck rumbled into the yard and failed to switch off its engine, which meant a swift turn-round.

Connor and Harry exchanged puzzled but hopeful looks. 'For us? A fun day out?'

'Or a ticket to nowhere?'

Their question was answered when the guards prodded their lean ribs and dragged them to the rear of the truck.

When Connor's legs crumpled beneath him, they swung their rifles and hit him in the backs of the knees. When he fell, they half lifted, then threw him in face down.

Lying on the wooden planks of the truck floor, he found himself face to face with a pair of boots next to a pair of feet. Both were in a bad way, the boots split and the toes of the bare feet blackened by foot rot. Harry was heaved in after him.

'You all right, cobber?'

'Antipodeans, are you?'

'If you mean Australians, then yeah. Your companions for the foreseeable future.'

Three pairs of hefty arms helped him, then Harry to sit up against the side of the truck. His gaze travelled over the ravaged faces and ragged clothes. A few still exuded an air of defiance but he could see from their faces that they'd all been through hell.

'Where we going?'

'Bali, mate. We're going to the island of the gods.'

'Excuse me for asking, but what would the gods want with us?' asked Harry.

'The Japanese airstrip there is in need of repair, thanks to the pasting they've been getting from Uncle Sam. They need labourers to rebuild it.'

'You mean slaves.'

'Of course I do, but, hey, I used to be hot on navigation back in Sydney. My brother-in-law had a sailing yacht and Bali is a damn sight closer to Darwin than Osaka. I'm going home, mate. One way or another, I'm going home.'

# 18

'Doctor, I wanted to ask you if we could borrow Dawn for the Christmas pantomime the society is putting on this year. I thought she would make a wonderful fairy and we have just enough pink net to make her a very pretty dress. With a bit of luck it will draw audience attention away from the shabby costumes of the rest of us. Are you in agreement?'

'I'm grateful to you for taking her under your wing.'

'We love her,' said Alice, perhaps a little too pointedly.

'She'll like being a fairy, Marjorie.'

'Takes my mind off things,' said Marjorie, ticking her list with an air of finality, another job well done.

Rowena watched Marjorie stride off across the yard with Dawn toddling at her side.

Her daughter had grown from a beautiful baby into a lovely little girl. Her black hair was as glossy as a blackbird's wing. Her face was pretty and she moved lightly but unsteadily on slim but sturdy legs. Despite the sickness, deprivation and death all around her, she had thrived and was happy, shielded from the worst aspects of imprisonment by Alice and O'Malley.

Rowena let them take charge of her child, throwing herself into her work, taking on more shifts and responsibilities than anyone else, purposely laying herself open to the most infectious diseases. She claimed, quite truthfully, to be too tired to play with or feed the child.

It was early evening, the sun had gone down and night sounds filled the air. Rowena leaned against a pillar outside the main entrance. She turned towards the sound of a mouth organ being played by somebody at the pantomime rehearsals, which was followed by a loud, though out of tune rendering of 'Only a Rose'.

'Marjorie,' she murmured, and smiled.

Marjorie's voice was resonant, and she began humming along, thinking of Connor and wondering how he was faring in Japan.

'Mind if I join you?' O'Malley didn't wait for her to respond but offered her a cigarette, which Rowena refused.

'I hear Dawn is to be a fairy in *Snow White and the Seven Dwarfs*.'

'I didn't know there was a fairy in *Snow White*.'

'Marjorie created the part just for Dawn so that she feels wanted.'

Rowena winced at the implication. 'That's very kind.'

'Somebody has to be.' O'Malley blew smoke rings and her eyes slid sidelong to Rowena, who noticeably bridled at her comment.

'Dawn is very happy.'

'But you're not. I've seen the way you look at her sometimes, pushing her away if she attempts to put her arms around you. It won't do, Rowena. It won't do at all.'

'She's well taken care of.'

'Yes, and perhaps deep down you love her, but you don't show it and it's time you did. You're a doctor and have some idea of how children's minds work and how their treatment in the early years can affect them in later life.'

Rowena folded her arms and ground her teeth. 'I...' She'd been about to make excuses or tell O'Malley it was none of her business, but she stopped herself. 'You don't understand. I look at her face and see them. I didn't want a child and I certainly didn't want one of *them* to be its father. It happened and I can't help thinking that somehow I'm partly to blame.'

'Blame? How can you be? To put it in the old-fashioned way, you were taken by force, Rowena. Showing the child kindness is no admission of guilt. You didn't encourage those men and Dawn didn't ask to be born. She can't help being half Japanese and neither of you is guilty.'

Rowena rounded on her hotly. 'Of course I'm not guilty. That's not how it is. Anyway, she's happy enough, especially with the attention you, Alice and Marjorie shower on her.'

O'Malley raised pencil-thin eyebrows. 'That's now, but what about when we finally leave here? It's going to be just the two of you. What then, Rowena? You will be stared at and you will be asked questions. What then?'

Rowena rubbed at her tired eyes. She was working every hour she could, just to get through. She'd only half considered the future once the war ended, but there were options.

'When she's old enough I'll send her to boarding school.'

'So you'll keep her at a distance. But there are still holidays, Rowena – and, anyway, it's more than that. A growing girl will need her mother more as she gets older.'

Rowena tossed her head and tapped her fingers against her folded arms. 'We might never leave here. The Japanese will win the war and then it won't matter, will it?'

'You don't really believe that.'

'Perhaps I do.'

'You have a family at home?'

'A brother. Our parents are dead.'

'Does he have a family?'

'I believe so. We're not in touch that often. As you may have noticed, there's not a bright red pillar-box in sight!'

'No need to be facetious. And the future may not be like that at all. Do you have a sweetheart?'

Connor's blue eyes and tenor voice came immediately to mind, and she smiled faintly at the thought of him. 'I think so.'

O'Malley looked thoughtful. 'And you're thinking this is a secret you'd prefer him not to know about.'

Rowena locked eyes with her. 'I grant you some men are willing to accept another man's child, even an illegitimate one. But a child fathered by a Japanese?' She shook her head. 'He's in Japan, probably being worked to death. Imagine it. "My daughter is half Japanese, Connor. How do you feel about adopting her?" No. Let me be, O'Malley. Let's see where this war's going.'

'Have you ever considered that her father is already dead?'

'I don't need to. I know he is.'

O'Malley frowned.

Rowena turned away, unwilling to enlighten her about a man who held Hong Kong in the palm of his hand. 'Anyway, thanks for our little chat.'

Determined to have the last word, O'Malley called after her. 'Oh, and Dawn called Alice Mummy. The child's confused, Rowena. She needs you to put her straight. Now that's my final word on the matter.'

It was Rowena's final word too. Trying to survive the privations in the camp was bad enough and, no matter her feelings towards her daughter, she had every intention of ensuring her survival.

Conversations between the women often consisted of wondering what might have happened if they had done that instead of this. Rowena had her own version.

Back in the summer of 1941 Clifford, her brother, had written, suggesting she come home for Christmas since she hadn't been able to make it for his wedding. In letter after letter he'd enthused about Wendy, his fiancée, and how she would make him a wonderful wife and how much he wanted them to meet: '*I'm sure you'll get on well together and Wendy is looking forward to meeting someone who's spent so much of their time abroad. She hasn't gone much further than Bognor Regis, but then, she loves her home more than she wants to see foreign climes.*'

It was debatable that she and her sister-in-law would get on, but even so she regretted not going back, perhaps not regretting attending the wedding, but not being there for Christmas 1941. What Clifford failed to grasp was how dangerous it was to travel back. The only possible route was around the Cape of Good Hope in South Africa, and even then there was danger from submarines and surface raiders. '*Wendy says that families matter and I agree with her. Quite frankly, sis, we want to have children as quickly as possible. There, I'm blushing...*'

In time when the war was over – and surely it had to be over at some point – she would see him again and meet his wife, with whatever children he had. But how would she explain Dawn? Clifford had never been that broad-minded – and as for his wife, was a woman who'd never gone much further than Bognor Regis be accepting of a mixed race child?


Shimmy was one of the more approachable guards, who had gained the familiarity of a nickname. His real name was Shimida, and as the task of guarding women was regarded by his superiors and compatriots as demeaning, it was usually given to the lowest of the low. It was rumoured that as a civilian he'd been a simple fisherman who had had to sell his daughters to train as geishas because he couldn't afford to keep them.

As such, his comrades in arms shunned his company. As a consequence he did more guard duty than they did, preferring to do something rather than sit alone. It was his job to keep an eye on all that was going on, while the others smoked and played card games out of sight of the commandant.

Shimmy had taken a liking to the lonely little girl, who seemed to have aunties but whose mother was always tending the sick in the long single room on the ground floor that served as a hospital.

While he guarded the women, Shimmy whittled pieces of wood. Dawn proved a willing audience, fascinated by the shavings, which she picked up and curled around her fingers. Rowena had not paid him much attention until now, her mind on other things, and nobody having mentioned his fondness for her little girl. On that particular morning she happened to see him from the ward window where she was about to draw down a blind to keep the sun off a patient.

Alice looked over her shoulder. 'Looks like Shimmy's made your daughter a wooden doll. How kind.'

Leaving his rifle leaning against the wall behind him, a smiling Shimmy was indeed handing the doll he'd made to Dawn, who looked very pleased.

Rowena saw red. 'Not from his filthy hands!'

In a trice she veered away from her patient, from Alice and from the ward, and ran for the door.

Dust kicked up behind her. 'Get away from her,' she shouted, as she ran towards him, waving her arms. 'Get away from my child.'

A look of surprise came to Shimmy's usually bland face.

Rowena grabbed the carved figure from Dawn and threw it at Shimmy's feet, her eyes blazing. 'She doesn't want your doll. Leave her alone. Just leave her alone.'

Dawn raised her arms, her fingers making clutching movements. 'Dolly. Dolly.'

'You're not having it.'

Dawn burst into tears.

Rowena stood there, her chest heaving and hatred in her eyes.

Shimmy, being of a conciliatory nature, spoke softly and when that didn't work, brought out a soft leather wallet from within his uniform. From the wallet he took out a photo, murmuring in Japanese and inviting her to look.

'Dr Rossiter. Doctor!'

Marjorie Greenbank was bearing down on her. She was still an imposing woman, though she'd shed a good deal of weight and her round face was now haggard, her hair thinner and greyer than it had been. She stood between Rowena and Shimmy.

'Doctor,' she said, dropping her voice, 'Shimmy is only trying to be friendly. He's showing you his family photo.

He misses them just as much as we miss our own families. He's a kindly man and also barters for us. We'd all have been dead a long time ago if it wasn't for him.'

'If he's that kind, why doesn't he leave here and go home?'

'Because he's no choice and his wife would starve if he wasn't here. His two daughters are apprenticed as geishas and his wife has moved in with his mother in a place called Hiroshima. Believe me, I've spoken with him and know that he's desperate to go home. He hates being here.'

Dawn's wails attracted the attention of other women who, misunderstanding, picked up the wooden mannequin and gave it to her.

The wails stopped.

Rowena clenched her jaw and, aware of everyone looking at her and even patting Shimmy's shoulder, she backed down.


'I hate this place,' she said to Alice later.

'We all do, dear. It's just a case of muddling through until we're rescued by our knights in shining armour. I only hope they bring a large steak with them. And a dozen eggs. I'd eat the bloody lot.'


Roughly a week later, Rowena was watching Dawn playing with the wooden doll, rocking it in her arms and continually wrapping and unwrapping it in a scrap of material that Alice had given her.

Alice was encouraging her to sing 'Rock-a-bye, Baby'.

'Come on, darling. Rock the baby backwards and forwards like this. "*Rock-a-bye, Baby, on the tree top...*"'

Alice sang so badly that even Dawn looked at her askance.

'Alice, you've got a voice like a cracked drain,' Rowena told her.

'And you can do better?'

'I prefer something a bit more classical...'

'"*Go to sleep, my baby, Close your pretty eyes...*"'

Her voice, so clear and strong, affected those standing around who stopped what they were doing to listen awhile.

'Well, ain't that a beaut,' murmured one of the Australian nurses.

Engrossed in her singing, only a few women had noticed the sleek car purring through the main gate and stopping in front of the bungalow once occupied by a senior executive officer of the British administration. As usual it was an Australian who took in the details and made a flippant comment.

'What say we ask him for a ride out of here? Hey, Doc. You don't happen to know him, do you? He's looking directly at you.'

On hearing the remarks, Rowena turned and looked to where they were looking.

It was Kim.

Her heart raced. He was looking directly at her. What was he doing here?

Alice noticed too. 'It's the foreigner. My goodness, Doc, you must have made an impression.'

Rowena turned cold as, with slow deliberation, Kim Pheloung took his hat from his head, clasped his hands together and bowed.

The commandant's right-hand man came out of the office and bowed almost reverentially to the tall, slender Asiatic, and the guards either side stood to immediate attention.

Kim glanced once more in her direction, then disappeared into the commandant's office.

'Audrey's right. He's looking at you. Do you know him?' Marjorie sounded curious.

'I used to. His name's Kim Pheloung. He has a house in Kowloon Walled City and an office in Nathan Road.'

'What does he do?'

She had no inclination to go into details, except one. 'He killed the men who raped me.'

'My word.'

'He calls himself a businessman.'

'Your tone suggests he's a criminal. Did you know he was coming?'

She shook her head. Now he'd seen her anything was possible.

★

Rowena looked down at the peaceful face of an elderly lady who had breathed her last. Her limbs were no thicker than twigs and she was the third to die that week. Familiarity with death didn't make dealing with it any easier.

'I need some air,' she muttered to the Australian nurse, the one who had spotted Kim Pheloung's car on his last visit.

'Hey. It's him again. The bloke in the pale green car. The one who stared at you so hard.'

Rowena went to the window. It was definitely Kim's car, but not him at the wheel.

'I wonder what's brought him back,' the nurse added.

'It's not him. It's another man driving.'

Even though it was not Kim, she felt a knot of apprehension tighten in her stomach. She watched him take packages from the back of the car and carry them in to the commandant. Gifts intended to bribe, no doubt. Kim had to be doing business with the occupying army. One part of her was disgusted. Another understood that Kim Pheloung would indeed do whatever he had to not just to survive, but to prosper.

The car left. The excitement was over.

Rowena turned back to dealing with the dead woman's meagre artefacts, looking for a home address so the relatives could be informed.

The only item worth returning was a wooden box, containing tresses of hair – perhaps those of her children?

Her husband? Letters, the writing faded, the corners curled.

*My darling Cynthia...*

She'd known the woman only as Mrs Creighton.

'Mrs Creighton's gone, then.'

Alice was in the doorway, the body inside the baggy clothes reminding Rowena of dolls she used to make from clothes pegs – a stick of wood covered with scraps of material.

She glanced at the first line of the letter, folded it and placed it in a brown-paper bag along with other letters destined for relatives who didn't yet know they were grieving. The distance between where they were and home was immense. 'Her name was Cynthia. She used to be in her twenties and in love. We don't think of old people having once been young. That's why we instinctively refer to them formally, which means we never get close to them.'

'You're sounding a bit down.'

'It's been a long day. *Did I see Marjorie's been summoned to the commandant's office?*'

'*You did.* Did you also see our friend Kim's car? Somebody else was driving it. Looked as though he was making some kind of delivery. Whisky, I expect. Our dear commandant is very fond of highland dew. I hear Johnnie Walker is his favourite. Cup of tea?'

'Do we have any?'

'It's a bit weak but by now it might have stewed enough to make a decent brew.'

They sat down on two rickety chairs either side of an equally rickety table in a small alcove under the stairs. The rest of the ward was taken up with beds, mosquito nets and the small supply of medicine and bandages, which had to be boiled and reused. There were also a few surgical instruments that had to be kept scrupulously clean without the aid of disinfectants.

'Wish we could get some of that Johnnie Walker,' said Rowena.

'To drink or to use as an antiseptic?'

'Both.'

It was while they were sipping tea without milk or sugar that Marjorie came in carrying a parcel beneath her arm. 'I'm perplexed,' she said, in a very affected manner.

'Will a cup of tea help?'

She sank onto a stool that had been a chair until they'd needed wood for a winter fire. Chopping the back off had been an acceptable compromise.

'Dr Rossiter, may I speak to you alone?' Marjorie seemed puzzled.

The Australian nurse had left and only Alice remained. At first Rowena was inclined to say that Alice could stay, they had no secrets, but Marjorie, a woman of stout manner and clipped words, seemed unusually awkward.

Alice saw her expression and got up. 'I'll go.'

Marjorie sat down heavily and laid her hands over the cushion of brown paper.

'Dr Rossiter. I know nothing about your history with the owner of the terribly smart car that's just left, except that you said he'd executed the men who... attacked you. I don't think I want to know anything else. But I've been asked to pass you this and to tell you to be ready for the car to pick you up at six this evening.'

Rowena's eyes flicked between Marjorie's face and the brown-paper parcel that now lay on her lap. She frowned, then tentatively unwrapped it so the paper would not tear or crumple. Everything could be reused, included such a simple thing as this. It was a habit she was sure would remain with her.

A swathe of heavy silk fell out of the parcel. She caught the rest with both hands, unfolded it and found herself looking at a red silk dress – a cheongsam embroidered with gold thread.

'My word. It's beautiful.'

Rowena sprang to her feet. 'This is ridiculous. It cannot be happening.' 'It seems that it is.'

'I'm not going. I got away from him once. I don't want to go back.'

'Is he dangerous?'

'Let's put it this way. If he sees something he likes he takes it. He deals in opium. He deals in everything.'

Marjorie frowned. 'I suppose I could tell the commandant that you refuse to go, though I'm not sure it will do any good.'

Rowena rubbed her forehead in an effort to quell the ache behind her eyes: a vision of Kim, his naked chest, his dark hair and his way of slowly insinuating control.

It hadn't been so evident while she'd been with him, but now, at a distance, she could hear the way he spoke, see the things he did – having her waiting at a time he had stipulated, his reaction to her having dared to eat when he hadn't appeared. Now it seemed clear, but at the time she'd been confused, tired and in need of healing.

'Where is he taking me?'

Marjorie shrugged. 'I don't know. You're to be ready at six. That's all I was told.'

Rowena lowered her eyes. Kim had found her by chance. It must have surprised him to see her the other day when he'd taken off his hat and bowed from the waist. 'I can't go. I promised Dawn I'd read to her.'

'You have no choice. I'll read to her.'

Then: 'What will the others think?'

'They'll be envious.'

She looked at Marjorie with pleading in her eyes. 'I didn't ask for this, Marjorie. I don't want to go. What if he won't let me come back?'

'I shouldn't think the commandant would allow that and... funnily enough, I think your friends, your true friends, will enjoy being party to your date with a handsome man, helping you bathe – if we have enough water – washing your hair, getting you dressed.' She smiled. 'It will be as though we all have a place at the table for your night out.'

Every part of Rowena was very still, except her trembling hands.

'Alice told me he bribed the Japanese to let you go,' Marjorie went on, 'and you lived in his house for a while. That must have been quite sumptuous compared to this. Please don't think I'm prying, my dear, or judging you, but was there any particular reason you didn't stay with him?'

Rowena couldn't help the sheepish grin. 'His grandmother was jealous. One day she loaded me into the car, then we transferred to a rickshaw and she turned me in. I wonder whether she's still alive.'

'No matter. He obviously has a soft spot for you.' She paused. Rowena thought she knew what was coming next and was instantly proved right. 'If you can, see if he can get us a few little luxuries. A bar of soap would be nice. And medicines, of course, but that's your domain. You've probably already considered it.'

'You'll look after Dawn if I don't come back?' Rowena blurted, her voice shaking.

Marjorie's eyes were full of compassion. 'Some women say you're indifferent to the child. I'm not one of them. Neither is Alice. We know what you went through and how hard it must be to both love and hate at the same time. You love her, but it's hard to show it. In time you will, my dear. In time I'm sure you will.'


Marjorie was proved right. There was genuine excitement in helping the only female doctor in the camp get ready for a big night out.

Leanne Kemp was a Eurasian girl married to a sailor she hadn't seen for some time. Her hair was as long and thick as Rowena's. 'Wear these,' she said, handing over three mother-of-pearl combs. 'I'll help you put your hair up if you like.'

'They're beautiful. Are you sure?'

Leanne nodded. 'Bob bought them for me. I can't bear to wear them now. He was on the *Repulse*, you know, but was transferred before it was sunk. I don't know where he is now.'

Rowena thanked her. Another woman lent her a nub of soap consisting of bits and pieces she'd collected from everyone else and made into a usable portion.

Marjorie was the last person she'd expected to own a bottle of French perfume.

'Just a dab or two behind the ears, my dear. As you can see, there's not a lot left.'

Rowena regarded her reflection in a mirror. It hung on the wall and was far from perfect, a large crack running down the side, thanks to a bullet hole in one corner. Casting her mind back, she realised she'd worn the dress before, though she didn't fill it as well as she had done then.

Her hair was pinned up, her face made up and she no longer smelt of dried blood and medicine. The sight of her shining self was downright surreal. 'I shouldn't be going.'

'Yes, you should. We all think so. And we want to know every detail. It'll do us all good.'

Alice nodded in agreement with Marjorie's observation.

At first Rowena had thought their interest shallow and schoolgirlish until Marjorie reminded her of the more serious aspects. 'It's a means to an end, Rowena. That man could make our stay here much more comfortable, even if only for a little while.'

★

The car was on time, sweeping in through the gates and stopping outside the commandant's office. Kim was driving.

She stood there shivering, aware of the envious faces of the women and the lascivious grins of the Japanese soldiers, who exchanged wry looks with their colleagues, all surmising what might transpire when the two were alone in the car together.

She blushed at the thought of what they were thinking, of what might happen. Everything about her, from her silky hair, to her silky dress to her shiny shoes, hinted at a pre-war life of parties, receptions and intimate dinners with officers and naval attachés.

Kim got out, took off his hat and inclined his head, his eyes never leaving her face when he opened the front passenger door. He didn't look any different – perhaps a little sleeker, a little more affluent. 'Please. Get in.'

She slid silently onto the lush leather upholstery, which was warm beneath her, yet she huddled beneath the

Kashmir shawl borrowed from a woman who had spent some time in India.

He put the car into reverse before making a tight U-turn.

Unsmiling and afraid, she turned her head to face her friends.

Their expressions for the most part were happy, though some looked more serious, even concerned. One small figure stood out in the crowd, the only child who wasn't chasing a ball or playing chase. She was the only person to raise her hand and wave goodbye.

The streets and turnings were familiar.

'Where are we going?'

'For a spin, as the Americans say.'

'That's not a destination.'

'Because there is none.'

He drove very fast away from Fort Stanley and into such little of the countryside as there was in Hong Kong. As they hurtled along, rickshaws and people carrying panniers and piles of merchandise dived out of their way.

The unique smell of sampans and salt water heralded their arrival at Victoria Harbour where Kim brought the car to a stop.

Her stomach churned. 'Are you taking me back to Kowloon?'

'No. I am taking you for a drive. We will discuss the next step in your life and all that has happened and all that we wish to happen.'

He stopped talking. His hands tightened on the steering wheel.

The cliff road wound away from the tenements, the bustling alleys, the noise of people and war. After only a few miles, he pulled into a recess at the side of the road. From there they looked down on Victoria Harbour, the Perfumed Harbour of former times.

She wanted him to speak first and tell her how he had managed to arrange this without her having to ask.

Suddenly his arms were around her and his lips were on hers. It took her totally by surprise. On breaking the kiss he held her at arms' length. 'Why did you leave? I gave you everything. You were safe. I would never hurt you. That night I intended making love to you. You should have known that.'

Rowena looked at him, dumbfounded. 'I didn't leave you. Your grandmother turned me in.'

Now he was dumbfounded, which swiftly turned to anger. 'Tell me, and I will tell you if I believe you.'

She told him how it had been, going for a drive, getting out, walking a little way, getting into a rickshaw.

'Grandmother would never travel in a rickshaw.'

'She would if it meant getting rid of me. There was nobody to see her turn me in. Your driver was left with the car. It was impossible for him to follow.'

A different look came to his eyes that she could not entirely comprehend. 'My grandmother can be a little possessive.' He nodded thoughtfully, then stopped when his mind was made up. 'We can begin again.'

'What do you mean?'

'You will come to my house again.'

'But your grandmother?'

'I will leave her in Kowloon and take you to my house in Shanghai. You recall me saying I have a house in Shanghai?'

'You mentioned it.'

'My favourite house. You will be safe. There will be food and clean clothes. All you have to do is trust me. As I trust you. Everyone trusts doctors.'

'We're only human, just like everybody else.'

'Doctors always speak the truth, I think.'

'Most of the time.'

'Have you ever lied? I do not think so. But we will not refer to you being a doctor. I prefer to speak of other things.'

She did not contradict him. Telling a lie had resulted in a man's death, which was against everything she stood for. If the man who had killed himself had not been Japanese, she would never have lied, but whatever he was, the guilt was still with her. Sometimes it surfaced and made her feel an unworthy member of her profession. Telling herself it had been her way of fighting back helped but did not bring total forgiveness. Only time would heal.

She looked down at her hands, their whiteness against the rich red and gold of her dress, so luxurious, so different from the second-hand cotton dresses she wore in the camp.

His presence lifted her spirits, but she knew she

couldn't possibly leave her friends and she had to make him understand that.

'There's something I have to tell you.'

His eyes narrowed. His arm was around her shoulders, his breath warm on the side of her face.

'I have a child. A daughter fathered by one of the men you killed. Don't ask me which one. I don't know.' She went on to tell him she couldn't leave her daughter behind, and that the woman he'd wished to possess no longer existed. He seemed to think about this, his face turned away, his jaw compressed, his eyes looking seawards.

At last he spoke. 'You may leave her at the camp.'

'I will do no such thing!' Despite her fear of him, she didn't hold back. 'My child goes wherever I go.'

'How strange.'

'It is not strange. You have a grandmother who loves you and I love my daughter. I will not go with you.'

He seemed to be thinking about it. 'A girl, you say?'

'Yes,' she snapped, feeling the heat rise to her face.

'Girls can be more easily accommodated. They are much more biddable than boys. They are more easily trained to obey. It is in their nature, whereas boys...' He laughed, a short bark, like taking a bite out of the air. 'Boys like their own way. I should know.'

His hand travelled imperceptibly to the nape of her neck, his cool fingers tracing circles that gave her goose bumps and sent shivers down her spine.

'Do you recall the first time we met? I gave you a cigarette lighter. Do you still have it?'

'No. I bartered it for food and medicine.' It was only half a lie, but she feared telling him about Connor, what he might imagine had happened between them.

The moving fingers slowed and stopped.

'You don't mind, do you?'

'No. I prefer you fed and here with me, than dead of starvation or disease.'

Having made this statement, his fingers began moving again, leaving her cheek and running through her hair. 'I do not like this style. I prefer your hair to be loose and long. It pleases me.'

He took out the first comb and a third of her hair tumbled down.

'You did not get to know me so well before. In Shanghai you will know me better. You and your daughter.'

'I will go nowhere without her.'

She started when he reached out and plucked the second comb from her hair so it fell like a black veil onto her shoulder. All that remained was the third.

'No more kowtowing to Japanese officers who do not deserve it.'

'Do you not bow when you do business with them?' The last tress fell down and tickled her shoulder blades. She looked into his eyes and caught something dart across them – like a black beetle that shuns daylight and lives only in darkness.

'Only those who are useful to me. Not the peasants who now think themselves soldiers. And I am useful to them. Without me Hong Kong would be more difficult to control and I am very good at controlling the island. I keep certain elements of its character under control.'

One arm around her, one hand cupping her face, his lips found hers. They were surprisingly cold and as mesmerising as the mysterious look in his eyes. Again he was playing with her hair. 'I think I would prefer it like this. That is more to my liking,' he said, as he appraised his handiwork.

'You like things to be as you want them.'

His smile was slow and had something triumphal about it. 'Always.'

'Do you know what the women at the camp desire most of all?'

A knowing expression came to his face. 'You are going to tell me and ask me to satisfy that desire – which I will do at a price. Everything I do is at a price. I think you know that.'

She did, but she asked him anyway. Soap, medicine, towelling and other feminine items.

'I will do this. Now we go.'

The evening out had been a glorious change from the routine, away from dirt, disease and boredom, a short time in which to remember what it was like to be a woman going out with a man. And he hadn't attempted to have sex with her. She'd contemplated what to do if he'd pressed himself on her, and decided she had her price too. Her fellow prisoners were in need of just about everything, and if she could get things for them she would. Such a small price, she thought, in return for comforts that might lengthen the lives of her fellow prisoners. But it wasn't only that. Her body still stirred for his attention.

As they drove back she eyed his profile, the high brow, the aquiline nose, the wide, sensual mouth. She knew then what her life would be with him. He would require total submission, like a concubine of the old Chinese emperors. There was something both alluring and romantic about it, but also something a little frightening. Suddenly realising she would be giving up her freedom made her change her mind. No matter the deprivations her friends suffered, she just couldn't do it.

The car was waved through the main gate and stopped outside the commandant's office.

'I will go in and make arrangements,' said Kim.

She felt the warmth of his hand encompassing hers, which felt as cold as fallen snow. 'No. Don't. I'm sorry, Kim. I'm not coming with you. I'm staying here. Sorry,' she said again, and turned on her heel. Then she stopped and looked over her shoulder. 'I'll parcel up the dress and get it back to you.'

She ran and dared not look back, sensing that he was furious but sure she had done the right thing.

# 19

The one good thing about being in the hold of the *Ashada Maru* was that there were no guards to bully or steal what possessions the men had left. Not that they had much. The rest was all bad: the stinking latrines, too few to take the effluent of five hundred men, the reek of oil, the putrid bilge water washing around their ankles. The portholes were high and let in little light. They were in a dark, oily world where fresh air and daylight were an infrequent luxury.

Connor took out the lighter Rowena had given him. Their meetings had been brief, yet he could still smell her hair, see the dark grey eyes, the swan-like neck. Such small details kept him going. There had been many instances when he could have traded the lighter for food, tobacco or some other small luxury, but the memories it instilled were luxury enough. It kept his heart beating, his lungs breathing.

A bulkhead door opened and a shaft of light lifted

the gloom. The daily ration of rice balls and water had arrived.

Fingers filthy on account of his surroundings, Connor swiftly tucked the lighter back into his loincloth. That and the lighter were his only possessions. His uniform had turned to mildewed rags long ago.

Food was swiftly consumed, as was the water, though it tasted brackish. Sleeping was difficult but welcome. Sleep helped him forget how hungry he was.

Time passed. Night was preferable to day.

The engines throbbed with an incessant rhythm. A sudden change in their tempo woke him. He looked up at the light coming from a deck prism, a thick piece of glass set into the deck through which came a feeble beam of light. The throb of the engines lulled them to sleep, but they heard their note change.

Harry looked up at him. 'We've changed direction.'

'And speeded up.'

Ears were primed for the slightest sound.

Another twenty minutes. Unsecured in the dingy hold, they lurched from side to side, bony bodies packed tightly, which at least helped prevent serious injury.

Another change of direction swiftly followed the first.

'We're zigzagging.'

Tension increased, men murmuring, questioning, and those of a naval background confirming what was going on.

'There's a submarine close by.'

'A US submarine, no doubt.'

'A torpedo is a torpedo and we're dead.'

Eyes were raised to the overhead girders, the metalwork dripping with condensation blackened by grease and oil. Droplets fell on their upturned faces. Somebody asked if anyone had spotted a red cross on the side of the ship or anything to denote that Allied prisoners were aboard.

'The Japanese don't do that, old boy. If they're attacked, we are too.'

Harry sounded his usual blasé self, but Connor heard the fear in his voice and, even in the gloom, saw the nerve twitch beneath his right eye and the trembling in his dirty fingers.

Suddenly the ship vibrated violently, lifted up, then smashed down, metalwork twisting as the side of the vessel was ripped open, like a sardine can.

Rivets pinged like bullets.

Water came rushing in, a dark green and thrusting power.

The door was gone, the darkness was gone. They thrashed against the incoming water, kicked until they were on the surface, flailing in the first light of dawn.

The oil was still with them, covering their bodies, siphoned into their lungs, smearing the sea with a black, clogging slick.

At first Connor found himself below the surface. It was blue and cool but turbulent with the antics of men and the death throes of a sinking ship. With every ounce of his strength he kicked his way to the surface, then powered himself away from the vessel. All around him those still alive were doing the same thing, cruelly aware that when the ship went down it would suck them with it if they didn't get clear.

There were no waves and the sea was warm but it was hard to see. Dawn had broken but the oil got into eyes, noses, throats and ears. Connor wiped away the oil from his eyes, stalled his stroke and looked for something solid to hold onto. Some distance away he spotted a grey object, not a boat or a life raft but an object blown off the ship that promised stability.

Summoning every last ounce of strength, he struck out for it and knew that Harry was doing the same. Once it was within his grasp, he saw it was a bulkhead door, possibly the one that had kept them confined in the hold.

A glance over his shoulder confirmed that Harry was right behind him. As he hauled himself onto the door, it felt warm, from the explosion, and somehow comforting. His lungs heaving for air, he checked Harry's progress. He had almost reached the piece of jetsam, though he was struggling, his hair floating behind him, his beard black and filthy.

Connor dragged him aboard, and they looked to where the ship's bow pointed skyward. All around it men were getting into the lifeboats kept on deck, only accessible to the crew.

On seeing the lifeboats being lowered and the ship still there, though badly damaged, those prisoners who had swum away turned back in the vain hope that they would be taken aboard.

Connor and Harry exchanged a questioning look. Should they swim for it too and fight their way aboard a lifeboat?

Connor shook his head. He kept his eyes on the men, willing them to succeed even if it meant throwing the enemy sailors into the sea.

It wasn't to be. Suddenly the whole sky seemed to catch fire as a second explosion ripped the ship apart, flame and smoke leaping upward. Debris rained down on Connor and Harry as they threw themselves flat onto the metallic surface. When they looked up there were only flames and smoke, a deafening roar and the sound of residual ammunition going up in smoke.

Some distance from the ship bodies floated, blackened and immobile.

There was no sign of a single lifeboat.

Connor cupped a patch of uncontaminated seawater and bathed his scalding eyes. Harry had been luckier: black saliva dribbled from his mouth but his eyes were clear. Forcing himself to straighten his arms, he looked all around. 'Where's the submarine?'

'Gone.'

'Gone? Well, that's just not cricket. They could have picked up the survivors even if it's only two of us.'

'They don't play cricket and they're not going to hang around and get sunk by a Jap destroyer.'

'So what do we do now?'

Connor was fumbling in his loincloth for the lighter. It

entered his head that if he still had that there was hope and he'd live to give it back to her.

For a moment he could see nothing as a light breeze blew his hair across his face. All around him was death, but he didn't want to die. He dared to look towards the ship and the mass of floating bodies. They were caught in a current, which meant they were moving to – where?

'Do you see what I see?'

Harry looked. 'The bodies are coming this way.'

'No. We're all going in the same direction. We're caught in a current. All I want to know is, where is it heading?'

He swallowed and wished they'd had the chance to bring water. As it was, they were both half naked and the sun would roast them like chickens. Without water they would dehydrate quickly.

'Connor, I'm reading your mind. The only thing I've got that might help is this.'

Harry brought out his tin cup, his one and only prized possession.

Connor grinned. 'That's a start. All we need now is some rain.'

The far horizon shimmered with light.

'The rising sun is that way, the port side in nautical terms, which means the current flows south.'

'Understood, old boy.'

'It's a slim chance but it could be taking us to Bali.'

'Are you sure?'

He nodded. He couldn't be certain, but hope would keep their spirits up. 'I don't know what speed we were doing on that old tub, and can only guess at our longitude and latitude, but there's a chance. Just a chance.'

'Good,' said Harry, pulling his tangled hair over his face. 'This should keep off the sunstroke, that plus a little swim now and again.'

'Not yet,' said Connor, and pointed to where more than one triangular fin was drifting through the mass of dead bodies. The sharks were coming to feast. The water was turning red.

'At least they won't bother us when there's that much free meat.'

Connor turned again to the horizon. 'We might make it. It's a strong current.'

'About seven knots would you say?'

'Yes. If I remember rightly the horizon is roughly twenty miles away.'

'So how long will it take us to get there?'

'Anything from five to eight hours.'

'Well, that's something.'

'It's just the horizon. I didn't say I could see any land.'

'But if we get there...'

'It could be another twenty miles to land, or fifty, or a hundred, it all depends on the current and the wind. It would help if we had a wind behind us.'

Harry didn't ask anything else, but sank down and slept. Connor did the same, glad the sea was calm and that the sharks were preoccupied. All they had to do now was pray for rain tonight and tomorrow they could share a mug between them.

# 20

'Rowena, I'm sorry. You can't come in here.'

Rowena frowned. 'Why? I want to do my job.'

Dr Anderson shook his head. Marjorie Greenbank was standing beside him wringing her hands and looking very worried.

'It's on the orders of the commandant. He summoned me just before midday and said you are no longer to be allowed to practise.'

'That's crazy! Why not?'

Marjorie cleared her throat. 'I was ordered to see Dr Anderson first, then you. You're to pack your and Dawn's things and report outside the commandant's office in one hour.'

With increased dismay, she saw what was going on. 'It's him. Kim Pheloung. I refused to go with him and now he's trying to force me. I won't go.'

Marjorie looked perplexed. 'Is that what this is about? I thought that perhaps you were being moved to another camp, one that's a bit more comfortable – if there is such a thing.'

'Well, I'm not going. No man is going to force me to do something I don't want to do ever again!' She turned on her heel, her jaw set, Marjorie trailing along behind her. Usually the older woman had a brisk stride, but today Rowena was faster.

'I don't think the commandant will listen, but if you want to give it a try, I'll go with you.'

'I'm quite capable of dealing with it myself.'

'No, you're not. You don't speak Japanese or Cantonese fluently, do you? No, I thought not. That's the advantage of being married to a diplomat. You get posted all over the place so have to make use of your time. I occupied myself with languages.' Marjorie was keeping pace with her now. 'You're looking rebellious, Rowena, and that's dangerous here.'

'I don't care. I'm not going. Some time ago, after I lied to the soldier with crabs, I was thinking I wasn't up to being a doctor, that I'd broken my oath to do no harm, but now I've decided I am a doctor and that I'm needed here. I will not abandon ship.'

'You may have to.'

Marjorie's tone had changed. Rowena looked up and saw why. Two guards had entered the ward and they were heading her way.

There was no need for Marjorie's interpretative skills. They wanted her to come with them and she knew better than to disobey. They'd been known to injure or kill a patient if a doctor did not do as they were ordered.

Feeling sick, she went with them.

The day was bright and at first she squinted after leaving the shade of the ward. Using her hand to shield her eyes, she saw his car had arrived. Kim Pheloung had come to claim her, regardless of whether she wanted to go with him or not.

'I've brought your things. They told me to pack them for you.'

It was Alice with Rowena's few belongings wrapped in the brown paper the dress had arrived in.

'This is nonsense.' Rowena rubbed her aching temples. 'I don't want to go. I won't go.'

'Rowena...'

Alice's voice was gentle, but the finger that pointed to Kim's open-top car was shaking.

Rowena saw what she was pointing at and gasped. One of Kim's men was acting as chauffeur. Kim was sitting in the back, one arm around Dawn, who was standing on the leather seat next to him.

'Mummeee!' The little girl waved. She sounded excited.

Rowena was scared. Her brave talk about refusing to go with him melted away. Her heart pounded against her ribs.

He was holding Dawn more tightly now, though from her smile, the little girl hadn't understood that.

Kim was not smiling but wore a challenging look, inviting her to test his resolve even though he would have things his way.

'That's it, Dawn. Wave to your mother and tell her to hurry up. We're waiting to go. We're going on a long drive away from here and if Mummy doesn't hurry up we'll have to go without her.'

She felt Alice pressing the brown-paper parcel against her clenched fist. She had no option but to accept it, no option but to go with him or he would take her daughter anyway.

She made her way to the car, his eyes fixed on her. A Japanese guard opened the rear door and she stepped in, trembling as she sat on the soft leather seating.

The door closed after her with a hushed thud – like a prison door. She felt she had entered a cage.

He did not relinquish his hold on Dawn, but rested his chin on the child's head. His smile was stiff and lacked warmth. His eyes were obsidian.

'Now we can go far away from here, your mother and I, safe within the walls of a house that has been standing for centuries. We will all be happy there because I, Kim Pheloung, insist on it.'

She sat silently during the car journey, then the sea crossing from Hong Kong to mainland China, her spine poker stiff.

'Fresh air,' he said loudly, waving his hat into the wind as the boat ploughed the troughs and rose on the peaks of a choppy sea. 'Is this not fun, Dawn?'

Dawn agreed that it was.

Clenching Rowena's wrist, he encouraged Dawn to run free. 'Show your mother you have good sea legs, Dawn. Go on, little girl, run all over the deck, if you like. Your mother and I will be watching, and then we will go below for some tea. Would you like that?'

'No! She's just a baby. She could get swept away in this sea.'

Kim stepped between mother and daughter, catching Rowena's wrists and twisting them slightly. 'I insist she is allowed to run free. You Westerners have a tendency to overprotect your children. Asian children are allowed to roam at will. Some as young as five work in the paddies or on the street from dawn till dusk.' He looked over his shoulder. 'Go on. Run away from us. Hide and we will try to find you.'

Rowena was terrified. 'But the sea!'

'She is coping. Come. In here.'

He pushed her towards the companionway that led down into a small saloon for the use of passengers. Ordinarily they would have taken a ferry from Hong Kong to the New Territories, but they were heading for Jiangsu, the province in which Shanghai was situated. It was a longer sea voyage but avoided driving along roads manned by Japanese soldiers of little education and a peasant background. They were likely to kill anyone regardless of whether or not they had a pass.

The saloon was empty of any other guests because Kim owned the vessel and used it for various purposes. His car had been lifted aboard by crane, the operation watched with amazement by the occupying army, who knew the man was important and wealthy, and gazed enviously at the car once it was firmly secured on the foredeck.

A servant wearing traditional garb stood ready at the door, his head bowed as though Kim was an emperor, not the criminal she knew him to be.

Kim clicked his fingers and pointed to the door.

The servant, his thin goatee beard almost reaching his chest, bowed his way out and shut the door behind him.

Rowena faced him with blazing eyes and a feeling that she was no more than a rabbit in a trap. 'I do not want to be here.'

'Irrelevant. It does not matter what you want. I want you to be here.'

'Then let me out to see where my daughter has got to. She might have fallen overboard. You saw that sea. This boat is leaping around. The sea is rough.'

'The child is enjoying herself, let out at last from the camp. Would you deny her the freedom she has never known? Can you believe it is better in that stinking camp, with its privations and diseases, than here with me? No longer will you lie on a bug-ridden mattress. No longer will you dress in washed-out rags.'

He indicated the dress she was wearing. 'I won't insist you change now, but you will before we touch land. You still have the dress I gave you?'

'Yes, but... I'm sorry, I can't take this in properly when my daughter is outside.'

'We will play hide and seek,' he said, throwing his arms wide, encouraging her to feel that all was well and she had nothing to fear from him. 'She will enjoy that. You will enjoy it, as will I.'

'Can we go and find her now?'

He nodded. 'Yes. I think we've given her enough time to hide. Come. Please...'

She did not protest when he put his arm around her and guided her back onto the deck. The wind was fresh and feathery puffs of spume were blowing across the deck. Every so often the bow dipped into the waves and water flooded towards them, not enough to knock them off their feet, but enough to topple a child – or drag her into the sea.

The boat was no more than a hundred feet long, big enough to go to sea and only just big enough to take a sufficient amount of cargo to make its journeys pay. He was holding her tightly, but when the boat slewed forward then reared up, she broke free and raced to the forepeak where Dawn had run.

'Rowena!'

He sounded angry behind her, but her shoes were without heels so she ran quickly.

In front of her was the car and in front of the car's sleek bonnet she saw the driver. His back was towards her, but when she shouted he turned. Dawn was tucked in front of him. His hands were on her shoulders but he was holding her only loosely.

'Dawn!'

As her mother sprang forward, Dawn escaped the driver's clutches.

Kim was right behind her, reaching out, his hands landing claw-like on her shoulders.

'There. I said she was all right. Ching was with her.'

He said something in Cantonese to which the driver replied.

'He said he saw she was going forward and he stopped her. It was lucky he was here.'

Unsure whether to believe him, Rowena smoothed her daughter's hair back from her face and held her close. 'Dawn, stay with mummy. There's a good girl.'

Her daughter nodded solemnly.

The sea calmed, but not once did Rowena leave her child alone. During this journey at least, she would forget the circumstances of Dawn's conception. She had a duty of care, much as she did towards any human life. She would protect her, keep her distance from Kim as far as she could, though in time she knew there would be a price to pay. If it came to it, she would sacrifice herself for Dawn's safety.

# 21

The scariest thing Connor O'Connor knew about the Pacific Ocean was that it covered almost a third of the earth's surface and their chance of hitting land was slim. That they had no provisions contributed to the hopelessness of their predicament.

'Don't move. Don't speak.'

'I know. Unless strictly necessary. We've got a long journey ahead of us.'

'Too many words already.'

Words and moving used energy they could ill afford.

Their long hair kept the worst of the sunburn at bay though their lips were cracked, their shoulders red and sore.

Connor awoke each morning at the same time, his eyes checking the sunrise and finding they were still travelling in a southerly direction. Hopefully they would eventually arrive at Bali, though any island would do, a small atoll with or without water. If there was no fresh water, they could set up some kind of collecting system for when it rained. Until it did they would avail themselves of coconuts hanging in clusters and filled with milk. Their main preference was that the island was not already home to a battalion of enemy soldiers.

Their lips were blistered, their bodies dehydrated, and their spirits were failing until an overnight downpour.

Torrential rain overnight caused pools of water to collect in the central door panel held there by the band of metal that formed its frame.

While it rained, Harry filled and refilled his tin mug and they drank. 'Now perhaps God might furnish us with dinner,' said Harry, once the rain had stopped and the sun was like a burnished doubloon in an azure sky.

'God, must have been listening,' Connor declared, when a trio of flying fish leaped on board.

Harry was just about to eat one raw, but Connor stopped him. 'Save the sashimi for the Japanese. We're cooking tonight.'

He fumbled in his pocket for the lighter which was still wrapped in a square of canvas. It took a few attempts, but luckily the lighter had escaped the worst of the water. On the fourth attempt a yellow flame sprang into life with which he seared the silvery flesh, and they ate it between them, bones and all, then opened the other two and laid them to dry in the sun.

'What I wouldn't give for a slice of pork and roast potatoes cooked in goose fat. Our cook did the best roast potatoes ever. Did I ever tell you that?' Harry sounded tired, and Connor felt pretty much the same. From midday onwards was the hottest time of day but all day the sun shone and that was when they slept. At night they tried to stay awake, their eyes scanning the horizon for any sign of a light – a light on land, a light from a fishing boat, a light from a warship. They didn't much care about the nationality of a rescuer – any flag would do.

It was around midnight. The moon was high and the night still when Harry slumped onto the wet metal, throwing his arms over his face. 'Damn it. My eyes are falling out. There's nothing out there, old chap. Nothing at all. We're going to die. That's it and all about it.'

Connor made no comment but stared silently ahead of their surprisingly sturdy vessel.

He got out the lighter. There wasn't much fuel left, but perhaps it might be enough to attract attention. With that in mind he lit the lighter, stood up and began waving it above his head. 'For Christ's sake, come and rescue us!'

Harry looked up at him. 'What are you doing?'

'Light travels a long way at night when you're at sea. Somebody might see us.'

'It's a false hope, old chap, and only a small lighter.' Harry's voice cracked with dryness when he laughed.

'It was my own angel gave it to me.'

'Then I should hold onto it, old boy. We'll be meeting with a few more before very long if we go on like this.'

The lighter went out, but Connor remained standing, his eyes narrowed and sudden hope rising in his breast. 'I saw a light.'

'You're hallucinating. We've had it.'

'Like hell we have! Come on. Use your hands. Start paddling.'

Hearing unmistakable urgency in Connor's voice, Harry struggled onto his knees and began using his hands as paddles on one side of their raft, Connor doing the same on the opposite side. Although he knew that their efforts weren't likely to improve their speed by much, Connor thought it might keep Harry focused and help boost their jaded morale.

By the time dawn broke, their shoulders felt as hard as granite and their arms were shaking with tiredness. Their biggest worry was that the water that had gathered in the belly of the door was no more than an inch deep.

A day and a half went by when all they had to eat was the last half of the last fish.

'Come on, flying fish,' Harry shouted across the water.

Connor rubbed the nape of his neck where his aching muscles had knotted, hard and sharp. His eyes were sore from staring into the darkness but he willed himself to keep looking, scared that if he glanced away, he might miss something.

'Are you sure you saw a light?'

'Yes. There's something ahead of us. Wish I had a pair of binoculars.'

'I'll look too, old man, just in case you miss something.'

Harry was on all fours, peering ahead as dawn pushed back the darkness.

Half an hour of the encroaching dawn and Harry finally agreed with him. 'There is something! I'm sure I can see a hump of land.' He dragged himself into a sitting position and gazed straight ahead. 'How far do you think that is?'

Connor calculated. A sailor had once told him that the horizon was twenty miles away. The current was fast-moving, four knots at least, perhaps even six. He opted for five. 'Another day. We'll take it in turns to paddle. I'll go first.'

By nightfall the last of the fish was gone and no other fish had obliged them by jumping on board. What water they hadn't managed to store in the mug had evaporated.

'So close yet so far,' said Harry, as he slumped back after taking his turn to paddle.

'See?' Connor pointed. 'Closer. Look. There's a light.'

By the time Harry looked it had gone. 'I'm tired of looking.' He sounded fed up.

'Look, damn you!' shouted Connor, his patience running out. He grabbed a handful of Harry's filthy hair and thrust his head round so he was facing forward.

Harry blinked, then wiped the salt from his eyes. 'There's a light.'

'Is it moving?'

'No.'

'Then it's not a light from a fishing boat.'

The light blurred into mist as dawn approached in a

pale beige sky laced with indigo. The light was gone. In its place a mauve shape divided the sea from the sky, closer than the horizon, its colour changing from pale to deeper mauve the closer they got. The current was taking them there.

'One more day,' whispered Connor, his mouth parched, his face blistered.

They paddled furiously, their hands wrinkled and sore from continued immersion in salt water. Slowly the land mass, the island they hoped would be unoccupied, came closer.

'I wish I could tell what island it is by the shape of those hills, but I can't. If it's deserted, all well and good. If not, that's good too.'

'But if the Japs are there we could be shot.'

'Don't be a pessimist. Look on the bright side and believe it's unoccupied – or if it is occupied, pray that the Americans have taken it.'

'And in the meantime?'

Connor stopped paddling. He looked at the water. 'Let's leave the sea to get us there. We need to preserve our strength now. There could be obstacles to overcome. We might need to climb rocks to get ashore. We might need to swim. So get some sleep and we'll explore afresh tomorrow. Tonight we get some rest.'


As it always does in the tropics, night fell like the black back curtain of a splendid theatre, blocking out the sun and the blueness of the sky just as it would blot out the hand-painted scenery.

Some hours later, Connor woke, aware that something had changed. Hungry, thirsty and fatigued, he eased himself into a sitting position, his eyes narrowed and his ears alert to the sound that had awoken him. He gave Harry's shoulder a shake. 'Harry. Wake up. Do you hear that? Harry!'

Groggily Harry propped himself on his elbows and listened. 'Thunder? Faraway thunder?'

'Surf.'

Connor shook his shoulder again, joyfully this time. 'Surf! It's the bloody surf we're hearing, which means it's running onto a beach.'

'What if it's surf crashing over rocks?'

'No, damn it, no. You're a pessimist and that's for sure, Harry Gracey. Put a picture of a golden beach in your mind and that's what it will be.'

Harry shrugged. 'The power of thought? Well, I've heard of the power of prayer, so why not?'

Hours later, the palm trees bordering the beach were turning from black to grey as they came more clearly into view.

Connor was suddenly agitated. 'We need to get ashore before it's light. Start paddling. As soon as we're close enough, we go over the side and swim.'

'Connor, an officer is only as good as his sergeant, and

you're the best. I'm the officer. I should have been the one making the decisions and giving the orders.'

'Orders be buggered.'

Ribbons of surf spread like dirty lace across the surface of the water, moving inexorably to the land.

At a point about two hundred yards from the beach, they slid quietly into the ocean and struck out for the land, finally dragging themselves ashore, their chests heaving with exhaustion.

Harry raised his head. 'Do you think there might be a welcome party of the Japanese persuasion?'

'We need to hide until we've had a good look round.'

Legs weak from their long days at sea, they half staggered, half crawled over the warm white sand and into the dense vegetation just beyond the fringe of beachside palms. Among the greenery, shaded by the palms, they fell onto a mossy bed and slept.


Connor woke when Harry shoved something weighty into his chest. 'Here. Breakfast. A coconut. One each. I've made holes with my penknife. Forgot I'd tucked it into my pocket. I knew being a Boy Scout would one day come in useful.'

Connor grabbed it with both hands, tilted his head back and poured the milk into his mouth.

'I didn't even have to climb to pick it,' crowed Harry. 'There's a few scattered around. Should keep us going for now until we go inland and find a village willing to feed us.'

'Let's get our strength first.'

'Now, now, old boy. It's my turn to be in charge and I say we go and take a look around. We need to have some idea of where we are. Who knows? That current may have brought us to Northern Australia.'

'No chance.'

'I suppose that is wishful thinking. Still, might be some way of getting there from here – borrowing a fishing boat perhaps.'

They drank the milk of three coconuts each, then proceeded to smash them open on a sharp rock and eat the flesh.

Connor peered up at the sky. 'Looks like rain.'

'Nonsense,' said Harry, narrowing his eyes as he followed suit. 'Just puffballs.'

A little later, the tropical downpour washed every vestige of salt from their bodies, and if they'd had the strength they would have danced in it.

The lazy surf that had brought them ashore now swept up the beach in angry heaps.

'No fishing today,' Harry said glumly, coughed and spat a mixture of salt water and blood onto the ground. 'My chest is painful. My mother told me to look after my chest. Should have listened,' he said, smiling ruefully. He was joking, but Connor knew he was worried.

He studied the rising water. If this was an atoll then

there was a chance of it being buried by the sea almost as quickly as it had risen. It might still be Bali, but there was no way of knowing.

They stayed in their hiding place for another night, listening to the storm as it thundered overhead, soaked by the water running in rivulets from drooping palm leaves.

The following day dawned clear. The sea had calmed, the water now sweeping ashore with less vigour.

Failing to secure the scattered coconuts prior to the storm proved a mistake. More had been torn from the trees, but the sea swirling up onto the beach had taken them. There was only enough for immediate use and no surplus to take with them into the interior of the island.

Hand on his chest, Harry coughed and spat.

'Well?' He looked at Connor. 'What do you think? Stay here or explore?'

'The sea will be rough for at least another day, so no fishing for our supper. I think we need to find civilisation and food other than coconuts – if there is any.'

The vegetation they'd found pleasantly reviving grew more sparse and the rain had turned the firm earth into a viscous slop.

They struggled to trudge through it. Sometimes their knees gave out and their muscles ached. When their limbs screamed for rest, they fell onto their hands and knees or even their bellies, forced to use their elbows to propel themselves forward.

The mud cooled their sore skin, seeping into the cavities where once they'd had flesh.

Harry fell face down so he was almost breathing mud. 'I think I could sleep in this stuff.' His voice was muffled.

'Don't be ridiculous.'

'At least it's soft. Like cream.'

'You're going soft in the bloody head, man.'

'Watch it, Sergeant Major. That's insubordination. I'm the senior officer. Remember?'

Connor didn't laugh. He was too weak for that. They'd been starved, beaten and tortured for so long, they were not like men any longer, their flesh almost gone, nothing but the skeleton remaining – but against all the odds, they were still alive.

'On. We have to go on. On, Harry. Come on. Shift yourself.'

High above, monkeys capered in the treetops, stopping to look down at them and scream their warnings.

'I envy them,' said Connor. 'They're free, athletic and noisy.'

The two men could not be noisy. Despite the jungle foliage, noise travelled fast and was best left to the monkeys. At least they had the choice of coming to the ground or climbing into the trees.

The light began to fade at the same time as their hunger came back to gnaw at their shrunken stomachs.

Harry lifted his head and sniffed the air, like a dog on the scent of a bitch, though sex was the last thing on his mind. 'I smell a village.'

Connor raised his head and did the same.

Limbs clicking into place, like those of old men, they staggered to their feet, each grasping the shoulder of the other. Hope renewed their failing energy. Bedraggled and caked with mud, they moved slowly through the twilight, screeched at by macaques, bitten by myriad insects, moths fluttering blindly into their faces.

Dark forest behind them, they emerged into a clearing, their hopes leaping at the sight of children playing, a handsome woman with a baby strapped to her back. On seeing the two men, the children ran to their startled mothers who looked up from their cooking pots, their faces glossy with moisture. Others shouted and screamed, older children running into the village huts and between them into the greenery beyond.

Drawn by the cries of alarm, men filtered into the clearing from wherever they had been. One man, grey, wrinkled and elderly, stepped proud of the others. Holding his head high, the headman gazed at them, a slight frown needling his forehead in pencil-thin furrows.

Harry crumpled to his knees, pressed his palms together and begged for rice. Connor remained standing, swaying slightly, shoulders hunched, arms limp at his sides. He would have crumpled too if he hadn't forced himself to imagine a coat hook between his shoulder blades that was holding him upright.

The tense atmosphere dissipated, long brown hands beckoned them forward, invited them to sit, gave them water. Bowls of rice, with a little fruit and fish, appeared, then more coconuts, which had been hollowed out and contained fresh water. Thanking their hosts with clasped hands, their bowed heads drew friendly smiles from soft brown faces.

That night they rested, sleeping on bare earth that, under the circumstances, was as comfortable as a feather bed. Being close to one of the cooking fires was a luxury, the dying embers warming their tired bones and heating their ragged loincloths so that they steamed.

Harry was staring into the fire and smiling. 'If Heaven is like this, then I'm all for going there,' he murmured, his eyes half closed.

Connor didn't answer. He was staring up at the stars and thinking of those he knew who were experiencing the same starry night. He wished Harry would shut up about Heaven. He'd heard enough of that kind of talk from the priests back in Ireland.

'Can I remind you of that favour I asked you a while ago? Get me home. In pieces if you have to. And I'll do the same for you. Mind you, I don't intend going home any time soon. I think I'd like to stay here.'

'But you still want your ashes taken back? Even if you think you've found Paradise?'

'It's a family thing. Anyway, I won't need my body and its many amazing attributes when I'm dead, will I?'

Connor made himself comfortable, closed his eyes and prepared to sleep.

'I wonder where we are.'

'For the moment I don't care. In the morning I'll ask if the Japanese Army is hereabouts.'

Feeling warmer and more content than they had for days, they closed their eyes against the night, but the nightmares were still in their heads – the slaughter they'd seen, the privations they'd endured.

A hand shook Connor's shoulder and the dream was dispelled.

'Quick. You hide. Quick. Japanese.'

'Harry. The bastards are here.'

Harry didn't need a second urging.

People were rushing in all directions. There was screaming and crying all round, hurrying feet, mothers with babies in their arms, men looking confused – peaceful men who were farmers not fighters.

Although still feeling the after-effects of their voyage, fear straightened their limbs.

Supporting each other got them halfway to the edge of the village before Harry erupted in a coughing fit that bent him double. 'Go. You can run faster than me.'

'I won't do that.'

'Get going. I'm right behind you.'

In the surge of frightened villagers attempting to escape, Connor found himself running into the thick greenery they'd tripped out of earlier in the evening.

When he looked round, Harry had gone in the other direction.

He was faced with a choice: run back across the compound or stay where he was.

Figures seemed to be milling beneath a hut. Harry was among them. The huts were set on stilts above the ground, away from snakes and vermin.

Was it his imagination, or were the milling humans diminishing?

Minute by minute, the figures became fewer until they had gone. He guessed then that the wily villagers, who had experienced the enemy raids before, had a hiding place beneath the hut.

Making himself as small as possible, he melted into the vegetation and watched unseen as hordes of bayonet-wielding Japanese flooded into the clearing, kicking at the cooking fires and pots, killing the dogs that still barked and harried.

A few villagers were caught in the open. The sound of gunfire mingled with cordite and blood.

He kept low and still, eyes closed. He heard somebody speaking, then laughter.

Being careful not to give himself away, he parted the bushes and peered through. His heart sank.

The soldiers were bending down, looking beneath the hut where the hiding place was situated, laughing and pointing – and doing something else.

An order was snapped by the officer in charge, a

thickset man with round glasses. A number of soldiers fumbled with something fastened to their belts.

Grenades.

The explosions blew the soldiers backwards and bits of bodies flew through the air then fell in lumps, thudding as they hit the ground.

He wanted to scream in horror, but all he could manage was a silent retch.

Flames engulfed most of the huts. Nobody came running when the soldiers left. He found himself feeling glad that the dogs had been killed. Dead meat was dead meat and they would have feasted for days on the human remains scattered across the ground.

Unable to look any longer, he tore his eyes away. If he kept looking, remembering the details, he would go insane. He closed his eyes, placed his hands over his ears and rocked backwards and forwards, like a child trying to console itself.

By the time dawn came, his head was still buried between his knees, but he sat as still as a tombstone in a silent graveyard. He had no idea how long he remained in the strange limbo, his mind a blank and the world nothing but a void that he wished would never be real again.

*Harry is gone.*

*Harry is gone.*

*Harry is gone.*

*Harry is gone.*

He rose slowly from behind the bush that had screened him and kept him safe.

A fire was blazing in the middle of the compound. He recognised the village elder, heard a frail wailing of men and women alike. They were all gathered around the fire, throwing on more wood, pushing at it with long sticks in an effort to encourage more heat.

The fire was wide and sprawling, unlike the earlier ones, above which had hung cooking pots. This had trellises of wooden stakes over it, which he recognised as a funeral pyre. The bits of bodies were being burned.

He sat there, thinking of Harry. Only last night his senior officer and friend had said this place was his idea of Heaven, which, after all they'd been through, was a reasonable enough observation.

*Take my ashes home to my mother.*

Ashes.

He heard the roaring of flames and saw the fire was burning more fiercely now.

Later in the day as the flames began to die, the ashes were raked from the fire.

How was he supposed to know which ashes were Harry's among the heap from the bodies that had been burned?

*You won't know.*

But his mother. I've to take his ashes to his mother.

*And she won't know either. Nobody will know.*

The villagers understood and gave him a blue and white jar with a lid.

He stared at the cold ashes that didn't just belong to Harry but to everybody who had died in the explosion.

He sat by those ashes for some time trying to come to terms with what had happened. It would be a long while before he could – if ever.

As night began to fall and the daytime horror became cloaked in darkness, he used his bare hands to fill the jar, his tears running into his beard. When the jar was full he held up his trembling hands before his face and whispered Harry's name.

More body pieces were found among the vegetation. The villagers attempted to relight the fire, but their movements were listless, worn out by despair and the effort of making the main fire.

Connor got the lighter out from within his loincloth. He hoped it would light, its fuel somewhat diminished. He clicked it three times before it sparked then put it to the dried grass piled beneath wood and body parts.

The flames grew. Smoke rose.

Connor looked at the lighter, the Chinese characters on the bottom that probably spelled out the name of Kim Pheloung. It wasn't him he was thinking of but the raven-haired woman who had given it to him. He recalled singing 'Star of the County Down' when she'd been in the bar, a song about an Irish girl with chestnut hair. He'd seen her raven hair, her grey eyes, and her image replaced that of the girl in the song. If they both survived he would find her. Returning Harry's ashes to his mother was the promise he'd made to his best friend. Returning the lighter to Rowena Rossiter was a promise to himself.

# 22

The house in Shanghai was larger than the one in Kowloon and, as Kim had indicated, older and built in a grand style. It, too, was protected by an outer wall enclosing one compound and an inner wall enclosing a second.

The outer wall bounded the ancillary compound where the car was parked, the gates wide enough to take transport. The next gate set into the interior wall was what the Chinese called a 'moon gate', a circular opening as round as the moon and offset out of line with the main gate and the main entrance to the house. The crooked path between the doors was meant to prevent a demon entering the house.

The pagoda-style roof of luminescent blue tiles ended in great swallowtails at each outer corner, its dugong rafters painted black above white pillars, green lanterns and red walls.

Inside was cool and smelt of spices, ebony and rosewater. Women in silk robes and traditional garb bowed deeply as they passed.

Rowena held Dawn's hand as they entered, aware of the child's innocence, her face lit with wonder as she eyed the high ceilings, the rich furnishings, the dragons that girdled the base of the roof.

Dawn looked around her wide eyed and touched her mother's thigh, grasping a handful of her dress.

'It's all right, darling. We're safe now.'

'Yes,' declared Kim. 'A palace compared to where you were before. My palace.'

'Or a prison,' murmured Rowena, which earned her a sharp look from her host.

'It will be far more comfortable than where you were.'

'Yes. You're right. I'm very grateful to you.'

He clapped his hands. 'You will be even more grateful. I have a surprise for you. You will be much pleased.'

A figure she recognised stepped forward from among the other women, dressed traditionally in dark blue, a colour deemed suitable for a servant.

Luli bowed, then raised her head and smiled shyly. 'Doctor.'

Kim frowned. 'Not doctor. You call her madam. She is no longer a doctor while she is under my roof.'

Luli blanched and lowered her eyes.

'She will be the child's nurse,' Kim announced.

Luli raised her eyes, smiled shyly at Rowena and then at Dawn.

Dawn smiled back.

'You will take the child to see the carp. Now.'

Luli repeated the instruction as though it were natural for his command to take root, like a Buddhist prayer.

Remembering the scene on the boat Rowena was momentarily compelled to cling to her daughter's hand.

Kim gently prised away her fingers. 'My dear, Luli will take the child.' He smiled as he said it, then leaned closer so that only she could hear: 'Or there will be no child.'

A sense of helplessness fell over her. Reassuring herself that Luli had always been kind, she let go of her daughter's hand and watched her toddle after the Han girl.

'What did you mean?' she asked him.

'I am not a brute, my dear, but if you insist, I will return both of you to the camp. You have a better chance of survival here, where the child will be well cared-for and so will you. You have endured horrors and have now returned to a higher standard of living. The child has gone through a period of neglect. She needs to recover. She also deserves a nurse.'

The way he spoke was meant to reassure, but she couldn't help thinking that he'd meant what he'd said as a threat. Yet why should he?

'You are overtired and weakened by your experiences.'

Taking hold of her shoulders, he turned her to face him. When he smiled she forgot what he was.

'Soon I will visit you, but only when you are fully recovered from your ordeal.' His fingers stroked her tangled hair back from her face. 'Trust me, my dear, and all will be well.'

★

Her clothes were burned and replaced with sumptuous robes and dresses, tunics and trousers, mostly in silk, some in fine wool and cashmere. Her hair was washed, a bath was filled, and oils, creams and Western-style make-up were put at her disposal.

She asked him if she could see Dawn more than once a day. 'I could do with the company. There's nothing else for me to do.'

'You are still feeling tired?'

She agreed that she was.

'You may be carrying some illness from the camp.'

'I'm a doctor. I would know if I was.'

'Ah! Physician, heal thyself. Listen to what I say. It is not an ordeal to be taken lightly. You need good food, drink and medicines to make you whole again. And rest. Plenty of rest. The child is being taken care of. You will rest and regain your strength. You are very much thinner than when I first saw you.'

To some extent she had to concede that he was right about her physical state. She was far thinner than she had been, her hair less glossy, and at first her stomach rebelled at the food she was offered.

Kim was especially attentive and appeared to have

thought of everything. 'I have given instructions that you are given only plain food, which will not upset your stomach. We also have a cure to purge any parasites from your body.'

She had to agree that what he said was only basic common sense. A number of her fellow prisoners had suffered from parasitic infections. She'd done her best to treat them, but she'd lacked both Eastern and Western medicine, so her task had been difficult.

Once she was subject to the new food regime, she found that she slept the whole night through, but woke in the morning only slowly. The glossiness returned to her hair, her skin cleared, and her nails were less brittle.

The truth was there for her to face. Sickness and death stalked and claimed those weakened by lack of food, fresh water and medicine. There was no telling when she might have succumbed to disease and ended up in the ground where so many she'd known were already buried. Gradually she had to concede that Kim had saved their lives and did not deserve her condemnation. All the same, she felt terribly alone and persisted in asking to see Dawn more than once a day.

'I've been alone all day. I would like to dine with my daughter.'

'You need to rest.'

'I am rested.'

'You saw your daughter this morning?'

'Yes.'

'Then tonight I will dine with you. Dress yourself as though we were going out to dine at the Savoy in London. Can you do that?'

'Yes,' she said, a sudden wave of happiness flooding her. 'I look forward to it.'

She felt almost girlish as she made herself ready, as though about to embark on her very first date. It seemed an age since she had not been working on a ward or living from hand to mouth in a prisoner-of-war camp.

The light was fading when he kept his promise, sweeping into her room followed by a servant with a tray of food, which was set down on a black-japanned table inset with figures made from pale shades of mother-of-pearl.

The servant dismissed, he flung his robe out behind him and sat beside her on the wide divan.

At first her eyes were drawn to his bare chest, but by lowering her eyelids perhaps it didn't seem as though she was looking.

Kim appeared not to notice. He handed her a pair of chopsticks. 'I recommend the fish. It is very good for you.'

'You're right. It looks delicious, but I've never been very good with chopsticks.'

'Then I will do it for you.'

With delicate precision he picked out small portions of fish and fed her, as a father might a child.

She insisted she could manage the wine glass herself, but still he held it for her, the rich liquid seeping into her mouth and tingling on her tongue. 'That's a whole glass,' she said.

'Just one. You can manage two. It is French. A fine vintage. Here.'

The wine nudged her memory, reminding her of a family holiday when they'd driven through French vineyards and she'd taken her first sip of wine. Such a long time ago but fondly remembered. The thought, like the wine, took her back to a time before she'd experienced the horrors of war and in her dreams there were no ugly faces but a blue sky and rows of vines ripening in the French sunshine.

That night she sensed his shadow falling over her bed and feared what might happen next. Her heart raced. She squeezed her eyes shut and waited for him to make his presence known.

His shadow receded and she heard the door closing. One half of her was relieved. The other wanted him to come back, but it was too late. The moment of decision was over but she knew there would come a time when it would have to be made. Resistance is futile, she thought, smiling as a line from a novel she'd once read sprang into her mind. In fact, she wasn't sure she would resist. She'd only know that when the time finally came.

The routine of dining together prevailed, and as she began to know him better, her initial distrust vanished. She was beginning to enjoy these moments.

Each morning Dawn was brought to her. On occasion they had breakfast together. Rowena noted that the little girl was filling out, thanks to the better food, and the same was happening to her.

The days seemed long but she had taken note of Kim's advice to rest and regain her strength. With each day she found herself looking forward to the evening when they would dine together, although she had still not mastered the art of using chopsticks. Not that she was in any rush to do so. She liked things the way they were.

She laughed when he used the chopsticks to tease her, offering food then taking it away. He did the same with the wine, passing the glass under her nose, then retrieving it.

After half of the second glass had been consumed, he held the wine equidistant between them at face level, his expression serene. A sudden smile flickered at one corner of his mouth, so he looked almost quizzical.

'Do you want more wine?'

She smiled. 'Yes.'

'Very much?'

'Yes, please. It's very good wine.'

'Is it?' He arched his eyebrows.

'I've just told you it is.'

'What will you do for one more taste of it?'

Unsure how she should answer, she tilted her head to one side. 'What do you want me to do?'

A slow smile lit his face. He said nothing but raised the glass and tipped it against his chest. The little wine spilled from the glass trickled down the crease between his well defined chest muscles.

Without a moment's hesitation, she leaned across and licked the wine. She was lost. Her tongue travelled on down, her senses revelling in his scent and the slight saltiness of his body.

She felt his hands peeling off her robe, but couldn't have stopped him even if she wanted to. And she didn't want to. What he was offering was sex on her terms. He had invited her to indulge. She had not been forced and that in itself was a kind of healing.

The robe fell in a silken heap leaving her shoulders bare. He brought her head back up so they were facing. His lips were cool on her lips and her shoulders. His hands cupped her breasts, his fingers gently caressing her nipples.

The divan was wide enough to take both of them, their robes floating to the floor.

Nothing about sex with him bore any resemblance to that other time, those other men, whom he had killed.

She'd often considered his admission of having killed those men, and not once had she felt sorry for them. They had violated her, left her pregnant and wary of ever trusting a man again. Kim might have been a criminal, but she could forgive that because he'd made her feel whole again and for that she was eternally grateful.

He ran a hand down her back caressing one buttock then the other. 'You are regaining some weight.'

'Too much?' she asked, in mock disappointment.

'Just enough,' he responded, both hands now resting on her behind.

She felt no shame at doing this with him, no fear of getting pregnant because somehow she expected he'd taken care of everything. That was the kind of man he was. She had no need to worry about anything, just to receive the gentleness of his body, the warmth of his breath, like the sound of a waterfall against her ear.

They lay there afterwards, his arms around her, his face buried in her hair.

'The child. Tell me how it happened.'

Rowena froze. 'I don't want to.'

'I understand. How did you feel once the child was born?'

She closed her eyes, pushing the painful memory of rape deep into her subconscious. And then she told him, unburdening her soul in a way she'd never done before. 'I didn't want her. How could I? It wasn't her fault she was born but every time I looked at her I saw them – their faces. I know you had them killed, but it doesn't make any difference. It happened and is still in my mind.'

'Do you still feel that way now?'

She frowned as she thought about it. 'I'm her mother. It's my duty to look after her.'

'That's not what I asked.'

'I would never want any harm to come to her.'

'I realise that. But it must be difficult.'

'It's better now.'

'You could have her adopted.'

'No. I couldn't do that. I've adjusted. Everything will be all right.'

His lips brushed her shoulder; his fingers fondled the nape of her neck. 'But each time you look at her you see them.'

As she squeezed her eyes shut, a tear seeped from one corner. 'Sometimes.'

'Come here.'

She rolled underneath. He rolled on top, his exertion as gentle as it was before.

In the morning he was gone.

The following morning, she felt guilty, not so much because of the lovemaking but because she'd told him how she'd felt about her daughter. He'd promised to dine with her that evening. She hoped also there would be more sex. She hadn't realised how much she'd missed it.

Dawn had adapted well to her new life. Dressed in a silk pyjama suit that echoed an adult ensemble, she bubbled with excitement, trying to form words like fish and monkey, the latter tied to a long rope in the room she shared with Luli.

Rowena's mind wandered as she listened to the child's babble, shivering at the thought of him, tingling at the experienced and gentle way in which he'd touched her until she felt as though her body was bursting into flame.

Thinking of the undoubted skill of his lovemaking brought a question to mind.

She asked Luli the whereabouts of the other women she had seen when first entering the house. 'I see them in the garden sometimes and thought I heard children laughing.'

'That is what your daughter has been telling you. She has been playing with the other children. Did you not see them outside?'

Rowena had to admit that she had, but had presumed them to be servants' children. 'Are they here in this house?'

'They have their own quarters. Not with you.'

A thought entered her head. 'Do they live in a harem?'

'I do not know this word.'

'A seraglio.'

'This word is also unknown to me.'

'Do they have a separate dining hall?'

'They have meal wherever they want. Outside when sunny, inside when rainy or cold.'

'Are they all servants?'

Luli blushed. 'Not servants.'

'So what are they?'

'*Pinfei.*'

'*Pinfei*? What does that mean?'

'Not wives. *Pinfei.*'

'Concubines. Am I a concubine?'

Luli looked away, picking up a red silk tassel and inviting Dawn to reach for it. 'I do not know.'

She frowned, poured herself water. Somehow the whole idea of Kim having taken her to be a concubine seemed quite ludicrous, the stuff of cheap novels. She had felt great joy in their lovemaking, but now it was as if she'd let herself down.

She took a sip of water and thought about how she was feeling. I want him again, she thought. I want to be his above all others. Now if that isn't the stuff of romantic fiction, I don't know what is.

She waited for him that night, sitting in a loose black robe, the food on the table, the male servant who waited on them every night standing by.

He didn't come. On the last occasion he'd been late for a meal, in Hong Kong, he'd swept the food onto the floor declaring it unfit to pass his lips, and blazed with anger when she'd admitted eating some sweetmeats.

Even though her stomach was rumbling, she ate nothing, wanting to please him, wanting him to feed her again and afterwards make love to her.

The candles burned low. The lanterns in the courtyard outside attracted myriad moths and still there was no sign of him. Ordering the food removed, she took to her bed, staring through the darkness, her ears tuned for any sound that heralded his return.

Alone in the darkness she ran her hands down her body, a feeble alternative to having the hard body of a man who exuded danger and desire in equal measures. The mix was exciting and, despite all that had happened, he made her feel as though she was his and his alone.

The next morning, breakfast arrived, and because she'd had nothing the night before, she ate hungrily. Once bathed and dressed, she waited for Luli to bring Dawn to her.

Time passed but they didn't come.

On hearing the sound of chattering children out in the courtyard she looked out, saw Dawn with the other children, marching in crocodile formation and disappearing out of the gate. Luli was one of the women accompanying them.

Swiftly donning a pair of slippers and an extra shawl, she headed for the door and found it locked.

'Let me out!'

Her shouts and the hammering of her fists brought no response.

She went back to the window. The courtyard was empty now but she thought she heard the sound of a vehicle and was immediately filled with dread.

'Where are they taking her?'

Just when she was considering climbing out of the window, even though it was too narrow to squeeze through, she saw Luli running back into the courtyard and looking as though she was coming her way.

When she waved, Luli waved back. At the same time she heard the bar being slid back on the outside of the door and within minutes there was Luli, her cheeks pink from running.

'Where's Dawn?'

'Gone to mission. To school.'

'She's too young for school.'

'Nursery. The mission has a nursery and Dawn wanted to go. She is happy with other children.'

'But why didn't you bring her to me first?'

'No time.'

Exasperated, Rowena didn't press her to say why there had been no time. 'Then I'll see her when she gets back. You will let me know when she returns?'

Although Luli nodded her eyes evaded Rowena's.

'Is it the same mission school where you went?'

Luli nodded. 'Yes.'

The sudden sound of footsteps came from overhead and made her look up. 'The other women?' She refrained from saying 'concubines' but Luli knew whom she meant.

'Yes.'

'Sometimes I see them over there on that balcony. Are some of the children theirs?'

'Yes.'

'Can I meet these women?'

Luli blinked. 'I don't know.'

'Can you ask them if I may visit, or they may prefer to visit me? I promise I won't get you into trouble. I'm sure the *luoban* won't mind,' she added, seeing fear on Luli's face.

Luli still seemed undecided.

'Can you ask them? For me?'

It was not a very enthusiastic nod, but at least she'd agreed.

Like some latterday Mother Goose, she followed Luli out into the courtyard holding back to wait for approval.

Luli's expression was strained as though she was still undecided.

'Go on,' whispered Rowena.

A final decision and Luli was running up the opposite staircase and along the balcony on which three of the women had appeared. She saw them bend their heads, then eye each other in amazement as Luli explained.

Three white faces and heads surmounted by pillows of glossy black hair turned to look across the courtyard in her direction, then at each other before nodding in unison.

Rowena followed Luli across the courtyard and up the steps. At the top she slid back the retaining bar.

Their rooms were unremarkable in that they were as beautiful as her own with panelled walls, ebony fretwork and a painted dragon slithering across the ceiling.

She returned the women's welcoming bows and smiled. Two of the women smiled shyly back at her. The third, slightly taller than the others and exceptionally beautiful, retained a guarded look and did not attempt to rise from her divan.

Rowena kept smiling. 'Would you tell them my name, Luli?'

'They already know it.'

'Oh. Then perhaps I could know their names.'

The two who had smiled were introduced as Sai Po

and Dai Lee. The haughtier woman was named Koto.

'I'm very pleased to meet you all.'

The opening formalities over, she accepted Sai Po's invitation to sit down.

Nobody offered her tea. Their discomfort was almost palpable, as was hers. To alleviate the situation, she fixed on the pink flower pinned in Sai Po's hair. 'That's very pretty.'

Luli translated.

Sai Po blushed and raised her hand to stroke the bloom, as though she'd forgotten it was there.

She noticed Dai Lee was rubbing her ink-stained fingers with a cloth. 'Have you been writing?'

'Dai Lee cannot write.'

'Can she read?'

Luli shook her head. 'No. Not allowed.'

'Tell them I think they are very pretty.'

Once her comment was translated, the two women smiled bashfully and nodded in a gesture of thanks.

The third woman continued to stare at her, her stunningly beautiful eyes larger and more feline than those of the other two. Out of the three she was the most beautiful, yet there was something in those eyes and the tight red lips that made her think Koto would rather she had not come.

After exchanging a few words, Sai Po and Dai Lee seemed to come to a sudden decision. Whatever the conclusion was, they mentioned it to Koto, who jerked her chin in agreement, her steely gaze remaining fixed on Rowena's face.

Sai Po went to the door and pulled across a piece of wood, barring entry. Rowena and Luli watched as the two women went to the back wall, which was panelled in squares of red and green and held in place by black framework. Between them the women removed a panel consisting of four squares, two red and two green, revealing a small aperture. Placing the panel carefully to one side, they knelt down and reached into the revealed cavity.

'Luli, what are they doing?'

'It is a secret. We must not tell.'

Luli got up and went to take a closer look. Rowena thought about doing the same but Koto's frown stilled her.

Having completed their task, the two came back carrying rolled-up pieces of paper, making small comments to each other before unfurling them one by one, laying each in front of Rowena and inviting her to comment.

One was an exquisite watercolour of floating water lilies beneath drooping willow trees in front of far blue mountain peaks. The other was of two figures running from a pagoda to cross a bridge, more weeping willows on the other side and two birds that looked like swallows swooping in the sky.

Each woman said something, pointed at the paper, then at themselves, patting their chests.

Rowena realised why Dai Lee had been wiping stains

from her fingers. She had been painting and the works of art had been hidden before she'd arrived – their secret hobby that Kim did not know about. Sai Po claimed the water lilies and Dai Lee the two lovers running across the bridge to be turned into swallows or bluebirds on the other side – a story repeated on dinner plates set on many British tables, thought Rowena. 'They're beautiful. Tell them so, Luli. They're beautiful.'

The two women basked in her praise, their clear porcelain cheeks suffused with pink.

Koto had said nothing, sitting on the divan as though she was made of a rare pale jade.

Having won over the others, Rowena decided it was time to break through Koto's prickly manner. 'And you, Koto? Do you also paint?'

Before Luli had a chance to interpret, Koto snapped an order. Luli started then leaped to obey, getting down on her hands and knees and groping inside the secret cavity.

The expression now on Koto's face was less hostile, instead seeming to challenge Rowena to dare criticise whatever she was about to see.

Clearly Luli wasn't moving fast enough: Koto snapped at her again.

Dust clinging to her hair, her face red with effort, Luli came back with yet another roll of paper. Rowena prepared herself for yet another delightful, though predictable painting of flowers, trees and birds. Koto's work took her by surprise and she leaned forward for a closer look. She found herself gazing at something very different indeed. Laid on the floor in front of her was what looked like a pictorial map of the kind that was done in Europe in the early middle ages. There was little in the way of writing, but plenty of detail – alleys, streets and a waterfront. A group of Chinese characters was painted in the most elegant calligraphy in the bottom right-hand corner. The pictures of flowers had been beautiful, but this was exquisitely executed and refined.

She raised her eyes. Koto was still sitting rigidly, like a cat: watchful and ready to pounce should she say the wrong thing. Rowena turned to Luli. 'Tell her this is glorious. I've never seen anything like it.'

Koto turned her head slightly as Luli interpreted Rowena's comments. Her expression seemed to soften and she spoke.

'It is a map of Shanghai as she remembers it,' Luli said.

'She was born there?'

'Yes. Until her parents sold her to a warlord when she was thirteen years old. He sold her to the *luoban*.'

'It's a work of art. Even I could find my way around Shanghai with a map like that.'

Whispered warnings ran from one woman to the next, Koto sounding more urgent than the others.

The paintings were returned speedily to their hiding place where, no doubt, the paints were also stored. The panel was reinserted and the door unbarred.

Tea was fetched, and although Koto was still not entirely at ease, she seemed satisfied that Rowena had meant what she'd said.

Through Luli she asked them why they hid their paintings.

'It is not allowed.'

'So what do they do all day?'

'Devise ways to entertain.'

Rowena frowned. 'Time must drag if they're not allowed to do anything else. And they can't read.'

Luli repeated her comments to the women. 'They are not allowed to read, but they do have a book.'

Koto pressed for an immediate interpretation. Once she knew what had been said, she tucked her hand under a cushion, brought out a book and gave it to her.

'Ah,' said Rowena, on seeing the title. 'They don't speak English.'

'Have you read this?' asked Luli. The others leaned forward, expectant interest alight in their eyes.

'Yes. A long time ago.'

It was *The War of the Worlds* by H. G. Wells.

'I brought it from the mission,' said Luli. 'The pastor and his wife knew English but didn't want too many people to speak it, especially a book like this. A Bible in English was acceptable, but not this.'

Rowena turned the book in her hands, noting the gilt swirls down the spine. She thought of the long hours alone in her room, waiting for a single hour in the morning with her daughter, some time at night with her lover, the anticipation of him coming either to dine or sleep with her building up throughout the day. She imagined these women did the same. The book would help pass the time.

Surely Kim wouldn't object to her reading. Just as she couldn't believe he would object to the women painting to pass their time.

'May I have it?'

'Yes. It is too difficult for me to read and translate to them. Anyway, they prefer stories about handsome princes, fairies and genies.'

'What about their children? They do have children?'

'Yes.'

'Do they live here with them?'

'Yes. This is the house of women. Only women and children are allowed here.'

'But why hide the paintings?'

'Women must do womanly things that do not tax their minds.'

'Like thinking,' murmured Rowena, under her breath.

'Sometimes Zu Mu comes here to search through their things.'

'Ah,' said Rowena, nodding. It seemed Kim had only recently ordered his grandmother to remain in Kowloon.

Luli was becoming agitated. 'The children will be home soon. We have to go.'

Her first inclination was to ask Luli to bring Dawn to her the minute she got back, but she refrained. Somebody, perhaps the cook, one of the men guarding the gate or even one of these sweet-faced women, might tell Kim. If this arrangement – having other children around her and going to school – made the little girl happy, there was no reason to alter it. Not for the first time Rowena felt guilty at relinquishing control over her daughter's life. There were still times when she looked at Dawn's pretty face and remembered how brutal her conception had been. Never would she forget those faces.

Before the door closed behind them, she saw Koto raising her feet onto the divan, an opium pipe cradled in her arms. 'I will not fall into that trap,' she muttered grimly. At least I'll have a book to read, she thought, as she made her way back across the courtyard clutching the handsome tome.

Within an hour of being back in her own room, she heard excited laughter as the children ran into the courtyard towards the carp pond. She smiled at the sight of her daughter's glossy head, her black hair falling around her face. A movement to one side drew her attention and there was Ching, the man on the boat whom she'd suspected of being about to toss her daughter into the sea.

Chilled, she ran to the door, meaning to go out and drag her daughter away regardless of what Kim might say when he found out.

Tug as she might, the door did not budge. Somebody had been ordered to bar it once she was back in her room.

It would do no good to shout. Nobody would come.

From behind a fretwork screen, her heart pounding, she eyed the view outside her window hearing the children's laughter as they ran around the pond, ornamental but also a source of food. Her fear lessened on seeing that Ching had disappeared. There was only Luli, Dai Lee and

Sai Po. In the midst of the excited babble, she heard her daughter singing 'Old MacDonald Had a Farm', which Luli had taught her.

Hearing a song in English brought back the times when she'd sung at the camp, and before when she'd sung with Connor. His features, especially his blue eyes, came easily to mind as did the sound of his voice and his Irish songs. She smiled at the thought of his singing, at Dawn's singing and also of the time immediately before their world had shattered. She remembered the sight of him asleep beneath the stars in the grounds of the hospital, an opium pipe cradled in his arm – just like Koto.

The food was prepared and she'd taken extra care in dressing to please him. Nine o'clock was again the designated time, so there she sat, waiting for him to come.

The food looked and smelt delicious, but when yet again he failed to appear, she did not eat, even though she was very hungry. He would come eventually.

Two hours went by. Without being ordered to do so, a serving man, wearing black satin and soft shoes, came and began clearing everything away.

It crossed her mind to grab something and gobble it before she went to bed, but she restrained herself. The thought of him coming to her bed reinforced her will. She wanted to please him and in doing so perhaps gain some small indulgences, time with the other women, with her daughter, a drive in the car, even to accompany him, though on reflection she might end up disliking him if she saw what he did at first hand.

She went to bed where, accompanied by the sound of crickets and caged birds, she read for a while, then followed the other women's example and hid the book.

She was disturbed by the sound of his footsteps, then the hush of silk garments falling to the floor as he removed his clothes. Her first inclination was to remark that he had been late in coming home, but she said instead, 'I've missed you.'

She waited for him to slide under the heavily embroidered silk eiderdown and enfold her in his arms and was disappointed when he remained on top of the bedding, his naked body glistening in the glow of the single lantern that was still alight.

'Have you eaten?'

'No. I was waiting for you.'

'Good.'

She wanted to ask whether he had eaten but held back because, deep down, she knew that he had.

His lips were cool on hers as he stroked her hair, fanning it on the pillow, like a great sunburst of blackness.

He heaved a great sigh against her hair but when he moved away she saw that his mouth was set in a grim line. 'What did you do with the book?'

'Book?'

He moved his hand, the weight of it against her windpipe, his fingers applying pressure in a light but ultimately lethal squeeze. 'The one they gave you.'

'It's in the clothes chest. I don't understand...'

'I did not say you could have a book.'

'Please...'

Her head slammed against the pillow when he let her go. Then he got off the bed and went to the clothes chest, took out the book and proceeded to tear out the pages. 'Just paper,' he said, as page after page fluttered to the floor.

In that one act, all her desire for him vanished.

'I want to read it.'

It was the wrong thing to say. The slap sent her flying back onto the bed.

His eyes remained fixed on her face, as though he had no desire for her body, only for her soul.

The realisation shook her. So did the fact that one of the three women who painted so beautifully had betrayed her. Perhaps Koto, who had given her the book and eyed her with such hostility.

He left her there with her cheek burning.

In the morning she awaited breakfast, but it didn't come. She awaited her prescribed visit from Dawn and Luli but they didn't appear.

Even before she tugged at the door to her room, she knew it wouldn't open. She was locked in without food or water, smoke from the burning pages of the book rising from a bronze brazier with dragon claw legs.

All that day she paced the room or lay down on the divan, nursing her sore face.

*War of the Worlds*. That's what had happened here.

Her predicament was as a consequence of war: war between the cultures of East and West, war now seething between her and the exotic man who, she thought, had cured her disgust with men, but who now had reignited it.

He was playing with her, like a child with a pet dog, one moment making it feel truly loved, then teasing it, scolding it and slowly bending it to his will. That, she decided, was what he wanted.

All day then all night without food or water. On the following morning her breakfast was brought by the silent man with the soft shoes, and even before he'd left the room, she snatched at the fruit and drank from the bowl of milky broth laced with honey. Then she fell into a deep sleep.

When she awoke the lights were lit outside, their glow diffused through the fretwork screens that had been closed from the outside therefore restricting her view of the courtyard and the rest of the house. The only movement she could discern was of the chrysanthemums nodding in the breeze, as if to say, 'I told you so.'

Food had been left on the low japanned table, sweetmeats, fruit and another bowl of the milky broth laced with honey.

Her hunger partly satiated, she ate only part of what had been left for her. Again she fell asleep, waking mid-morning to find the same fare waiting for her again. Although the outside shutters were still closed sunbeams darted through the intricate pattern, like golden rods lifting the gloom. A shadow seemed suddenly to prevent them entering. At first she thought more solid shutters had been closed and panicked at the thought of seeing no daylight at all.

Then she heard a faint sound. 'Psst.'

Struggling to her feet, she staggered to the window, her fingers hanging on to the patterned wood to keep her upright.

'Luli?'

'Are you all right, madam?'

'I feel drowsy.'

'Ah, yes.'

Ah, yes? What was that supposed to mean?

'How long have I been here?'

'Four days.'

She gave a little cry of alarm. Four days! Yet to her it seemed only half that. 'The others. Are they all right?'

'Yes. They were punished for allowing you to visit. Sai Po and Dai Lee handed over their drawings and Koto mentioned giving you a book.'

'And you? Were you punished for taking me there?'

'They beat the soles of my feet. It does not hurt too much. They said they were sorry afterwards. They did not want to do it.'

Luli was referring to the three women. Kim hadn't beaten her: he'd made them do it.

Meanwhile she was imprisoned.

'Where's Dawn?'

'At the mission.'

Rowena sighed with relief. It seemed her daughter was out of harm's way. 'How long am I to stay in my room?'

'I don't know.'

Sensing somebody was coming, Luli rushed away and Rowena dragged herself back to her bed.

Her head hurt, her throat was dry and her heart was pounding. Something about the room had changed. Something was there that had not been before.

The brazier, now cold and containing only ashes, was still there. Laid out on the window sill next to it was an opium pipe and plugs of the expensive, destructive drug on which Kim had made his fortune.

Overcome by an unfamiliar lethargy, she tried to get her thoughts in some order. There had to be a reason why she felt as she did. If Kim came to her in the night, she was not aware of it. Then why should he? What possible reason was there for wanting her to be here if it wasn't a mutual passion?

The following morning there was fruit and again the bowl of milky broth laced with honey.

She had already decided that her lethargy had to be due to what she was eating and drinking. Fruit was not a good vehicle for administering a sleeping draught or poison. The sweetmeats were a possibility, but the broth had to be the cause of her exhaustion.

Deciding her eating habits might be reported, she picked up the spoon as though she would eat the bowl's contents first. The glum-faced servant retreated.

Spitting out the sole spoonful she had eaten, she looked

for a way to make it seem as though she had finished the broth and rebuked herself for being a fool. She should have realised sooner that her food was being drugged.

'Now what?' she murmured. 'Plan,' came the immediate answer. 'You must plan this carefully.'

The dish must be empty of food. She looked round for somewhere to pour it. A tall jar, almost of human height and complete with a lid, occupied one corner. After scraping the contents of the bowl into it, she replaced the lid and ate the fruit.

It was half an hour or more before she heard the approach of shuffling footsteps. Faking sleep, she heard the things being gathered up, a pause as though the gatherer was studying her, perhaps making sure she was as near comatose as she usually was at this time of day.

She heard the door being closed. Once she was sure she was alone, she got up quietly but without thought of escape, not yet. The first thing she had to do was evaluate her chance of getting away, which was now her only option.

There wasn't much to see through the fretwork shutters, but she recalled most of the details before they'd been locked and barred against her. The suggestion of movement came from the upper floors where the three residents bobbed around on the balcony.

She recalled her visit to the kitchen and the wide opening in the southern part of the house, the moon door in the outer courtyard. Go through the first, then the moon door, and she would be almost free, but free to do what?

All she knew was that she was in a house on the periphery of Shanghai, but where would she go after that? The world was still at war. As far as she knew, Hong Kong was still occupied. Going back there would mean returning to the camp.

The harsh truth was that this was China and she was a foreigner. If it was just her escaping she might stand a chance, but she had Dawn to think of. She couldn't leave her behind. She just couldn't.

Kim disappeared for days on end, then reappeared, and when he did, she had to seem to be under the influence of whatever was added to the broth.

At the slightest sound from outside, she fell back onto her bed feigning unconsciousness. Everything depended on her keeping up the pretence of being drugged, her voice softly slurred, her head lolling as though her neck was made of rubber.

To her great relief he seemed persuaded, his fingers tracing lines across her brow. She was supposed to feel languorous, but she felt only revulsion.

'You need more rest. The child will not be brought to you any longer. She has a new mother.'

She wanted to protest that Dawn was her daughter and remembered Luli saying she was at the mission, where she should have been safe. But this new mother? Who was she?

Time was now of the utmost importance. She would have preferred more time to plan but that did not seem possible. She had to grab whatever opportunity came along.

He no longer made love to her when he came to her but he did try to persuade her to smoke the opium pipe. Each time she turned her head away, feigning weakness.

This appeared to exasperate him. 'You will learn it is best to obey me. Bow to me.'

She felt herself sliding onto the floor, his hands maintaining pressure on her shoulders. 'Bow to me.'

Pride and fear battled for her mind. Fear for her child won. She let herself slide, bowed to him, her head between his feet.

The jar was big enough to take a lot of the food she was pouring into it. Some of the evening meal had to follow, but it was more difficult to decide which dishes had been drugged and which were safe to eat.

She decided rice was the safest, and proved this when she gave some of the meaty sauce to one of the cats that prowled outside the window. The cat lay down and was soon sound asleep. The only problem was that she couldn't give it all the food because then it would die, which in itself might prove suspicious. That, too, had to go into the jar.

She thought through the consequences. The food would not be detected while the weather was cool but in warm weather the stench of rot might escape despite the lid.

Time dragged with nothing to do and no visits from either her daughter or him. At night her sleep was lighter than it had been with the drugged broth, which she guessed was being administered so that she took more easily to smoking opium. She supposed the other women had been through the same experience and pitied them.

The door was still locked. Nobody gained entry except for those servants who did not speak English.

She squeezed her eyes tightly shut, steeling herself. She'd do anything to regain access to her child. Only Luli could help her with that.

She braced herself when she heard him enter the room that night and felt a cool draught of air as he lifted the coverlet and studied her naked form.

To her relief the silk coverlet fell back over her body and she smelt the mix of fresh male sweat and sweet-scented body oil as his arm wound around her.

She wondered what would happen if she sat up and confronted him.

Whether he sensed she was not properly asleep, she didn't know, but the next morning there was only fruit and dried fish for breakfast. The room was bathed with light. The outer shutters had been removed.

The sound of laughter outside drew her attention. Dawn was dipping her hand into the carp pond, Luli beside her. Rowena washed and dressed quickly, in a green silk tunic and trousers, then sped outside.

Beaming with delight, she headed for Dawn, ready to hug her as she'd never hugged her before.

Luli grabbed her. 'Madam. Do not touch her. Bad things will happen if you touch her.'

Rowena frowned. 'What things?'

'The master will lock you away again if you do so. I am to tell you this. He gave me permission to bring her from the mission to say goodbye.'

'Goodbye?'

'That's what he said. She is to live at the mission.'

She was immediately bombarded with mixed emotions. On the one hand Dawn was her child. On the other, if she failed to escape Dawn would be safer at a Christian mission than she would under Kim's roof.

Luli leaned close and bowed her head. 'I have to tell you that you may now eat with the other women – if you want to.'

'Until the master decides otherwise,' she murmured, but accepted that this might be a defining moment.

Later she went with Luli to put Dawn down for her afternoon nap. Tears stung her eyes as she considered what was happening. Dawn was the child to whom she had been unable to show affection and now she was banned from doing so.

For a moment she stood looking at the sleeping child. How could anything so beautiful have come into being in such a cruel manner?

★

That evening a handwritten note was brought to her room: *Tonight this noble house has guests. I would like you to act as my hostess and mistress of my house. The dress I wish you to wear will be brought to you and you will wear your hair down.*

Was it an invitation or an order? She wasn't sure.

The cheongsam-style dress was delivered just after she'd bathed and pinned up her hair. It was red and displeasing. The colour was too bright and the slits in the side went far too high, exposing the smooth flesh of her thighs, like the prostitute she'd seen with dragon tattoos up her thighs. Throwing it to one side, she took out the one he'd first given her. Despite its design there was something classic about its cut, the gilded mandarin collar, the gold thread writhing like plant tendrils over its glossy surface.

Kim was formal in a traditional black outfit. He smiled as he entered her room. The smile faded on seeing what she was wearing. 'I want you to wear the red dress I sent you today.'

She pulled a face. 'But this is a red dress. Besides, the other one makes me look like a whore.'

'I wish you to wear it. And your hair. I wish you to wear it down. Your lips must also be red.'

He didn't give her a chance to say that she preferred her hair pinned up, that a formal style suited an evening event. Her hair unpinned and falling around her shoulders tended to be wild and made her look like a gypsy – or worse.

He plucked out the pins and ruffled her hair as it fell, then watched her peel off one dress and put on the other.

'Quickly. And the shoes I sent you.'

She'd totally forgotten about the shoes, which were of the same red as the dress and had high heels – not at all Chinese and not as comfortable as the slippers she'd come to love wearing.

'There,' he said at last. 'That is how I want you to look.'

She caught sight of her reflection and gasped. 'I look like a high-class tart.'

'You will look as I want you to look.'

She felt a knot of fear in her stomach as she wondered at his purpose for dressing her like this. Was he going to sell her to a house of ill-repute, of the kind that proliferated around the docks of Hong Kong?

'I won't do it!'

He frowned. 'You will. If you don't, you will never see your child again. Now come. We have guests waiting. Follow.'

Scared of what he would do if she didn't, she did as ordered, her black hair bouncing, the red silk dress slithering around her thighs.

# 23

The house guests were not at all what Rowena had expected.

Gerhard and Maretha Grobler were in their forties, Lutheran missionaries from Johannesburg who, by virtue of their German ancestry, were allowed to live within an old cantonment especially designed and built for foreigners. They greeted her warmly enough, but their expressions were judgemental.

Gerhard fixed his gaze firmly on her face as though she were a profanity that hurt his eyes. His wife's countenance flickered with disapproval as her eyes travelled from Rowena's tumbling hair over her red dress to her shoes.

'So what did you do before you met Kim?' Maretha asked.

'I was a doctor.'

She saw Kim's condemning glare before he stepped in to expand her response. 'But then she was taken sick and had to stop. Now she is here she no longer needs to do that.'

The old Rowena wouldn't have failed to protest. The new one was obliged not to because she wanted to know what was going on. Dawn was spending more and more time at the mission and she wanted to ask them how she'd settled in.

'Doctors are responsible people. You do not look like this,' said Maretha, once again eyeing the red dress and tumbled hair. 'A man's job, I think.'

'I think so too,' said Kim, flashing a warning look when it seemed likely she was going to defend her corner.

'Not safe out here for a woman,' said the heavy-set German padre.

'Is it safe for you to be in China?' snapped Rowena.

'We have survived, but we are of German descent. We are not enemies,' said Maretha. She pointedly looked Rowena up and down, seeming to think her an enemy on more than one count if her outfit was anything to go by.

'The church requires us to administer wherever the need is greatest,' Gerhard explained over his second glass of sherry. 'Are you a Christian, Mr Pheloung?'

'Buddhist,' Kim replied.

Rowena tried not to let him see her sneer. Buddhist indeed. Firstly Buddhists didn't believe in a god, and secondly Kim only believed in himself.

'And you, Rowena?'

'Christian, but I don't attend church as often as I should.'

'Evidently,' said Maretha. 'Has your daughter been baptised?'

'No. The only minister in the prison camp I was in died before she was born.'

Maretha looked surprised. 'But that can be rectified.'

'I haven't got round to it.'

'Tell me, with the circumstances of her conception, did you not think to have her adopted when she was born, or put into an orphanage?'

'In war?'

'Ah, yes. The war. We thought about running an orphanage, but decided that God did not require us to go in that direction. We need to preach. We need to bring the heathen and the fallen to the Lord, and that includes a child of mixed parentage.'

Rowena had the feeling that she was one of those fallen, a woman of wanton appearance. As for her child, was it really so wrong that she hadn't yet been baptised?

When they at last got up to leave, she thought it only polite to offer to shake hands, but neither offered theirs, instead bowing curtly from the waist, almost as if there was something soiled about her touch.

She attempted to follow them out, thinking to go beyond the moon door and learn more about the surrounding terrain, the road leading to Shanghai and perhaps to freedom.

Kim stopped her. 'Stay here. They are my guests, not yours.'

'So what was I supposed to be tonight?'

'A brood mare.'

'I will not be that.'

'You will be anything I want you to be.'

'Or you'll beat me black and blue?'

'No. I will beat your child black and blue.'

Rebellion, she realised, had to be kept in check if she was to allay his suspicions while she made plans for her and Dawn to escape.

That week the Groblers came for a second visit. On this occasion she was left with Maretha, Kim making an excuse of showing Gerhard the aviary where he kept finches, song thrushes and brightly coloured lovebirds.

'I have always wanted a daughter,' Maretha said, over a low table of dark green tea.

'And you had only a son?'

'Please don't misunderstand. I adore my son and am so grateful I have him. But I would so love a daughter, even one who was not flesh of my flesh. We can give the child we choose a very good home and, of course, a strict Christian upbringing.'

'I hope you find a child deserving of your charity.'

Rowena felt her blood chill when Maretha beamed broadly. 'We think we have, my dear. We truly think we have.'

They visited a few more times, but it wasn't until some weeks later when the swallows were diving after the last insects of the day, that the first steps of losing her child were put into operation.

That night, when she lounged naked beneath a silk robe, Kim arrived unannounced and without knocking.

He proceeded to lie on the opposite sofa, smoke from a sensor sitting on the table rising in a leisurely skein before his eyes. 'I have a question for you.'

'I hope I can answer it.'

'What would you do for the most precious thing in your life?'

She had a feeling she knew where this was going, but kept her fear in check. 'That depends.'

'Your child. What would you do for your child?'

'I think you already know the answer to that.'

'The life of your child is in my hands. She will live or she will die. It depends on you.'

She could barely believe what she had heard and was too frightened to say the wrong thing.

'I bought you. I bought both of you.'

She looked at him, thinking of when she'd first seen him in Kowloon: she had been charmed by his courtesy and enthralled by the classic lines of his face, the way he'd come to their rescue.

'You've rescued me a number of times.'

'Rescued. Yes. I decided I wanted you the first time I saw you in the hospital. A female doctor. A fine mind. Not one who submits easily. That is you.'

It was not quite what she'd expected. 'From the time you saw me in the hospital?'

'I thought you a beautiful and enticing challenge. I

wasn't sure I could achieve my objective but, as it turned out, the fates and this war played a helping hand.'

'I still don't understand.'

'Then I will explain, my dear. You see, I have a hobby. I enjoy moulding people into what I want them to be. That is what I shall do with you. The other women are my earlier accomplishments. They would die for me. Their days are empty in order that I and I alone am the focus of their lives. When not administering to my needs, they satisfy their dreary days in dreams of opium – which you, my dear, will eventually use to fill your time. Not administer to the sick. Not read books. I will mould the children too. They will not know any other way of living and have no will of their own. Women and children. I also love beautiful objects. The moment I saw you I thought what a challenge it would be to mould an educated woman, a doctor and Westerner at that, to something I want her to be, not what she wants to be.'

'You're...' She stopped herself saying he was insane.

'A scientist. Mind-bending I believe they call it.'

Her every nerve tingled with disgust and horror. 'You will not bend me.'

'Come. Follow me to the reason you will become what I want you to be.'

Through dimly lit rooms he took her to where Dawn was sleeping in a small bed made especially for a child. There were others in the room, the small figures of children rounded beneath the heavy cotton coverlets.

'See how she sleeps,' he said, as he ran his fingers over Dawn's cheek.

She stirred at his touch, but did not wake.

'The sleep of one with nothing to fear, who knows she is loved but will soon know abandonment. That is what she will be told, that her mother has abandoned her.'

She forced herself not to show any emotion, not to do anything that would cause him to react because she could not know what he would do. Inside she felt a sick and terrible fear and also a deep resolve. She had to get her daughter and herself out of there.

'Come.'

He took her hand and guided her through the darkened house to the garden. He undid the thin ribbons holding her robe closed and it fell from her shoulders, pooling around her ankles and leaving her naked.

Everything around her was silk: the velvet dark night lit only by paper lanterns, his voice, her skin.

'Please let me go, or let my child go. I'll stay here with you willingly if you allow me to do that.'

'Come, come. I decide who goes where. I was surprised to see that you had a child. It was not part of my plan but, as I told you, I avenged myself on the perpetrators for raping you in the first place – not so much revenge for you, my dear, but for myself.'

He pulled the piled silk back up around her shoulders and turned away. His head fell forward, his hair loose around his shoulders as he lit a cheroot, his words mingling with the rising smoke.

'You will accompany me to Kowloon. Yes. I think that is a good idea.'

'And my daughter?'

'She will not be coming with us. She is no longer yours but the daughter of the Groblers, who will baptise and educate her as they see fit.'

'I don't want her to be adopted.'

'She lives apart from you or she dies. That is what I have decided. Luli will no longer be your servant. Following our return here, my grandmother will come and administer to your needs.'

Rowena felt like one of his birds, trapped in a cage. 'But your grandmother—'

'She will do as I tell her. It is her place to do so and she is sorry she took you away from me.' He laughed. 'As a punishment I took her walking stick from her. At one stage she could barely stand, so went down on hands and knees and crawled everywhere. Yes, she knows she did wrong. But now you are back and I can resume where I left off. You will no longer pin up your hair. You will wear only the clothes in the colours I wish you to wear. Your life is mine. Your child's life is mine.'

'How could you be so cruel?'

'I can do whatever I want. I am master in my own house. In the interim I am moving you from your present room into the one adjoining mine. I want to watch you fall apart before I put you back together.'

'You're not human!'

'I thought you were going to say that I was a monster. No, my dear, I am not human. I am better than human. I am a human who orders the lives of other humans, from the opium addict making me rich from his habit, to the Chinese general who wishes bribes paid that will make him a warlord or the Japanese commander who relishes the comforts of life.'

She searched around for an excuse to keep her distance from him.

'But that's Koto's room.'

'I have tired of her moon face and her tiny feet, which, incidentally, I instructed her to bind. The exercise was only partially successful. Her toes are still straight and whole. She is no longer challenging, whereas you, my dear Rowena...'

'I am not your dear Rowena. I am Dr Rossiter. You can't keep me here. I will be missed. Someone will come looking for me.'

'Nonsense. Your relatives in England will think you're dead. There will be many posted as missing once this war is over. There is also little chance of escape. You would find it hard to escape with a child. And even if you decided to escape alone, I would spread the word that she is half Japanese. At best the Chinese to whom I told her parentage would treat her cruelly, at worst they would kill her. Gossip travels fast. Anyway, the Groblers have offered a good price.'

'You're selling her! But I'm her mother!'

He shrugged his lithe frame and eyed her speculatively, all the time his hands running up and down the arms of the silk robe.

'I have noticed you are not in the habit of showing her affection. Could it be that your ordeal at the hands of the Imperial Army has left you traumatised? Discard her along with your past, your education and your free will. I am your present and immediate future.'

'But eventually, once I'm what you want me to be, you will discard me just as you will Koto.'

He spread his arms wide. 'In the lap of the gods. We people of the Orient set great store in what the gods want for us.'

'I can't do it. I cannot abandon my child and I cannot believe you would kill her.'

'No. I would not kill her. Not personally. The vengeful Chinese would kill her once they were made aware by whom she was fathered. But I am not a monster. You may have her with you for the next seven days until the Groblers have paid the price in full. They are not the most generous of people – or the richest. But she will attend the mission school every day with the other children. Make the most of it. Be as you were before. Do not touch her. Do not cling.'

She shivered as his long, sensuous fingers drew circles at the nape of her neck. With grim determination, she bunched the silk robe at neck level so her skin was hidden. The time for escape had come and so had restraint. He must not suspect what she was planning.

★

Day after day, night after night, she went through the process of living, her mind whirring with escape scenarios, some of which were extreme, others half formed.

It gave her no pleasure to move into the more opulent room next to Kim's, which had been occupied by Koto. She thought she now understood the woman's sour expression. Kim had insisted her feet be bound, that she endured the pain because he wanted her to. Sometime in the past she must have been a happy, pretty woman but Kim had taken her mind and warped it to suit his own selfish desires and fed her opium.

On her first night in that room she saw her clothes strewn all over the floor, the red dress that Kim so loved cut into shreds. Luli saw her smiling as she fingered the fine silk and tucked her chin deferentially into her chest. 'I am so sorry, madam.'

Rowena circled the room, eyeing the destruction. 'Koto did this?'

Luli nodded.

'Tell her she did me a favour.'

Luli frowned.

'It's Kim's favourite dress, not mine. I hate it. I just don't understand why she bothered.'

'She is unhappy. Her feet are painful, as the master wishes them to be, and she walks as those who really possess lotus feet, but she is very unhappy.'

'Please tell her that it was not my idea. I don't want

her room. I don't want to remain in this house. I want to go home.'

Luli looked surprised. 'No want room?'

'No. Where's Dawn?'

'Gone to the mission school.'

'I see.'

He'd said seven days, but she should have known better. Making a promise, building up hope, then breaking it apart was how he intended controlling her.

That evening she awaited the return of the bus with the other women, peering over their shoulders as the ramshackle vehicle pulled in to decant the eager pupils. It would have been full length at one time, but perhaps through accident or design, it was now only half what it used to be, an odd clumsy thing that bounced along the road as though suspended on broken bedsprings.

One by one, boys and girls alighted, clothes askew, their happy faces displaying their delight at being home, tumbling into the shady interior of the old house, with its smells and superstitions, the women following them.

Rowena craned her neck. All the children had left the bus except one. 'Where's Dawn?'

Overcome with panic, she ran along the side of the bus, looking through the windows until she came to the open door where the driver was preparing to pull away. 'My daughter. Dawn. Where's my daughter?'

He said something, shrugged his shoulders and, encased in a cloud of dust, drove out of the compound.

She was left to stare after it until, assured that no magic would make her daughter appear, she spun round and looked for Luli.

The girl was standing next to Koto, talking to her avidly, which resulted in a frown. Koto spoke just as avidly back to her and both held their hands over their mouths as though they were sharing a secret.

'Luli. Where is Dawn? Why hasn't she come back?'

Luli started. Hesitantly she explained. 'She stays with the reverend.'

'Stay?' She grabbed the girl's shoulders and shook her. She was angry, scared, desperate, and totally lost control. 'What do you mean, stay? She's my daughter. Don't you understand? She's my daughter!'

Luli looked terrified.

Realising she was hurting her, Rowena let go of her shoulders. 'It isn't your fault, Luli. I'm sorry.'

Luli ran back into the house, Rowena following behind her.

Koto was waiting for them, standing in the middle of Rowena's new room.

The girl Luli exchanged a brief glance with Koto that was difficult to interpret.

Rowena repeated her question. 'Luli. Where is the master?'

'Home soon.'

Ripped clothes scattered around her, she sat there, not attempting to pick them up but seething with a rage that would not be subdued. She recalled Maretha Grobler informing her that she had found the child she wanted to adopt and that child was Dawn.

So far she had been careful in what she said to him, aware that a serpent writhed beneath his elegant exterior, but the time had come for her to act in whatever way she could to reclaim her child. She had to take action. Even if she had to kill him, she would fight all the way to keep her child.

Dusk was falling and outside lanterns bobbed into light when Kim walked into the room looking pleased with himself. With deep loathing, she wondered what violence he had done that day, how many people had suffered at the hands of his agents and the delirium caused by the opium he traded in.

His self-satisfied smile disappeared on seeing the torn clothes scattered all around the room. He frowned disapprovingly. 'This is a mess.'

'So am I.'

He ignored her pointed response.

'Where's Dawn?'

He looked totally unfazed. 'Forget her. She is no longer part of your life.'

'She's my daughter. You told me I had seven days.'

'I changed my mind. You will do as I say and be the human being I wish you to be.'

'I won't be happy.'

'I do not need you to be happy. I want you to be unhappy.'

She eyed him fiercely. 'What do you have in mind?'

Tucking one leg beneath him, he settled on the end of the bed looking thoughtful.

'You will be the woman I presented to the Groblers. The opposite of a physician who cures disease. I will make you a woman who spreads disease.'

'A whore.' She said it in a hushed voice tinged with disbelief and horror.

'In another life I would have been a scientist, one who experiments with the human psyche, for I revel in making people what I want them to be. It is very challenging – and very interesting.'

She willed herself to keep a cool mind, to take charge of this situation, to plan steps that would remove her from this horror, from this place.

To protect Dawn was paramount. It would be easier to escape alone but she couldn't do that. Kim was insane, that much was clear, but perhaps many criminals who ordered killings as a matter of course were insane and considered themselves superior to their fellow men.

Suddenly he noticed that she'd pinned her hair up when he'd specifically told her not to.

His mouth grim, he reached out, clenched her chin with one hand and plucked out a pin with the other. 'I told you not to pin your hair up. I do not like it.'

As her hair fell, he slapped her so hard that she fell across the bed.

'No!' she shouted, thinking he would fall on top of her and take what he wanted.

'No.' He shook his head. 'Tonight no food, no drink.'

★

Those next few days were a nightmare and her dreams were nightmares. She couldn't eat and her eyes were red-rimmed.

'This is so desperate,' she whispered to herself, to the night, to her tear-stained pillow.

It was three days later, and only two before he would take her to Kowloon, that Luli and Koto came knocking at her door.

Luli was feverishly excited. Koto had a bruised face.

Luli quietly closed the door behind her.

They looked at each other as though sharing a great secret, their movements slow and careful, their footsteps light, as though they were walking on eggshells.

'What is it?'

The two women exchanged brief looks.

'We have a plan to help you escape.'

'I'm not going without my daughter.'

Koto said something.

Luli translated.

'She says she quite understands. She would not wish to be parted from her son.'

'Is Koto his wife?'

She shook her head. 'She was number one until you came. He will send her to the House of Women in

Kowloon if you stay. She does not wish to go. She wishes to be with him.'

'And she wants me gone.'

Luli translated for Koto and they both looked extremely happy that everything was so clear. 'She says she wants her room back.'

'And Kim – the master? She wants him back too?'

'Yes. She loves him.'

Rowena shook her head. 'I'm amazed.'

Green tea was brought, with little sweetmeats. Judging from Koto's exclamations and hand signals, she'd made them herself.

Feeling a little more hopeful, Rowena remembered she hadn't eaten much in days and she really needed to keep her strength up. To her mind the only chance she had of escape was going to Kowloon with Kim, where she hoped an opportunity would present itself. She expressed this to Luli. 'But how do I get Dawn there with me?'

The two women talked excitedly in Cantonese delivered as swiftly as machine-gun fire, then silence as they considered problems, then back to rapid Cantonese before Luli translated into English.

'It is agreed. We will get the child to you.'

In a mixture of English and Chinese, they rattled out the details. As planned, Rowena would go with Kim to the house in Kowloon. Luli reminded her that she had been educated by the Groblers and knew the mission very well. 'While you are with Master, I will go there at night. I know where she will be sleeping. I will climb in and take her. Koto's cousin is a rickshaw driver. He will take me there, then take both of us into Shanghai. Other relatives will hide her until we can get her to Kowloon. Then to Hong Kong.'

Rowena nodded, though until this point she'd had made no plans as to where she wanted to go.

They went on to discuss further details, making contact once she was in Kowloon.

'Then I will have to get to wherever you are.' Rowena thought about the grandmother's ruse of going out for a drive in the car, then transferring to a rickshaw. Their eyes lit up when she related the details. 'It might be easier if I could escape from the house in the walled city and hide in Kowloon until you get there.'

Luli nodded sagely. 'Do you know somebody there who will hide you?'

She thought of the face she'd recognised at Connor's Bar: Yang the barman. 'Yes. I believe I do.'

'When I get there, I too will go on to Hong Kong, perhaps even Australia.' Luli grinned cheekily. 'I would like that.'

'You won't come back here?' Kim had already told her that Zu Mu would take Luli's place but she decided not to mention it to Luli.

As it turned out Luli had taken that into account. 'Koto will say I planned it all so no blame falls on her. That is best. I do not want to stay here or in Kowloon with the old grandmother, who likes to beat me with her walking stick. I want a new life in the new world that will come to be when the Japanese go home.'

Overcome with gratitude, Rowena gave Luli a hug, then the same to Koto. 'How can I ever thank you both?'

Collusion was evident in the looks they gave each other.

'Koto says no need. She will have everything she wants when you are gone.'

Rowena doubted Koto's life would return to what it had been. It shook her to think that Koto was not merely subservient to Kim: she loved him.

As with all travel, there would be costs involved.

'I haven't any money. I'll need some.'

She looked around the room. All she had here belonged to Kim and there were only dresses. How far would a torn red one get her?

'This.'

It was the one English word she'd ever heard Koto utter. The other woman held a small silk package in a nest of long, painted nails.

She explained her intentions to Luli, who translated: 'She says you are to take this. It is jade, very old and very valuable. She says it belonged to one of her ancestors, the favourite concubine to a great warlord. It is yours now.'

'I can't possibly…'

Koto's hands folded over hers. 'Yes.'


'A few days and we will begin your education.'

She resisted the urge to tremble and didn't protest when he ordered her to sit on a low stool, circled her and told her which days of the week he would allow her to eat, and those days when food and drink would be denied her.

Adopting a look that was winsomely sad, she dined with him, only eating those things he allowed her to eat and even then in very small quantities.

She sat with eyes demurely cast down when she accompanied him in the car along the grand avenues of Shanghai where many world banks had their headquarters. She was not expected to have a will of her own. There was only his will that must always be obeyed.

Acting had never been of great interest to her – she'd never had any desire to be a movie star – but she had some idea of how it was done.

That night she held back the threatening shiver as he lay next to her, teasing her as to whether or not he would make love to her. Either way she had no choice but to give in, let him do anything he wanted to her or have her do anything to him. Everything was at his pleasure.

He joined her, his naked loins against her back, his arm around her neck so she had no choice but to stretch her head back or she wouldn't be able to breathe.

His hand explored the front of her body, shoulder, arm, breast, ribcage and over the curve of her hip until it finally rested on her belly.

'You will smoke the pipe?' he asked suddenly.

'No. I can't.'

'I want you to.'

'I'll be sick.'

Suddenly he kicked her. 'Get out of this bed.'

Not understanding, she held onto the covers. 'No.'

'Out!'

His kick was violent and before he lashed out again, she was out of the bed.

Kim spread himself across it.

Rowena headed for the divan.

'No. You sleep on the floor.'

He didn't deny her the cushion she pulled down from the divan or the discarded dressing-gown.

She lay there shivering but wouldn't dare disobey. He had to think that she was becoming what he wanted her to be and she vowed never to be that. The cold concentrated her mind, and as her hatred for him grew, she thought of happier times in the past when she'd sung in a bar with a big bluff Irishman.

*She looked so neat from her bare brown feet,*
*To the tip of her chestnut hair...*

Over and over again the words sang in her head keeping her mind focused and the chilly night at bay.

Everything will be worth it, she thought. The present will pass and I'll be living in the future.

★

It was two days later when the message was delivered and from an unexpected source.

The children had not gone to school because the Groblers were attending the funeral of an old friend some miles distant and expected to be away for a few days.

As a consequence there was no school and Luli had been requisitioned to look after Dawn while the couple were away. This has to be our main chance, thought Rowena, and it turned out she was right.

Walking in the courtyard, she saw a guard she recognised snap off the head of a heavy chrysanthemum. Nobody else saw him. She wondered why he had done it and how angry Kim would be. Above everything else in the world, it seemed Kim's only love was for himself and the flowers.

She half turned away from him before remembering that he was the guard whose wound she had treated.

'Madam.' He handed her the flower.

She took it and thanked him.

Once he was back at his post and she was alone with nothing but chrysanthemums for company – she was quickly coming to hate them – she took a closer look at the bright yellow head and its tiny curling petals that made up the whole. Rolled into one of its petals was a slip of paper. She took it out, read it and felt her heartbeat quicken.

Dawn, and an address in Kowloon. All she had to do was get there and Kim was inadvertently providing her with the opportunity.

★

From the moment they arrived in Kowloon Kim's grandmother refused to look her in the face, looking away every time she appeared.

Dawn had been snatched to safety and the opportunity for her to escape had finally arisen but even Kim didn't know that yet.

Today was the day Zu Mu chose to go for a drive and Kim ordered Rowena to go too. She bowed to his will, hardly able to believe her luck. Out of his sight she refrained from skipping, but she couldn't stop herself smiling.

She secreted the address and the piece of jade on her person along with a few coins Koto had added to pay a rickshaw driver. She also put on two layers of clothes and a pair of black Chinese shoes with white rubber soles. High-heeled red shoes would be no use for what she had in mind.

To her dismay the old lady ordered the driver to take a country road away from the city.

She tried not to appear agitated, but calmed when the driver said something to the old lady that made her change her mind. The driver, the man who had brought her the message, changed direction and headed for the centre of Kowloon.

Crowded with street traders, the car slowed to walking pace. The old lady leaned forward, berating the driver, perhaps about his slow driving.

Rowena suspected he had purposely driven into the most crowded alley and Zu Mu was not amused. The car slowed to walking pace, nosing its way through the stranglehold of crowds. The drumming of her heart was so loud she was half afraid the old lady would hear it, but Zu Mu was too busy beating the driver about the shoulders, the pair shouting at each other.

It was too good an opportunity to miss. She opened the car door, got out into the milling crowds and was easily lost. Behind her she heard the old lady screaming at the top of her voice, guessing she was calling for assistance, that the woman in the green silk trousers and tunic was a thief and should be brought back to her immediately.

There was no way either of them would come after her. The driver would not leave the car and his employer's grandmother alone, and the old lady had bound feet so could barely walk, let alone run.

Crowded as it was, Rowena breathed in the scent of food being cooked in the open air and heard the shouts of tailors offering their services to make an outfit from silk. Freedom had never tasted so good. If it hadn't been for the fact that she was wearing Chinese garb, she could almost have believed she was back in 1941 when she and Alice had ventured there, visited Connor's Bar, first met Connor and also the man who had charmed them into sitting at his table.

As she ran she thought of Connor, her blue-eyed Irishman, and again heard him singing inside her head. Was he still alive? Would he one day come back to

Kowloon, reclaim his violin and reopen his bar?

Her heart skipped a beat at the thought of it. Things could have been so different if the colony had held out, or if the army and supporting medical staff had fallen back to Singapore and thence to Australia.

She was careful to keep her head down and not to stare at the off-duty Japanese soldiers picking at merchandise, laughing with their comrades, leering at the girls hanging over the balconies.

Having black hair and not too light a complexion was a definite plus. Nobody stopped her, nobody questioned where she was going, winding in and out of the crowds and the alleys into narrower alleys until she came to the address she'd been given. House of Peace, an address she knew was adjacent to Connor's Bar.

It was only a pile of rubble now, but behind it was an opening in the wall and a Chinese character she'd last seen on the entrance to the alley: one woman under one roof. This was it.

Powdery dust rose from the tumbled blocks as she clambered over them to what looked like a cave set among piled rubble. The front lintel was propped up with wooden trusses and a green tarpaulin formed a canopy that almost made it look like a proper shop. Only the tops of heads were visible in the blue shade of the interior.

She stopped, her heart thudding. What if those glossy-haired heads were Japanese? She had to take the chance.

'Is anyone there?'

A single head bobbed up, and there was Luli, grinning from ear to ear.

She reached down beside her and a smaller figure, which had been out of sight, also stood up. Hand in hand they waited until she was there, standing directly in front of them.

She was speechless. Tears streamed down her face as the full consequences of what she'd been through and what she'd escaped finally hit her.

'Honourable Doctor,' said Luli, and bowed.

Dawn bowed too. 'Mummy!' And threw herself into her mother's arms.

# 24

'It's over!'

It seemed that the whole of Hong Kong had erupted with joy, the shouting, the laughing, and the ever-present firecrackers combining to celebrate the final ending of the war.

Rowena had just delivered a breech birth, a baby boy. The hospitals were a place of fear, mostly frequented, as they were, by Japanese soldiers and medical staff, so the woman had given birth in her own home, her family sending for the doctor-midwife when complications arose.

More firecrackers exploded in the street.

She wiped her hands and asked the new mother's sister what was going on. 'It's not new year, is it?'

When she heard again the shout of 'It's all over!' she threw down the towel on which she'd wiped her hands, picked up her bag and dashed out into the street.

'It's over! It's over!'

People spilled onto the alley from their houses and shops, laughing, singing, shouting and letting off enough firecrackers to fill the air with blue smoke. Now the explosions would not result in death but inspire even more joy.

Hopping, skipping, running, barely able to keep her feet on the ground, she ran all the way back to the building that had been semi-derelict when she'd first arrived but was now partially rebuilt. Together she, Luli and Yang had laboured with heavy blocks, made mortar from whatever they could find to give them better shelter.

'Have you heard?' she shouted, as excited as a child about to blow out the candles on a birthday cake. 'The war is over. I heard it on the streets coming here. Japan has surrendered.'

Yang ran to find his own store of firecrackers. Luli got out a few faded paper lanterns from a box as well as a silk dragon, the head as big as a tea chest, its tail at least six feet long.

'Up here. We put it up here.'

As Dawn clapped her little hands, they hung it above the new entrance along with the old sign saying Connor's Bar.

'I only hope nobody thinks we're actually a bar. We've got no beer,' Rowena pointed out.

'Rice wine,' said Yang, bringing out a crate from the back.

'Now where did you get that?'

Yang tapped the side of his nose. 'You not know, you not say.'

He'd stolen it from some army storeroom.

'That looks good,' said Rowena, hands on hips as she stood back and admired the slightly tatty dragon they'd just hung up.

Still feeling good about the new world they were now part of, she suddenly became aware of Yang looking beyond her out into the alley, his expression less than friendly. On turning, she found herself face to face with a Japanese soldier. He looked a sorry sight, his face black and blue from the beatings the locals were meting out to any Japanese soldier unlucky enough to wander their way.

He looked straight at her. 'Doctor. I Shimida.'

'He's Japanese,' said Luli, her tone leaving Rowena in no doubt that she would rather see the man die than be treated.

'I know him. Shimmy?'

He nodded. It was indeed the guard from the camp who had made Dawn a wooden doll.

She took a step towards him, catching him just before he collapsed. Luli hung back, unwilling to help a man she regarded as an enemy.

Yang helped her get Shimmy indoors where he collapsed onto the floor.

'He was kind to Dawn,' she explained to Yang. 'Bandages. And fresh water. Do we have any?'

The water supply had been sporadic of late so they

had taken the precaution of storing quantities in buckets and tins, purely for those moments when there was only a trickle.

Shimmy's face was shiny with sweat, but swiftly growing paler as dark red blood seeped out of his guts and through his uniform. He winced as she began to undo his jacket, then caught her hand and said something in Japanese.

'I'm sorry. I don't speak Japanese.' She shouted at Yang to come and translate. Thanks to a little wheeling and dealing with the occupying forces, he'd picked up the language quite well.

Shimmy reached inside his tunic and brought out his wallet. She recalled seeing it before, the photograph of his wife and family inside.

He repeated what he'd said. Yang translated. 'He says he knows he is about to join his ancestors, his wife and family too.'

'Does he mean that his wife and family are dead? How does he know that?'

Yang again translated. 'His home is in Hiroshima. He heard about the great bomb that fell on his city, about the many dead.'

With shaking, clawing fingers, Shimmy laid his hand on her arm. His voice was weaker now. Yang had to get closer to hear what he was saying. 'He says your daughter reminded him of his youngest when she was small. He hopes she will live.'

She looked at the photograph of a pretty woman and

her two daughters, all dressed in their best to have their photo taken so her husband might have a memento to take with him to war.

He uttered a few more words.

'He wants you to keep these. He has nothing else to leave to anyone and nobody to leave it to. Everyone is gone.'

Another whispered few words...

'To remind the world of these times and to pray that they never happen again.'

'Amen,' Shimmy said.

From within his wallet she extracted a crucifix. Shimmy, the Japanese Christian.


They buried Shimmy in the cemetery of a ruined church. The photographs of his family Rowena placed, with her own few valuables, in a leather case Yang had purloined for her.

Shimmy stayed in her mind for days afterwards. She recalled the doll he'd made for Dawn and her own reaction, throwing it at his feet and telling him to keep away from her child. On account of his nationality, she'd thrown his offering back at him, and had not relented even when he'd shown her his family photo and Marjorie had explained that he smuggled in medicines and food. He had aroused painful memories and she could not, would not give in.

Yang had closed the man's eyes and tears had streamed

down Rowena's face, not just for him but for the stupidity and cruelty of the whole human race. That cruelty and stupidity had been emphasised when details began to circulate of what the bomb had done.

Leaving Dawn in the care of Luli, she made her way across the bay to mainland Hong Kong and Fort Stanley. The camp was a hive of activity as the inmates prepared to be processed and given the choice of staying in Hong Kong or going home – wherever home might be.

She recognised the stalwart figures of O'Malley and Alice, sitting in the sun, as the Red Cross and other medical assistance eddied around them, taking over the duties they had done.

Alice was leaning against a sun-splashed wall with her eyes closed. It was O'Malley who saw her first.

'Well, if it isn't Dr Rossiter. Excuse me if I don't get up, Doctor. I've had a case of dysentery and I might fall over.'

'Rowena?' Alice struggled to her feet.

She was thinner than ever but there was hope in her eyes.

The two women hugged.

Rowena reached down and clutched O'Malley's shoulder. 'So good to see you. Where's Marjorie?'

They shook their heads.

'Pneumonia.'

'How's that little imp of yours?'

'Dawn's fine. She wants to go to school. I'm not sure yet whether to return to England or stay here.'

Alice's eyes narrowed. 'You love it here. You wouldn't feel at home in England. There are no battles to fight.'

'I've had enough of war!'

'I said battles. You've fought your way through a few of the personal kind.'

'And come out the other side.'

She realised Alice had a point. 'I thought I might get involved in helping the refugees who are likely to flood into Hong Kong. That could be quite a battle, but I have Dawn to consider. I'm not sure how she'll fit into a post-war Hong Kong. It'll be a long time before the Chinese forgive the Japanese for what they've done.'

'Will you?'

'I never used to think so, but now?' She told them about Shimmy, his photo and her surprise to discover he was a Christian. 'I know that shouldn't make a difference, but up until then I was making assumptions, thinking they were all the same, that there was no good side to them, yet I know now Shimmy meant no harm. I just wasn't listening.'

O'Malley struggled to her feet. 'What next, I wonder?'

The Red Cross had set up a relief centre where they were given tea and biscuits.

Their mood lightened as they began discussing the future and what it might hold for all of them.

Alice said she would be going back to Sydney. 'My family have been writing to me for years but I've only just received their letters. I need to get back there so they see me in the flesh. Knowing my mother, she'll want to fatten me up. Steaks and lamb stews every day if she has her way.'

'I'm going to get married.'

Surprised, they both looked at O'Malley.

'Don't look at me as though I'm already a corpse. So what if I'm in my fifties? I'm not at the end of the trail just yet. There's a widower back home who told me before I left that he'd wait for me. I just hope somebody else hasn't snapped him up.'

There was much more talk and more laughter before they asked her about Kim.

'You look better than all of us.'

She shook her head. 'I've been in Kowloon for some time. Just the thought of him still gives me the creeps.'

'He didn't... well... you know...'

Alice was being hesitant and Rowena was grateful for that. It meant she could be hesitant too. 'That wasn't what he wanted. Our smooth-talking Prince Charming was not what he seemed.'

'A wolf in disguise?'

'No. A madman.'

They sensed the shivers she was suppressing and let the subject drop.

'Will you ever go back to England?'

'It holds no great attraction, but who knows what the future holds?'

O'Malley nodded. 'I can understand that. It won't be easy.'

'It also helps that I now speak some Cantonese, even a bit of Mandarin.'

Time flew, the teacups were emptied and refilled twice, but at last they fell into a comfortable silence, having agreed that they would keep in touch. They would share the same memories and would always feel warm commitment to their friendship.


Engrossed in her work, she gave no thought to returning to England until two separate things occurred. First, she received a letter from her brother asking her if she would like to invest in his new business venture, a pub on the side of a river in a beautiful spot. Second, she saw Kim Pheloung, who had a new car, which could only mean that he was back on form and was yet again taking advantage of whatever opportunities the aftermath of war offered.

It seemed that the only path open to her was to go back to England where he could not touch her. With that in mind she sent money to her brother on the understanding that he would provide her with a house in which she could bring up her child.

When she finally received a reply, she was living in an apartment in Hong Kong and Luli was there too, employed as nanny and housemaid, having been turned down by the Australian authorities.

The letter was straight and to the point.

*Dear Rowena,*

*I am very grateful for your offer to fund my business scheme and I think it might very well have worked if it was only you who was coming here.*

*After talking it over with Wendy, we agreed that it might be a bad idea seeing as you now have a child who is not of pure English blood.*

*My wife feels the only way it might work is if you send her to boarding school, perhaps one in Hong Kong? After all, that is where the child was born.*

*I know this might sound a bit harsh, and you are my sister after all, but we already have one half-caste child in this village, and having another, even of a different race, might not be a good idea.*

*Please try to understand our situation. I do hope you find somewhere here to suit your needs. In the meantime I remain as always,*

*Your loving brother, Clifford*


It was as she'd thought it might be. Dawn would not be accepted and she could not contemplate her daughter being unhappy.

'So be it,' she said to Alice, after she'd told her what Clifford had said.

'Poor you. Poor Dawn, but I did try to say...'

'That I should have her adopted? Is that what I should do, even now?'

'That isn't what I said.'

'No,' said Rowena, getting to her feet. 'It isn't. I'm off.

I have many Chinese and other refugees to look after – and they don't give a damn where I'm from.'

She fumed about it all night. In the early hours of the morning she felt her daughter sliding into bed beside her.

Men, women, children and babes in arms, poured into the refugee centre from China, their meagre possessions carried in bundles on their backs.

Some came through the crossing point above Kowloon. Others took a boat across, the vessels overloaded and filling with water by the time they made land.

Not all did so, their overburdened craft easily sinking in the most moderate seas.

Those who did disembark ended up either in one of the camps or, if they managed to side-step the border controls, built ramshackle houses in the walled city, some of which were now three, four or five storeys high. A city of only a few hundred inhabitants had swelled to many thousands.

For a while Rowena was content to help them, although at times she felt she could do more to repair what had happened over the last five years. The opportunity came not many months after she'd accepted a job with the Red Cross in Hong Kong.

'Dr Rossiter. I wonder if I could have a word.' Adrian Smith was a quietly spoken Australian doctor, who had come as part of the Red Cross contingent to help with the refugees fleeing the ongoing struggle in China. His office was situated in a one-storey flat-roofed building on the other side of the arterial road that circled the huts housing the refugees.

As she made herself comfortable she studied his rangy frame and the deliberate way in which he moved, as though he considered everything very thoroughly before he moved at all.

'Do you mind me leaving the window open?' he asked. 'I know some people dislike the smell of cooking coming from the camp.'

'I don't mind it at all.'

'Good. Neither do I. Their cooking has to be better than the stuff we're dishing up. Wish I could join them.'

He was sardonic but funny.

'Is anything wrong? I take it you're satisfied with my work.'

'Goodness me! You're an asset, Dr Rossiter, and I congratulate myself that I took you on.'

'I appreciate your faith in me.'

'We need you, Doctor. As I am sure you're aware, the Red Cross is currently overwhelmed, so many needs and not enough staff. Thanks to international support – from the United States and other countries – we have money to fund various projects, the latest being in Japan, but medical staff of your calibre are thin on the ground.'

She sensed he had paused to study her reaction. 'I hear there is a great need there.'

He nodded. 'Very. Unfortunately General MacArthur is very touchy about the whole situation there following the dropping of the atomic bomb and its ongoing impact on the Japanese civilian population.'

'Ongoing?'

'Side effects the powers that be are denying exist.'

She looked away at the busy people outside his window, carrying on with a makeshift life in their makeshift world. How long would they be there before they were processed and allowed to join the Hong Kong community?

She had a hunch where this was going and turned back to face him. 'You want me to join a Red Cross medical team in Japan?'

He nodded. 'That's exactly what I want. I think you would be a great asset to us, Doctor.'

'I don't speak Japanese.'

'Those people have been through horrors untold. The power of the sun was unleashed upon them, killing thousands, with thousands more dying in the aftermath. To say the people of the two cities destroyed are hostile is putting it mildly and it isn't only speaking their language that's capable of breaking down the barrier. You have something else that might make them trust you. Your daughter is half Japanese. Is that right?'

Nausea swept over her. She nodded but dared not open her mouth. Dr Smith had inadvertently brought it all back to her.

'Something is happening there, Doctor. Something we don't yet understand. Women and children who were not scarred by the inferno are becoming sick and dying. We need somebody the women will trust, someone who they can feel some empathy with.'

'I don't know how you can ask me this... not yet...'

He turned a page in his file, read something quickly, then looked up at her. 'I have to warn you that there is hostility towards the Allies, especially the Americans. We can provide you with an Indian passport, if you like, since your grandmother was from Bombay. I believe your grandfather was a subaltern in the Indian Army.'

She felt the colour drain from her face. 'You've dug into everything.'

'It wasn't that difficult. Army records are very thorough... Look, may I give you something to read? It was published by the *Daily Express* in London back in September by a man named Wilfred Burchett, an Australian journalist. It may help you make up your mind.'

When she didn't answer, he opened his desk drawer, got out a few pages of newsprint and placed them before her.

'Please. Read it at your leisure. I've got someone waiting to see me. I won't be long.'

He turned the newspaper the right way up before he left so she could read the headlines.

## THE ATOMIC PLAGUE
I write this as a warning to the world.

By the time she came to the end of the piece her hands were shaking. Feeling as cold as ice, she laid it back on the desk. Never had she read anything so harrowing – the frustration of the doctors and other medical staff as they tried their utmost to save lives. Already she had half made up her mind, though she would feel guilty at leaving the displaced persons who cooked and did their laundry beyond the wire fence.

When Dr Smith returned she was sitting stiffly, two factions fighting for her answer. He did not press her but went back behind his desk and sat down.

He was looking down at his ink blotter, both hands curled into tight fists and resting on the desk to either side of him. He glanced up and out of the window. Both fists thumped the desk. 'Do you see that man out there? Once the refugees are processed he comes here offering them shelter in the walled city – at a price. I've ordered that he is not to be allowed in again, but money talks and he has plenty. I believe he's an opium dealer.'

She looked out to the wide gravelled yard in front of the building and immediately recognised the pale green car. Kim was there and likely to find her. Japan seemed a safer option.

'I knew a man from Hiroshima. He made a doll for my daughter.'

'Does that mean you'll consider it?'

She dragged her gaze from the window. If Kim had contacts in the refugee camp it wouldn't be long before he found her. 'I will go to Japan.'

Before leaving she asked to visit St Stephen's, which was still operating as a military hospital. To enter she needed official clearance, but Dr Smith was more than willing to help when she told him the basics of her mission.

Once there, to the caretaker's surprise, she went down into the basement, to the cupboard behind the boiler and retrieved a dusty violin case.

# 25

*England, 1947*

'What the bloody hell am I doing here?'

Connor had packaged up the ash-filled ginger jar and sent it by registered post to Harry's mother. He'd expected that would be that, but now, more than a year later, she had tracked him down and asked him to visit. It had been the last thing he'd wanted to do because in facing Harry's mother his guilt might show on his face. He'd told her in the note he'd enclosed with the jar that it contained her son's remains, which wasn't quite true.

The glorious height of Granthorpe Hall loomed ahead above a red-brick wall and wrought-iron gates. The house was clearly visible at the end of a sweeping drive. A firm tug of the iron bell pull hanging from one side of the gate, and somebody would appear to let him in.

Hands stuffed into his pockets, he eyed the bell pull, the ornate leaves at its base. More like daggers, he thought. What was the bloody artist thinking of?

He asked himself for the third time that day what he was letting himself in for. Riddled with doubt, he began to pace up and down, wearing a shallow furrow in the ground.

His dog, an old mongrel named Bob, which reminded him of Vicky, eyed him.

'Why didn't you ring the bell?'

Deep in his own world, he had failed to notice the short, wide woman who dragged open the gate. She had a pert look, bright eyes and hair as fluffy as a dandelion head.

'I've been watching you pace up and down for the last half-hour and couldn't stand it any longer. Even from a distance you've been making me dizzy. Now, are you coming in or what?'

The moment he saw her he knew her name.

'I'm Louise Gracey. I take it you're Connor O'Connor. I won't say you haven't changed much since Harry sent me that picture of you both. He was very handy with a Box Brownie, though obviously he got somebody else to take it.'

'It was a corporal.'

'As good as anyone.'

He found himself looking into a pair of dark brown eyes. Her ladyship was wearing what looked like a man's checked shirt over faded green corduroys tucked into a pair of wellington boots. If she hadn't told him her name he would have assumed her to be staff – perhaps the cook or wife of the gardener, though her voice was crystal clear with rounded vowels. He recalled conversations with Harry as they'd lain in the dark, their stomachs rumbling with starvation. Mothers were discussed, as much as wives and sweethearts. Harry had described her succinctly but accurately. Different was the word best remembered. He felt her eyes on him.

'That's quite a head of hair you have. Same colour as my Harry's. Your eyes too.' She stopped as though at a sudden choke, which she swiftly turned into a hearty chuckle.

'What about a cup of tea? And there's cake. My old friend Minette brought it up. She lives down in the village.'

'I don't want to be wasting your time.'

'I've plenty to waste. One's faculties fade as one gets older and the social life goes with it. I have fewer visitors nowadays – unless for the horses and then they're not here to see me. With the exception of Minette, of course. Now, I insist you stay for tea and listen to what I have to say. Will you at least do that for me?'

She turned so quickly she almost left her boots behind.

'What about my dog?'

'I assumed he was coming with us. Don't mind dogs in the house, and he looks like a good 'un. He's getting on a bit. How old is he?'

'He was a stray and a bit grey around the muzzle so I think he's about eight.'

'I would guess that too. Good for his age. Shame they don't last as long as little yappers. Small dogs,' she said, on seeing his puzzled expression. 'Small dogs make up for their size with noise. Didn't you know that? No matter. Now, come along. We've given each other the once-over and I think we both like what we see. Let's find out if you and I really can judge a book by its cover.'

'Is Harry's father at home?'

'Dead.'

'I'm sorry. I don't remember Harry ever mentioning...'

'Don't be sorry. My husband was always going to fall from grace and get himself killed. The blame was entirely his. He was like an old stallion I used to have – couldn't accept that he was too old to be mounting the fillies. Hasty Gracey, I used to call him. In this instance he hastily followed a sweet young thing with a comfortable bosom and an ample backside. He forgot he was getting older and that his ambition was not matched by the capability of the heart to recover after strenuous exercise. After a particularly energetic tryst, he made the mistake of driving home on top of a few whiskies. It was a foolhardy combination that led to him swerving off the road and hitting a tree. My son's ashes were delivered on the day of my husband's funeral.'

'I'm sorry.'

'No need to be. I was glad to get them. Round here,' she said, swerving to the left off the driveway and onto a red-brick path bordered with fancy red tiles. 'Tradesmen's entrance, I'm afraid. I've been mucking out the stables. I've got help, but like to give a hand. The horses are used to me. Think I'm their mother – or I like to think they do, silly old mare that I am. My house-keeper Mabel huffs and puffs a bit if I go in stinking of horse shit – sorry, manure. Slip of the tongue. I use expletives in front of the stable lad, but make the effort to curb my language once I'm inside the house. My housekeeper doesn't like it.'

He followed her through a wide back door and along a flagstoned passage where she stepped out of her boots, kicking them beneath what looked like an old church pew. From there she trod onwards in knitted seamen's socks that, like the boots, seemed too big for her. The room they entered had a homely rather than a stately atmosphere. The furniture was old but handsome, the faded upholstery worn in places, and underfoot the Persian rugs had holes.

Hunting scenes in gilt frames hung alongside bigger portraits of poker-faced people from centuries past, against heavily embossed Victorian wallpaper. It might have been a riot of rich colouring in its day but was now faded.

She pointed a wrinkled finger at a winged armchair and the roundel of black fur sitting on it. 'Throw that cat off and take a seat.'

At first the animal seemed loath to move until Bob came out from behind Connor. Hissing, it showed its needle-fine fangs, then jumped down and high-tailed it out of the room.

Lady Gracey made herself comfortable in an armchair opposite the one in which the cat had been sleeping. Its horsehair stuffing and the webbing that was supposed to support it had fallen down. 'Whoops!' Her legs went up in the air as her backside sank into the chair's innards.

Connor sprang to her assistance, his strong arms pulling her upwards until she was balanced on what bit of the chair was still functional.

'So wonderful to have a pair of strong arms come to one's aid. I've never been used to that. Hasty Gracey's arms were usually to be found assisting another woman – mostly into bed.'

Huffing and puffing she was sitting fairly comfortably, her feet hovering some way off the floor. Patting the chair arms, she said, 'I really should get these old chairs repaired. I'll get Mabel to find someone to sort them out. I would have a go myself, but I just don't have the time. Too busy with the horses. Do you like horses, Sergeant Major?'

His attention wandered to the mantelpiece and the blue and white ginger jar sitting at one end. Why hadn't she buried or scattered Harry's ashes, perhaps over his father's grave?

'I said do you like horses?'

He tore his gaze away from the ginger jar, his eyes skimming past the photograph of him and Harry, two young men in uniform on the threshold of life.

'I like all animals,' he said, and nodded thoughtfully. 'I like them more than humans.'

'I don't blame you. I feel very much the same. Except for Harry, of course. I miss him, and nobody was ever going to take his place, but you...' She paused as her gaze drifted around the room. 'You were his friend. I'm so glad I tracked you down. Where is Mabel with that blessed tea? The woman's useless. I should have sacked her years ago, but there...' She shrugged. 'She has strange habits and a mind of her own. Her sweetheart ran away with the fishmonger so she never eats fish, not even on Friday. It was bad enough keeping staff after the Great War. It's even worse now. Nobody wants to go into service any more. If I upset Mabel, she'll take off in a huff and I'll have to go chasing after her and offer all sorts of bribes to get her back.'

With a crash of heavy wood against a stout wall, the door flew open, hitting the wall. When it rebounded a tall woman with bad-tempered features gave it a kick while balancing a heavy tray in both hands.

Lady Gracey carried on talking about something to do with horses, then about family, Harry and her ungracious husband. 'So many young women left our service after he'd put them in the family way.'

Connor was amazed at her matter-of-fact acceptance of her husband's indiscretions, which she recounted with great good humour.

Not until she'd come to the end of what she wanted to say did she acknowledge her housekeeper. 'Ah!' she declared, as though all was right with the world and Mabel the most amenable person living therein. 'Put it there on the table, Mabel, and then you can go. We'll help ourselves.'

Mabel, an elderly woman with age-speckled hands

and the scowl she wore looked to be a permanent fixture. 'The sandwiches are fish paste and the cake is supposed to be fruit cake though you won't find much fruit in it. You'll have to make do.'

'Really?'

Mabel's scowl deepened. 'It's all that's available.'

'If you say so. I thought somebody was making a coconut cake. I'm sure I smelt it cooking.'

'There is one.'

'When will it be ready?'

Mabel stopped at the door. 'It'll be ready when it's ready.' Then she was gone.

Her ladyship's eyes twinkled. 'See? I told you what she was like.' She gestured at the teapot. 'Do you mind pouring? You can reach it more easily than I can. That's the problem with being petite. Short legs.'

'Sure I will.'

'I think your dog likes the smell of the sandwiches. Have one yourself and give him one. I'm not going to eat any. I hate fish-paste sandwiches. I'm sure Mabel makes them purely to spite me.'

Connor gave Bob a sandwich but didn't take one himself. His mouth was too dry and his guts tight with apprehension. He recognised the taste of the Earl Grey tea from way back. He drank his, then poured himself a second cup.

'I wanted to meet you. I wanted to hear from you how Harry died. Do you mind telling me?'

He set down his cup. 'I have to warn you it's pretty harrowing.'

'All the same, I'd like to know. It wouldn't be a bad idea to write it all down, you know.'

'I don't think I want to remember – not all of it anyway.'

'You're not alone. It's been reported that a lot of the men find it difficult to talk about their experiences. War changes them.'

A dark frown furrowed Connor's brow. 'Yes. I've seen the worst in men and the best.'

'I know without needing to ask that my invitation came as something of a surprise, but I'll make no apologies. Before Harry went to war, I made him promise to come home – whether on his legs or in a box. I'd never considered a ginger jar, though must say I like it very much. I'm very grateful to you for getting him home, so if there's anything I can do, you have only to ask.'

'There's no need. I'm not the sort who needs the earth beneath his feet and a roof above his head.' He was unsure of how best to explain.

'Come, come, Mr O'Connor, you must get a bit lonely with only a dog for company.' She tilted her head to one side and eyed him speculatively. 'You must have loved, and before you blush and tell me anything, I knew my son very well, including his homosexuality, so nothing you say can shock me.'

Connor almost choked on his mouthful of tea. 'It wasn't like that.'

'You prefer women?'

'Yes.'

'Harry told me you sing and play the violin. He didn't say what sort of songs.'

'Toe-tapping songs and ballads.'

'Oh, lovely. I thought for a moment you were going to say you were a member of an orchestra. Don't get me wrong, I like classical music, but I also like to enjoy myself. A bit of music and a glass of sherry, what could be better?'

Connor felt her eyes on him as he placed his cup and saucer on the table. She had a direct look, the sort of woman who knows what you're thinking before you do.

'Was she pretty?'

The question took him by surprise. He looked down at his hands. It had been a while since he'd played the fiddle though his voice was fine. Bringing her to mind made his hands ache, as though they sought the curved neck of a violin and the feel of a bow in his hand.

'She was a rare beauty. I likened her to the Star of the County Down, though her hair was raven black not chestnut.'

'Raven black. What a telling description.'

The way she smiled was puzzling.

'I suppose an explanation is in order. You didn't merely describe her hair as black. You said raven black. It's very telling. I would guess you liked running your hand through it.'

He thought of the last occasion he'd been able to do

that and the times after when they'd eyed each other from afar, aching to touch, to console, to cling together against the world.

'So go on. Tell me what you and my son got up to.'

He smiled sheepishly and thought back to the choicest plums of his and Harry's friendship.

'He and I set up a bar in Kowloon.' He smiled at the memory. 'It was good while it lasted. We had all manner of customers. Chinese gamblers, lovers looking to meet in private. Even a man who dealt in opium.' His expression darkened at the thought of Kim Pheloung, then lightened when he thought of Rowena. 'And women who had no business being there, one in particular, but, oh, she had the sweetest voice.' He caught Lady Gracey's knowing smile. 'And raven-black hair.'

'I bet you and Harry had quite a time. I was so pleased when he sent me the photo. Your cheery smiles helped me cope with him being so far away.'

The silence that descended was like a lid closing on a box of memories they were both privy to, each in their own way. He was glad she knew about Harry. He would have found it difficult explaining, if he'd told her at all.

He went on to tell her about the two of them defending St Stephen's military hospital, the killings, though he held back on the more macabre details. He went on to talk about conditions in the prison camp, the stray dog that had become his constant companion, working in Japan, then the torpedo striking their ship on the way to Bali.

The bit he found the hardest to relate was Harry's

death, skirting around the exact details of the communal
funeral pyre.

She looked down into her teacup. 'At least he died with
his best friend by his side.'

'Aye.'

'You've no other close friends?'

'No. Just my dog. That's enough.'

'Ah, yes,' she said. 'Your dog. Animals ask nothing in
return for their love and loyalty. Just to be fed, watered
and taken care of when they fall sick. Still, don't you
think you should make the effort to find this beauty with
the raven hair?'

'I don't know if she's still alive even.'

'Do you read?'

'I've a few books.'

'Serious ones, I suppose. Most men read serious books.
You should read more romance. Then you might be
inspired to journey to the ends of the earth to find your
love.'

His thoughts went back to the evening when Rowena
Rossiter had joined in the chorus of 'Star of the County
Down', her voice soaring like a skylark's.

'I've no idea where to begin.'

She leaned closer, as much as the decrepit chair would
allow. 'Do you think she's dead?'

He thought of Kim and his blood boiled. 'I don't know.'

'Perhaps you don't want to know.'

His eyes met hers. 'Perhaps I don't. I've seen enough
death to last me a lifetime.'

Lady Gracey sighed. 'So many displaced people, lost people, and so many dead.' She tutted, then brightened. 'I wish the two of you had been able to get home on leave. It would have been wonderful if he'd brought you home with him.'

'Non-commissioned officer,' Connor said gruffly. The inherent hierarchy of the British Army still angered him. A sergeant major was there to take orders from a superior officer, not to be his friend.

'Ah, yes. He was an officer and you were a sergeant major. What I do know from my son and my husband is that the sergeant major is at the heart of any battalion or regiment, the man the senior officers depend on in the midst of battle to get them out of trouble.'

'I suppose so.'

'There's no "suppose" about it. I've learned enough to know that my son had the warmest respect for you, as do I.' She paused as though she had something more to say but wasn't sure she should say it. 'You're welcome to live here, if you like. It's a big house and there's plenty of room for lodgers.' She paused as though considering her next words very carefully. 'You were brought up in Ireland?'

'For the most part. I was born in England.'

'Where in England – if you don't mind me asking?'

'I'm not sure. My parents worked here for a while, and then we went back. I think my grandfather was ill and they were needed over there to work on the land.' He remembered the countryside being green, his father spending most of his time at the pub and his mother on her knees in church. He also remembered the beltings he'd taken – more numerous than those given to his siblings because they were all girls.

He became aware of her watching him intently, turning away when he looked at her.

'I want you to stay, Connor, though I think you already know that. You were the last person to see my son alive. You brought him home. Indulge an old woman and stay close to her heart. I would very much like that.'

Connor's rough palms made a rasping sound as he rubbed them together and he looked down at his clenched hands, the knuckles white with tension as he fought the urge to look at the ginger jar.

She wriggled in her chair. 'This chair is so difficult to get out of. I think I might christen it the Slough of Despond – shades of John Bunyan.' She held out her hand. 'Can you give me a good tug, Sergeant Major?'

Once he'd set her on her feet, she escorted him to the back door, his dog following politely.

'Tell me, why did you respond to my letter? You didn't have to come.'

'I wanted to explain.'

There. It was out. He wanted to explain, but where would he begin?

She heaved a sigh that, for a moment, seemed to erase the amusing persona she'd presented.

*

He got halfway down the drive then turned abruptly and went back to the house.

He didn't need to tell her the truth, but he had decided she deserved to know.

He found her in the stable yard standing in front of a pile of horse manure and rubbing at the hollow of her back. She saw him but did not question him on the reason for his sudden return.

'They shoot old horses, but this old mare will have to endure.'

'Let me give you a hand.'

His hair blew back from his face as he began to shovel the manure from the ground to the wheelbarrow.

She eyed him quizzically. 'You've something to tell me?'

'Yes.'

'That sounds a bit ominous. Have I got something to worry about?'

'I've a confession to make.'

She tilted her head to one side. 'Do you want to confess inside or out here?'

He had no wish to see the jar again. 'Out here's good enough.'

'This sounds like it might be a long confession so I'll make myself comfortable.'

She sat down on a bale of straw, folded her hands in her lap, eyed him expectantly and waited.

Connor shoved his hands into his pockets and thought carefully about what he was going to say and how to say it. 'As you know, Harry and I made a pact about bringing our remains home. As a Catholic, mine would have been the more difficult to bring back, cremation being frowned on, but he was more set on the idea than I was. So I promised I would do as he asked – I wasn't worried about my remains one way or another.'

'Go on.' She said it quietly as though she feared what she was about to hear.

Connor paced up and down. Once he had his mind firmly fixed on the matter, he stopped, threw his shoulders back and, feeling like a condemned man in the dock, turned to face her.

'It was the truth I related to you earlier. We escaped into the jungle and were alone for the most part until we came to a village where we begged food and water. They were kind and took us in. Two days we rested there, and then the enemy turned up.'

He told her how they'd got separated, that Harry had joined the villagers in the hiding place beneath the hut. On and on he went, letting it all come out, reliving with the words the terrible moment when Harry had died, the cremation of body parts, the wailing and lamentations of the villagers, their finding a jar in which to place some of the ashes – some of which were Harry's. 'It was impossible to know, to separate...'

His eyes were on fire and his throat had closed. He could see it behind his eyelids when he shut them, hear the exploding grenade, the sudden screams of innocent people.

After he'd told her everything he stood there silently, not daring to look at her, but feeling as though a great weight had been lifted off his chest. 'But they weren't Harry's ashes, not really.'

She shook her head. 'It doesn't matter, Connor. They came from the place where he died and the people he died with. What are ashes anyway? They're not him. Not really. My memories are of him, the baby, the boy, the man. My son.'

Connor took a deep breath, surprised at how much better he was feeling.

She paused, her bosom heaving. 'You see, I nearly fainted when I saw the photograph of you both. I suspect Harry thought the same as I did, hence taking it in the first place. I made enquiries but decided there was no point in pursuing them. Then Harry died and I made further enquiries. Tell me, am I right in thinking that your mother was named Bridget Riley and had a wonderful singing voice?'

Connor braced his thumbs in the waistband of his trousers. He was no fool. Everything she was saying had a purpose and was falling into place in a way he had not envisaged.

'You look so much like Harry. I told myself that I was jumping the gun in thinking you were sired by my husband. You would never believe how often we had to replace parlourmaids and housemaids. He couldn't resist. I found that out not long after we were married when I was expecting Harry.' She shrugged. 'But there you are. We were married and back then it was meant to be for life. Things aren't much different now. Who knows? In future it may become quite acceptable to have children without being married.'

Connor was staring into the distance. Most people would have been hit sideways by the news. He didn't feel that. The fact that he and Harry might well have been half brothers was oddly comforting, in fact he hoped indeed that it was so.

'My mother had a fine singing voice. And she was kind to kids and animals. She used to put bread and milk out for the hedgehogs and crumbs for the birds in winter. I wanted a dog, but my father refused to let me have one. Said it took all his money just to keep me and my sisters. I had five sisters, all younger than me.'

He swallowed hard. He'd rehearsed the words in his mind but too many words were uncalled for. Keep it simple.

'I hope you'll forgive me for that – telling a lie about the ashes.' A half-smile pulled at one side of her ladyship's lips and there was a sudden sparkle in her eyes. 'Come with me.'

They returned to the room where they'd taken tea, the tray still sitting on the table. At first he thought she was going to offer him another cup. What she did next took him completely by surprise.

With a sweep of her hand she knocked the jar from the

mantelpiece and onto the tiled surround of the fireplace, where it shattered into many pieces.

Connor stared open-mouthed. There was no sign of Harry's ashes. 'I don't understand.'

A sad look came to her face. 'It took me some time before I decided to put my boy's ashes to rest. I decided that "ashes to ashes, dust to dust" means just that. I wanted him to go back to the earth, to be part of nature and the universe, so I scattered them in the orchard. He always liked it there – in fact I think he climbed every tree in it.'

Connor felt numb. When he opened his mouth and nothing came out, she filled the void with a bittersweet truth that both startled and pleased him, and also made sense.

'You see, it doesn't matter that the ashes of others were in that jar. They were all victims and are now back where they came from. Floating up there with the clouds for all I know.'

# 26

The train back to London passed pastoral scenes, cows in fields, stone farmhouses and the tall steeples and towers of ancient churches. Above them were the clouds. His gaze kept straying to them.

One of the occupants of the carriage tried to strike up a conversation. 'Looks just as it did before the war. I don't know about you, but I'm glad to see that nothing's changed. Rule Britannia and all that.'

'We lost a lot.'

The man bristled. 'I was in the army, mate. I know what it was like.'

'Do you now.'

'Were you one of them conscientious-objector johnnies – or, rather, Paddies in your case? Weren't the Irish neutral?' he asked accusingly.

Connor didn't answer. His attention had been drawn elsewhere.

The man sitting opposite him was hidden behind a

newspaper. The woman next to him had folded over the page of a magazine that appeared to cater for women. He couldn't see the headline of the article, but the photograph was clear and he recognised her immediately.

'Excuse me. Can I borrow that a moment?'

She hesitated, somewhat surprised by the sudden demand of a complete stranger.

'Please,' he begged. 'I think it's someone I know.'

Looking slightly puzzled, she handed it over.

Connor stared at her picture before studying the headline.

## ANGEL OF MERCY SPEAKS OUT

Once he'd drunk in the familiar details of her face, he began to read how a woman doctor had observed people in the cities of Hiroshima and Nagasaki were dying of a sickness the Allied authorities were refusing to acknowledge as being a side effect of the atomic bomb. These people, who had not been in the immediate vicinity of the blast, were dying. The woman doctor concerned had insisted the symptoms were consistent with large doses of radiation from X-rays that must have come from the bombs that were dropped. Those connected to the team who had developed the bomb insisted it was not proven.

The article went on to describe wounds that wouldn't heal. "Even when I inject someone with penicillin – which only slightly improves the situation but does not cure it

– the puncture wound becomes infected. It's as though the patient's immune system has been totally destroyed. I'm no expert, but logically I would say that these people have been exposed to excessive amounts of radiation in far stronger doses than one would receive in a normal X-ray." It is believed by our trusted reporter that she is in Australia or perhaps Hong Kong. Following the publication of this article, Dr Rossiter was dismissed from her post and our reporter had his press pass rescinded. He has returned to London.'

After memorising the name of the reporter, one William Shaw, he passed the magazine back to its owner.

She looked concerned. 'Are you all right?'

Dazed, he managed to mutter that he was fine. Very fine indeed.

The man who had accused him of being a conscientious objector apparently thought better of pursuing his point once he'd seen a sudden fierceness come to Connor's eyes.

Connor thought deeply about what he'd just read. Apparently Rowena had upset the US censors in Japan and, in a bid to placate them, the Red Cross had sent her packing, transferring her to somewhere her ministrations were just as greatly needed.


William Shaw proved an amenable man who chain smoked and had the yellow fingers and brown teeth to prove it. Along with each cigarette he drank a pint of bitter with a whisky chaser. To Connor's mind he looked like a man with one foot on a bar of soap and the other in the grave.

'So you want to know more about Dr Rossiter. I take it you know her.'

'Yes. We knew each other back in Hong Kong before the Imperial Army came to call.'

'"Knew" in the Biblical sense?'

'None of your business. I want to know how she is and where she is.'

William – Bill, as he insisted on being called – polished off three rounds of drinks without paying for one. 'She struck me as a strong woman. Very attractive too.'

'You interviewed her.'

'I did. In depth. Only about her work, of course, but we did on occasion touch on her background. She spent some time in a prisoner-of-war camp. Fort Stanley, I believe. Speaks some Cantonese and a little Japanese. I did a ward round with her and a male doctor, an Australian bloke. What struck me was that the patients seemed to accept a woman more readily than they did a man. The hostility was still there, you see. I don't know whether they'll ever forgive the Yanks for dropping that bomb, but, still, the Japs did some evil things themselves. The Burma railway, Nanking and countless other atrocities. Totally unnecessary most of them.'

Connor could not disagree. He'd been through enough himself, seen enough to give him nightmares for the rest of his life.

Shaw ordered more drinks for himself, but Connor declined, resigned to paying for this round too.

'You don't mention her being married.'

'She wasn't, though she did have a kid, a little girl of mixed parentage. Chinese or Japanese.'

'Japanese.'

'Oh. Another reason they were more accepting of her. Did he die, the kid's father?'

Connor shrugged. 'I don't know.' He wasn't going to tell Shaw about the rape. The man had too much of an appetite for salacious scandal. 'You say she was deported to either Australia or Hong Kong. Do you know that for sure?'

He shook his head. 'I got chucked out myself after that. The bomb and its wider repercussions are a touchy subject. An Australian journalist was the first to report on the devastation, the dead and the living dead, and that was a month after the event. Had to use a Japanese press agency to get it through. Even then it never hit the American newspapers. I believe it was a London paper that printed it. Poor bloke was ostracised after that. Called a Commie and unpatriotic. You might try the Red Cross to find out where she is. It may take a few phone calls and telegrams, mind. It's a big outfit. Their offices in London may not hold the information – although, of course, if she's a British national...'

'She is.'

Bill Shaw was ordering another pint when Connor left, the only one he would have to pay for himself.

★

It took a few phone calls, letters and, finally, a visit to the offices of the Red Cross in London before he had the details he wanted.

The woman on the other side of the desk fingered through a bulky file. 'We may not be entirely up to date. You can imagine how long paperwork takes to travel between our Far East outposts and here. It makes things very difficult for me. From what I can gather...' A few more pages fluttered over. The woman traced down the open page in front of her with a blunt finger. 'Australia. Darwin. We operate from there for some of our projects in the area – and there are a lot of them. The war, you see. It was a very difficult time,' she said, as though being in charge of a mountain of paperwork was deserving of a medal.

'Yes. It was.'

He took the address she gave him and contemplated how much and how long a journey that was. Six weeks at least, but it would feel longer. It would feel like six years.

'A long journey if you go by sea. A lot less if you go by air – but the price of flying is prohibitive.'

He thanked her for the information. His mind was made up.

A poster advertising a trip to Australia that took only four days dominated the window of Imperial Airways in Regent Street. It did not mention a price, and when he went inside and asked, he could understand why they preferred not to mention it. He needed a chair to sit down and think it through. 'The flight actually terminates in Sydney and there are several stops on the way. Tripoli, Cairo, Karachi, Singapore, Darwin and then Sydney.'

He bought a ticket for Darwin.


'Connor! Mr O'Connor. Is that really you?'

Not having found Rowena at the address he'd been given, the person who'd answered the door suggested he try the hospital. 'I believe that was where Dr Rossiter was working. Somebody there might know where she's gone.'

The looks of the senior staff nurse striding towards him were familiar, though for the life of him he couldn't remember her name.

'Alice,' she said, on seeing his confusion. 'We met first in your bar, then a few less salubrious places after that. I take it you're looking for Dr Rossiter.'

'Is she all right?'

'Very. But she's not here. She's gone back to Hong Kong.'

'To stay?'

'I'm not sure about that and neither is she, but she's taken Dawn with her – you know, her daughter following that... incident.'

He couldn't help noticing the shaded look that came to her eyes, almost as though she was reluctant to admit

Rowena had a daughter or even to mention the word 'rape'. Describing it as an incident somehow lessened its horror. He guessed that was how she coped with it.

'And before you jump to conclusions, I don't think it's got anything to do with a man, if you know what I mean. I do know she wanted to pick up where she left off as regards the refugee issue. You know it's becoming a big problem there, don't you?'

'I did hear.'

'Can I treat you to a cup of tea before you go?'

Over tea and currant buns they talked of what they'd been through and Rowena's ordeal with Kim Pheloung.

'Funny man,' she said, frowning. 'Well, not so much funny as out of his mind. Liked to train humans as though they were dogs. That's what Rowena told me. She didn't like to talk about him much. Can't say I blame her. She gave me enough information to know he was a bad lot.'

He felt her studying his face.

'What happened to the officer in charge that Christmas Day?' she asked.

'Harry.' Connor shifted in his chair and fingered the edge of his saucer. 'He didn't make it. I survived on Bali for a while, courtesy of the locals. I've been a bit aimless ever since, not quite sure what to do or where to go next.'

Alice grinned. 'Well, you could open a bar.'

★

There were no flights from Darwin to Hong Kong but

there was a freighter that took a few passengers. It was a lot cheaper than flying or taking a passenger ship.

P and O, the old Peninsular and Oriental Line, was back in operation, for the most part ferrying civil servants and the administrators of international agencies back and forth. There was also a plethora of military staff, who shunned their own transport in favour of luxury.

The freighter suited him fine even though it took just over a week.


Victoria Harbour had changed little since the days when it was the staging point for trade with the Chinese mainland. As usual ships were at anchor, and it was easy to forget that a vast upheaval had taken place. The effects of the civil war on the mainland had been ongoing for years, but the occupation should have dented Hong Kong's eternal optimism, depending as it did on free movement throughout the Pacific Ocean and beyond.

Thanks to the shipping office in Darwin, he'd been able to send a telegram ahead of his arrival. Rowena hadn't given Alice her new address and she wasn't sure of the organisation she was working for, so Connor fell back on his own resources and sent a telegram to Yang, care of Connor's Bar, Kowloon. It was a faint chance but the only one he had and he wasn't a hundred per cent sure that the message would get through.

His spirits soared when he saw Yang, his one-time barman, standing on the quay waiting for him, waving his pork-pie hat and dressed like a waiter from the Savoy.

'Yang. Good to see you, old friend.'

They threw their arms around each other, not a natural greeting for either man, but they hadn't seen each other since the day the bomb had dropped on Connor's Bar.

'Good to see you, too, boss.'

Connor looked him up and down. 'That's a fine suit you're wearing. Have you got a job with the Hilton Hotel?'

'No, boss. This is my suit. I am boss so I dress like boss. Connor's Bar is Yang's Bar. We are doing very well.'

Connor shook his head. 'No, no. We ran out on you and left you to it. It's yours.'

'No. You my partner. You keep Kim Pheloung and his apes at bay. I grateful for that.' He paused. 'And Mr Harry?'

'He was killed. It's only me now to keep Pheloung's apes at bay. I came here looking for Dr Rossiter. Do you know where she is?'

'Yes. Of course I do. The offices of Kim Pheloung. That's where she is.'

Connor's face darkened. Without knowing it, Yang had voiced his worst fear. 'She's with him?'

'Oh, no, boss. She not with him. She at his offices. They filled with refugees now, not Pheloung.'

A great relief swept over him. 'Take me there, Yang. You can explain on the way.'

Yang talked and Connor listened as the rickshaw driver pedalled his way from the harbour to the place where Kim had taken Rowena on that fateful Sunday in 1941.

Piles of rubble still dotted the narrower streets but in the wider ones the metal carcasses of tall buildings were rising quickly, an army of Chinese labourers swarming over them.

The sound of pneumatic drills mixed with the rumble of increased traffic and the perennial racket of packed streets where tailors still shouted for custom but were almost drowned by clanking cranes reaching for the skyline.

'Pheloung think world would go on the same. He travel here, he travel there, Hong Kong, Kowloon and Shanghai. He do this too during war, keep on right side of Japanese. When it over he try to keep on right side of Chinese in Shanghai, but they know he collaborate with Japanese. They not like that. Not forgive him. They kill him. So that is that!'

He slapped his hands on his thighs and laughed. Connor couldn't blame him. Pheloung had destroyed Yang's business and Yang would have been killed if it hadn't been for Connor and Harry supplying the money and muscle. As they were representatives of the British Empire, Kim had been more wary of their response to intimidation. The one thing he had not wanted was those officers of the Hong Kong police who were not open to bribes looking too closely into his criminal activities.

'So he's dead.' Connor felt an incredible sense of relief and could see that Yang felt the same.

'Very dead. Head chopped off. Doctor very glad too. I tell her. She very happy. I too.'

'The future looks bright, Yang.'

'And now you back we run bar together. Very good bar. Posh bar where barmen wear suits, just like you and Mr Harry used to. Yes?'

Connor threw back his head so he could better feel the sun on his face and Yang wouldn't see the sadness in his eyes. 'Yes, Yang. Just like Mr Harry and I used to, though we drew a line at a hat like yours.'

'I like this hat.'

'That's all that matters.'

The sun was setting by the time the rickshaw drew up in front of what had been the centre of a criminal empire. A Red Cross banner fluttered over the front portico.

As he made to get out, Yang caught his arm. 'Wait. She say wait. She not be long. I have to check.'

The shadow of the building was lengthening into solid black, its stark lines accentuated by the rosy glow of sunset.

After a few minutes, Yang said, 'I go in now and see if she's ready. You stay.'

The little man in his dapper suit sprang down from the rickshaw and marched smartly indoors.

Connor waited, uncertain why he had to wait, but wanting to make everything perfect. If his waiting here would please her, then that was what he would do.

Half an hour went by and his impatience was becoming too much to bear. The springs on the old rickshaw squealed as though in pain as he swung his long legs out, both feet hitting the ground at the same time.

Just as he got to the bottom of the steps leading up to the entrance, Yang came out of the door.

'I have this,' he said. 'She tell me to give it to you.'

As Yang raised it chest high, Connor recognised his old violin case.

'She say we go round to garden at the back. I bring you drink. You wait there for doctor. She wants you to see.'

He had no idea what she wanted him to see, but the sight and feel of his beloved instrument thrilled him. His impatience vanished and, like a lamb, he followed Yang without question.

'This used to be Pheloung garden,' said Yang, as he pushed open a traditional gate complete with the painting of a dragon.

Connor found himself in what had been a pleasant garden of flowers, cherry trees and carp swimming in cool green pools. In the centre there was a dovecote in the form of a pagoda, its swallowtail roof ends climbing like spines from its base to its green-tiled apex.

A hundred pairs of eyes turned to stare at him. This was what Rowena wanted him to see and the sight pained him. Men and women of all ages, children and babies, their clothes ragged, their faces worn by months, perhaps years, of fleeing one slaughtering army after another.

'Nice garden,' he said to Yang. 'More people than flowers.'

'Dr Rossiter chop them down.'

'She doesn't like flowers? Well, there's a surprise.'

'Not those flowers. Big yellow ones. They were Pheloung's flowers. She gave them to the children to sell. "Nothing must go to waste," she said. The doves they ate.'

'So she doesn't like yellow flowers,' Connor muttered to himself, then watched as a smiling, nodding Yang handed out pieces of chocolate to the children, who continued to look at the European with wide-eyed suspicion.

When he sat down on a stone bench to watch the proceedings, their wariness was replaced by curiosity. One or two waved their fingers at him. Others began to smile.

He smiled back, attempted a few words, his pronunciation bringing forth outright laughter.

'Laughing is good,' he said mostly to himself, and it really was uplifting to hear them laugh. Then to Yang, 'It's a wonder they can still laugh after all they've been through, the things they must have seen.'

Yang agreed. 'No happy times. No school, no nothing.'

Connor ran his hands down the curved form of the violin case. The shape of a guitar or a cello was said to follow that of a woman's body, yet to his mind the violin had a more silken feel than either of those, more sylph-like. He smiled on recalling the last time he'd run his hands down Rowena's body. It seemed a lifetime ago.

Some of the children reached out and did as he did, running their small hands over the shape of the case, fingering the clasps that held it shut.

They started when he spoke to them, but did not pull away.

'I'd like to see you happy.'

More children drew near as he began to open the case. Even the adults began to take an interest. One or two nodded as they recognised this was an instrument and, whispering, got to their feet and edged closer.

'You're a bit the worse for wear,' he muttered to his fiddle, as he did his best to tighten and tune, finally deciding that he'd done his best. With slow deliberation he tucked it under his chin, picked up the bow and ran it across the strings.

All chattering ceased. He felt something stir in the air, and in the demeanour of the wasted people standing around him, it was as though he was about to open a door that had been closed to them for so long.

Both man and fiddle being out of practice, he decided on something steady that wouldn't overtax either the instrument or the musician.

A brief thought and he decided what it would be. Drawing the bow over the strings, he teased out the plaintive, gentle notes of 'The Londonderry Air'.

He closed his eyes and let the music waft over him.

The words came to mind, though he couldn't sing them for the words were painful and reminded him of Harry.

*Oh, Danny Boy, the pipes, the pipes are calling...*

Few people understood that the pipes were the pipes of war calling a young man to arms. So many young men had been called to fight, these last few years and many would never return.

*And I will wait in peace until you come to me.*

As the final notes fell away, the crowd pressed closer. They began talking among themselves, then exhorting Yang to intercede, to tell Connor they wanted more.

Connor smiled and shook his head when Yang told him. Not because he didn't want to play another tune, but because their enthusiasm filled him with such joy that he wanted to share it.

'Something a bit livelier, Yang. Something they can dance to. How would that be?'

'Good, Mr Connor. Very good.'

Yang's interpretation brought a gale of laughter and cheerful comments that Connor didn't need to understand. He could feel the joy of these displaced people. Words were not needed.

'Here we go!'

'Star of the County Down', faster-paced, undeniably merry and uplifting, had the children dancing and the adults laughing. Even an old man, with a string of a beard, shuffled his feet and tapped with his stick.

The words were in Connor's head, but he was

concentrating on the tune, playing the fiddle with stiff fingers, his foot tapping in time with its soaring, dancing notes, his eyes closed so he could remember better.

Nobody saw Rowena come into the garden, her face shaded but spellbound. It was as if he had stepped out from the page of the book she'd kept in her mind, a man against whom she would measure all others.

She saw the refugees beaming and clapping in time with the tune and, touching her most deeply, the children dancing.

His eyes were closed as he concentrated on the song, the one she'd sung with him on that night they'd met in a bar in Kowloon.

Just as they had back then, her feet began to tap in time with the fiddle's merry notes, her voice seized the melody and she sang the words:

'*At the harvest fair, she'll be surely there,*
*And I'll dress in my Sunday clothes,*
*With my shoes shone bright and my hat cocked right,*
*For a smile from my nut-brown rose.*'

She stepped out from the shade and, still singing, went to stand at his side.

His eyes were full of wonder.

Hers were full of tears.

They went on to the end, him playing the fiddle, her singing as she always seemed to do when they were together.

'No *pipe I'll smoke, no horse I'll yoke,*
*Till my plough it is rust-coloured brown,*
*Till my smiling bride by my own fireside,*
*Sits the Star of the County Down.*'

He joined her in the final chorus, his voice as strong as it used to be, the pair of them standing close so each could feel the warmth of their bodies.

'*From Bantry Bay, unto Derry Quay,*
*From Galway to Dublin Town.*
*No maid I've seen like the brown colleen,*
*That I met in the County Down.*'

There was more warmth in their embrace than there had ever been, yet they were not alone but standing in the midst of a crowd of humanity.

Fiddle hanging by his side, he clung to her tightly. 'Your voice is still as clear as a bell.'

'Your playing still stirs me to sing. And them to dance,' she said, indicating the people who had made a home of Kim Pheloung's garden.

'You kept my fiddle.'

'I hid it in the boiler room at St Stephen's.'

'You're a fine girl, Dr Rossiter.'

'And you're a fine man, Connor O'Connor.'

A ripple of approval ran through those watching as he kissed her deeply. 'It was quite a journey that brought me back here,' he said, his lips pressed into her hair, his eyes closed, as he breathed in her scent. 'Quite a journey. Back more or less where we started.'

'So we start all over again?'

'I wouldn't have it any other way.'

'Will you stay in Hong Kong?'

'Will you?'

'I have a lot of work to do.'

'So do I. It's been suggested that I should open a bar. What do you think of that?'

'Mummy!'

A small figure disengaged her hand from Luli's and ran to her mother. Rowena picked her up, hugged her close and kissed her. 'This is Dawn. My daughter. Named at the dawn of a new day.'

He cupped the child's cheek. 'And now hopefully the dawn of a new world. Peace at last.'

'Let's hope so.'

'But you still haven't answered my question.'

'What question was that?'

'The one I asked you before she was born.'

'You're a persistent man, Connor O'Connor.'

'And I won't take no for an answer.'

'You don't need to.'

# About the Author

Jean Moran was a columnist and editor before writing full-time. She has since published over fifty novels and been a bestseller in Germany. Jean was born and brought up in Bristol. She now lives in Bath.